ROBERT LOUIS STEVENSON'S

Treasure Island

THE GRAPHIC NOVEL

adapted by
Tim Hamilton

PUFFIN BOOKS

PUFFIN BOOKS
Published by the Penguin Group
Penguin Young Readers Group,
345 Hudson Street, New York, NY 10014 U.S.A.
Penguin Group (Canada), 10 Alcorn Avenue, Toronto, Ontario, Canada M4V 3B2
(a division of Pearson Penguin Canada Inc.)
Penguin Books Ltd, 80 Strand, London WC2R 0RL, England
Penguin Ireland, 25 St. Stephen's Green, Dublin 2, Ireland
(a division of Penguin Books Ltd)
Penguin Group (Australia), 250 Camberwell Road, Camberwell, Victoria 3124,
Australia (a division of Pearson Australia Group Pty Ltd)
Penguin Books India Pvt Ltd, 11 Community Centre, Panchsheel Park,
New Delhi – 110 017, India
Penguin Group (NZ), Cnr Airborne and Rosedale Roads, Albany, Auckland 1310,
New Zealand (a division of Pearson New Zealand Ltd)
Penguin Books (South Africa) (Pty) Ltd, 24 Sturdee Avenue, Rosebank,
Johannesburg 2196, South Africa

Registered Offices: Penguin Books Ltd, 80 Strand, London WC2R 0RL, England

First published by Puffin Books, a division of Penguin Young Readers Group, 2005

10 9 8 7 6

A Byron Preiss Book
Byron Preiss Visual Publications
24 West 25th Street, New York, NY 10010

Adapted by Tim Hamilton
Cover art by Tim Hamilton
Series Editor: Dwight Jon Zimmerman
Series Assistant Editor: April Isaacs
Interior design by Matt Postawa, Raul Carvajal and Gilda Hannah
Cover design by Matt Postawa

Puffin Books ISBN 978-0-14-240470-6

Printed in the United States of America

ROBERT LOUIS STEVENSON'S

Treasure Island

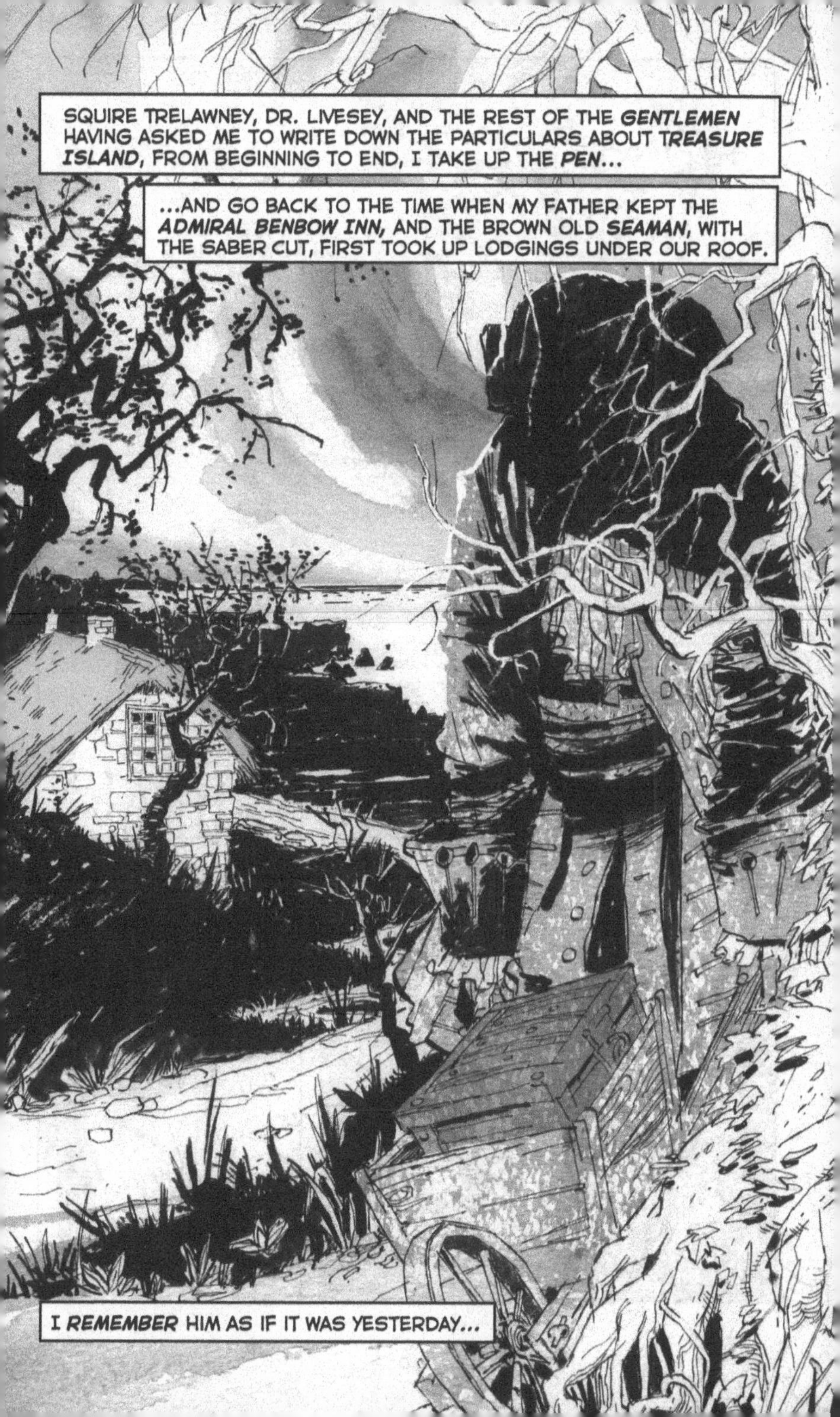
SQUIRE TRELAWNEY, DR. LIVESEY, AND THE REST OF THE *GENTLEMEN* HAVING ASKED ME TO WRITE DOWN THE PARTICULARS ABOUT *TREASURE ISLAND*, FROM BEGINNING TO END, I TAKE UP THE *PEN*...
...AND GO BACK TO THE TIME WHEN MY FATHER KEPT THE *ADMIRAL BENBOW INN,* AND THE BROWN OLD *SEAMAN,* WITH THE SABER CUT, FIRST TOOK UP LODGINGS UNDER OUR ROOF.
I *REMEMBER* HIM AS IF IT WAS YESTERDAY...

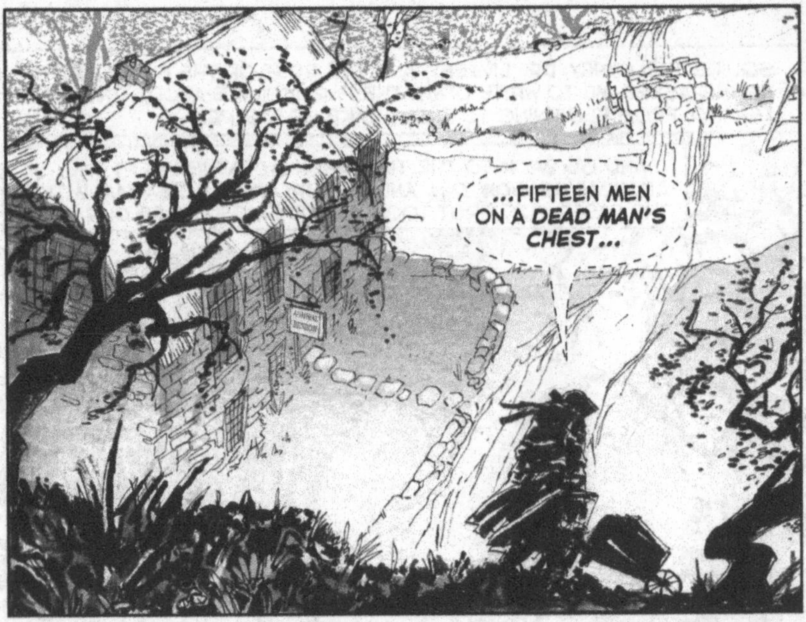
...FIFTEEN MEN ON A DEAD MAN'S CHEST...
ADMIRAL BENBOW

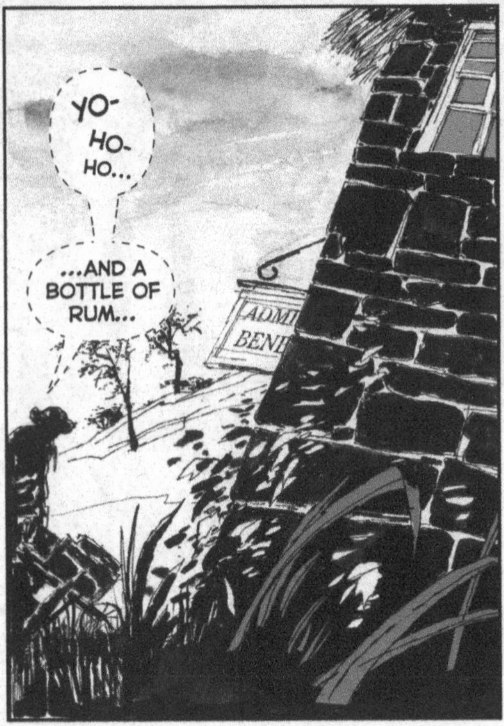
YO-HO-HO...
...AND A BOTTLE OF RUM...

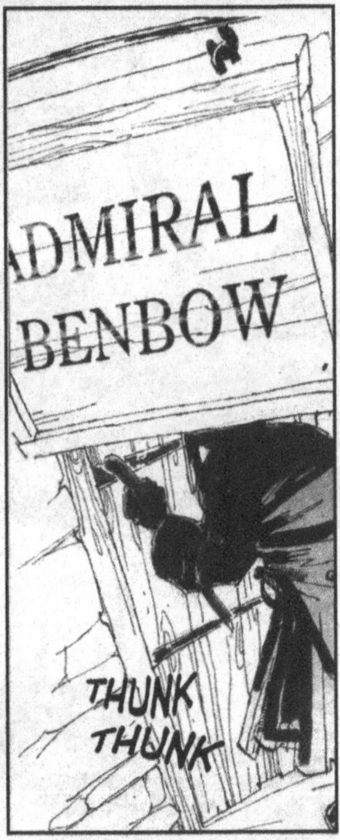
ADMIRAL BENBOW
THUNK THUNK

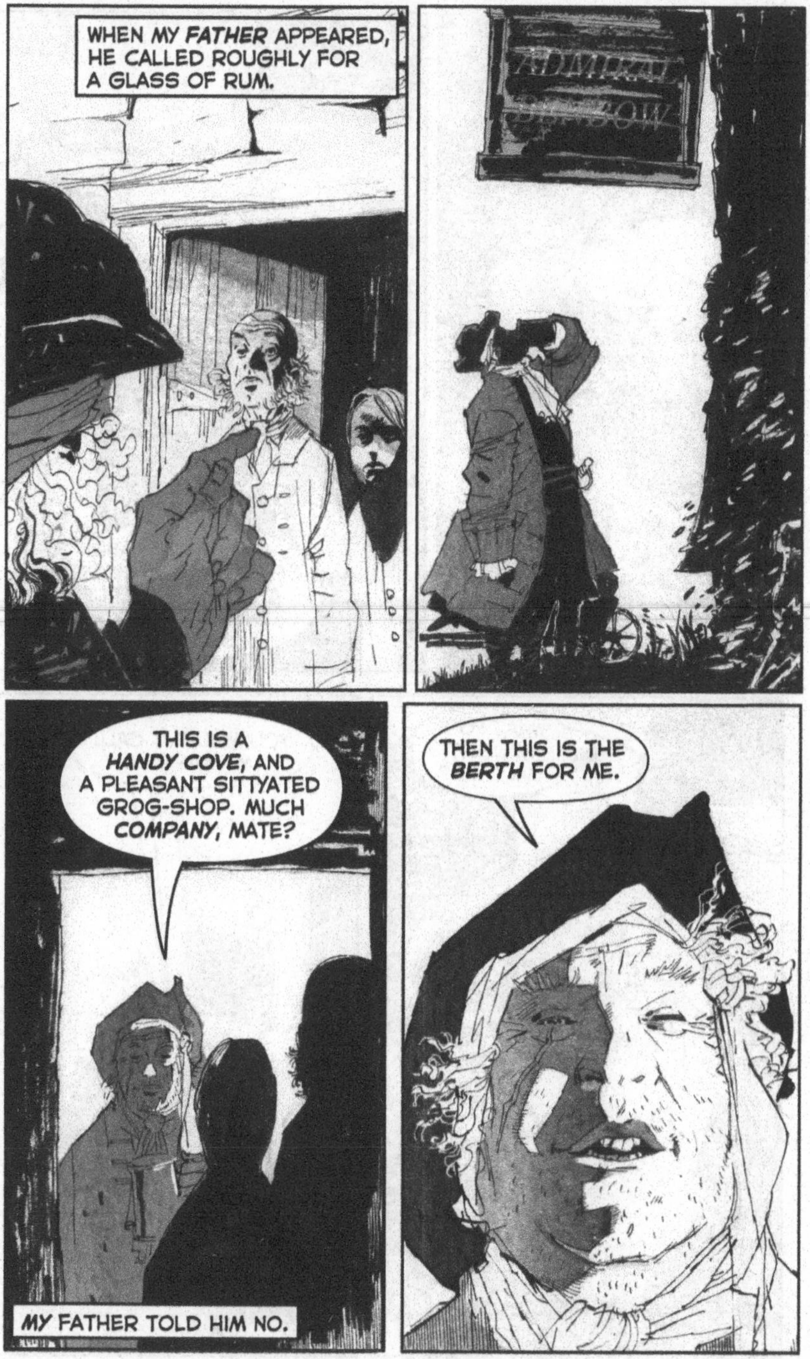
WHEN MY FATHER APPEARED, HE CALLED ROUGHLY FOR A GLASS OF RUM.
THIS IS A HANDY COVE, AND A PLEASANT SITTYATED GROG-SHOP. MUCH COMPANY, MATE?
MY FATHER TOLD HIM NO.
THEN THIS IS THE BERTH FOR ME.

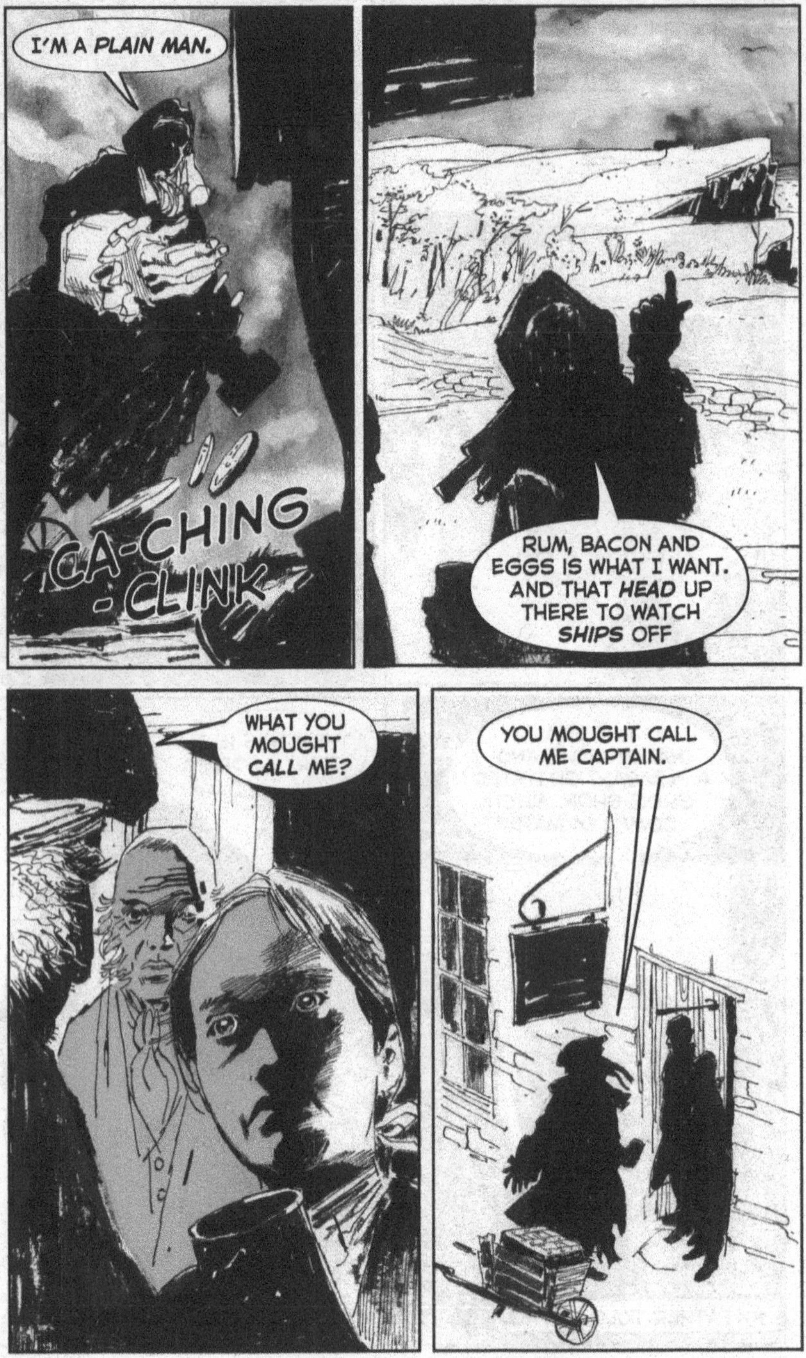
I'M A *PLAIN MAN.*
CA-CHING -CLINK
RUM, BACON AND EGGS IS WHAT I WANT. AND THAT *HEAD* UP THERE TO WATCH *SHIPS* OFF
WHAT YOU MOUGHT *CALL* ME?
YOU MOUGHT CALL ME CAPTAIN.

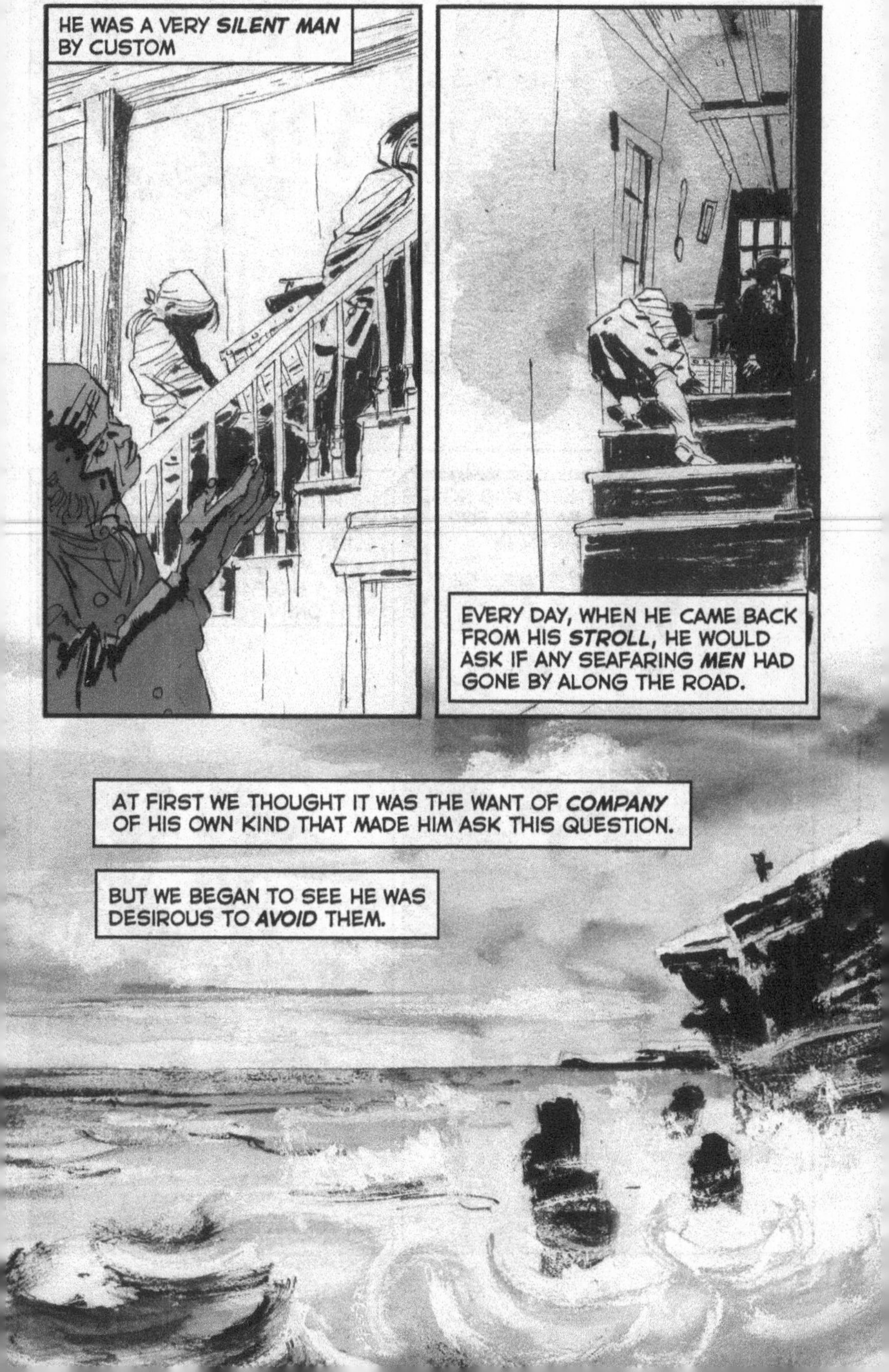
HE WAS A VERY SILENT MAN BY CUSTOM
EVERY DAY, WHEN HE CAME BACK FROM HIS STROLL, HE WOULD ASK IF ANY SEAFARING MEN HAD GONE BY ALONG THE ROAD.
AT FIRST WE THOUGHT IT WAS THE WANT OF COMPANY OF HIS OWN KIND THAT MADE HIM ASK THIS QUESTION.
BUT WE BEGAN TO SEE HE WAS DESIROUS TO AVOID THEM.

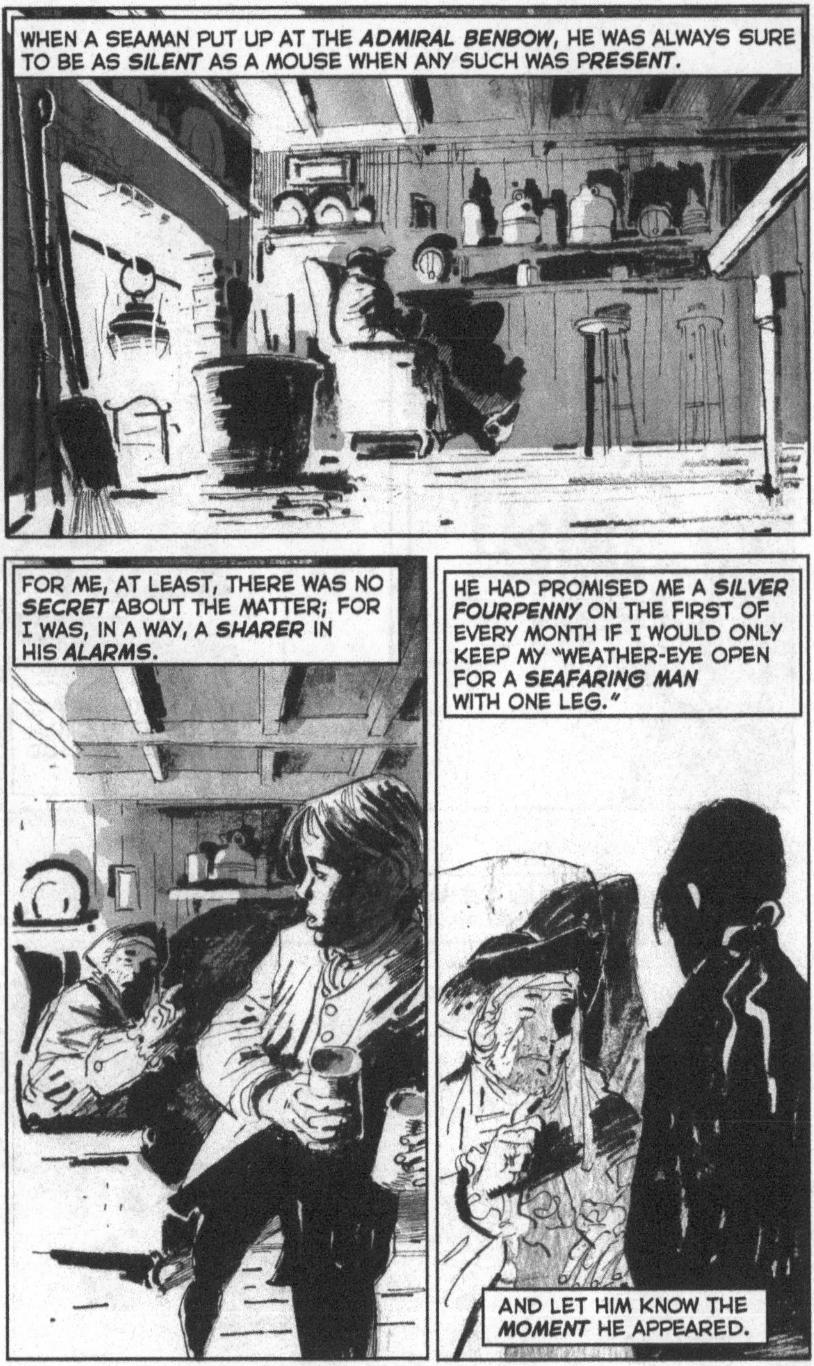
WHEN A SEAMAN PUT UP AT THE *ADMIRAL BENBOW*, HE WAS ALWAYS SURE TO BE AS *SILENT* AS A MOUSE WHEN ANY SUCH WAS *PRESENT*.
FOR ME, AT LEAST, THERE WAS NO *SECRET* ABOUT THE *MATTER*; FOR I WAS, IN A WAY, A *SHARER* IN HIS *ALARMS*.
HE HAD PROMISED ME A *SILVER FOURPENNY* ON THE FIRST OF EVERY MONTH IF I WOULD ONLY KEEP MY "WEATHER-EYE OPEN FOR A *SEAFARING MAN* WITH ONE LEG."
AND LET HIM KNOW THE *MOMENT* HE APPEARED.

"THE SEAFARING MAN WITH ONE *LEG.*"

HOW THAT PERSONAGE HAUNTED MY *DREAMS,* I NEED SCARCELY TELL YOU.

ON STORMY NIGHTS, I WOULD SEE HIM IN A *THOUSAND FORMS.*

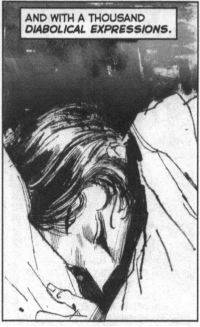

AND WITH A THOUSAND *DIABOLICAL EXPRESSIONS.*

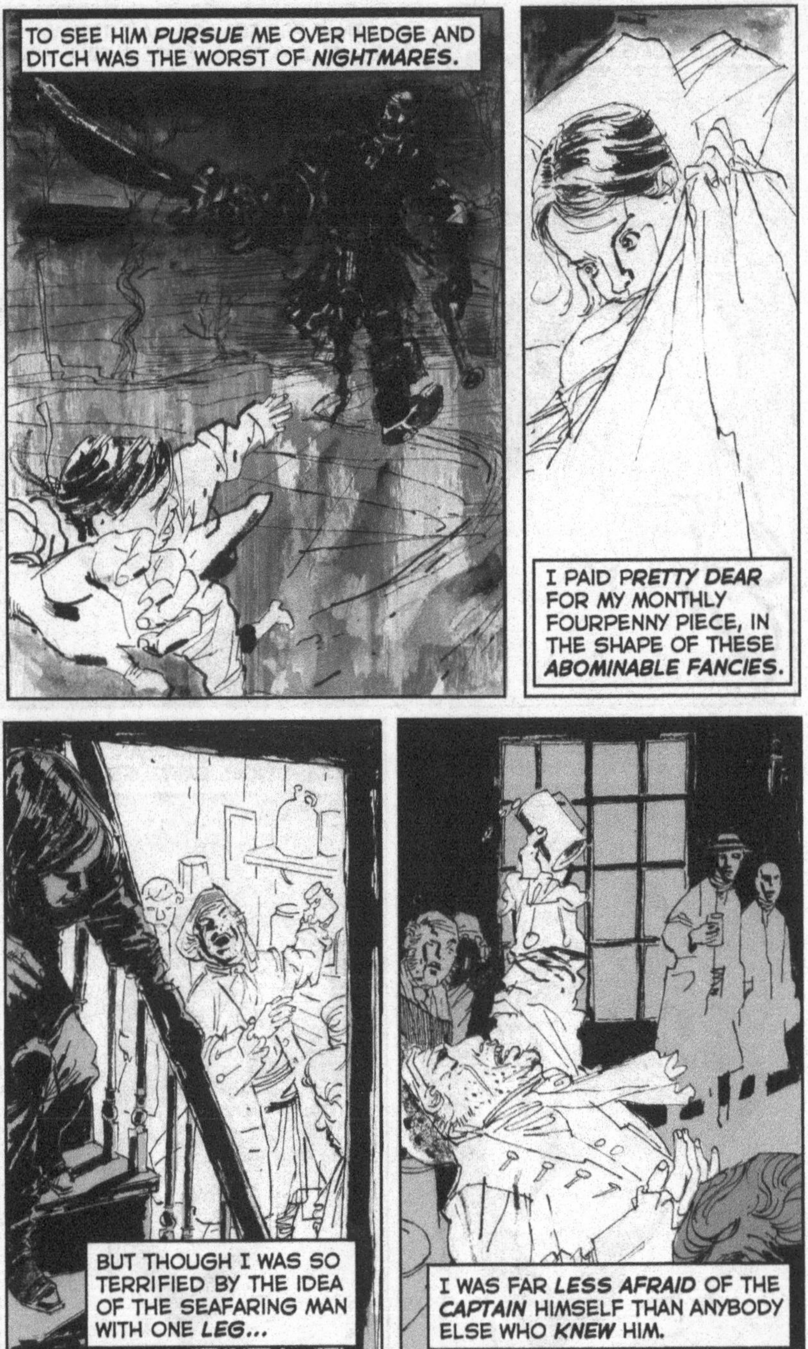
TO SEE HIM PURSUE ME OVER HEDGE AND DITCH WAS THE WORST OF NIGHTMARES.
I PAID PRETTY DEAR FOR MY MONTHLY FOURPENNY PIECE, IN THE SHAPE OF THESE ABOMINABLE FANCIES.
BUT THOUGH I WAS SO TERRIFIED BY THE IDEA OF THE SEAFARING MAN WITH ONE LEG...
I WAS FAR LESS AFRAID OF THE CAPTAIN HIMSELF THAN ANYBODY ELSE WHO KNEW HIM.

HIS *STORIES* WERE WHAT FRIGHTENED PEOPLE MOST OF ALL. MY *FATHER* WAS ALWAYS SAYING THE INN WOULD BE *RUINED.*

PEOPLE WERE *FRIGHTENED* AT THE TIME, BUT ON LOOKING BACK, THEY RATHER *LIKED* IT; IT WAS A FINE *EXCITEMENT* IN A QUIET COUNTRY LIFE.

HE WAS ONLY ONCE *CROSSED*, AND THAT WAS TOWARDS THE *END*.

WHEN MY POOR *FATHER* WAS FAR GONE IN A *DECLINE*.

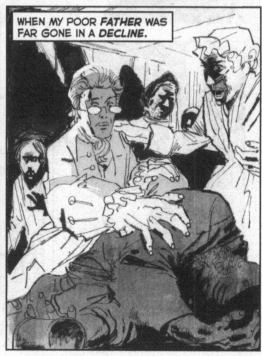

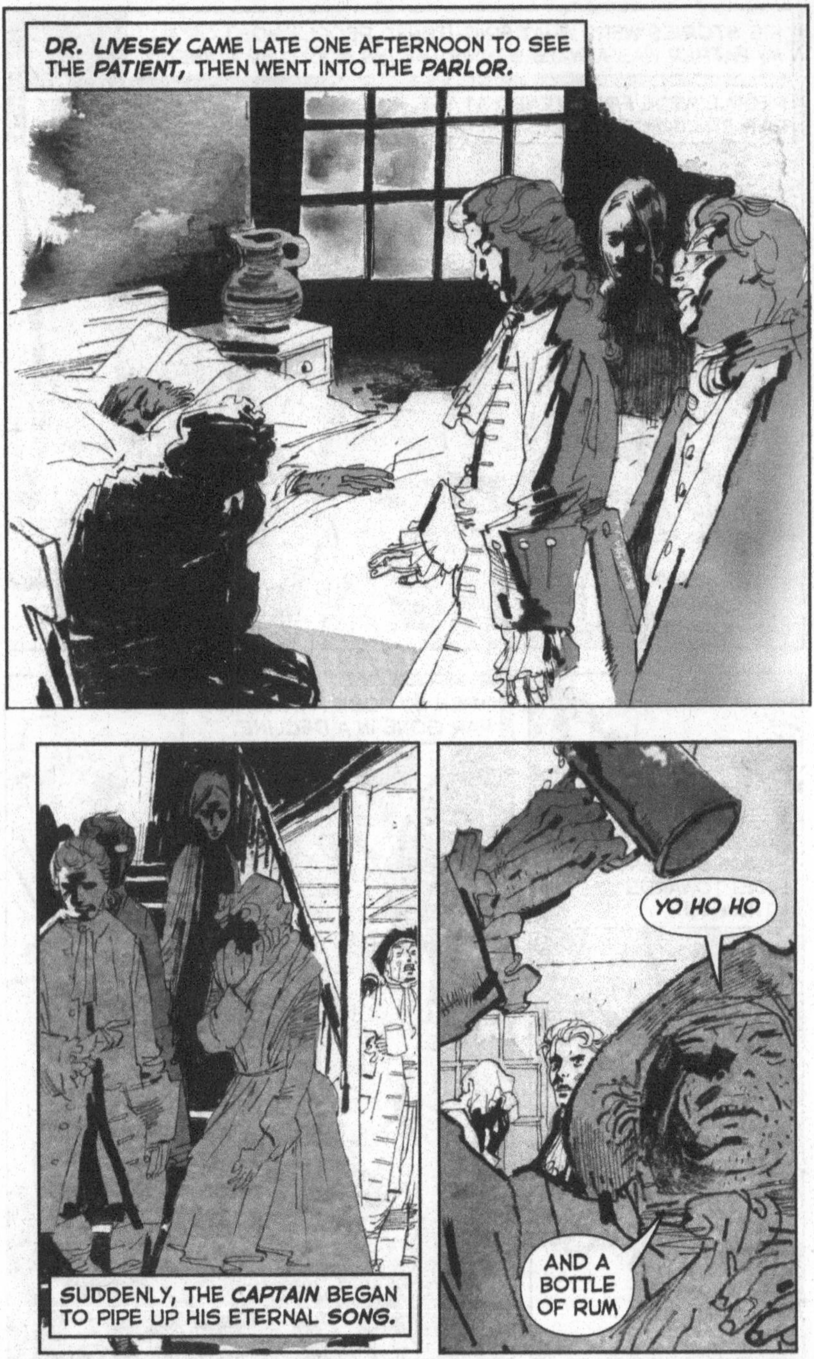
DR. LIVESEY CAME LATE ONE AFTERNOON TO SEE THE PATIENT, THEN WENT INTO THE PARLOR.
SUDDENLY, THE CAPTAIN BEGAN TO PIPE UP HIS ETERNAL SONG.
YO HO HO
AND A BOTTLE OF RUM

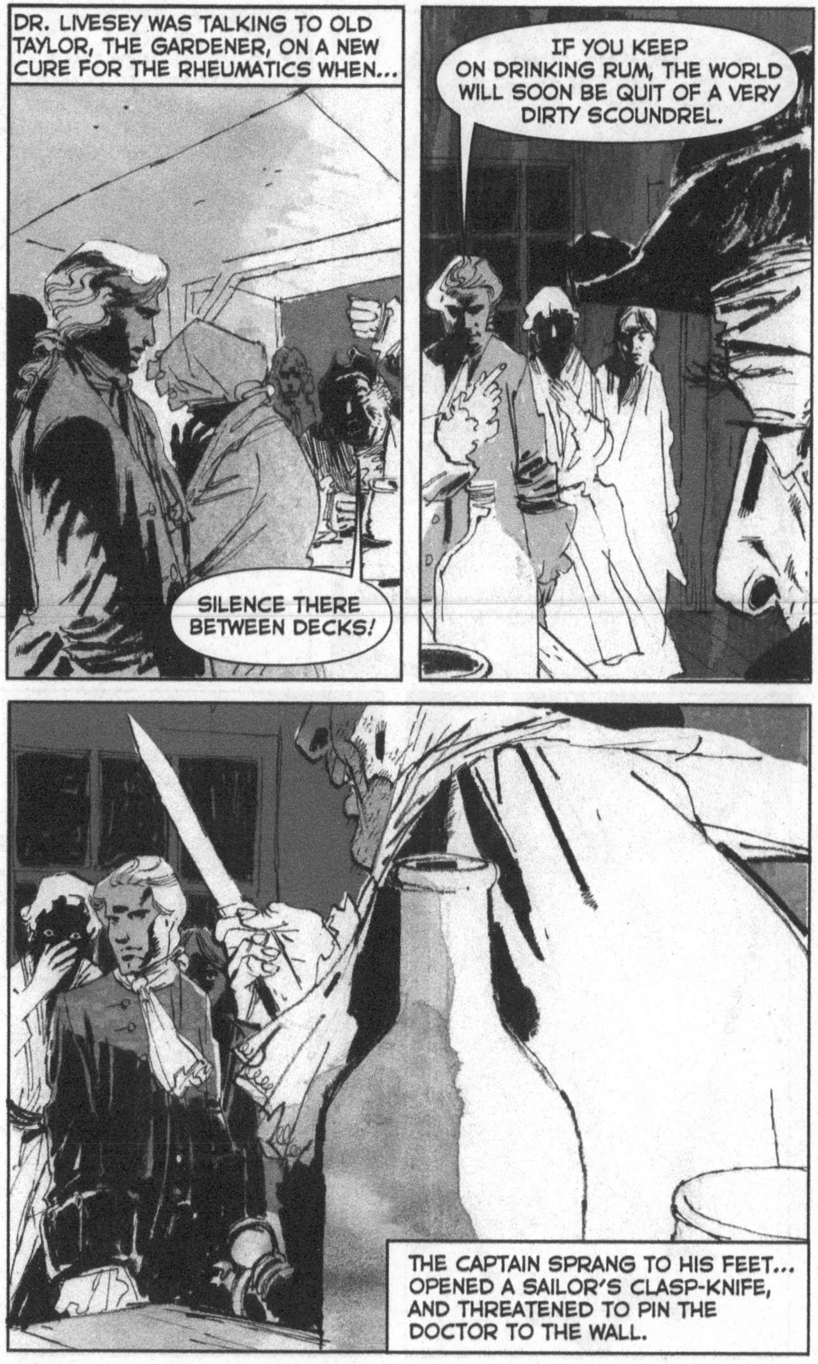
DR. LIVESEY WAS TALKING TO OLD TAYLOR, THE GARDENER, ON A NEW CURE FOR THE RHEUMATICS WHEN...
SILENCE THERE BETWEEN DECKS!
IF YOU KEEP ON DRINKING RUM, THE WORLD WILL SOON BE QUIT OF A VERY DIRTY SCOUNDREL.
THE CAPTAIN SPRANG TO HIS FEET... OPENED A SAILOR'S CLASP-KNIFE, AND THREATENED TO PIN THE DOCTOR TO THE WALL.

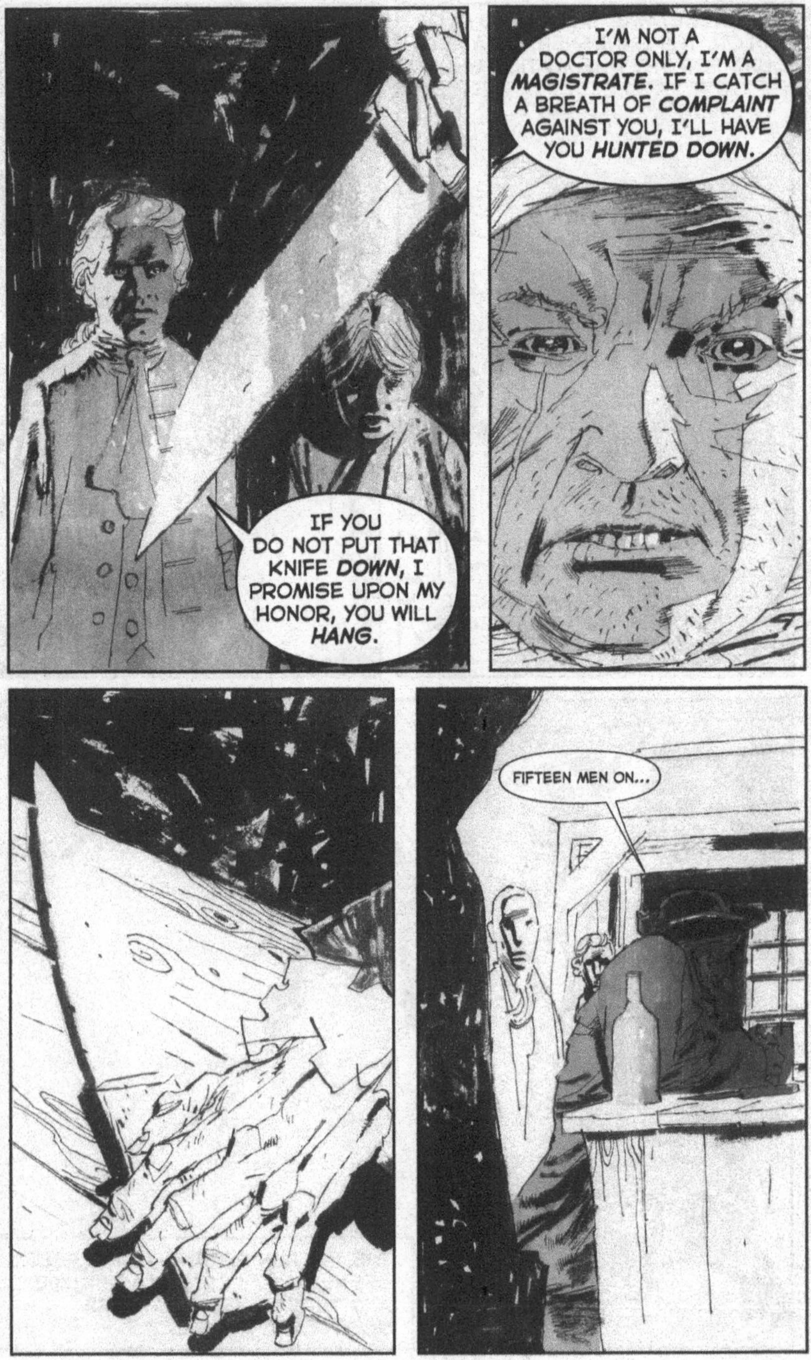
IF YOU DO NOT PUT THAT KNIFE DOWN, I PROMISE UPON MY HONOR, YOU WILL HANG.
I'M NOT A DOCTOR ONLY, I'M A MAGISTRATE. IF I CATCH A BREATH OF COMPLAINT AGAINST YOU, I'LL HAVE YOU HUNTED DOWN.
FIFTEEN MEN ON...

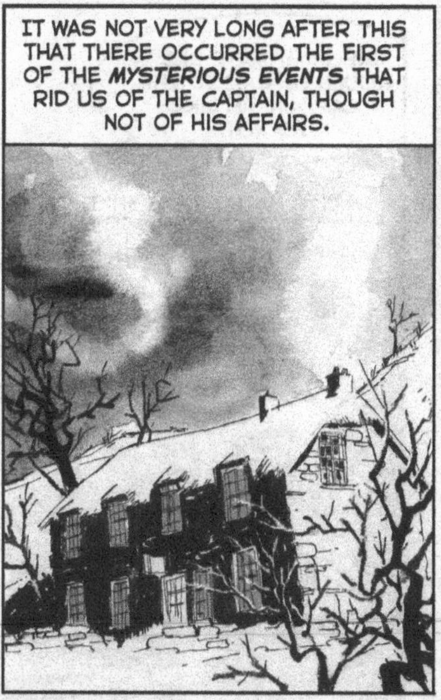
IT WAS NOT VERY LONG AFTER THIS THAT THERE OCCURRED THE FIRST OF THE *MYSTERIOUS EVENTS* THAT RID US OF THE CAPTAIN, THOUGH NOT OF HIS AFFAIRS.

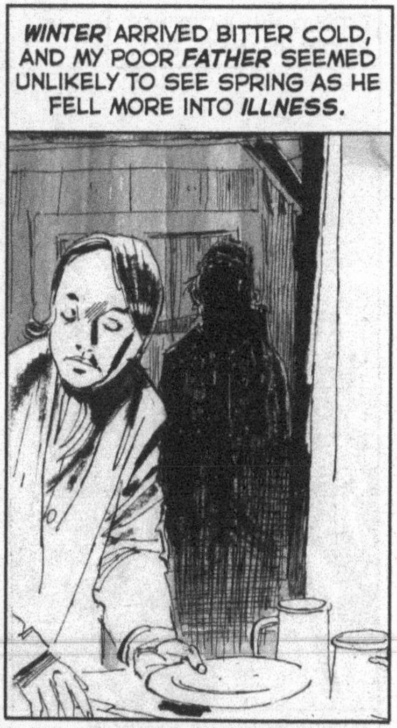
WINTER ARRIVED BITTER COLD, AND MY POOR *FATHER* SEEMED UNLIKELY TO SEE SPRING AS HE FELL MORE INTO *ILLNESS*.

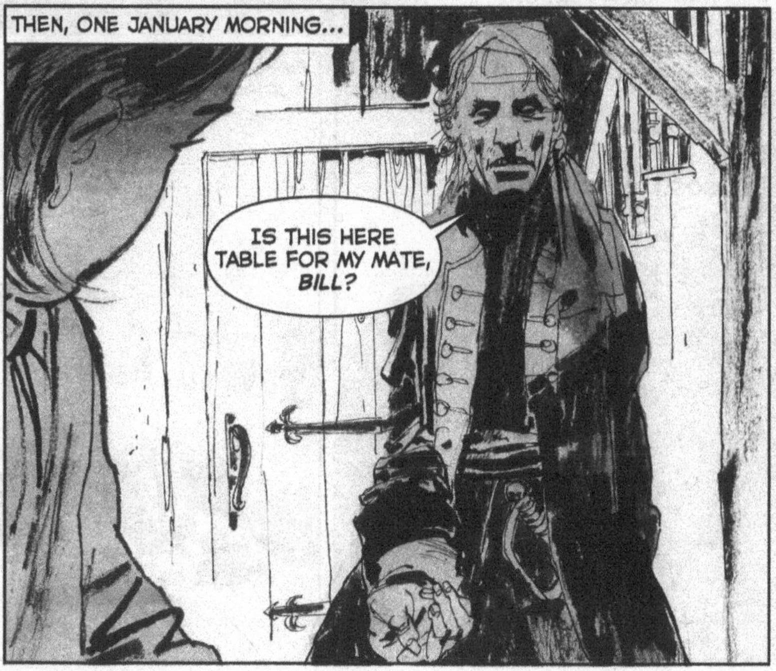
THEN, ONE JANUARY MORNING...
IS THIS HERE TABLE FOR MY MATE, *BILL*?

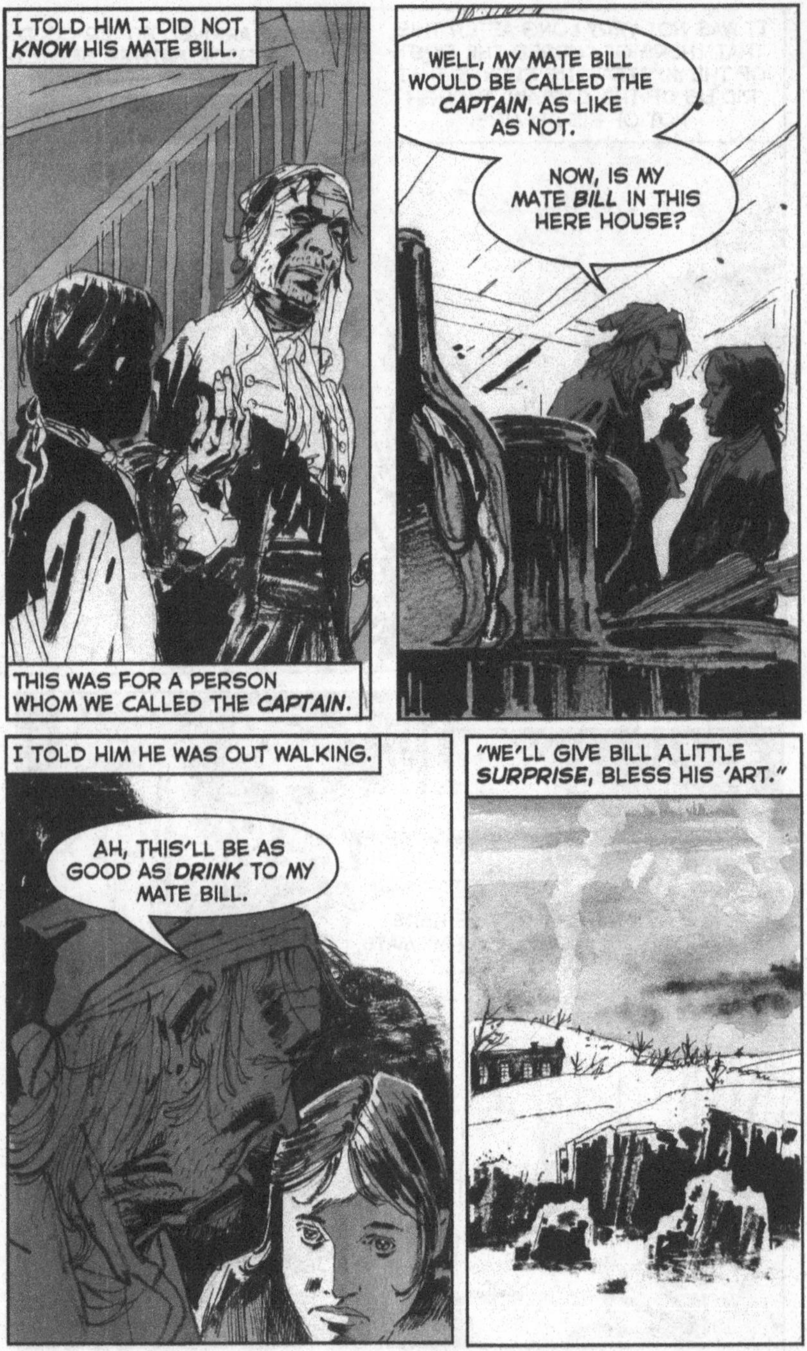
I TOLD HIM I DID NOT KNOW HIS MATE BILL.
THIS WAS FOR A PERSON WHOM WE CALLED THE CAPTAIN.
WELL, MY MATE BILL WOULD BE CALLED THE CAPTAIN, AS LIKE AS NOT.
NOW, IS MY MATE BILL IN THIS HERE HOUSE?
I TOLD HIM HE WAS OUT WALKING.
AH, THIS'LL BE AS GOOD AS DRINK TO MY MATE BILL.
"WE'LL GIVE BILL A LITTLE SURPRISE, BLESS HIS 'ART."

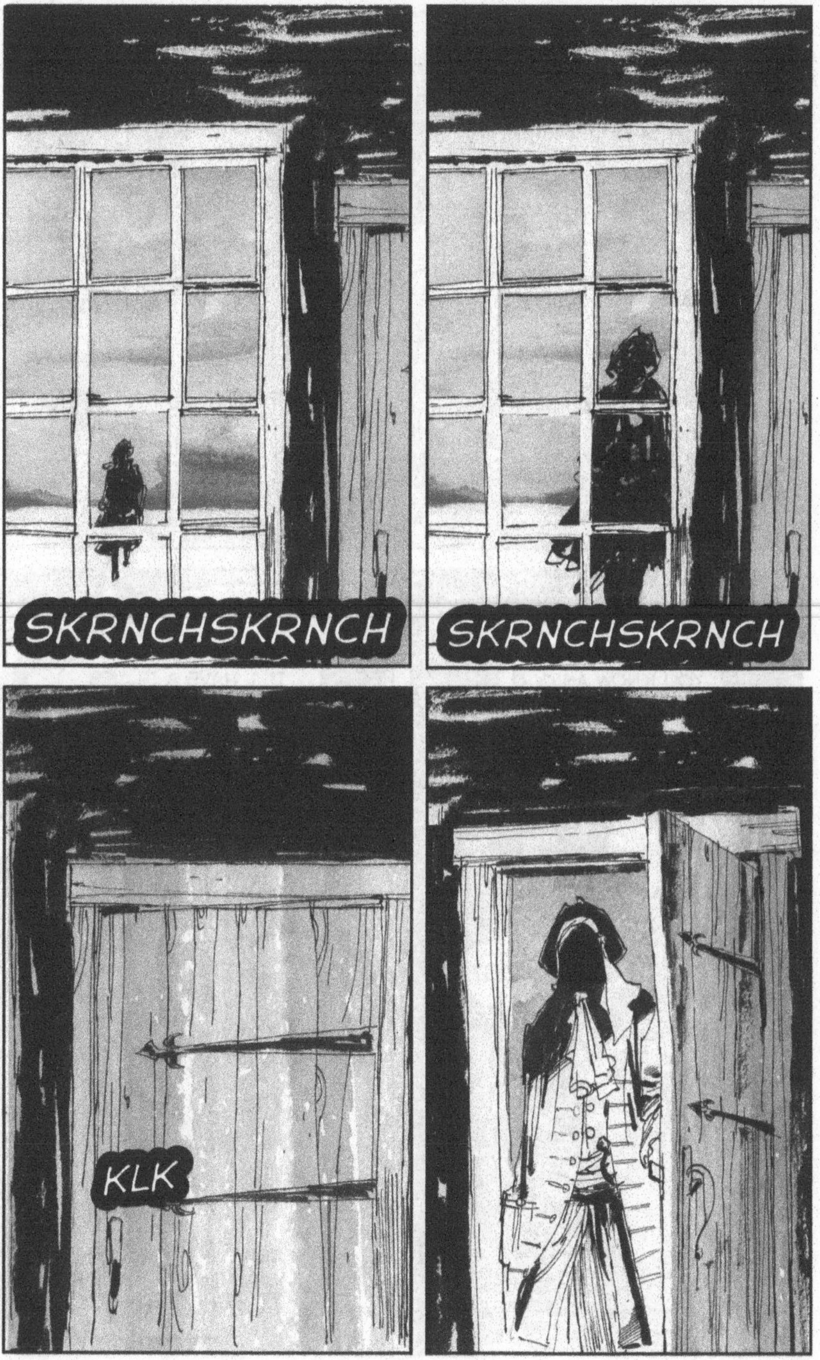
SKRNCHSKRNCH
SKRNCHSKRNCH
KLK

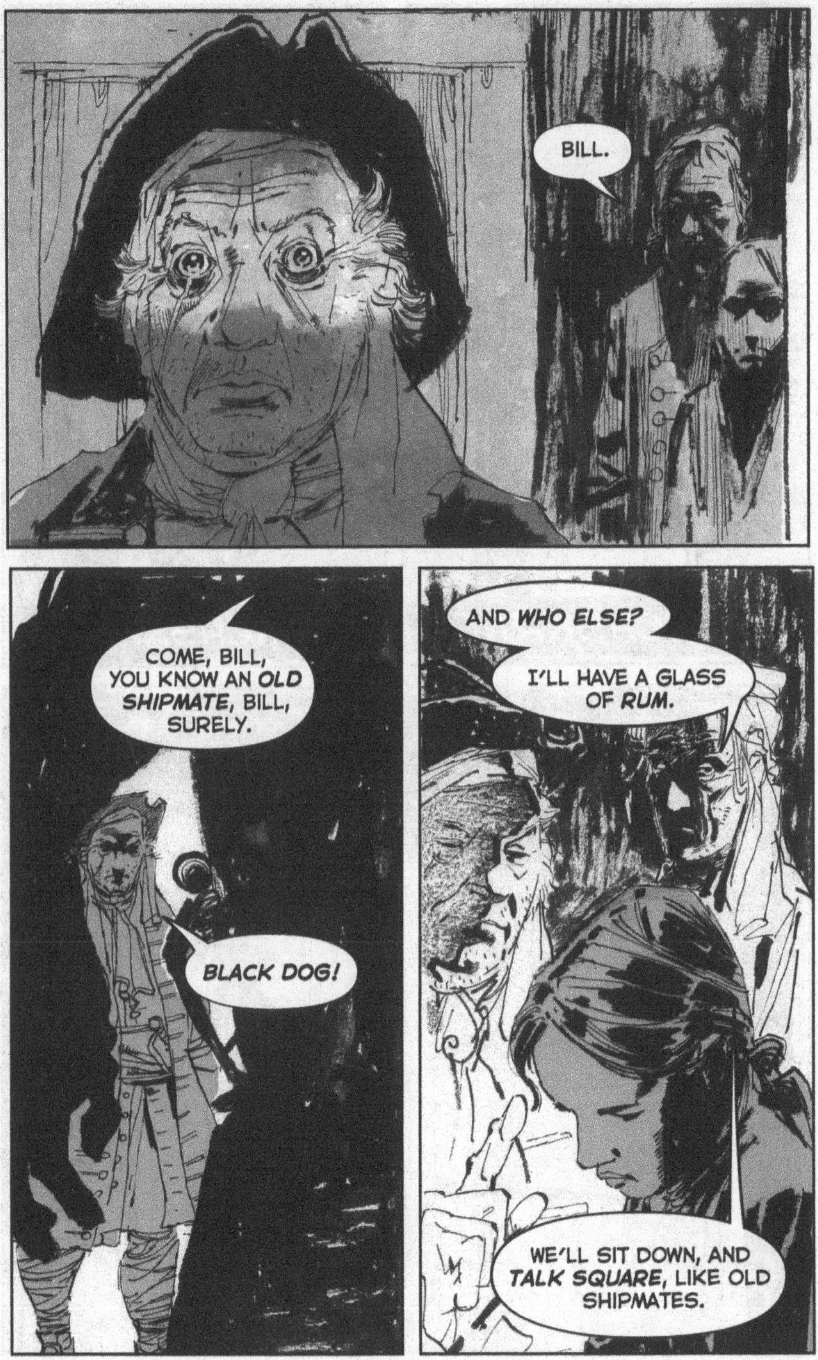
BILL.
COME, BILL, YOU KNOW AN OLD SHIPMATE, BILL, SURELY.
BLACK DOG!
AND WHO ELSE?
I'LL HAVE A GLASS OF RUM.
WE'LL SIT DOWN, AND TALK SQUARE, LIKE OLD SHIPMATES.

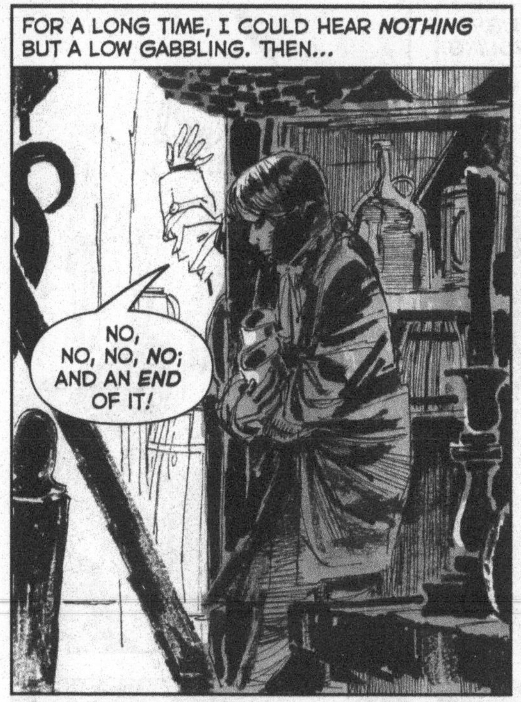
FOR A LONG TIME, I COULD HEAR *NOTHING* BUT A LOW GABBLING. THEN...
NO, NO, NO, *NO*; AND AN *END* OF IT!

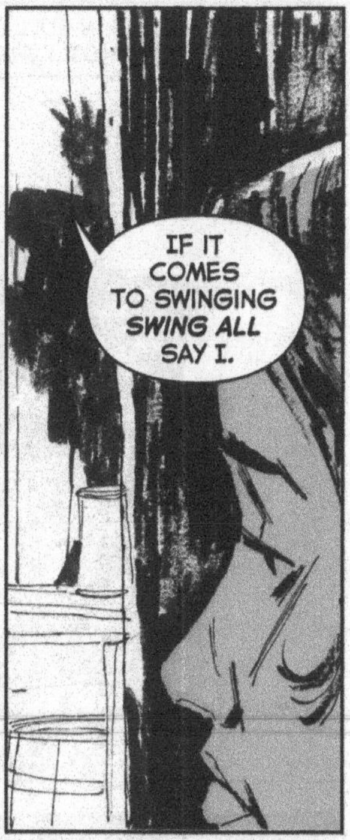
IF IT COMES TO SWINGING *SWING ALL* SAY I.

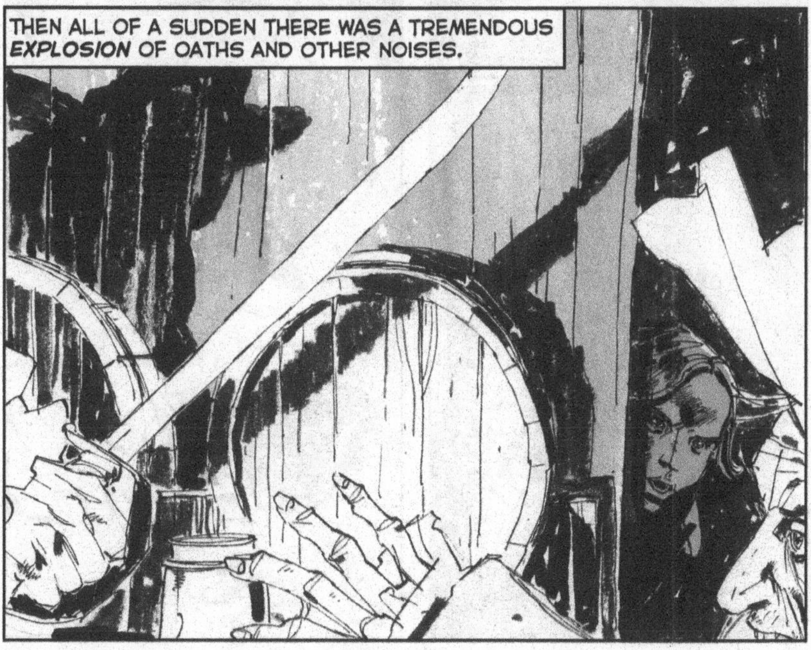
THEN ALL OF A SUDDEN THERE WAS A TREMENDOUS *EXPLOSION* OF OATHS AND OTHER NOISES.

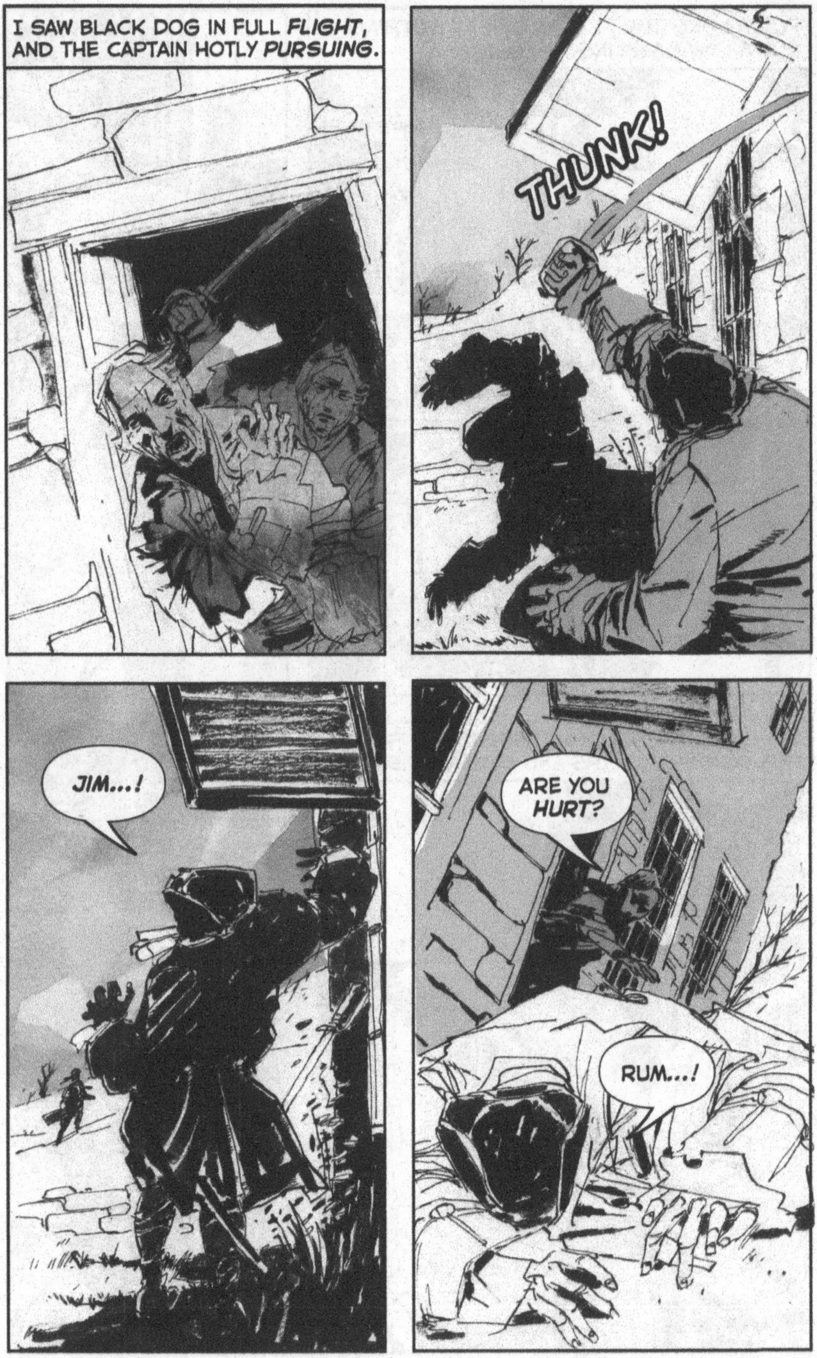
I SAW BLACK DOG IN FULL FLIGHT, AND THE CAPTAIN HOTLY PURSUING.
THUNK!
JIM...!
ARE YOU HURT?
RUM...!

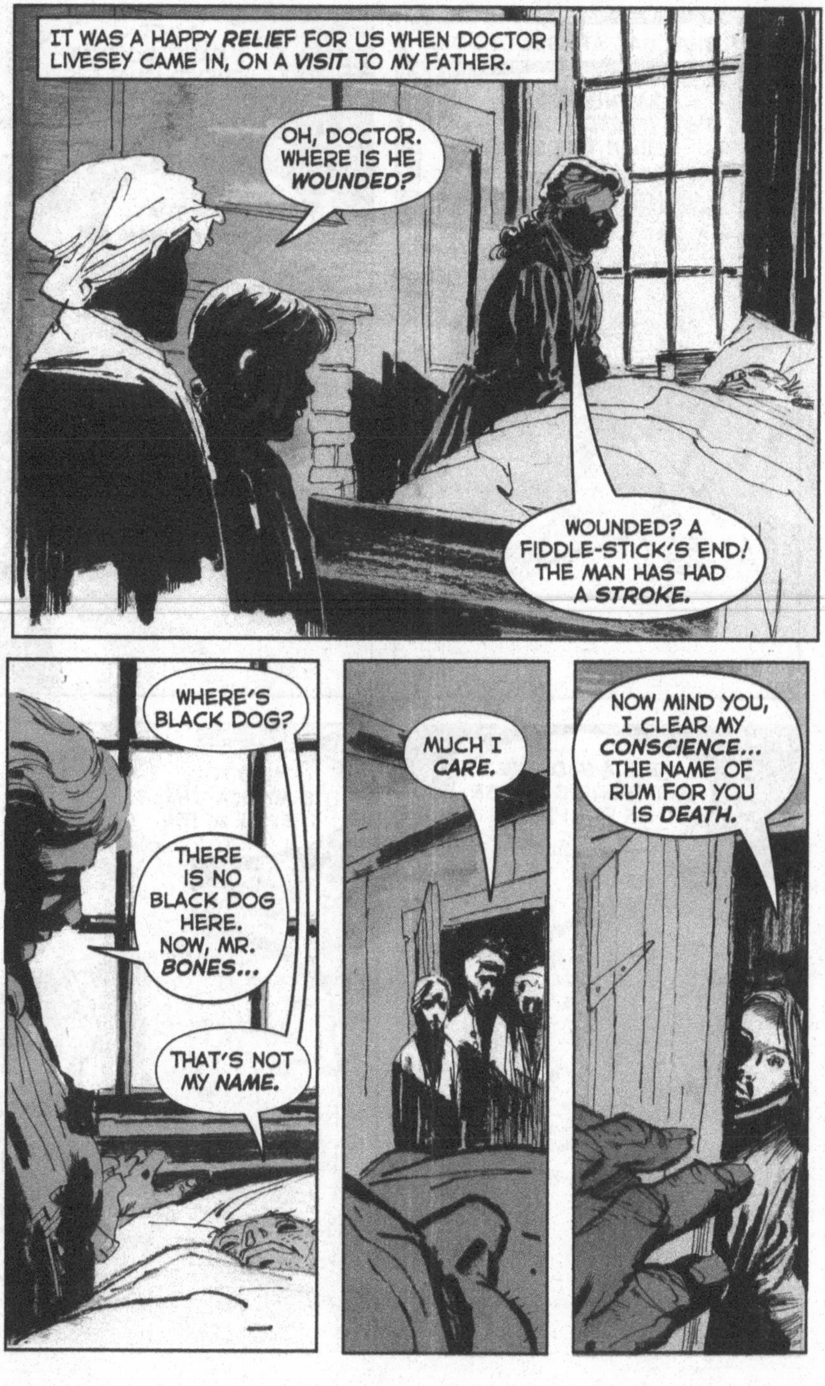
IT WAS A HAPPY RELIEF FOR US WHEN DOCTOR LIVESEY CAME IN, ON A VISIT TO MY FATHER.
OH, DOCTOR. WHERE IS HE WOUNDED?
WOUNDED? A FIDDLE-STICK'S END! THE MAN HAS HAD A STROKE.
WHERE'S BLACK DOG?
THERE IS NO BLACK DOG HERE. NOW, MR. BONES...
THAT'S NOT MY NAME.
MUCH I CARE.
NOW MIND YOU, I CLEAR MY CONSCIENCE... THE NAME OF RUM FOR YOU IS DEATH.

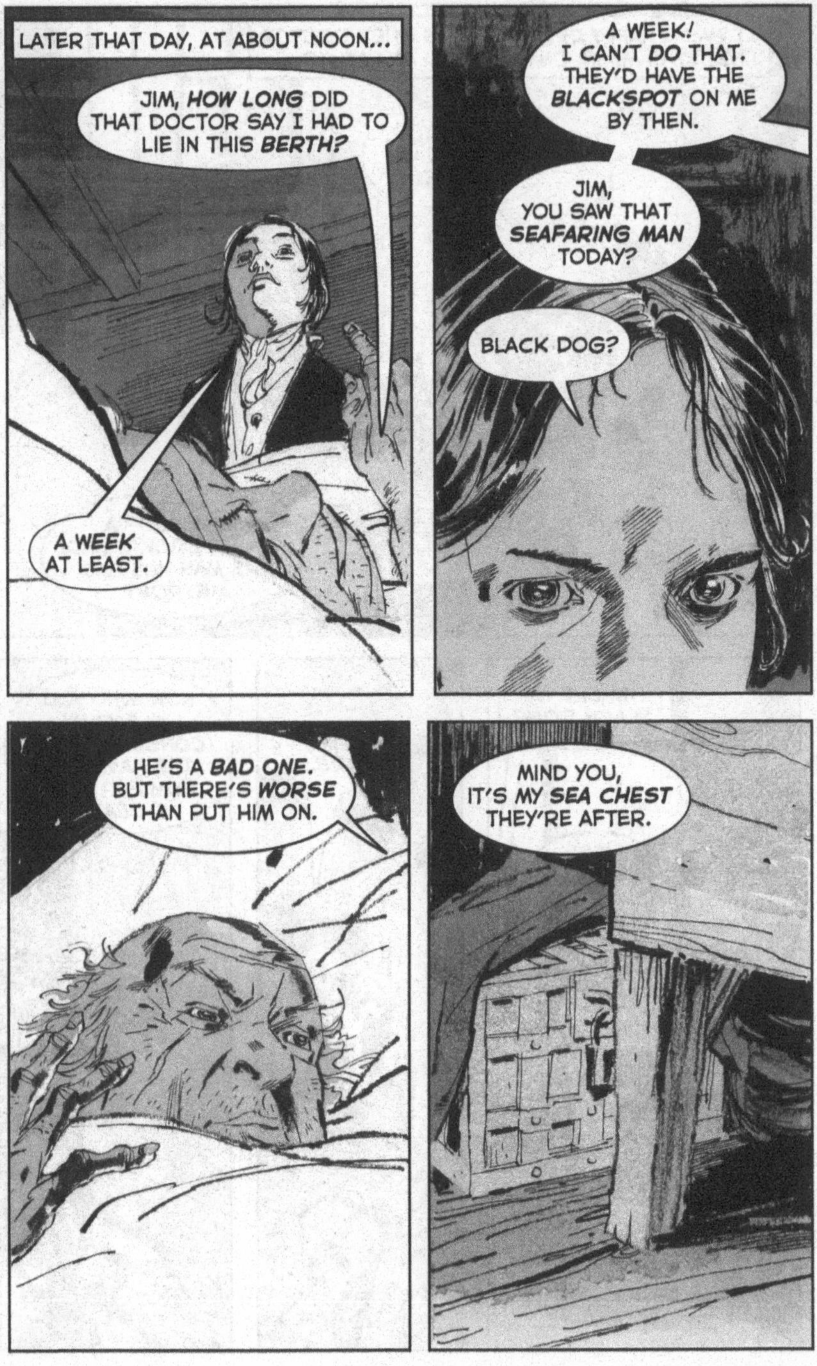
LATER THAT DAY, AT ABOUT NOON...
JIM, HOW LONG DID THAT DOCTOR SAY I HAD TO LIE IN THIS BERTH?
A WEEK AT LEAST.
A WEEK! I CAN'T DO THAT. THEY'D HAVE THE BLACKSPOT ON ME BY THEN.
JIM, YOU SAW THAT SEAFARING MAN TODAY?
BLACK DOG?
HE'S A BAD ONE. BUT THERE'S WORSE THAN PUT HIM ON.
MIND YOU, IT'S MY SEA CHEST THEY'RE AFTER.

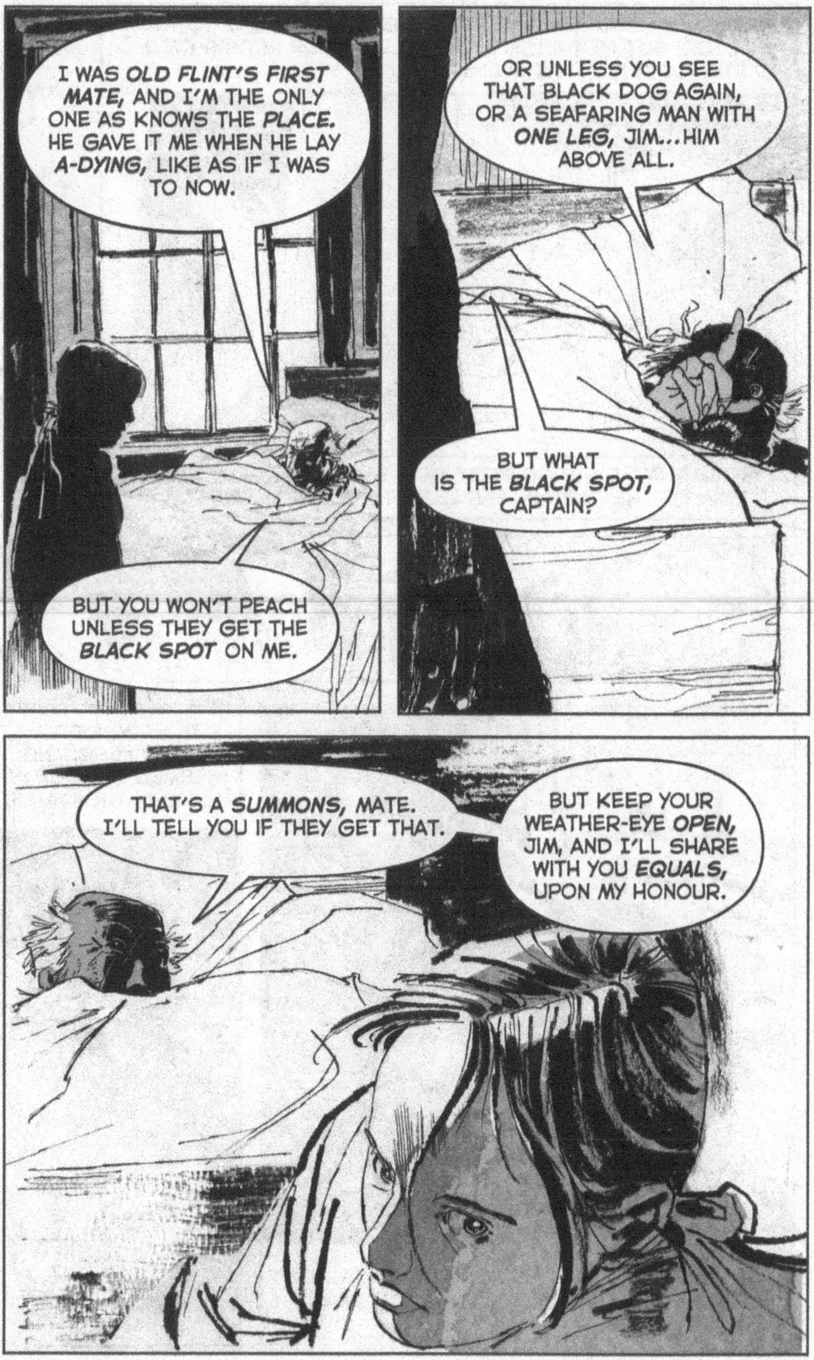
I WAS OLD FLINT'S FIRST MATE, AND I'M THE ONLY ONE AS KNOWS THE PLACE. HE GAVE IT ME WHEN HE LAY A-DYING, LIKE AS IF I WAS TO NOW.
BUT YOU WON'T PEACH UNLESS THEY GET THE BLACK SPOT ON ME.
OR UNLESS YOU SEE THAT BLACK DOG AGAIN, OR A SEAFARING MAN WITH ONE LEG, JIM...HIM ABOVE ALL.
BUT WHAT IS THE BLACK SPOT, CAPTAIN?
THAT'S A SUMMONS, MATE. I'LL TELL YOU IF THEY GET THAT.
BUT KEEP YOUR WEATHER-EYE OPEN, JIM, AND I'LL SHARE WITH YOU EQUALS, UPON MY HONOUR.

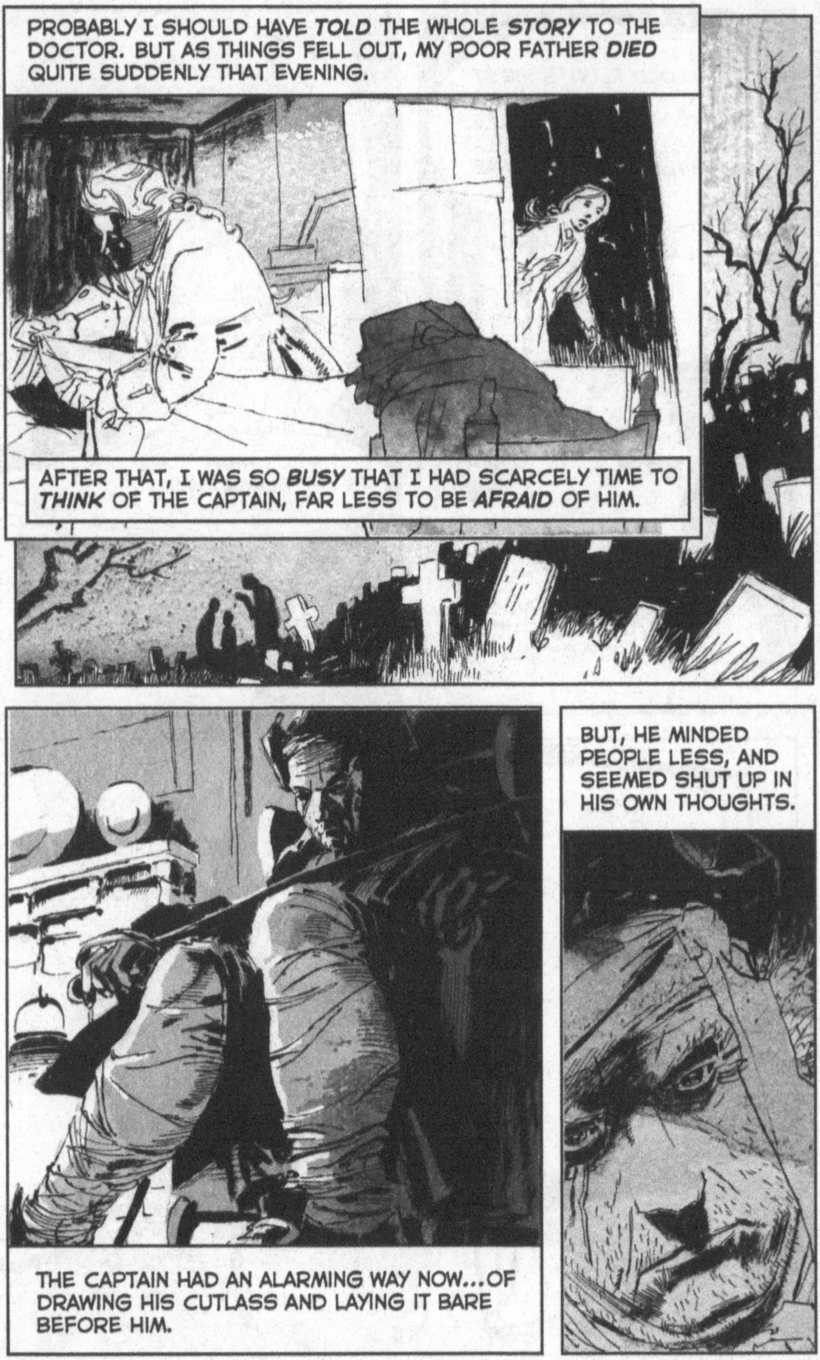
PROBABLY I SHOULD HAVE TOLD THE WHOLE STORY TO THE DOCTOR. BUT AS THINGS FELL OUT, MY POOR FATHER DIED QUITE SUDDENLY THAT EVENING.
AFTER THAT, I WAS SO BUSY THAT I HAD SCARCELY TIME TO THINK OF THE CAPTAIN, FAR LESS TO BE AFRAID OF HIM.
THE CAPTAIN HAD AN ALARMING WAY NOW...OF DRAWING HIS CUTLASS AND LAYING IT BARE BEFORE HIM.
BUT, HE MINDED PEOPLE LESS, AND SEEMED SHUT UP IN HIS OWN THOUGHTS.

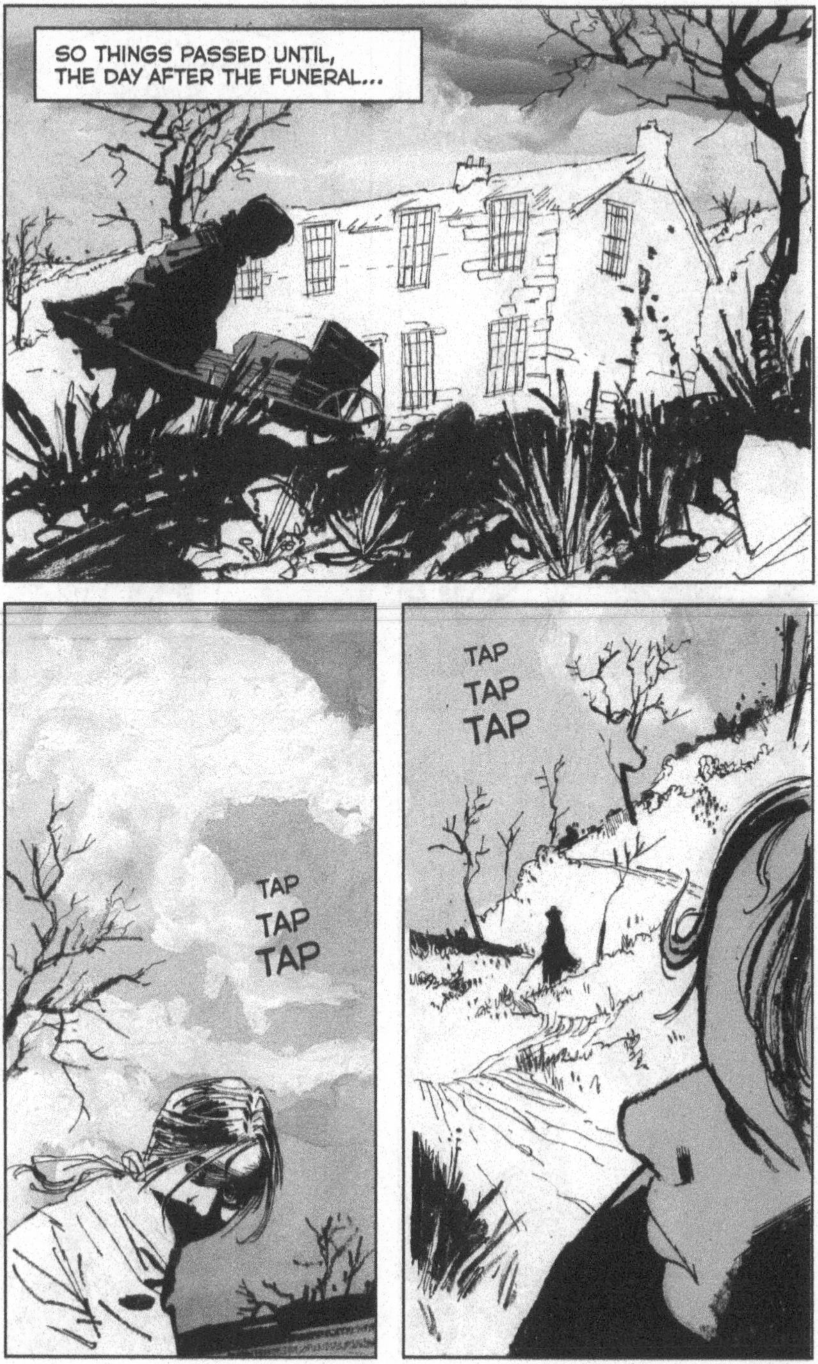
SO THINGS PASSED UNTIL, THE DAY AFTER THE FUNERAL...
TAP
TAP
TAP
TAP
TAP
TAP

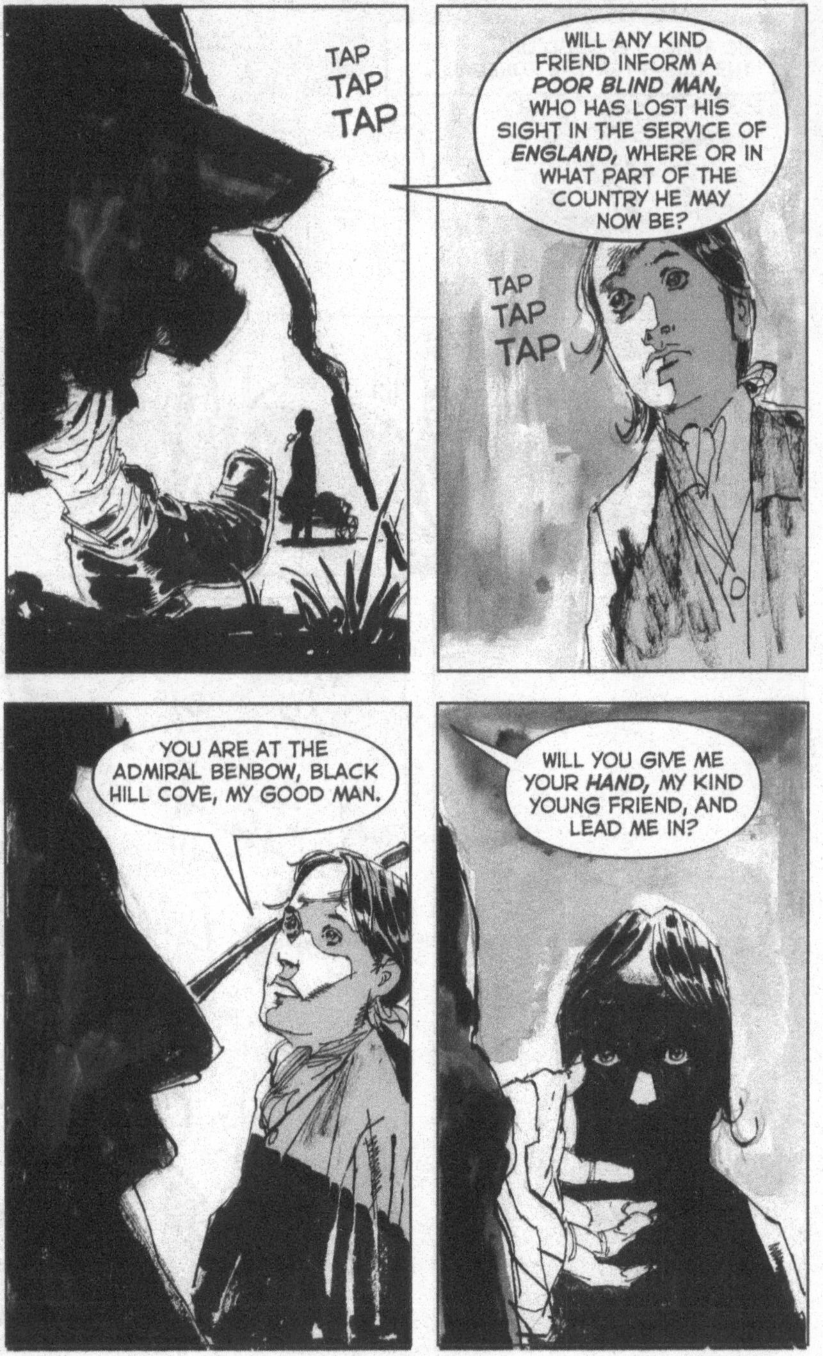
TAP TAP TAP
WILL ANY KIND FRIEND INFORM A POOR BLIND MAN, WHO HAS LOST HIS SIGHT IN THE SERVICE OF ENGLAND, WHERE OR IN WHAT PART OF THE COUNTRY HE MAY NOW BE?
TAP TAP TAP
YOU ARE AT THE ADMIRAL BENBOW, BLACK HILL COVE, MY GOOD MAN.
WILL YOU GIVE ME YOUR HAND, MY KIND YOUNG FRIEND, AND LEAD ME IN?

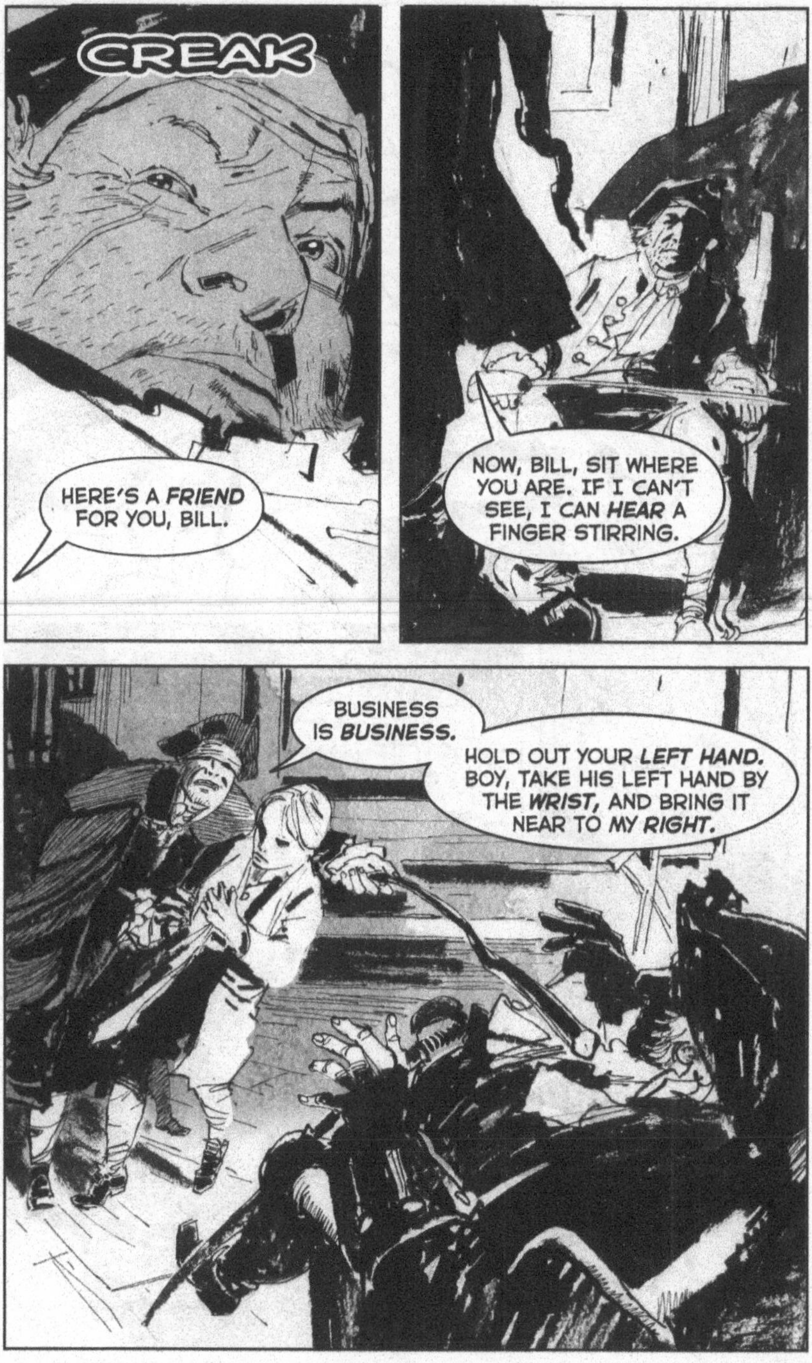
CREAK
HERE'S A FRIEND FOR YOU, BILL.
NOW, BILL, SIT WHERE YOU ARE. IF I CAN'T SEE, I CAN HEAR A FINGER STIRRING.
BUSINESS IS BUSINESS.
HOLD OUT YOUR LEFT HAND. BOY, TAKE HIS LEFT HAND BY THE WRIST, AND BRING IT NEAR TO MY RIGHT.

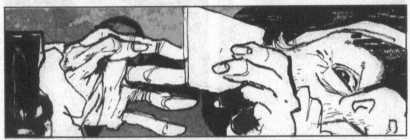

AND NOW THAT'S *DONE!*

TAP
TAP
TAP
TAP

TEN O'CLOCK! GIVES US *SIX HOURS.* WE'LL DO THEM *YET.*

SUDDENLY, HE *REELED*, PUT HIS HAND TO HIS *THROAT*, AND THEN *FELL.*

THE CAPTAIN HAD BEEN STRUCK *DEAD* BY THUNDERING *APOPLEXY.*

TAP
TAP
TAP

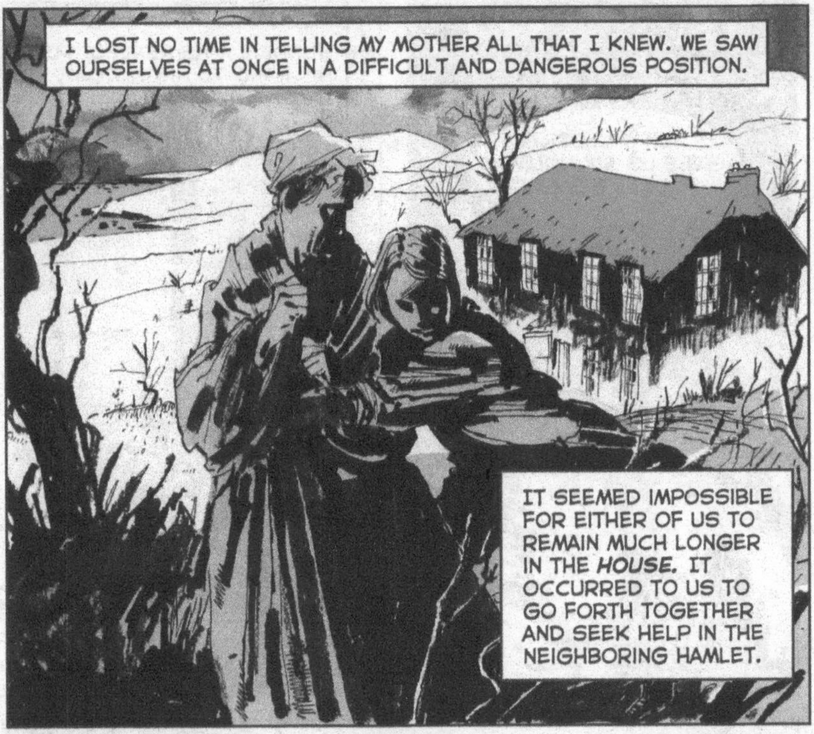
I LOST NO TIME IN TELLING MY MOTHER ALL THAT I KNEW. WE SAW OURSELVES AT ONCE IN A DIFFICULT AND DANGEROUS POSITION.
IT SEEMED IMPOSSIBLE FOR EITHER OF US TO REMAIN MUCH LONGER IN THE *HOUSE.* IT OCCURRED TO US TO GO FORTH TOGETHER AND SEEK HELP IN THE NEIGHBORING HAMLET.

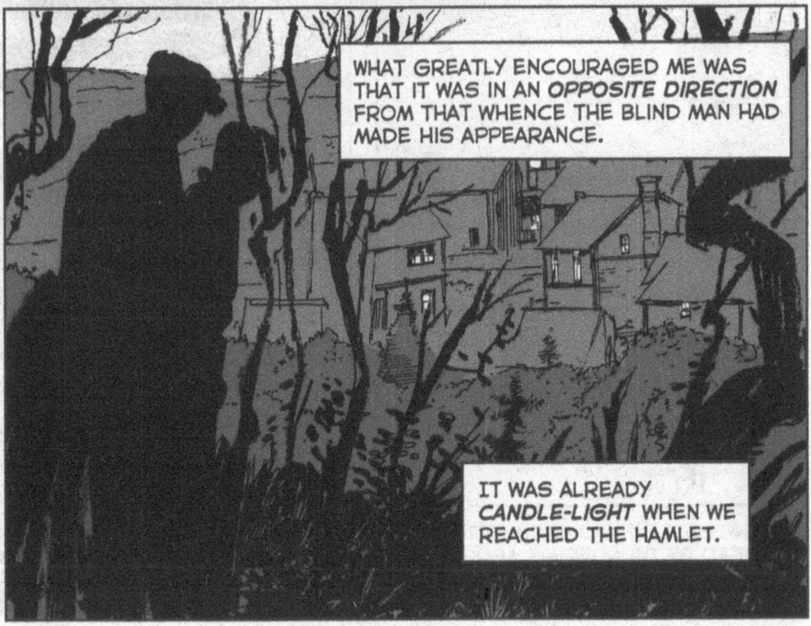
WHAT GREATLY ENCOURAGED ME WAS THAT IT WAS IN AN *OPPOSITE DIRECTION* FROM THAT WHENCE THE BLIND MAN HAD MADE HIS APPEARANCE.
IT WAS ALREADY *CANDLE-LIGHT* WHEN WE REACHED THE HAMLET.

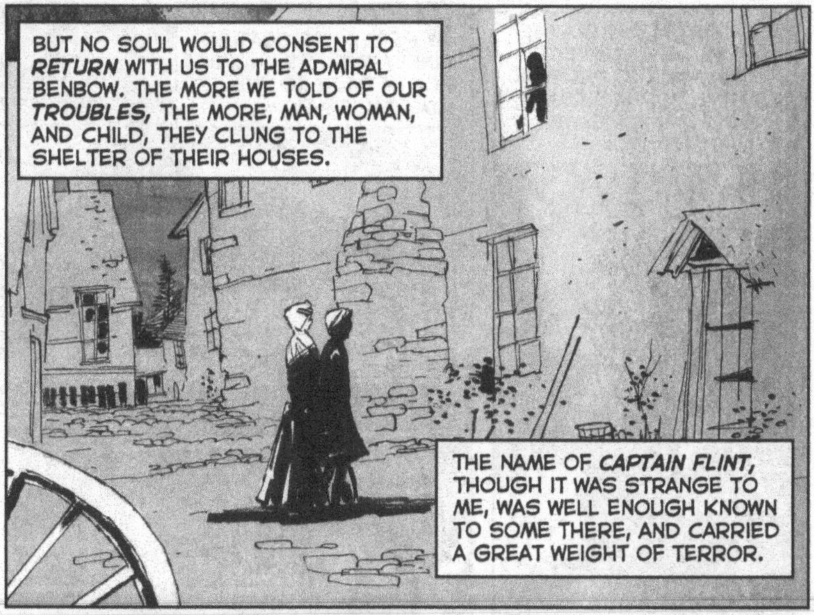
BUT NO SOUL WOULD CONSENT TO RETURN WITH US TO THE ADMIRAL BENBOW. THE MORE WE TOLD OF OUR TROUBLES, THE MORE, MAN, WOMAN, AND CHILD, THEY CLUNG TO THE SHELTER OF THEIR HOUSES.
THE NAME OF CAPTAIN FLINT, THOUGH IT WAS STRANGE TO ME, WAS WELL ENOUGH KNOWN TO SOME THERE, AND CARRIED A GREAT WEIGHT OF TERROR.

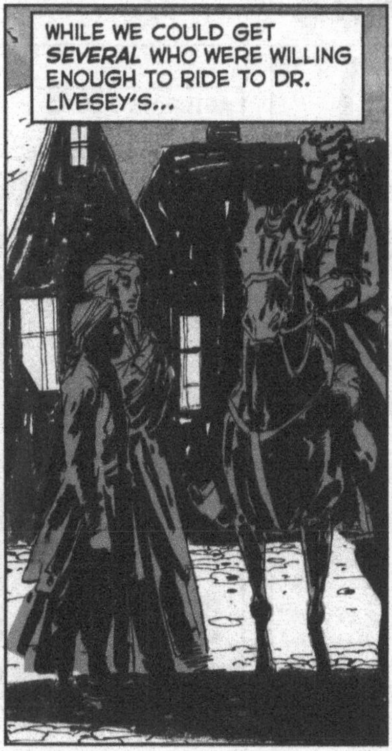
WHILE WE COULD GET SEVERAL WHO WERE WILLING ENOUGH TO RIDE TO DR. LIVESEY'S...

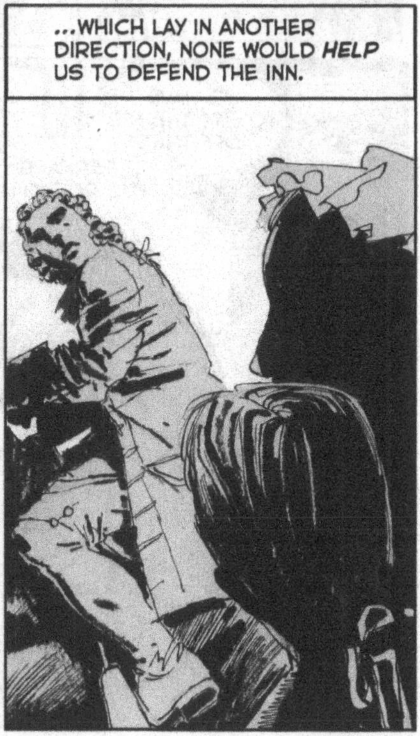
...WHICH LAY IN ANOTHER DIRECTION, NONE WOULD HELP US TO DEFEND THE INN.

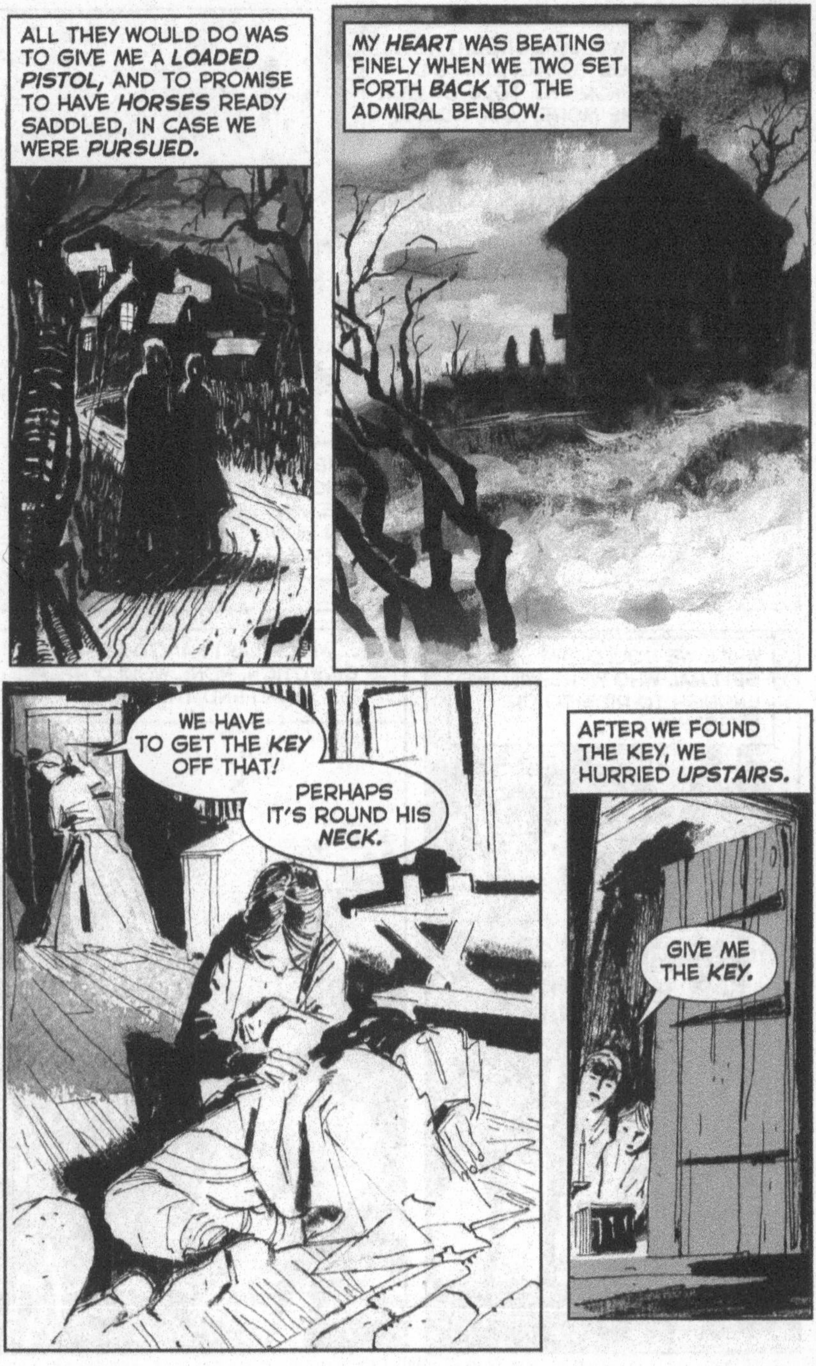
ALL THEY WOULD DO WAS TO GIVE ME A LOADED PISTOL, AND TO PROMISE TO HAVE HORSES READY SADDLED, IN CASE WE WERE PURSUED.
MY HEART WAS BEATING FINELY WHEN WE TWO SET FORTH BACK TO THE ADMIRAL BENBOW.
WE HAVE TO GET THE KEY OFF THAT!
PERHAPS IT'S ROUND HIS NECK.
AFTER WE FOUND THE KEY, WE HURRIED UPSTAIRS.
GIVE ME THE KEY.

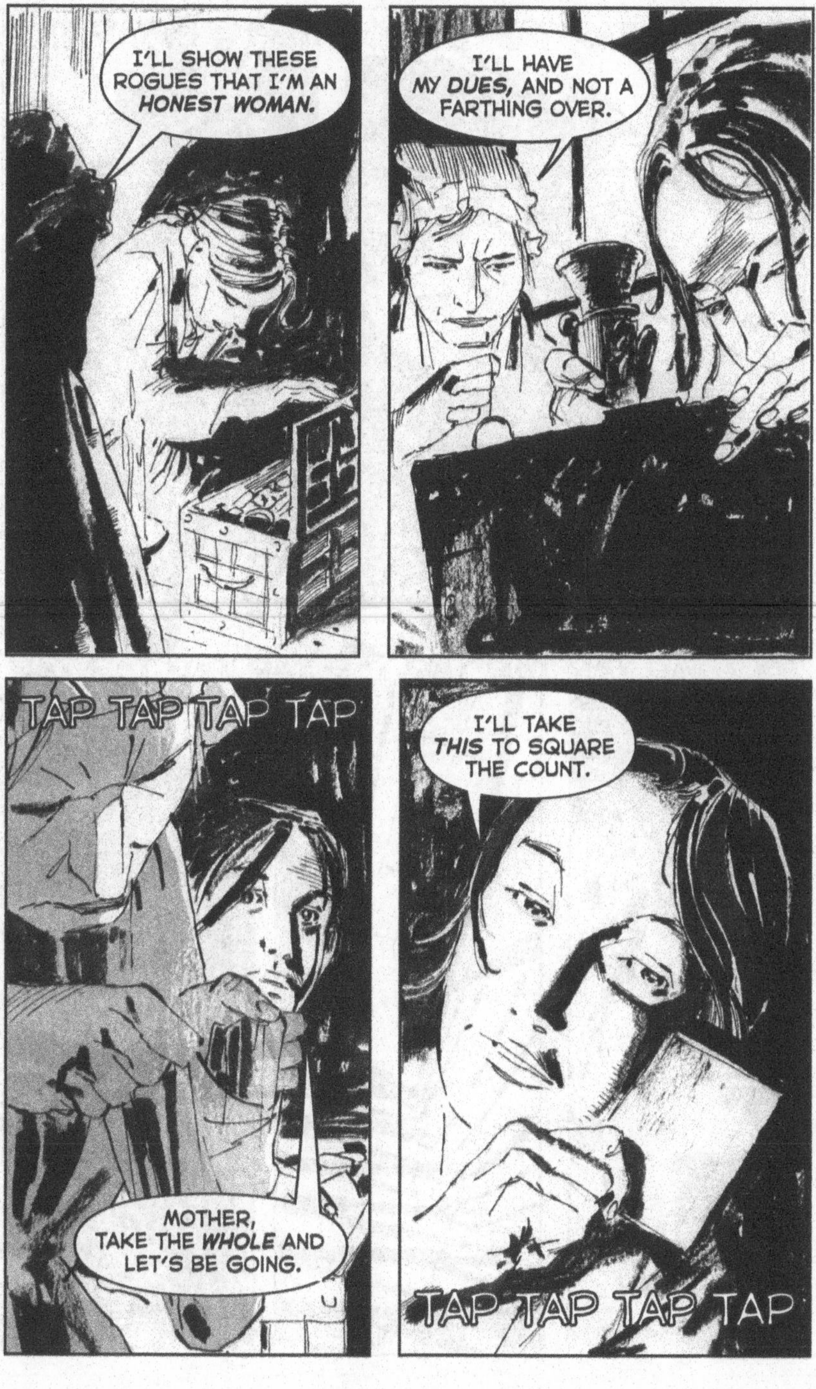
I'LL SHOW THESE ROGUES THAT I'M AN HONEST WOMAN.
I'LL HAVE MY DUES, AND NOT A FARTHING OVER.
TAP TAP TAP TAP
MOTHER, TAKE THE WHOLE AND LET'S BE GOING.
I'LL TAKE THIS TO SQUARE THE COUNT.
TAP TAP TAP TAP

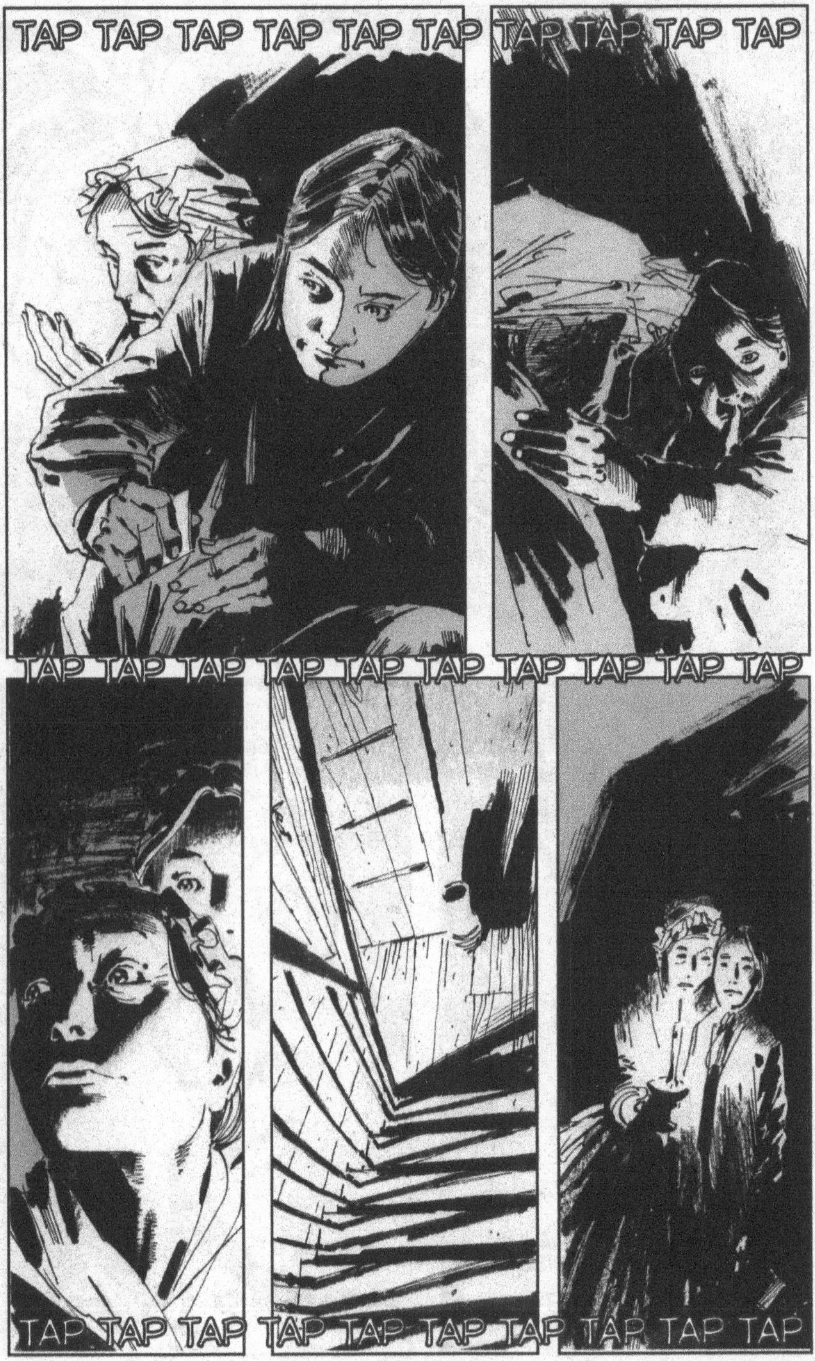
TAP TAP TAP TAP TAP TAP TAP TAP TAP TAP
TAP TAP TAP TAP TAP TAP TAP TAP TAP TAP
TAP TAP TAP TAP TAP TAP TAP TAP TAP TAP

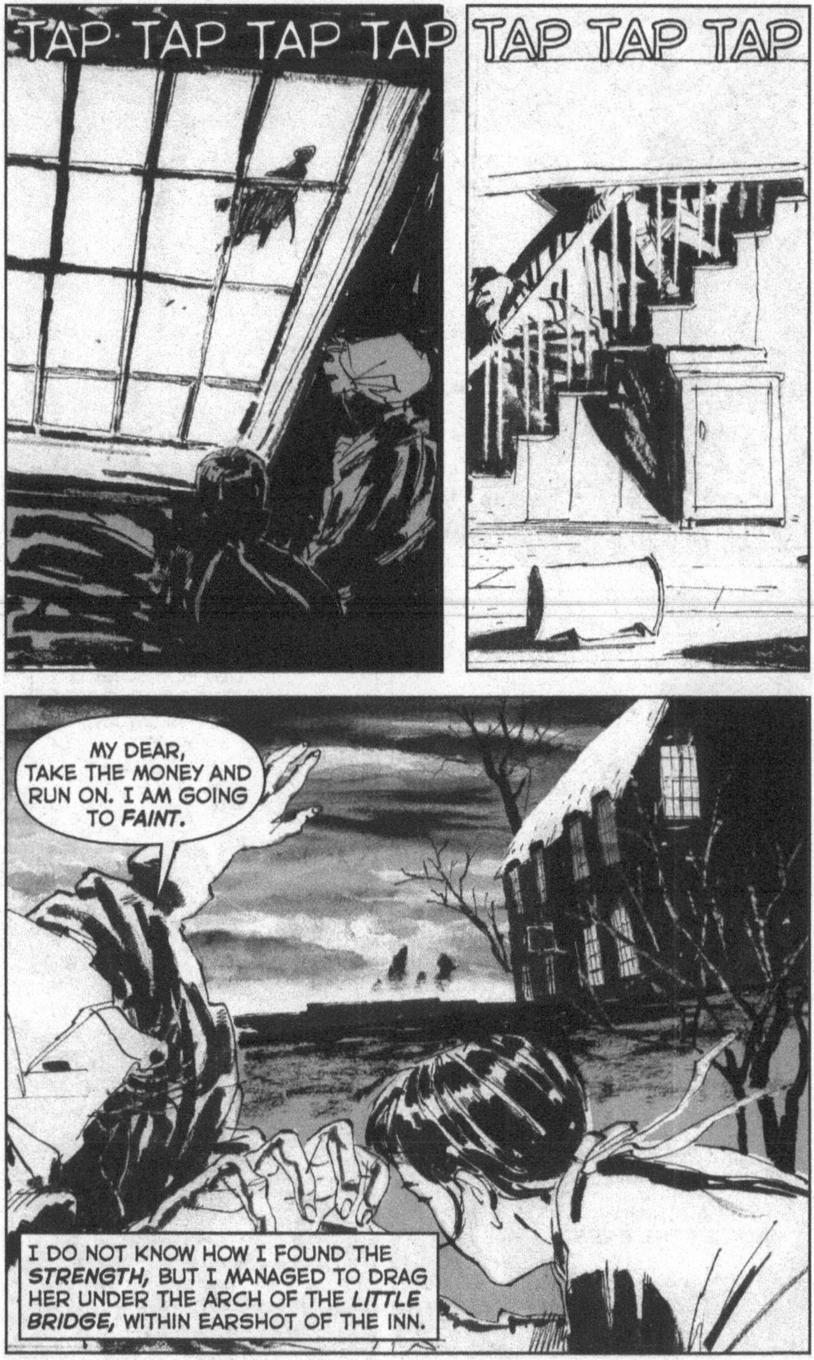
TAP TAP TAP TAP
TAP TAP TAP
MY DEAR, TAKE THE MONEY AND RUN ON. I AM GOING TO *FAINT*.
I DO NOT KNOW HOW I FOUND THE ***STRENGTH,*** BUT I MANAGED TO DRAG HER UNDER THE ARCH OF THE ***LITTLE BRIDGE,*** WITHIN EARSHOT OF THE INN.

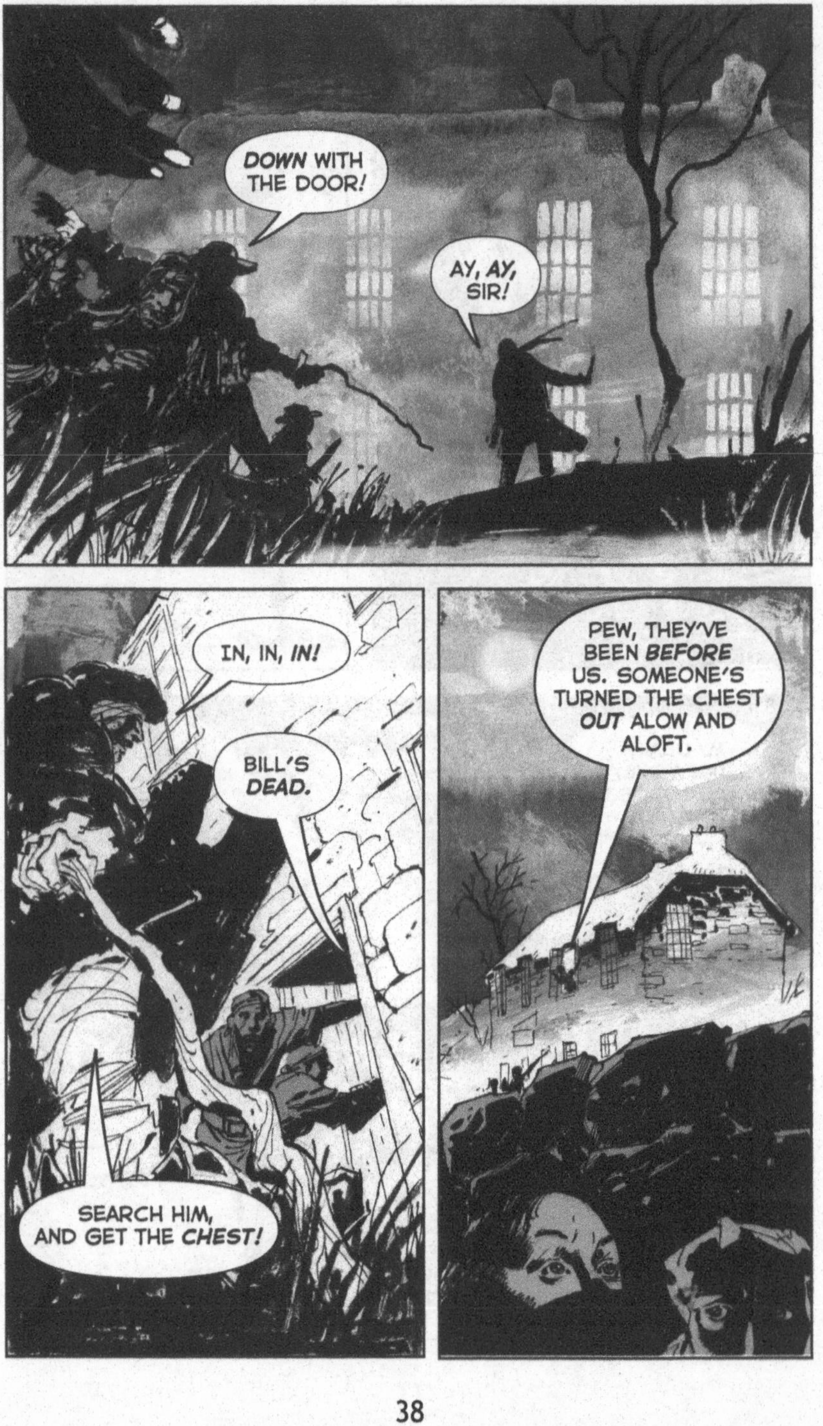
DOWN WITH THE DOOR!
AY, AY, SIR!
IN, IN, IN!
BILL'S DEAD.
SEARCH HIM, AND GET THE CHEST!
PEW, THEY'VE BEEN BEFORE US. SOMEONE'S TURNED THE CHEST OUT ALOW AND ALOFT.

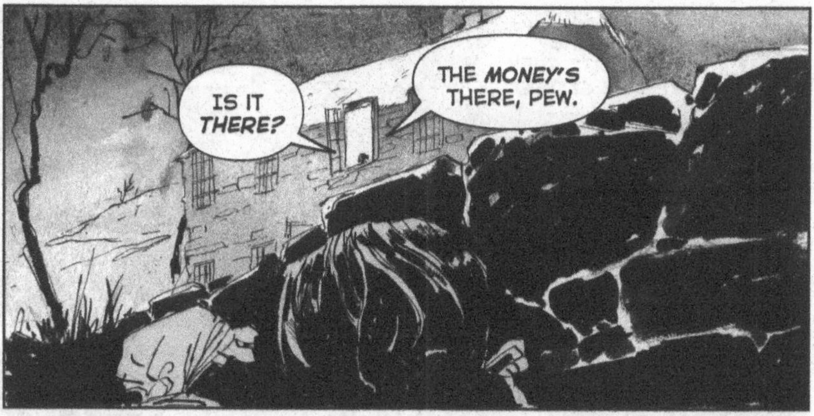
IS IT *THERE?*
THE *MONEY'S* THERE, PEW.

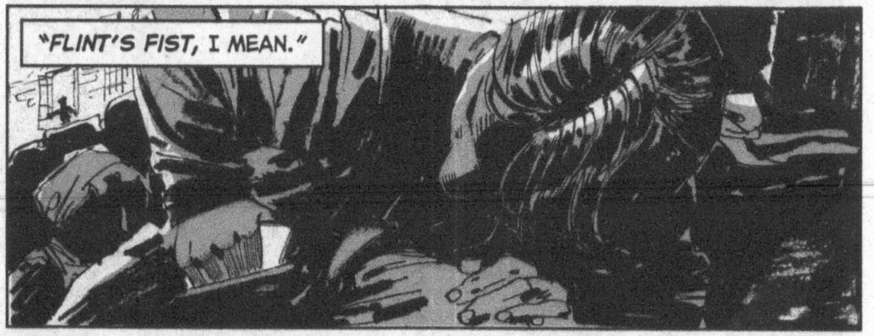
"FLINT'S FIST, I MEAN."

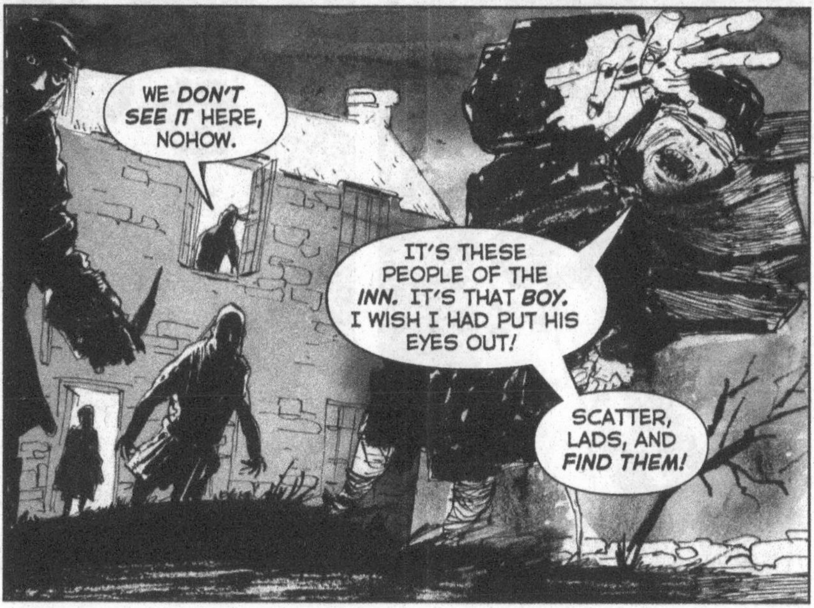
WE *DON'T* SEE *IT* HERE, NOHOW.
IT'S THESE PEOPLE OF THE *INN.* IT'S THAT *BOY.* I WISH I HAD PUT HIS EYES OUT!
SCATTER, LADS, AND *FIND THEM!*

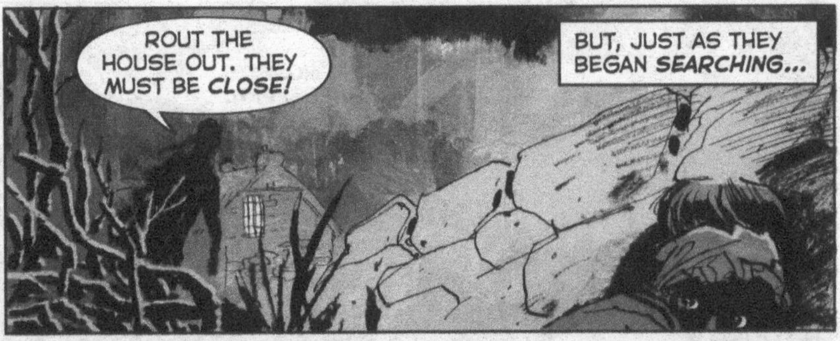
ROUT THE HOUSE OUT. THEY MUST BE CLOSE!
BUT, JUST AS THEY BEGAN SEARCHING...

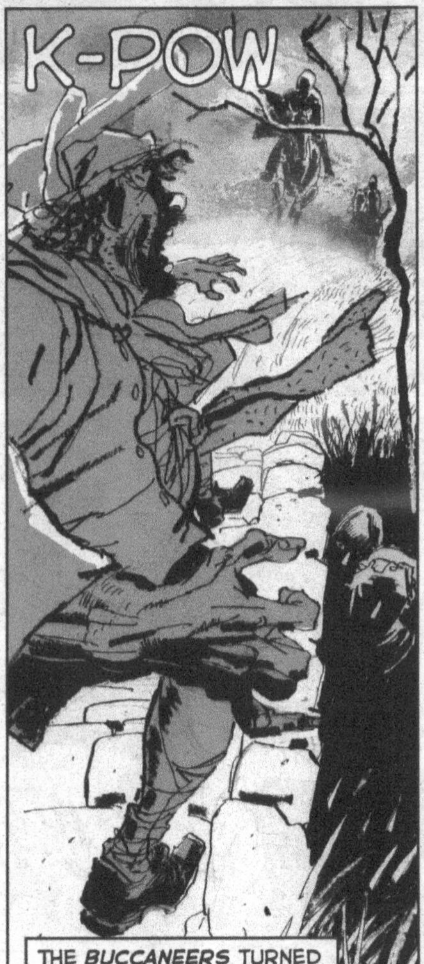
K-POW
THE BUCCANEERS TURNED AT ONCE AND RAN.

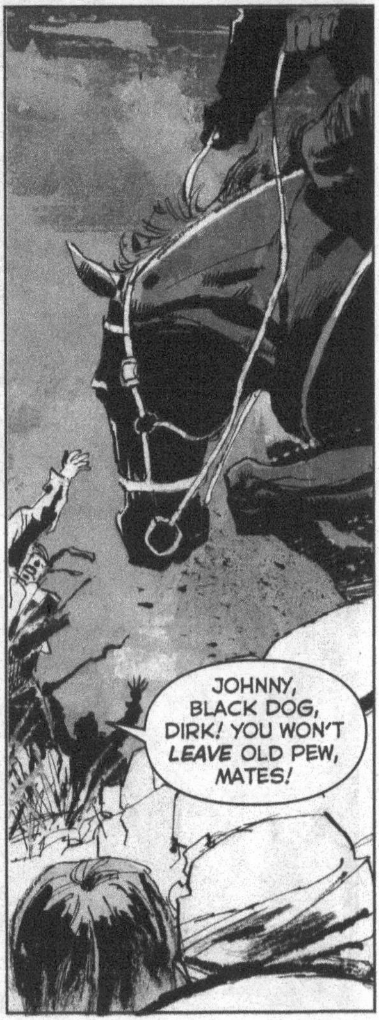
JOHNNY, BLACK DOG, DIRK! YOU WON'T LEAVE OLD PEW, MATES!

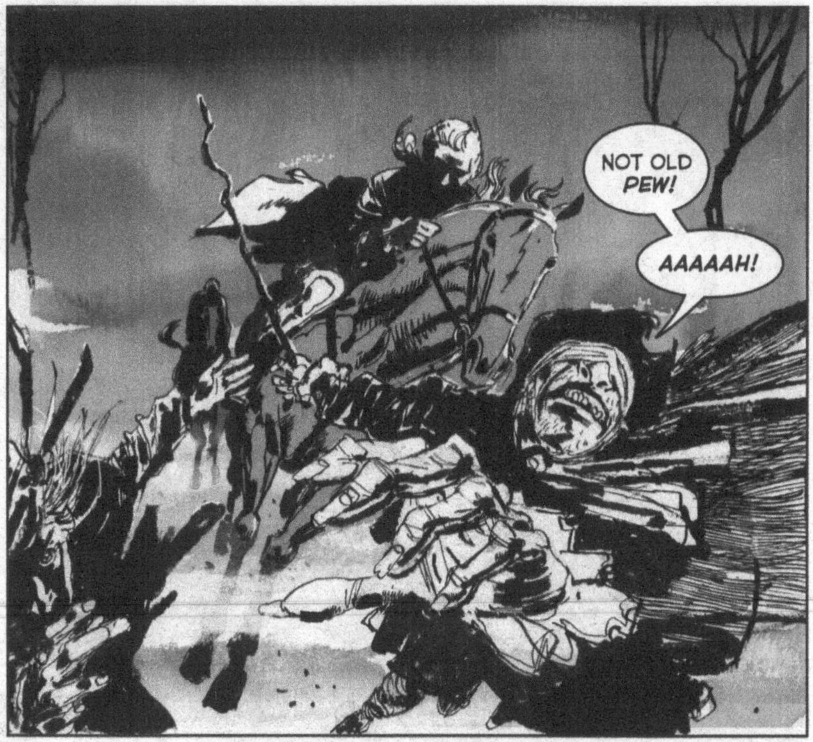
NOT OLD PEW!
AAAAAH!

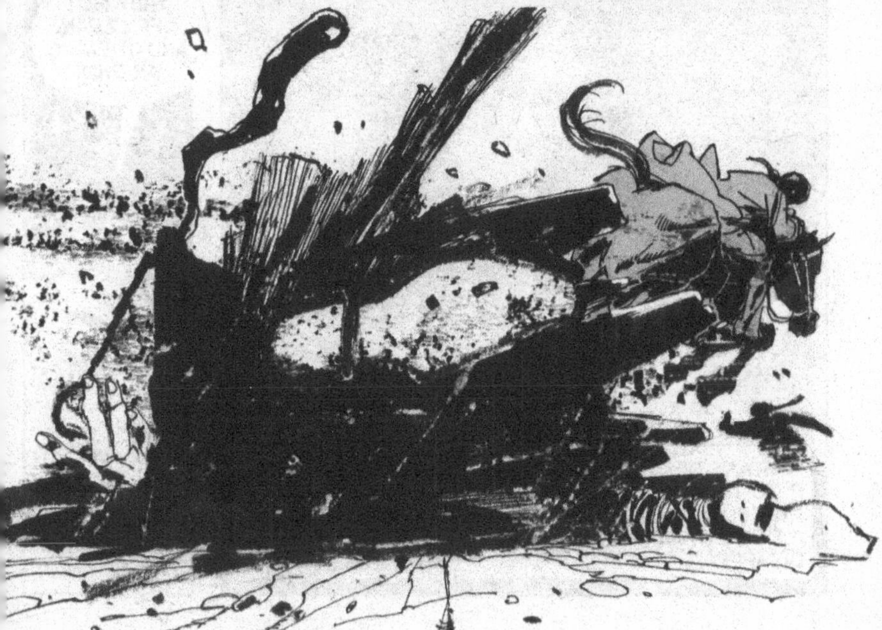

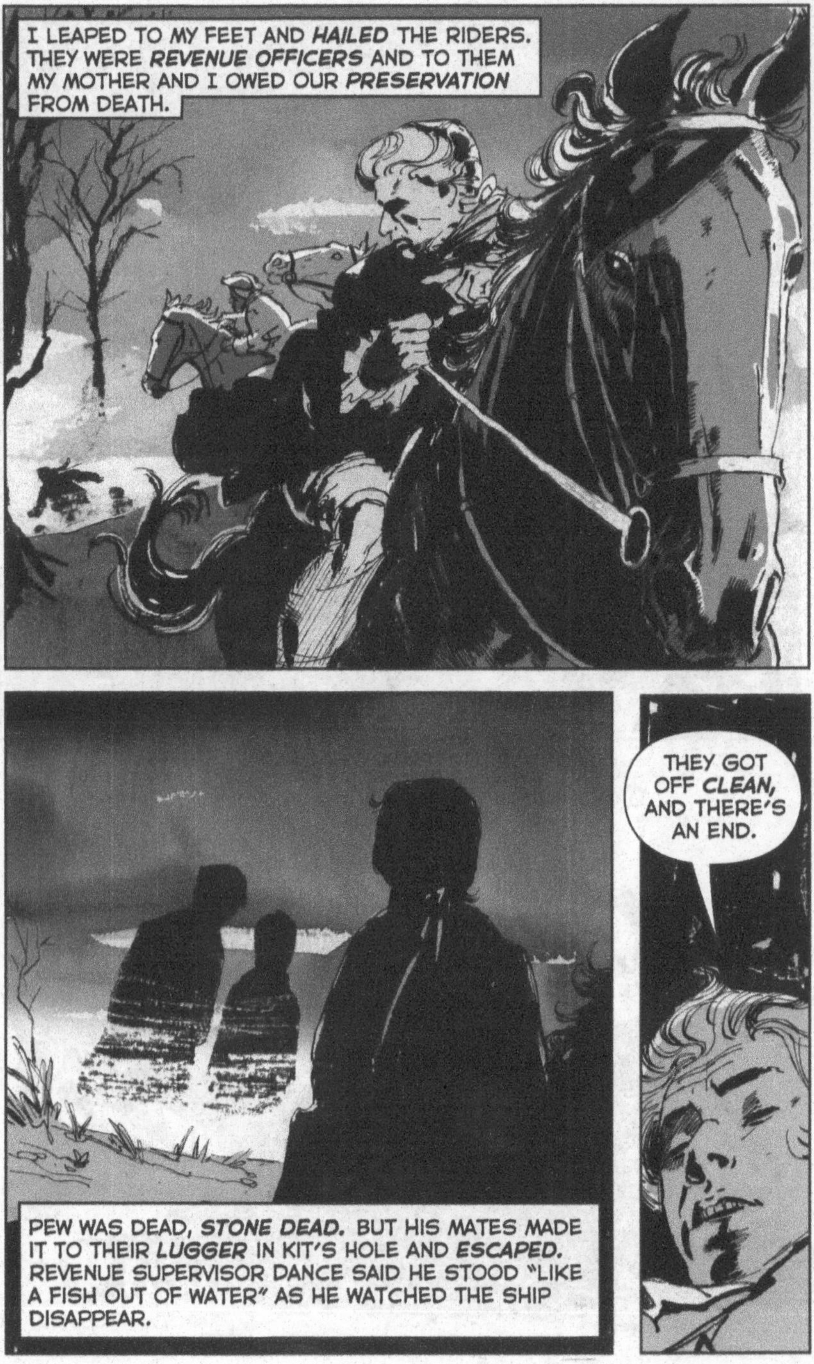
I LEAPED TO MY FEET AND HAILED THE RIDERS. THEY WERE REVENUE OFFICERS AND TO THEM MY MOTHER AND I OWED OUR PRESERVATION FROM DEATH.
PEW WAS DEAD, STONE DEAD. BUT HIS MATES MADE IT TO THEIR LUGGER IN KIT'S HOLE AND ESCAPED. REVENUE SUPERVISOR DANCE SAID HE STOOD "LIKE A FISH OUT OF WATER" AS HE WATCHED THE SHIP DISAPPEAR.
THEY GOT OFF CLEAN, AND THERE'S AN END.

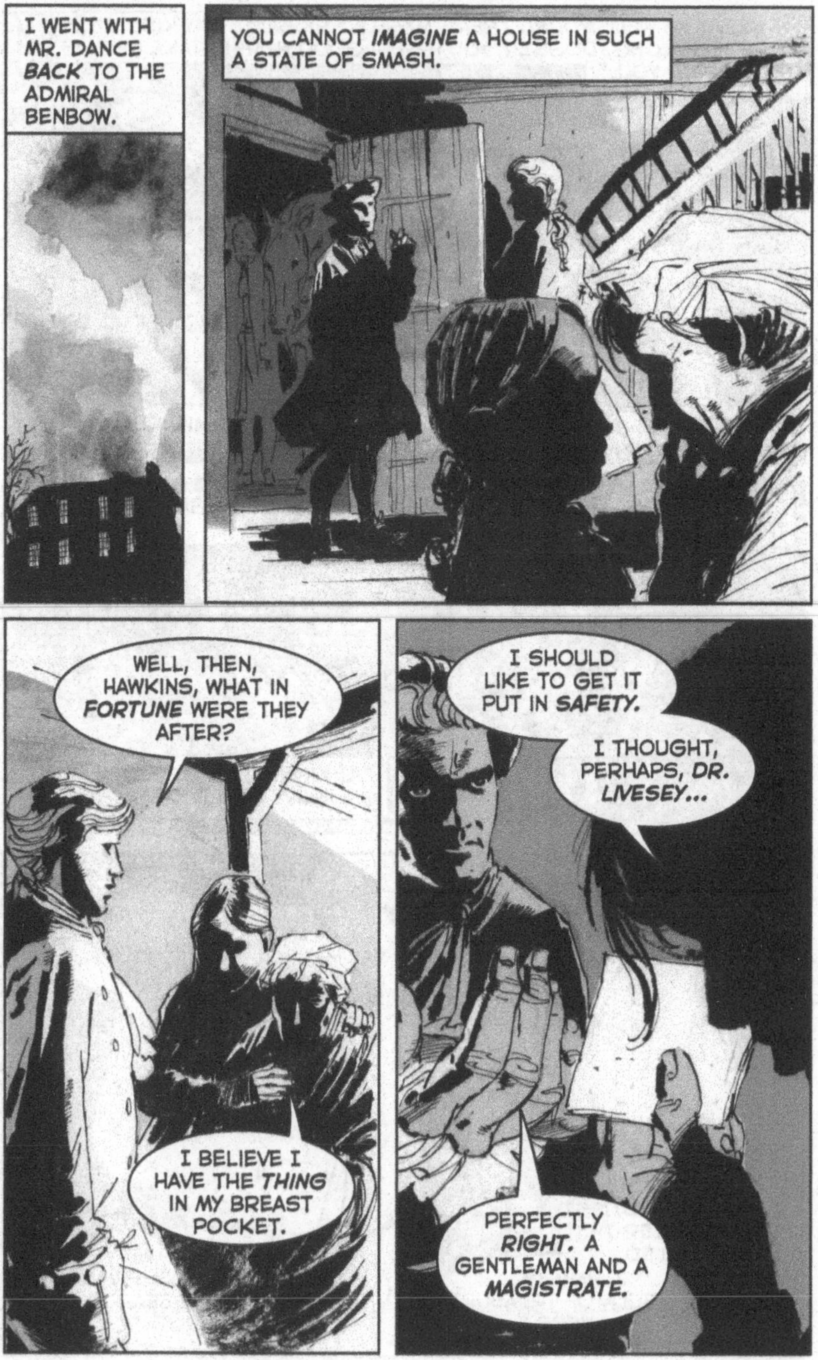
I WENT WITH MR. DANCE *BACK* TO THE ADMIRAL BENBOW.
YOU CANNOT *IMAGINE* A HOUSE IN SUCH A STATE OF SMASH.
WELL, THEN, HAWKINS, WHAT IN *FORTUNE* WERE THEY AFTER?
I BELIEVE I HAVE THE *THING* IN MY BREAST POCKET.
I SHOULD LIKE TO GET IT PUT IN *SAFETY.*
I THOUGHT, PERHAPS, *DR. LIVESEY...*
PERFECTLY *RIGHT.* A GENTLEMAN AND A *MAGISTRATE.*

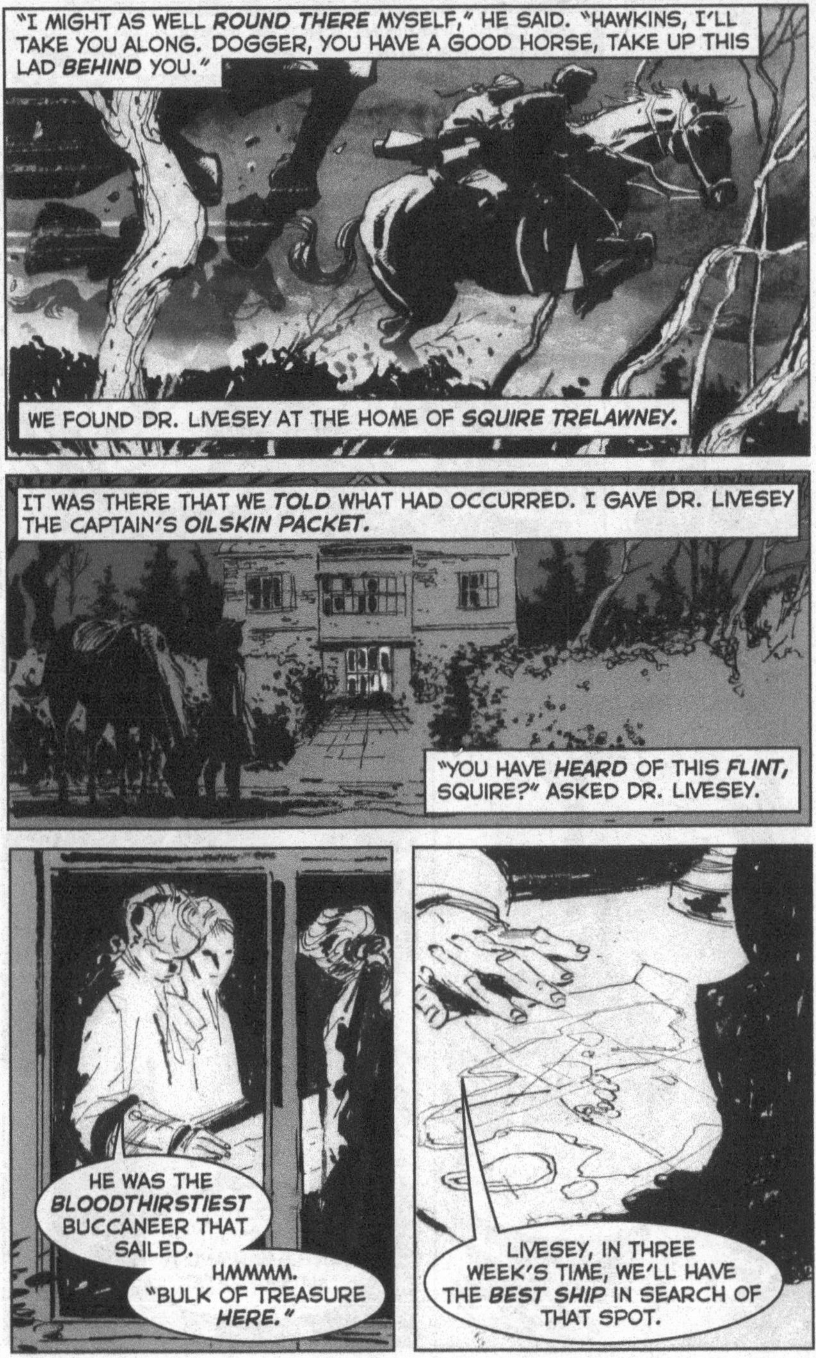
"I MIGHT AS WELL ROUND THERE MYSELF," HE SAID. "HAWKINS, I'LL TAKE YOU ALONG. DOGGER, YOU HAVE A GOOD HORSE, TAKE UP THIS LAD BEHIND YOU."
WE FOUND DR. LIVESEY AT THE HOME OF SQUIRE TRELAWNEY.
IT WAS THERE THAT WE TOLD WHAT HAD OCCURRED. I GAVE DR. LIVESEY THE CAPTAIN'S OILSKIN PACKET.
"YOU HAVE HEARD OF THIS FLINT, SQUIRE?" ASKED DR. LIVESEY.
HE WAS THE BLOODTHIRSTIEST BUCCANEER THAT SAILED.
HMMMM. "BULK OF TREASURE HERE."
LIVESEY, IN THREE WEEK'S TIME, WE'LL HAVE THE BEST SHIP IN SEARCH OF THAT SPOT.

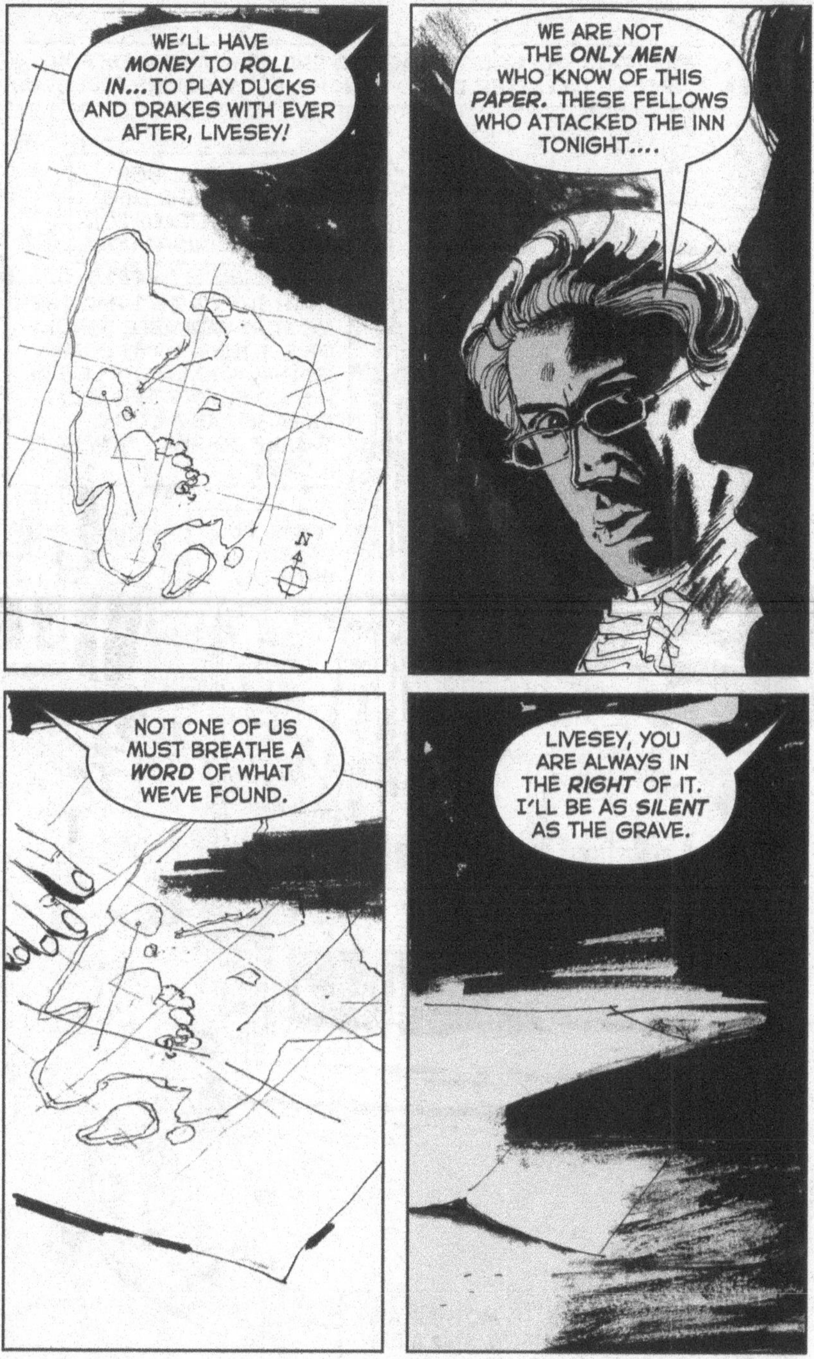
WE'LL HAVE MONEY TO ROLL IN...TO PLAY DUCKS AND DRAKES WITH EVER AFTER, LIVESEY!
WE ARE NOT THE ONLY MEN WHO KNOW OF THIS PAPER. THESE FELLOWS WHO ATTACKED THE INN TONIGHT....
NOT ONE OF US MUST BREATHE A WORD OF WHAT WE'VE FOUND.
LIVESEY, YOU ARE ALWAYS IN THE RIGHT OF IT. I'LL BE AS SILENT AS THE GRAVE.

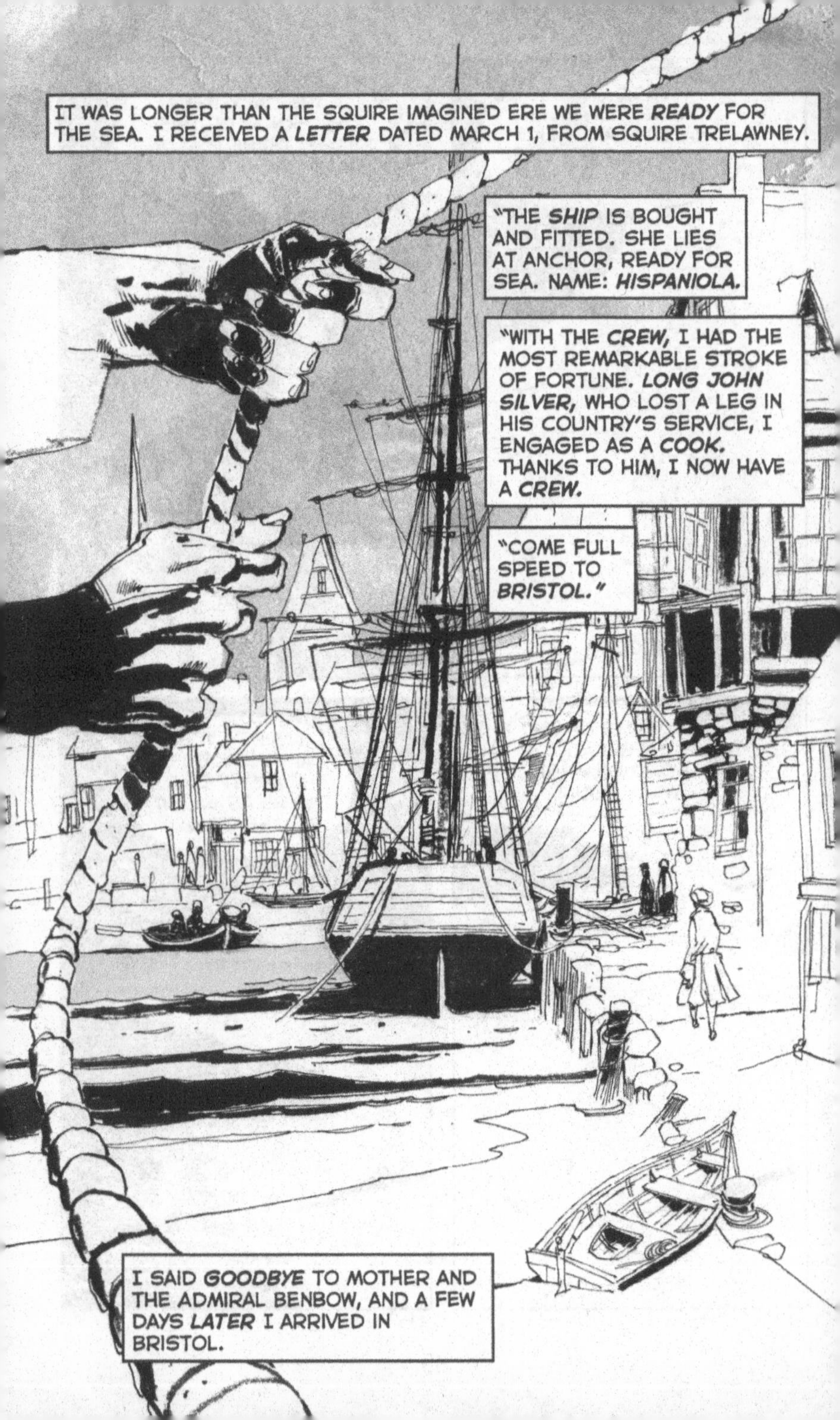
IT WAS LONGER THAN THE SQUIRE IMAGINED ERE WE WERE READY FOR THE SEA. I RECEIVED A LETTER DATED MARCH 1, FROM SQUIRE TRELAWNEY.
"THE SHIP IS BOUGHT AND FITTED. SHE LIES AT ANCHOR, READY FOR SEA. NAME: HISPANIOLA.
"WITH THE CREW, I HAD THE MOST REMARKABLE STROKE OF FORTUNE. LONG JOHN SILVER, WHO LOST A LEG IN HIS COUNTRY'S SERVICE, I ENGAGED AS A COOK. THANKS TO HIM, I NOW HAVE A CREW.
"COME FULL SPEED TO BRISTOL."
I SAID GOODBYE TO MOTHER AND THE ADMIRAL BENBOW, AND A FEW DAYS LATER I ARRIVED IN BRISTOL.

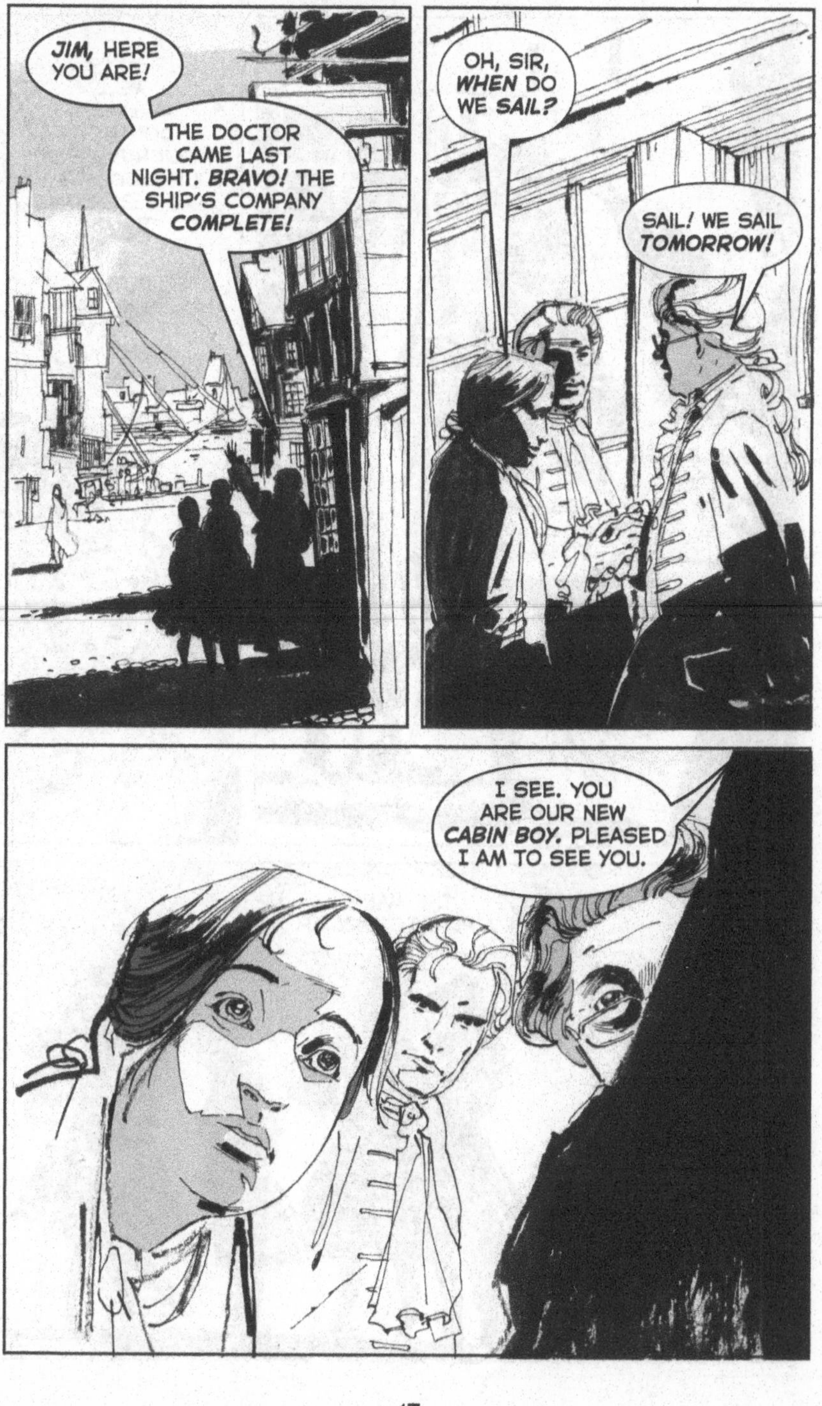
JIM, HERE YOU ARE!
THE DOCTOR CAME LAST NIGHT. BRAVO! THE SHIP'S COMPANY COMPLETE!
OH, SIR, WHEN DO WE SAIL?
SAIL! WE SAIL TOMORROW!
I SEE. YOU ARE OUR NEW CABIN BOY. PLEASED I AM TO SEE YOU.

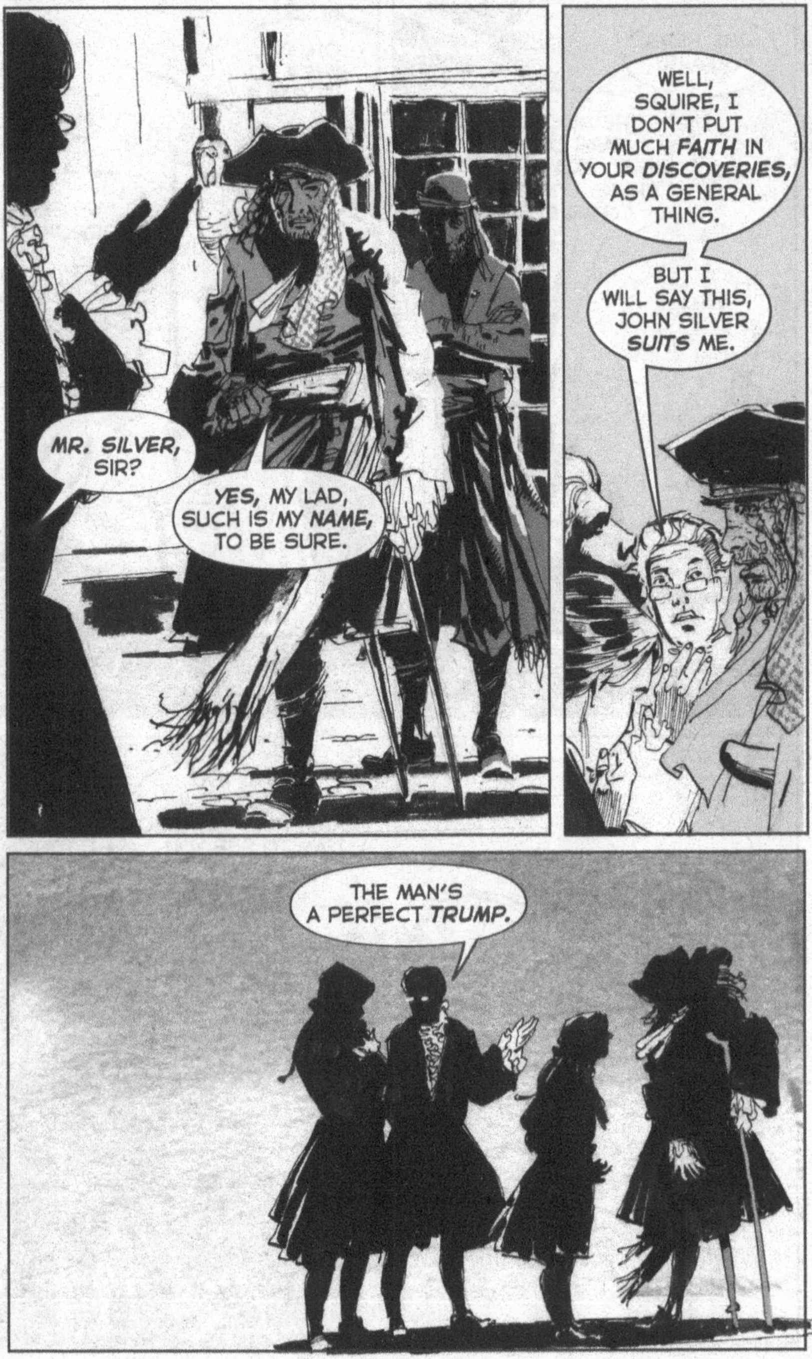
MR. SILVER, SIR?
YES, MY LAD, SUCH IS MY NAME, TO BE SURE.
WELL, SQUIRE, I DON'T PUT MUCH FAITH IN YOUR DISCOVERIES, AS A GENERAL THING.
BUT I WILL SAY THIS, JOHN SILVER SUITS ME.
THE MAN'S A PERFECT TRUMP.

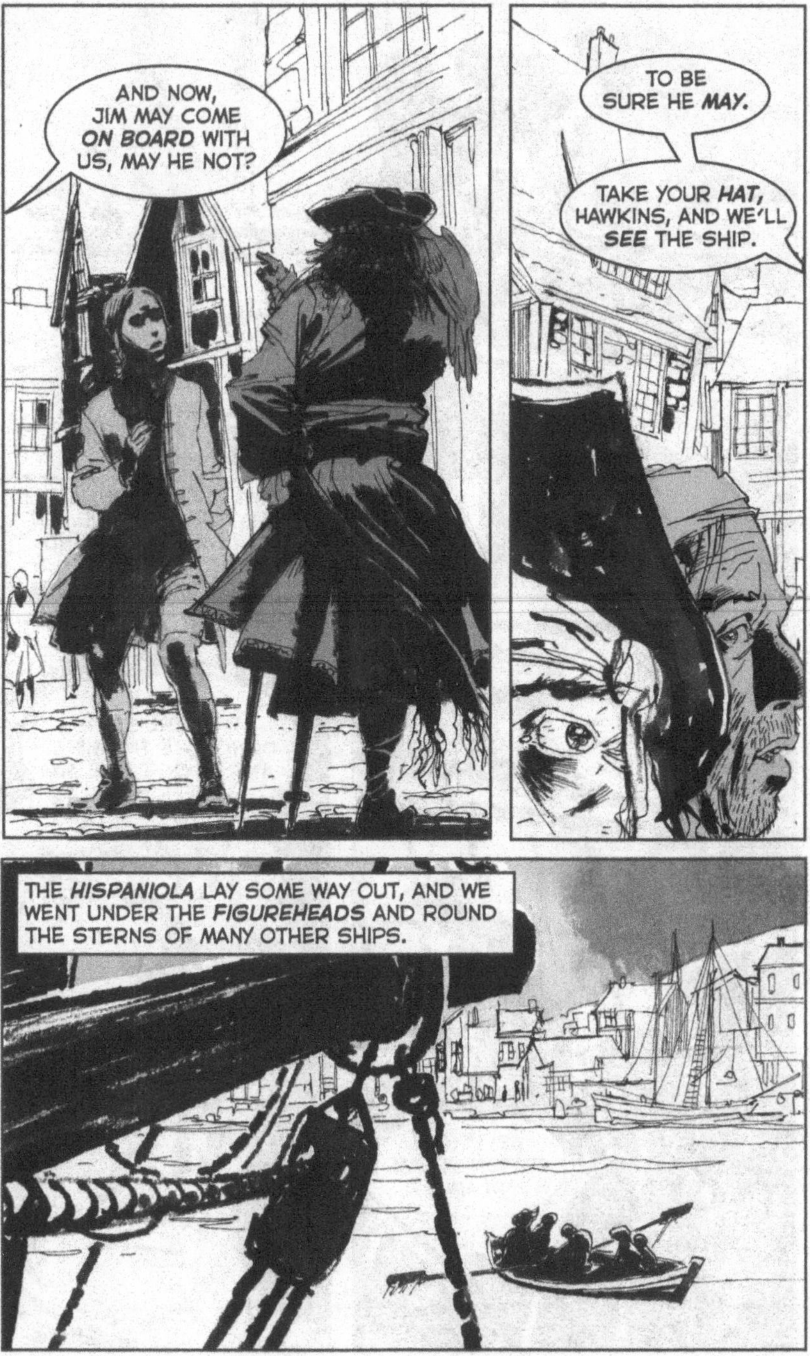
AND NOW, JIM MAY COME ON BOARD WITH US, MAY HE NOT?
TO BE SURE HE MAY.
TAKE YOUR HAT, HAWKINS, AND WE'LL SEE THE SHIP.
THE HISPANIOLA LAY SOME WAY OUT, AND WE WENT UNDER THE FIGUREHEADS AND ROUND THE STERNS OF MANY OTHER SHIPS.

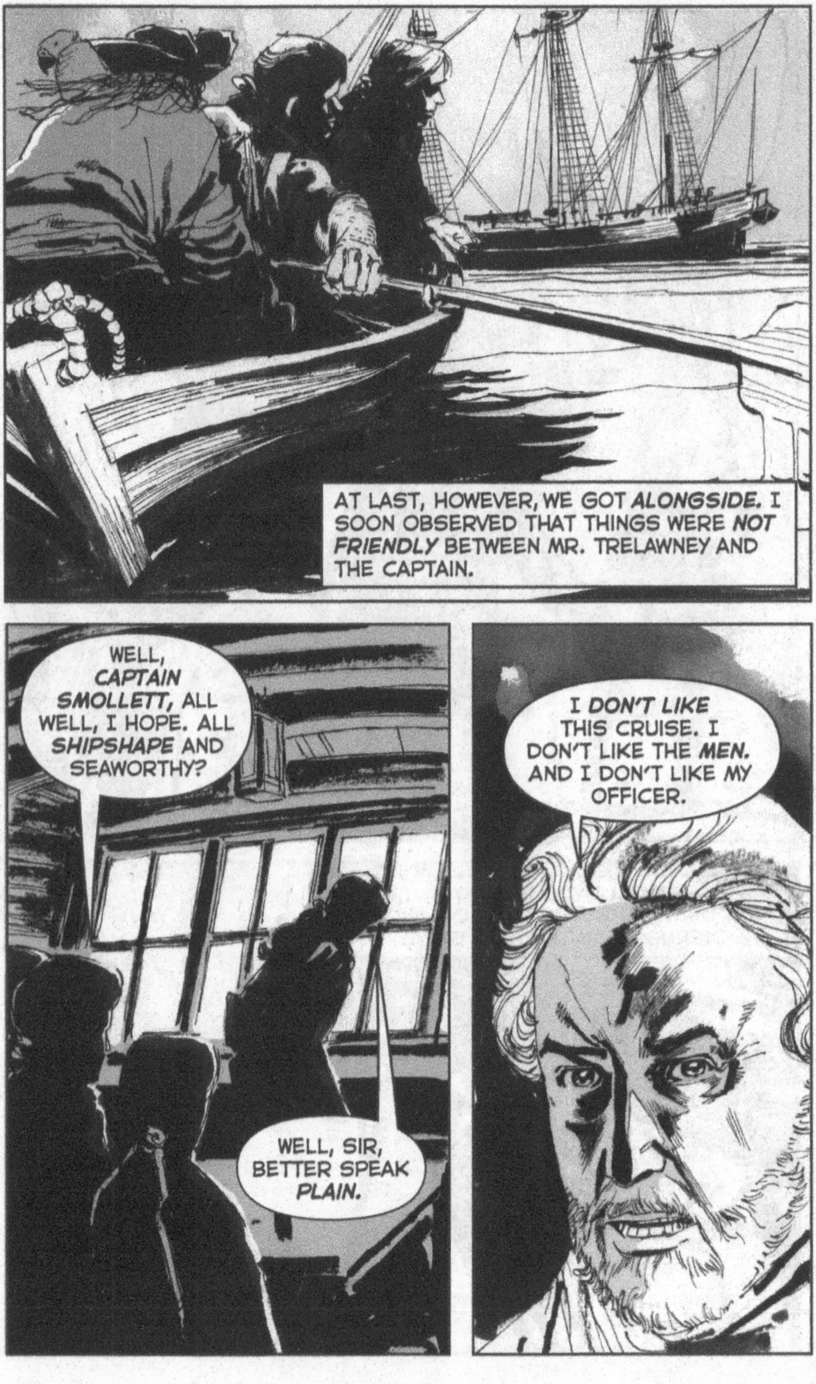
AT LAST, HOWEVER, WE GOT *ALONGSIDE.* I SOON OBSERVED THAT THINGS WERE *NOT FRIENDLY* BETWEEN MR. TRELAWNEY AND THE CAPTAIN.
WELL, *CAPTAIN SMOLLETT,* ALL WELL, I HOPE. ALL *SHIPSHAPE* AND SEAWORTHY?
WELL, SIR, BETTER SPEAK *PLAIN.*
I *DON'T LIKE* THIS CRUISE. I DON'T LIKE THE *MEN.* AND I DON'T LIKE MY OFFICER.

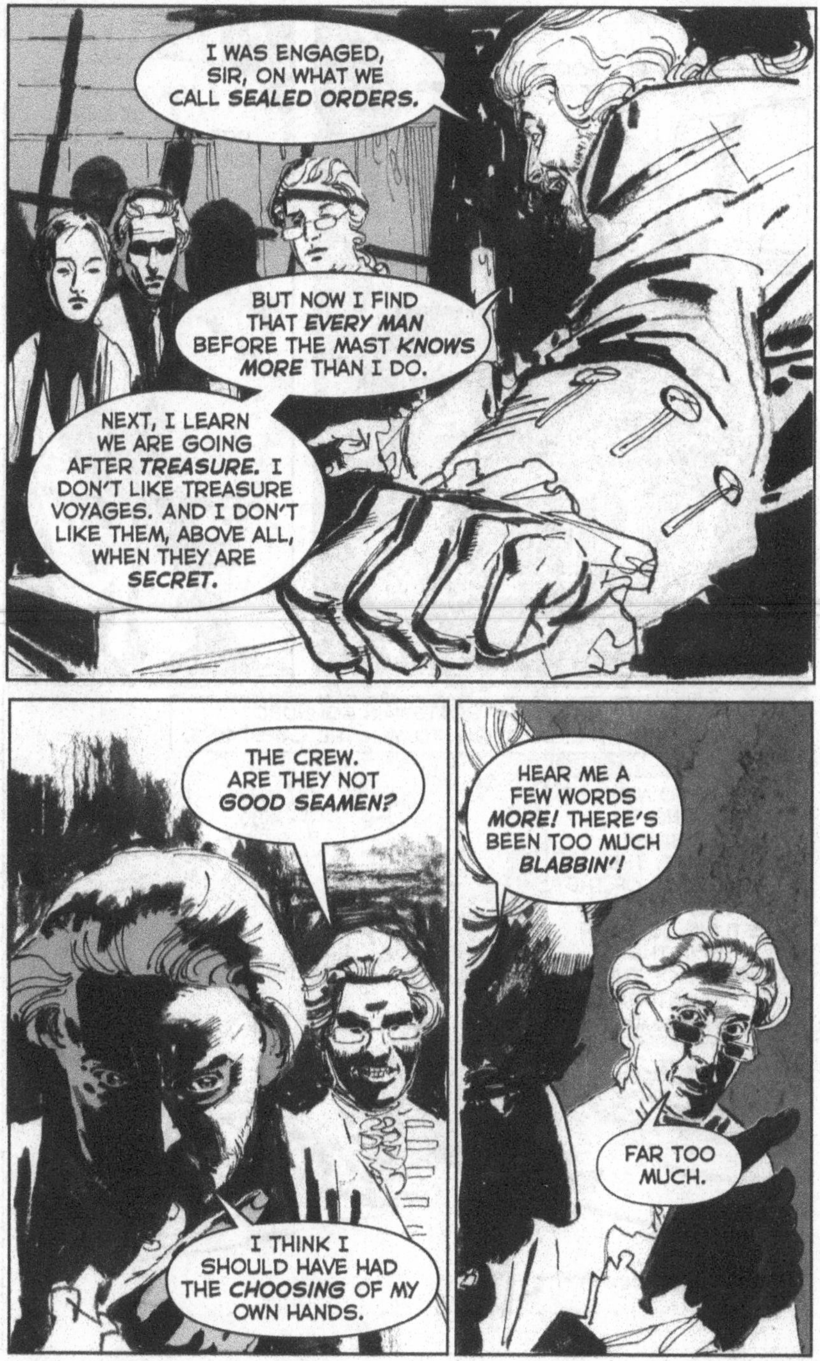
I WAS ENGAGED, SIR, ON WHAT WE CALL SEALED ORDERS.
BUT NOW I FIND THAT EVERY MAN BEFORE THE MAST KNOWS MORE THAN I DO.
NEXT, I LEARN WE ARE GOING AFTER TREASURE. I DON'T LIKE TREASURE VOYAGES. AND I DON'T LIKE THEM, ABOVE ALL, WHEN THEY ARE SECRET.
THE CREW. ARE THEY NOT GOOD SEAMEN?
I THINK I SHOULD HAVE HAD THE CHOOSING OF MY OWN HANDS.
HEAR ME A FEW WORDS MORE! THERE'S BEEN TOO MUCH BLABBIN'!
FAR TOO MUCH.

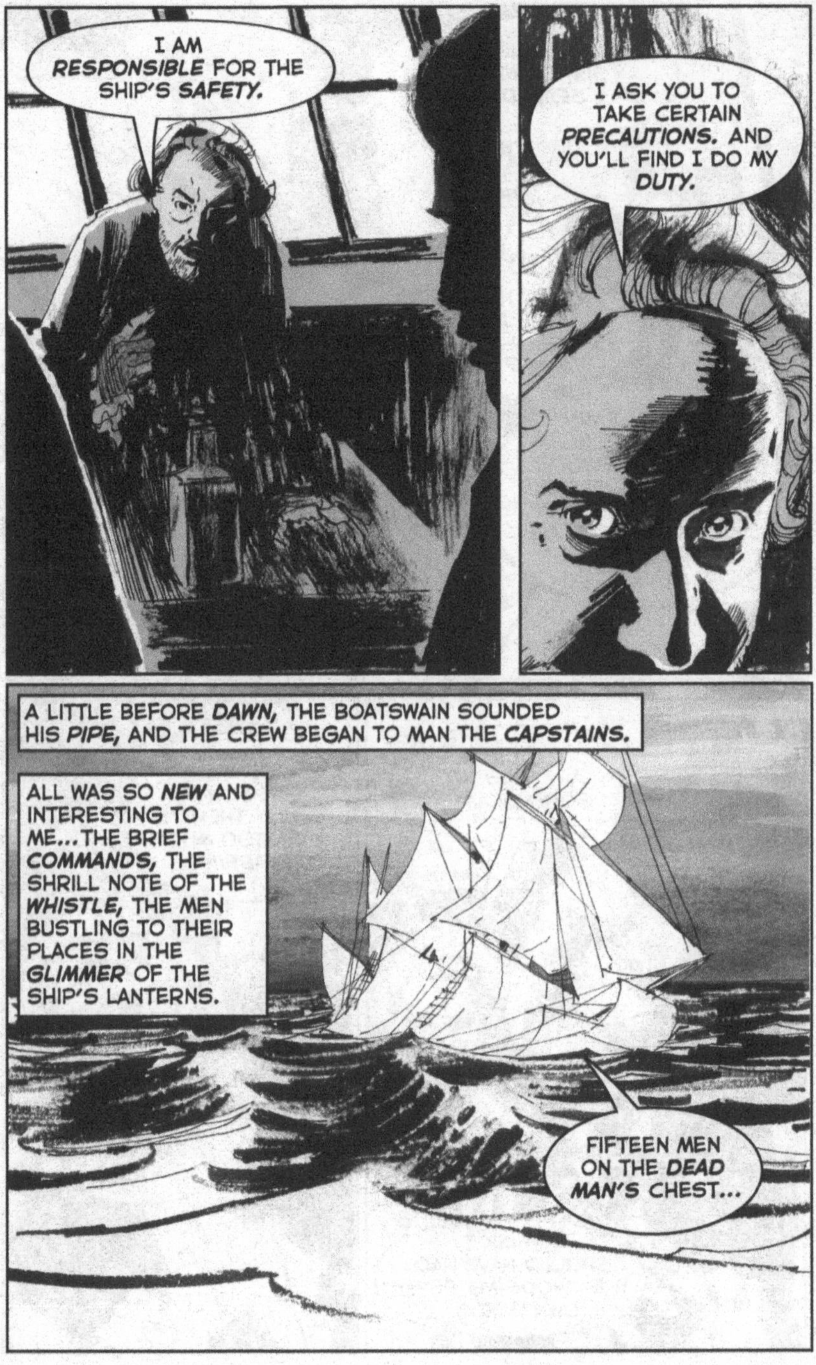
I AM RESPONSIBLE FOR THE SHIP'S SAFETY.
I ASK YOU TO TAKE CERTAIN PRECAUTIONS. AND YOU'LL FIND I DO MY DUTY.
A LITTLE BEFORE DAWN, THE BOATSWAIN SOUNDED HIS PIPE, AND THE CREW BEGAN TO MAN THE CAPSTAINS.
ALL WAS SO NEW AND INTERESTING TO ME...THE BRIEF COMMANDS, THE SHRILL NOTE OF THE WHISTLE, THE MEN BUSTLING TO THEIR PLACES IN THE GLIMMER OF THE SHIP'S LANTERNS.
FIFTEEN MEN ON THE DEAD MAN'S CHEST...

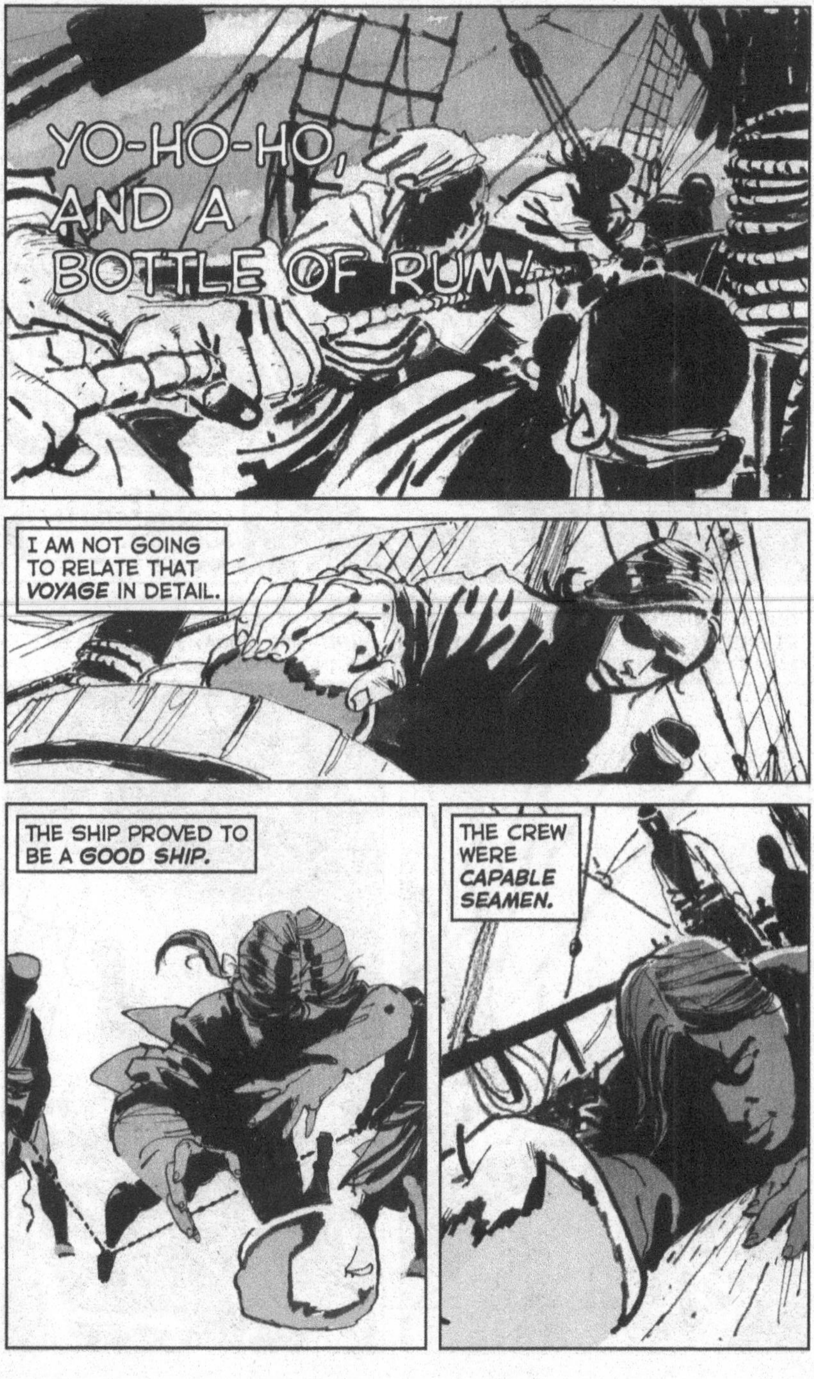
YO-HO-HO, AND A BOTTLE OF RUM!
I AM NOT GOING TO RELATE THAT *VOYAGE* IN DETAIL.
THE SHIP PROVED TO BE A *GOOD SHIP.*
THE CREW WERE *CAPABLE SEAMEN.*

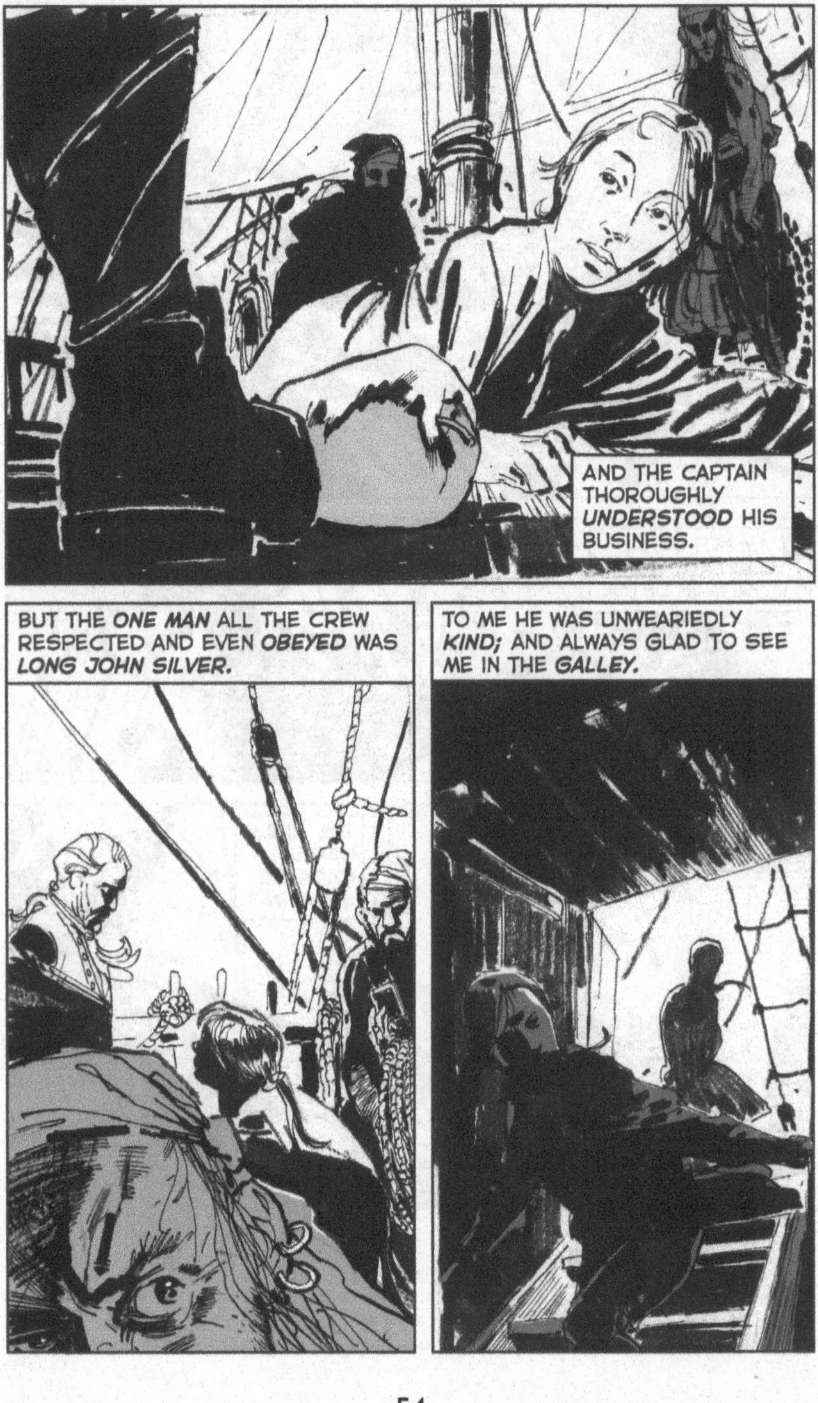
AND THE CAPTAIN THOROUGHLY UNDERSTOOD HIS BUSINESS.
BUT THE ONE MAN ALL THE CREW RESPECTED AND EVEN OBEYED WAS LONG JOHN SILVER.
TO ME HE WAS UNWEARIEDLY KIND; AND ALWAYS GLAD TO SEE ME IN THE GALLEY.

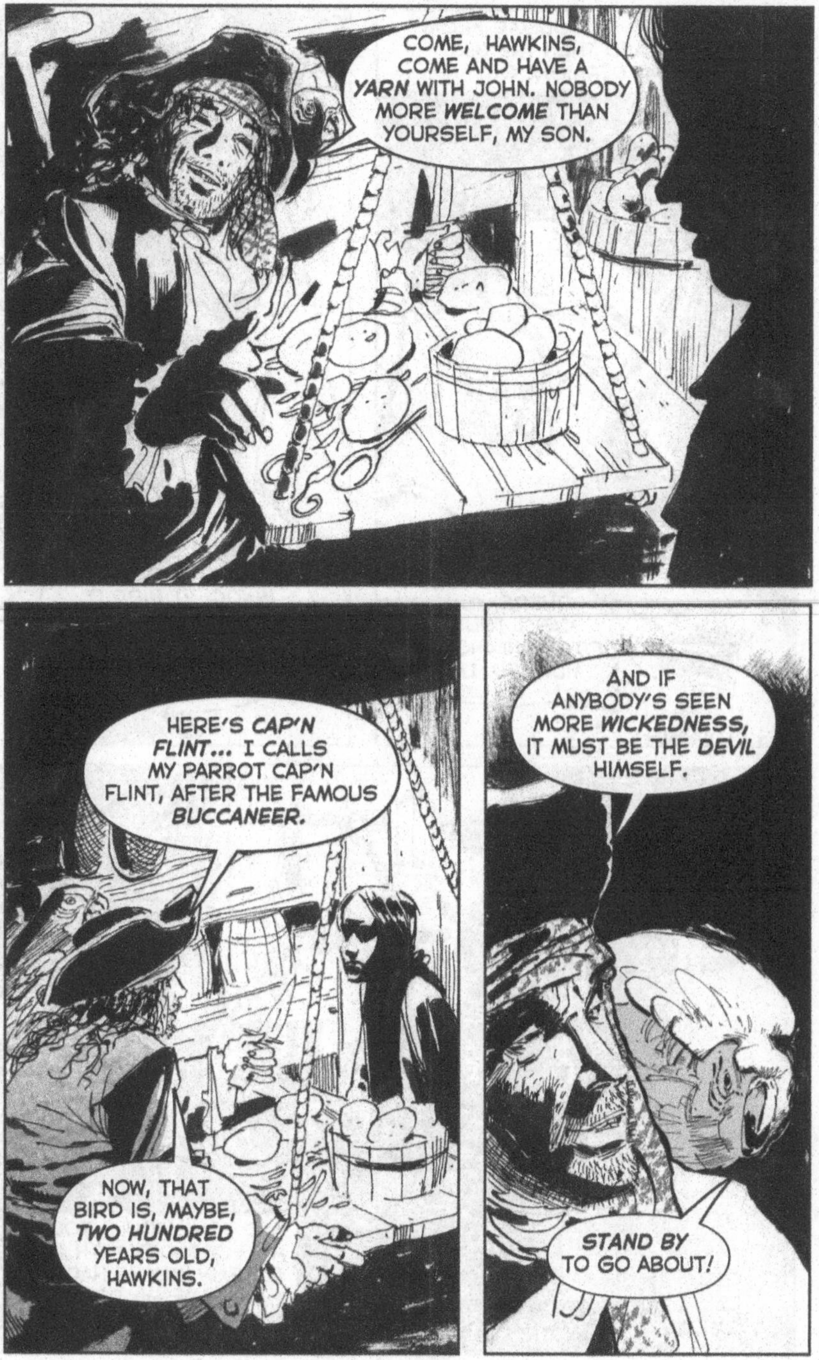
COME, HAWKINS, COME AND HAVE A YARN WITH JOHN. NOBODY MORE WELCOME THAN YOURSELF, MY SON.
HERE'S CAP'N FLINT... I CALLS MY PARROT CAP'N FLINT, AFTER THE FAMOUS BUCCANEER.
NOW, THAT BIRD IS, MAYBE, TWO HUNDRED YEARS OLD, HAWKINS.
AND IF ANYBODY'S SEEN MORE WICKEDNESS, IT MUST BE THE DEVIL HIMSELF.
STAND BY TO GO ABOUT!

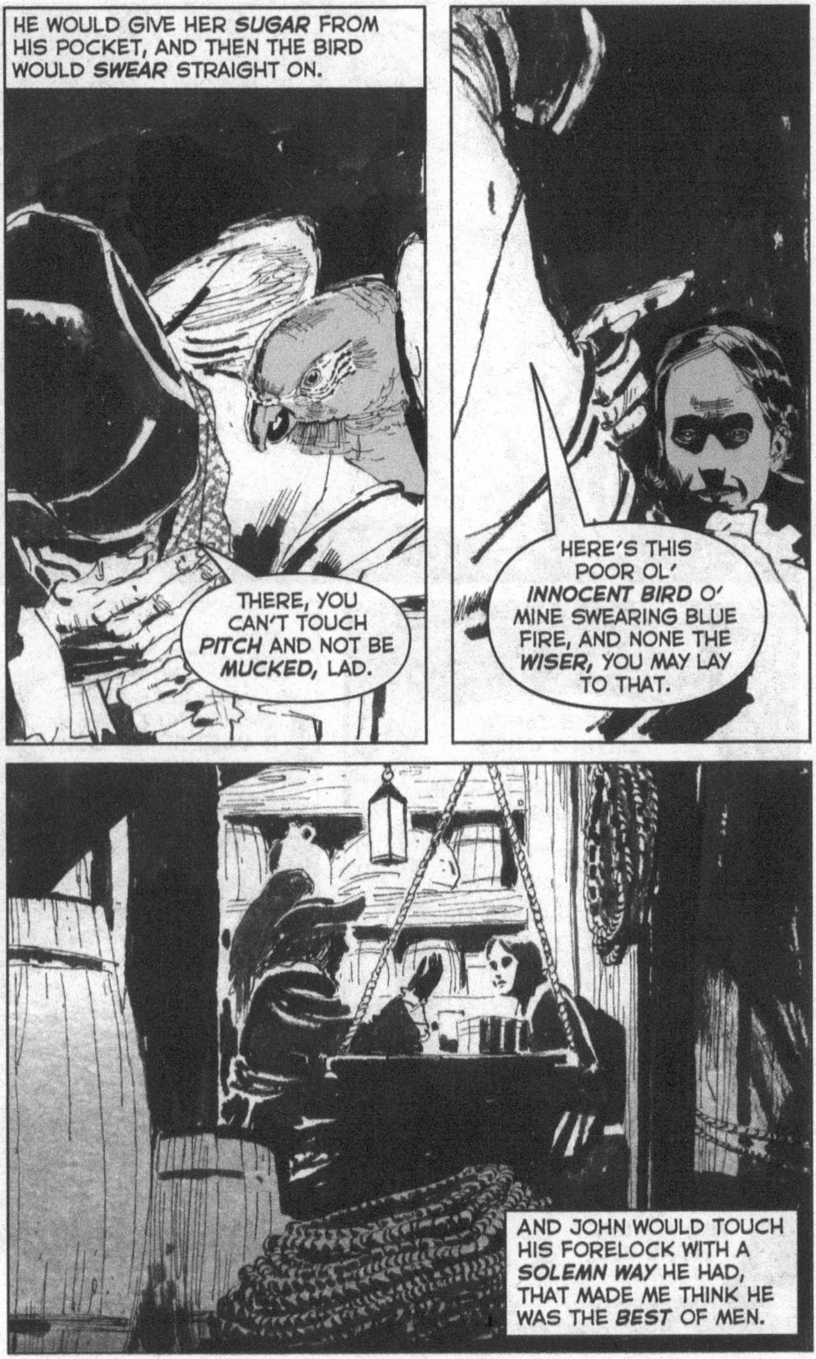
HE WOULD GIVE HER *SUGAR* FROM HIS POCKET, AND THEN THE BIRD WOULD *SWEAR* STRAIGHT ON.
THERE, YOU CAN'T TOUCH *PITCH* AND NOT BE *MUCKED,* LAD.
HERE'S THIS POOR OL' *INNOCENT BIRD* O' MINE SWEARING BLUE FIRE, AND NONE THE *WISER,* YOU MAY LAY TO THAT.
AND JOHN WOULD TOUCH HIS FORELOCK WITH A *SOLEMN WAY* HE HAD, THAT MADE ME THINK HE WAS THE *BEST* OF MEN.

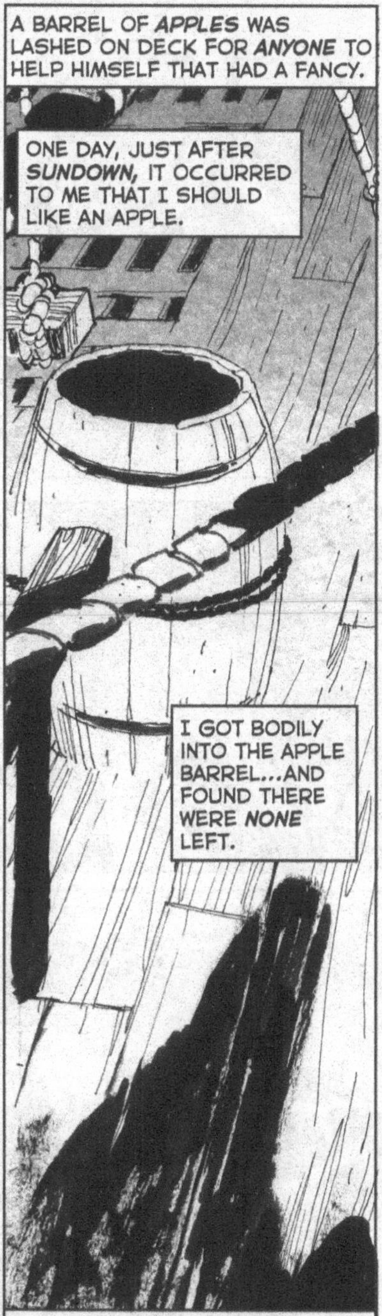
A BARREL OF *APPLES* WAS LASHED ON DECK FOR *ANYONE* TO HELP HIMSELF THAT HAD A FANCY.
ONE DAY, JUST AFTER *SUNDOWN,* IT OCCURRED TO ME THAT I SHOULD LIKE AN APPLE.
I GOT BODILY INTO THE APPLE BARREL...AND FOUND THERE WERE *NONE* LEFT.
BUT, BEFORE I COULD *LEAVE...*

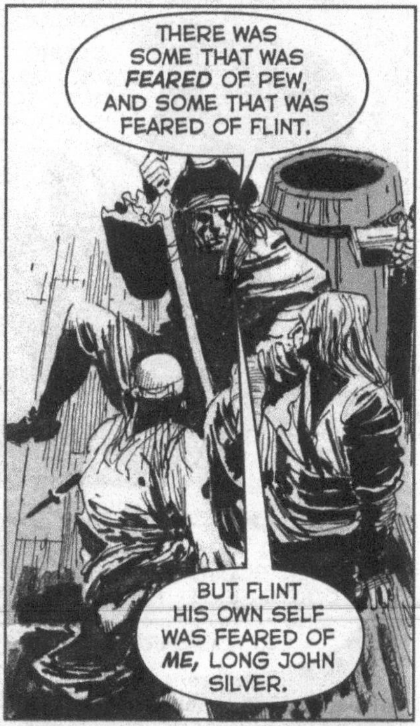
THERE WAS SOME THAT WAS *FEARED* OF PEW, AND SOME THAT WAS FEARED OF FLINT.
BUT FLINT HIS OWN SELF WAS FEARED OF *ME,* LONG JOHN SILVER.

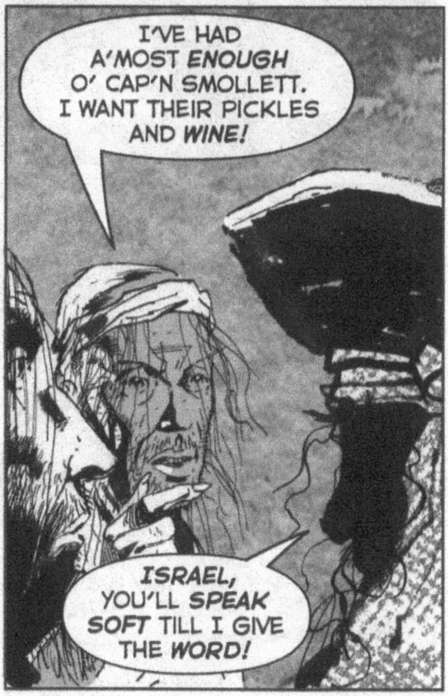
I'VE HAD A'MOST *ENOUGH* O' CAP'N SMOLLETT. I WANT THEIR PICKLES AND *WINE!*
ISRAEL, YOU'LL *SPEAK SOFT* TILL I GIVE THE *WORD!*

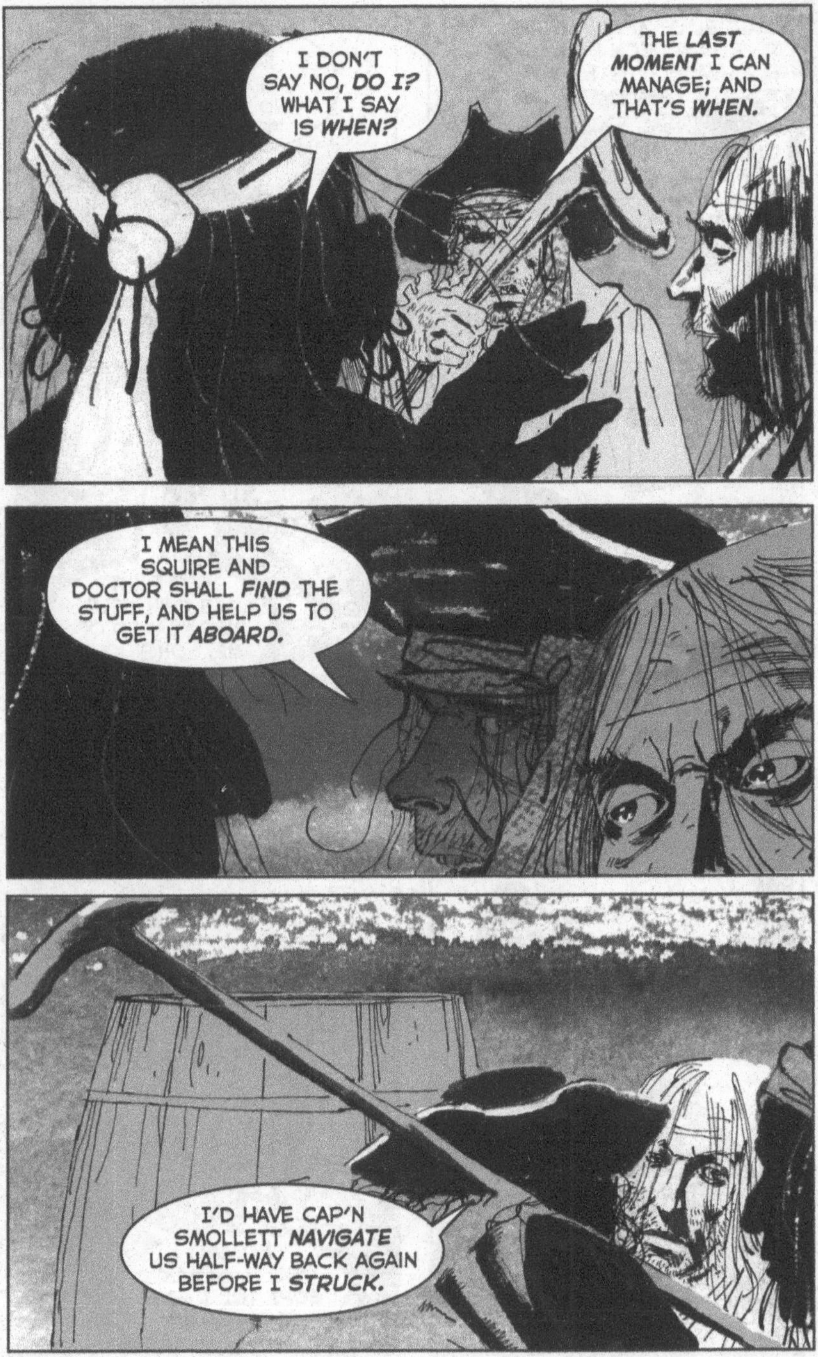
I DON'T SAY NO, DO I? WHAT I SAY IS WHEN?
THE LAST MOMENT I CAN MANAGE; AND THAT'S WHEN.
I MEAN THIS SQUIRE AND DOCTOR SHALL FIND THE STUFF, AND HELP US TO GET IT ABOARD.
I'D HAVE CAP'N SMOLLETT NAVIGATE US HALF-WAY BACK AGAIN BEFORE I STRUCK.

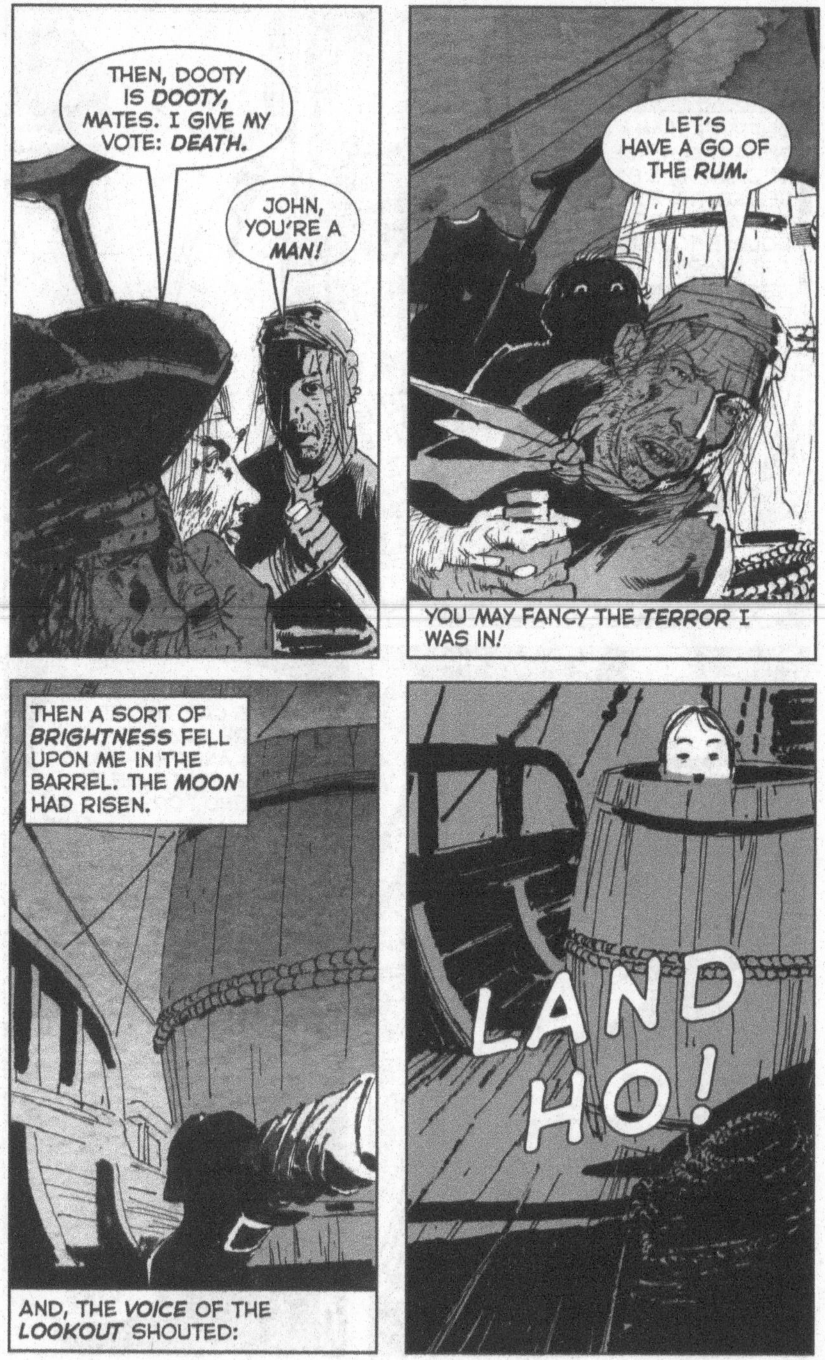
THEN, DOOTY IS DOOTY, MATES. I GIVE MY VOTE: DEATH.
JOHN, YOU'RE A MAN!
LET'S HAVE A GO OF THE RUM.
YOU MAY FANCY THE TERROR I WAS IN!
THEN A SORT OF BRIGHTNESS FELL UPON ME IN THE BARREL. THE MOON HAD RISEN.
AND, THE VOICE OF THE LOOKOUT SHOUTED:
LAND HO!

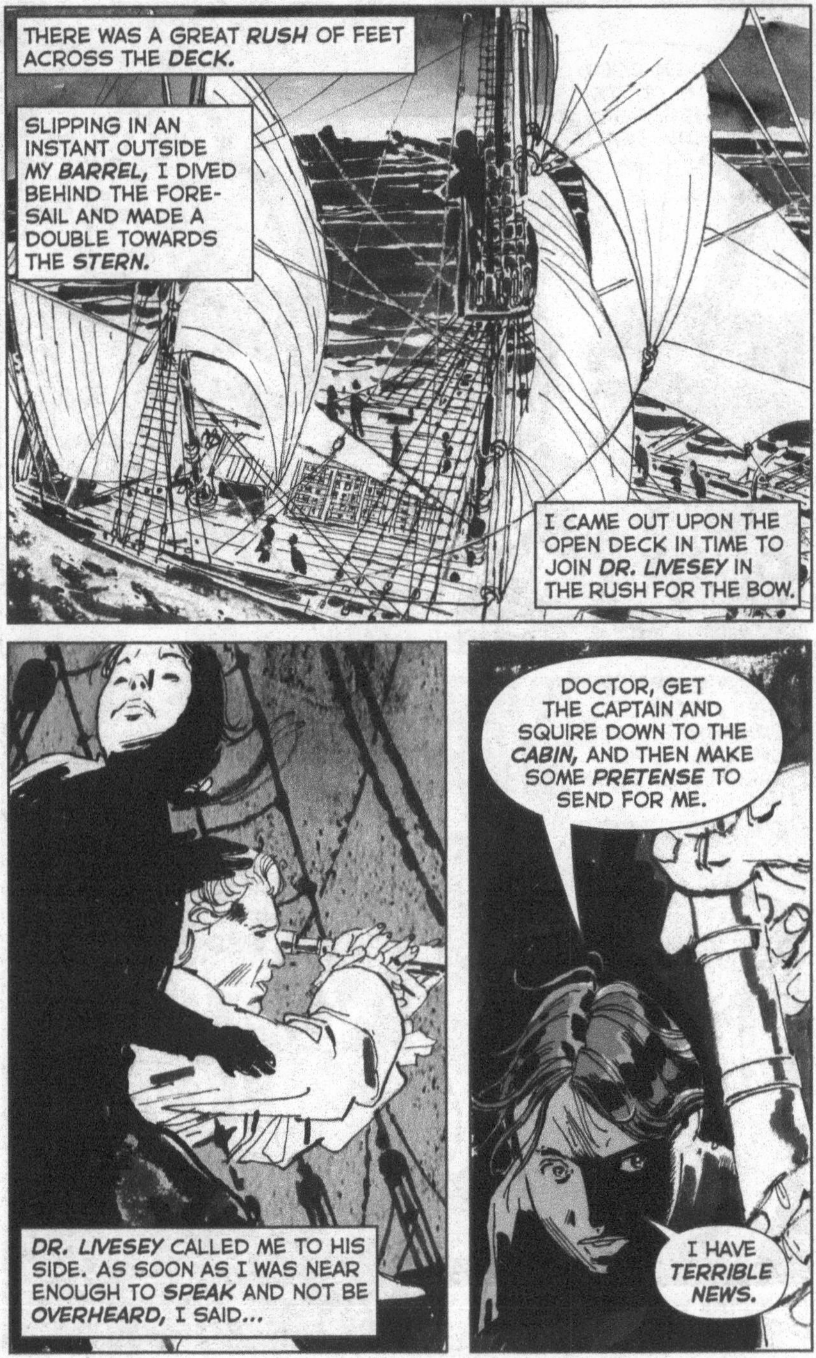
THERE WAS A GREAT *RUSH* OF FEET ACROSS THE *DECK.*
SLIPPING IN AN INSTANT OUTSIDE MY *BARREL,* I DIVED BEHIND THE FORE-SAIL AND MADE A DOUBLE TOWARDS THE *STERN.*
I CAME OUT UPON THE OPEN DECK IN TIME TO JOIN *DR. LIVESEY* IN THE RUSH FOR THE BOW.
DR. LIVESEY CALLED ME TO HIS SIDE. AS SOON AS I WAS NEAR ENOUGH TO *SPEAK* AND NOT BE *OVERHEARD,* I SAID...
DOCTOR, GET THE CAPTAIN AND SQUIRE DOWN TO THE *CABIN,* AND THEN MAKE SOME *PRETENSE* TO SEND FOR ME.
I HAVE *TERRIBLE* *NEWS.*

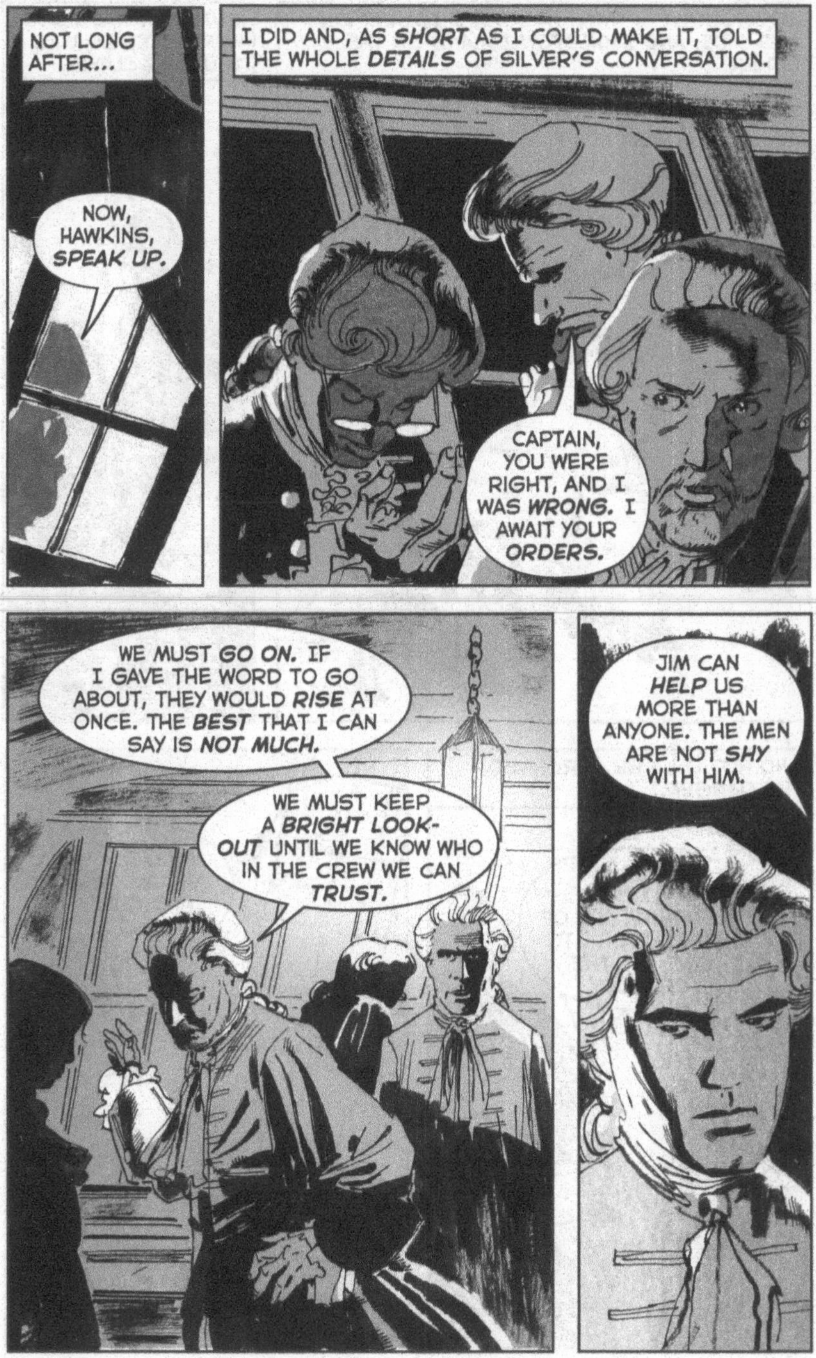
NOT LONG AFTER...
NOW, HAWKINS, SPEAK UP.
I DID AND, AS SHORT AS I COULD MAKE IT, TOLD THE WHOLE DETAILS OF SILVER'S CONVERSATION.
CAPTAIN, YOU WERE RIGHT, AND I WAS WRONG. I AWAIT YOUR ORDERS.
WE MUST GO ON. IF I GAVE THE WORD TO GO ABOUT, THEY WOULD RISE AT ONCE. THE BEST THAT I CAN SAY IS NOT MUCH.
WE MUST KEEP A BRIGHT LOOK-OUT UNTIL WE KNOW WHO IN THE CREW WE CAN TRUST.
JIM CAN HELP US MORE THAN ANYONE. THE MEN ARE NOT SHY WITH HIM.

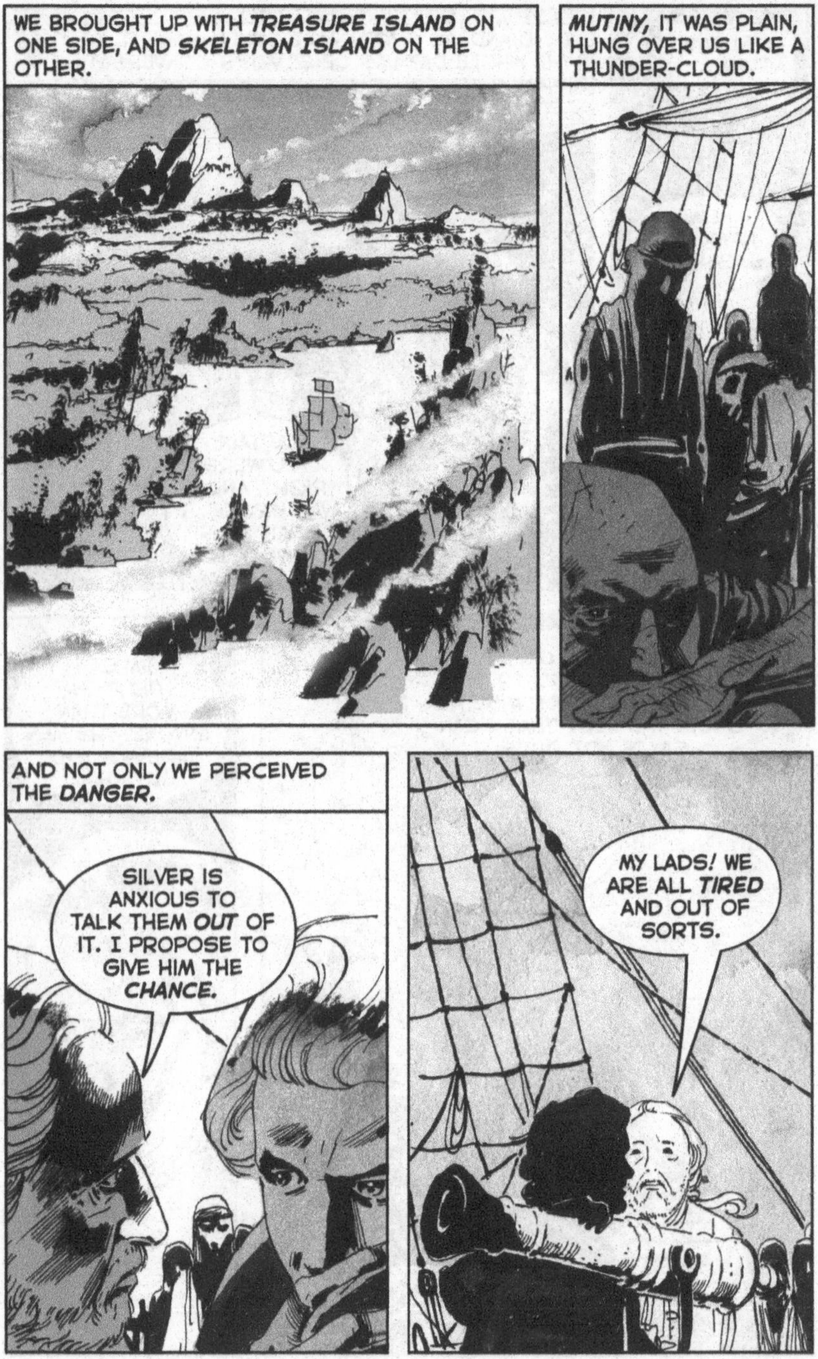
WE BROUGHT UP WITH *TREASURE ISLAND* ON ONE SIDE, AND *SKELETON ISLAND* ON THE OTHER.
MUTINY, IT WAS PLAIN, HUNG OVER US LIKE A THUNDER-CLOUD.
AND NOT ONLY WE PERCEIVED THE *DANGER.*
SILVER IS ANXIOUS TO TALK THEM *OUT* OF IT. I PROPOSE TO GIVE HIM THE *CHANCE.*
MY LADS! WE ARE ALL *TIRED* AND OUT OF SORTS.

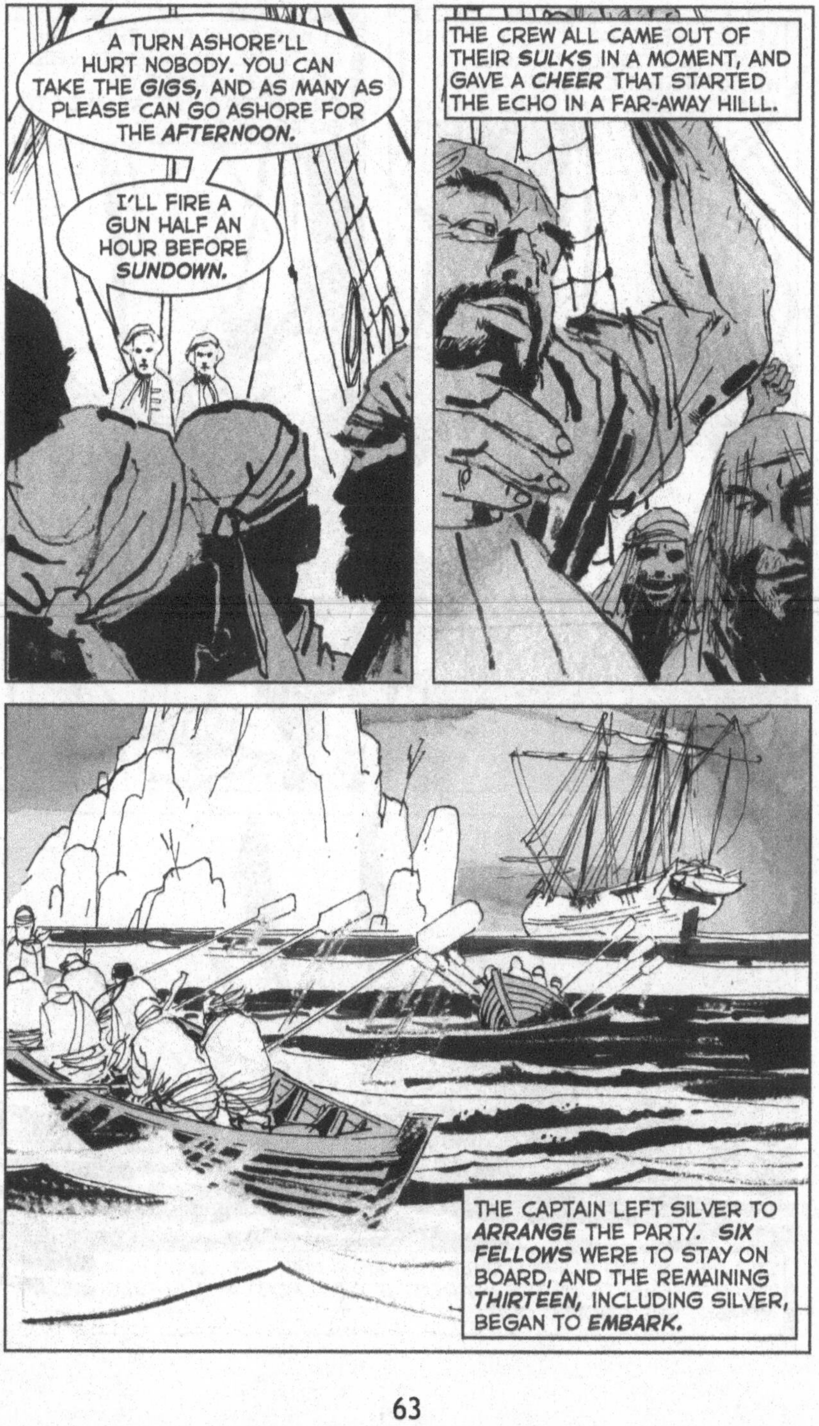
A TURN ASHORE'LL HURT NOBODY. YOU CAN TAKE THE GIGS, AND AS MANY AS PLEASE CAN GO ASHORE FOR THE AFTERNOON.
I'LL FIRE A GUN HALF AN HOUR BEFORE SUNDOWN.
THE CREW ALL CAME OUT OF THEIR SULKS IN A MOMENT, AND GAVE A CHEER THAT STARTED THE ECHO IN A FAR-AWAY HILLL.
THE CAPTAIN LEFT SILVER TO ARRANGE THE PARTY. SIX FELLOWS WERE TO STAY ON BOARD, AND THE REMAINING THIRTEEN, INCLUDING SILVER, BEGAN TO EMBARK.

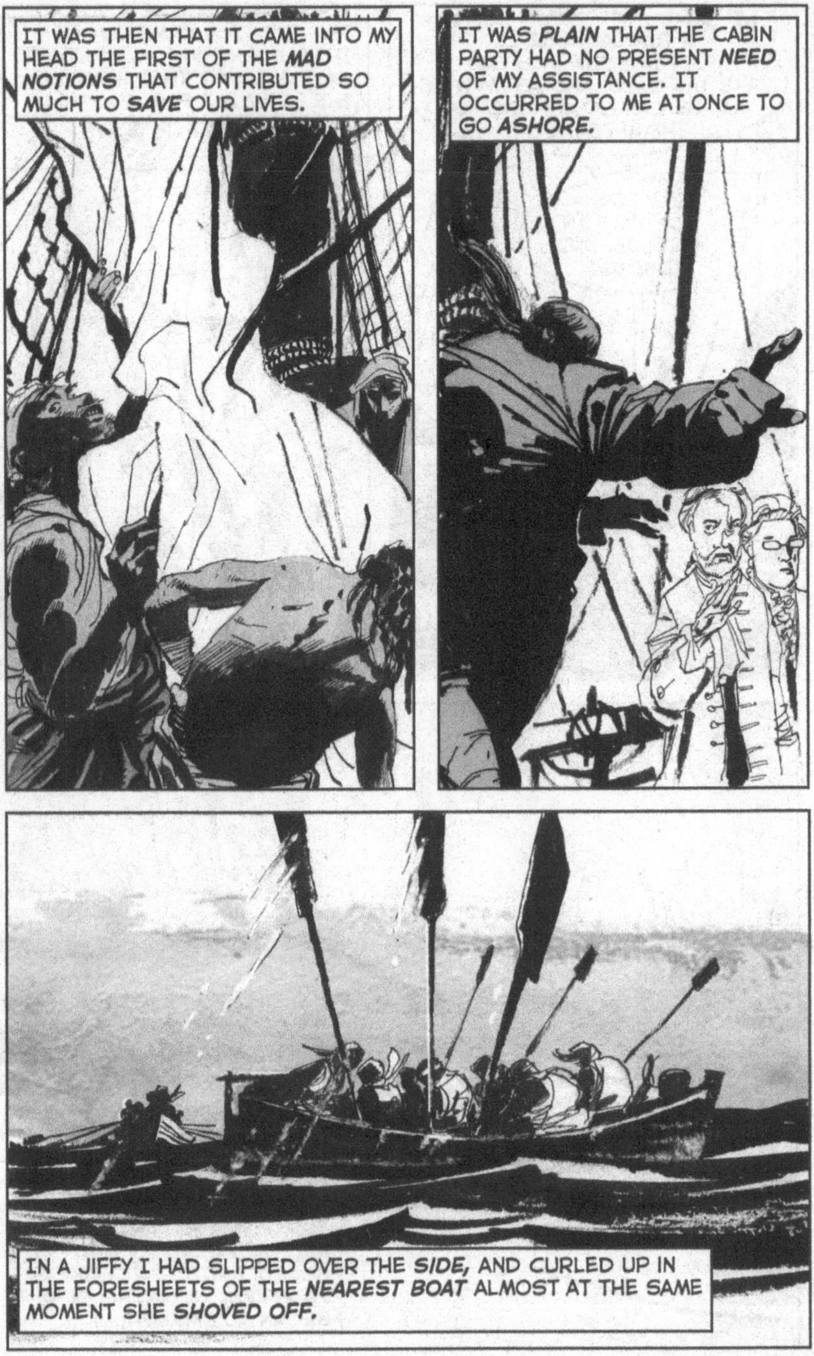
IT WAS THEN THAT IT CAME INTO MY HEAD THE FIRST OF THE *MAD NOTIONS* THAT CONTRIBUTED SO MUCH TO *SAVE* OUR LIVES.
IT WAS *PLAIN* THAT THE CABIN PARTY HAD NO PRESENT *NEED* OF MY ASSISTANCE. IT OCCURRED TO ME AT ONCE TO GO *ASHORE.*
IN A JIFFY I HAD SLIPPED OVER THE *SIDE,* AND CURLED UP IN THE FORESHEETS OF THE *NEAREST BOAT* ALMOST AT THE SAME MOMENT SHE *SHOVED OFF.*

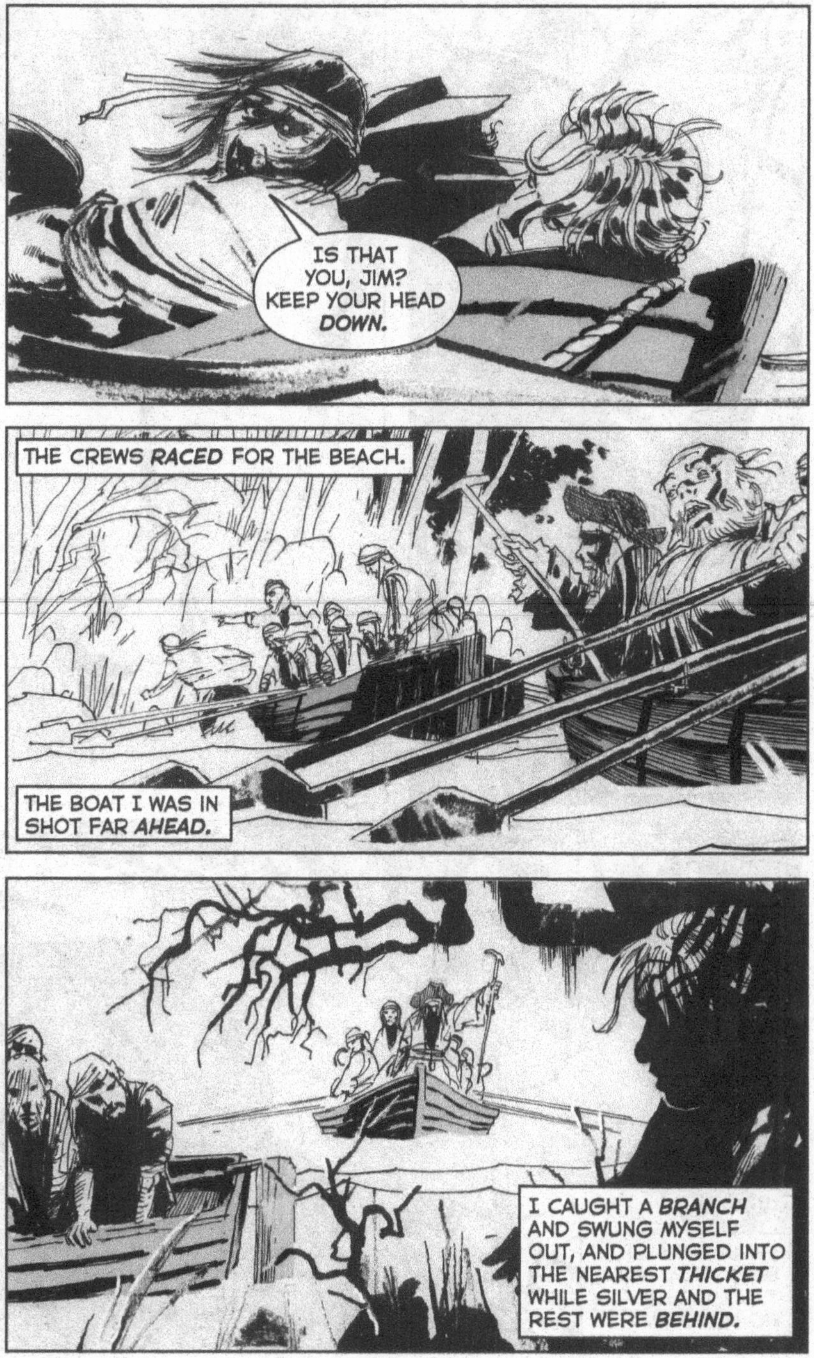
IS THAT YOU, JIM? KEEP YOUR HEAD DOWN.
THE CREWS RACED FOR THE BEACH.
THE BOAT I WAS IN SHOT FAR AHEAD.
I CAUGHT A BRANCH AND SWUNG MYSELF OUT, AND PLUNGED INTO THE NEAREST THICKET WHILE SILVER AND THE REST WERE BEHIND.

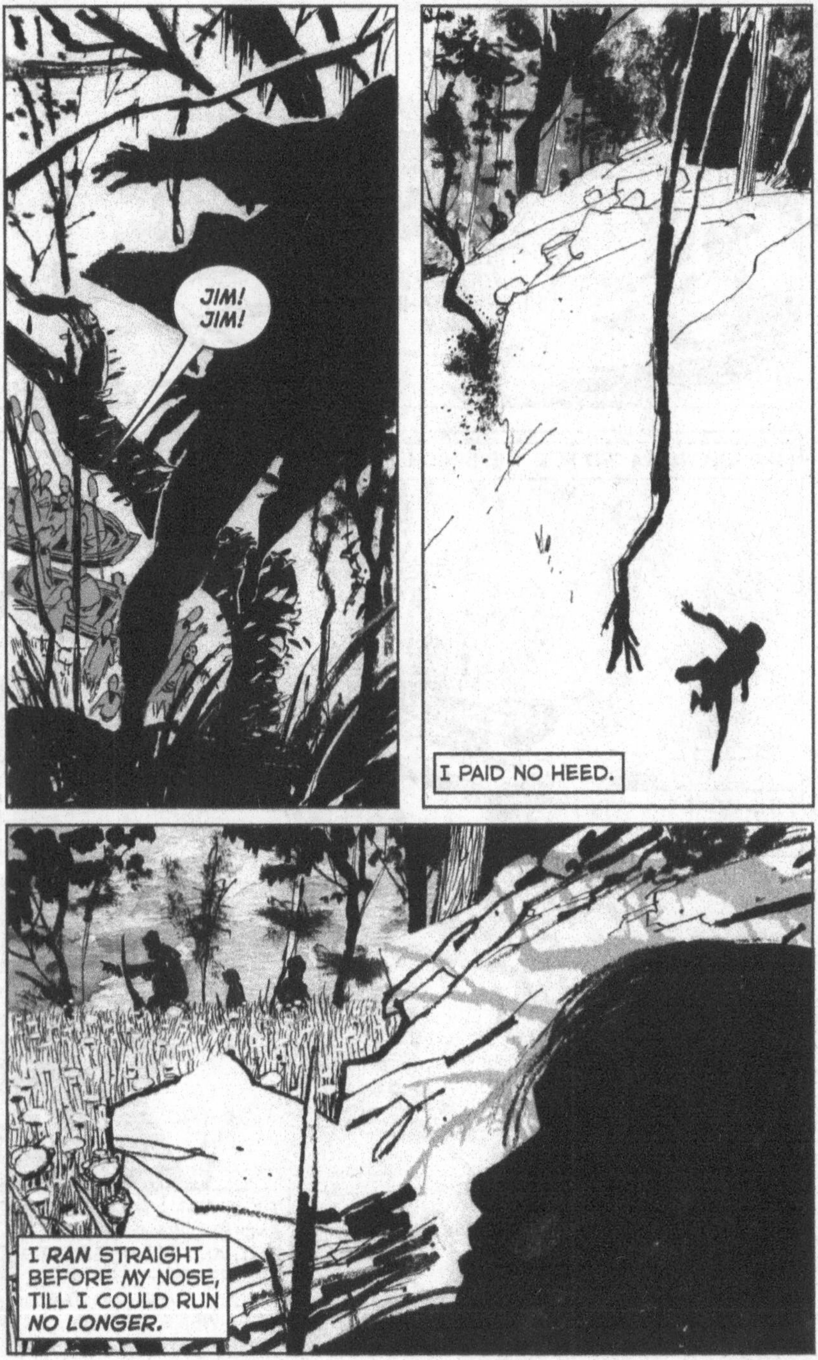
JIM!
JIM!
I PAID NO HEED.
I RAN STRAIGHT BEFORE MY NOSE, TILL I COULD RUN NO LONGER.

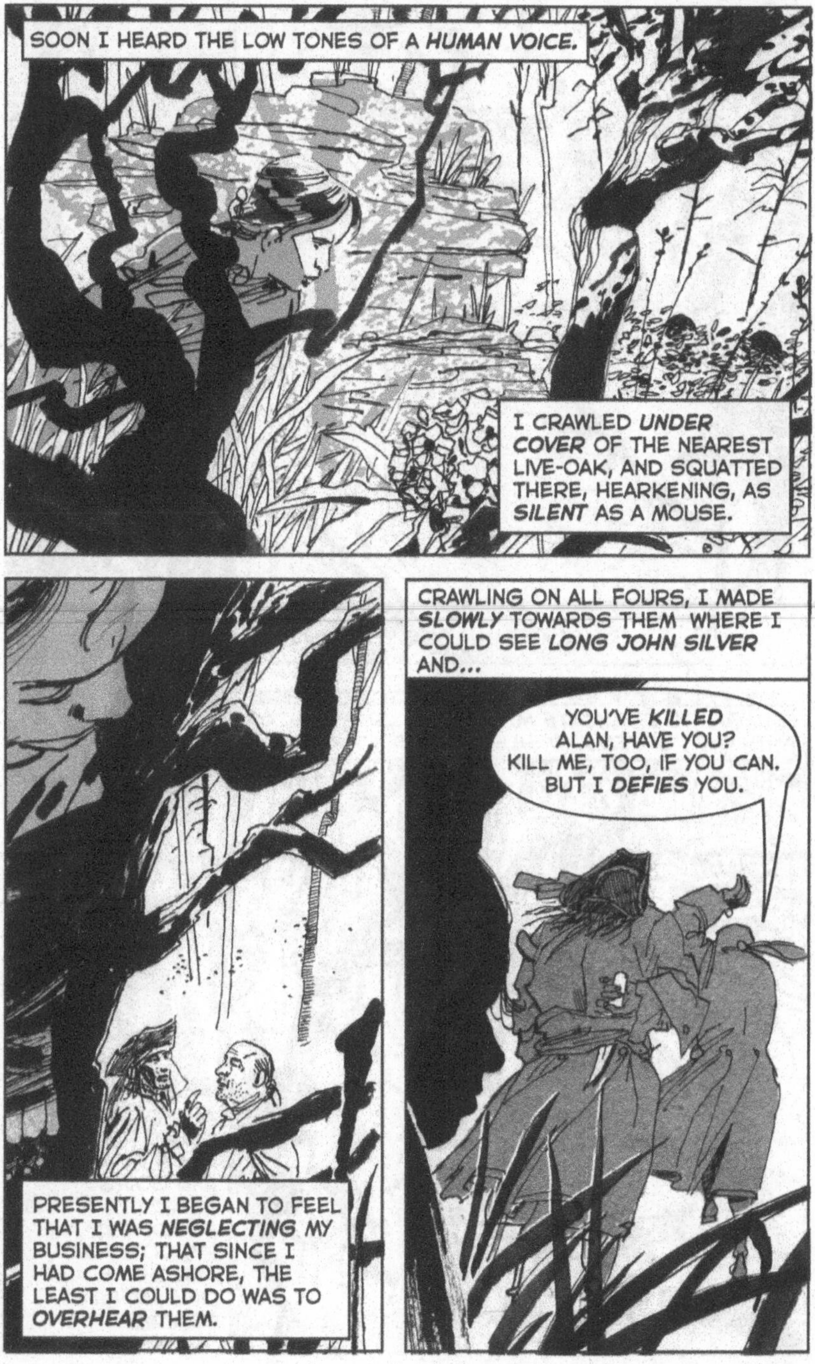
SOON I HEARD THE LOW TONES OF A HUMAN VOICE.
I CRAWLED UNDER COVER OF THE NEAREST LIVE-OAK, AND SQUATTED THERE, HEARKENING, AS SILENT AS A MOUSE.
PRESENTLY I BEGAN TO FEEL THAT I WAS NEGLECTING MY BUSINESS; THAT SINCE I HAD COME ASHORE, THE LEAST I COULD DO WAS TO OVERHEAR THEM.
CRAWLING ON ALL FOURS, I MADE SLOWLY TOWARDS THEM WHERE I COULD SEE LONG JOHN SILVER AND...
YOU'VE KILLED ALAN, HAVE YOU? KILL ME, TOO, IF YOU CAN. BUT I DEFIES YOU.

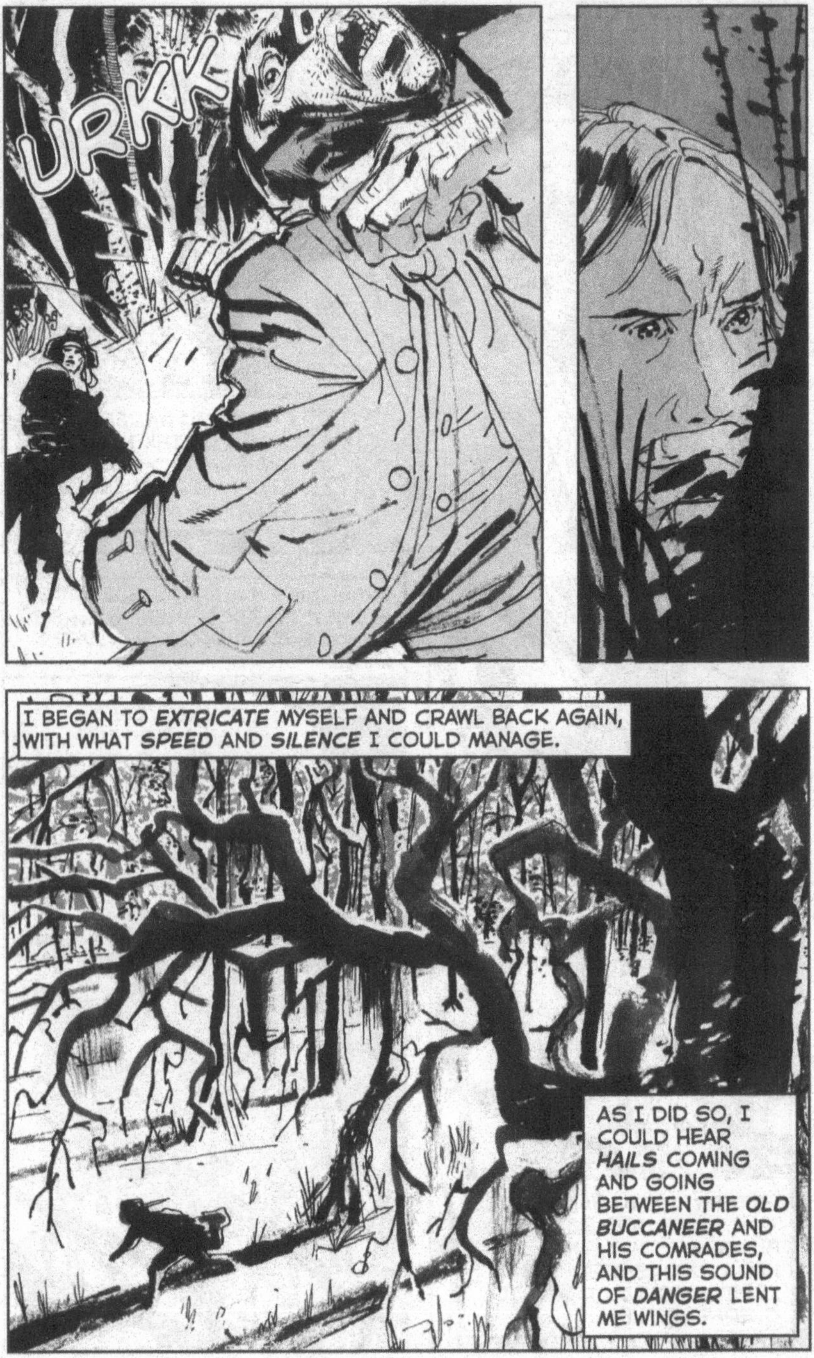
URKK
I BEGAN TO EXTRICATE MYSELF AND CRAWL BACK AGAIN, WITH WHAT SPEED AND SILENCE I COULD MANAGE.
AS I DID SO, I COULD HEAR HAILS COMING AND GOING BETWEEN THE OLD BUCCANEER AND HIS COMRADES, AND THIS SOUND OF DANGER LENT ME WINGS.

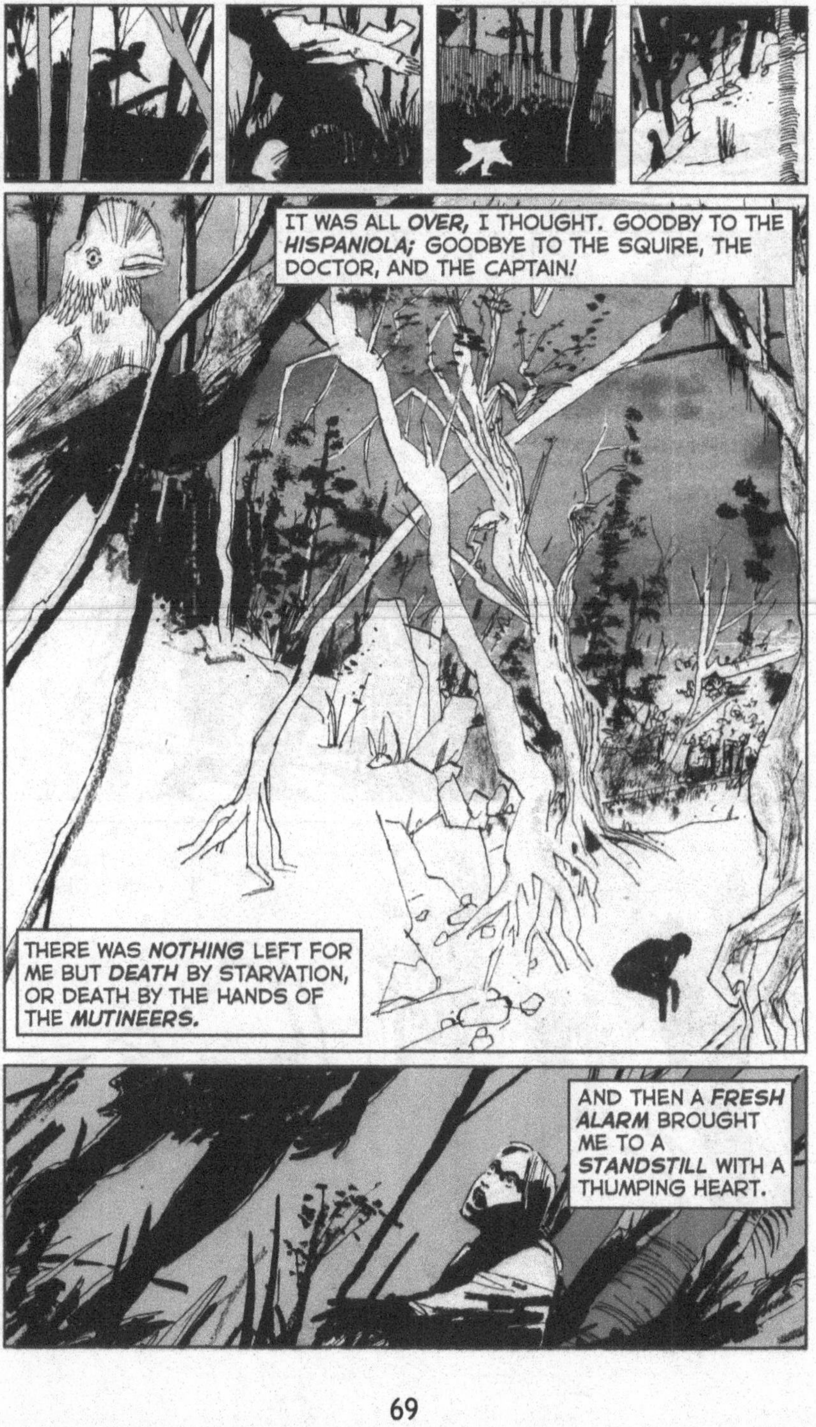
IT WAS ALL OVER, I THOUGHT. GOODBY TO THE HISPANIOLA; GOODBYE TO THE SQUIRE, THE DOCTOR, AND THE CAPTAIN!
THERE WAS NOTHING LEFT FOR ME BUT DEATH BY STARVATION, OR DEATH BY THE HANDS OF THE MUTINEERS.
AND THEN A FRESH ALARM BROUGHT ME TO A STANDSTILL WITH A THUMPING HEART.

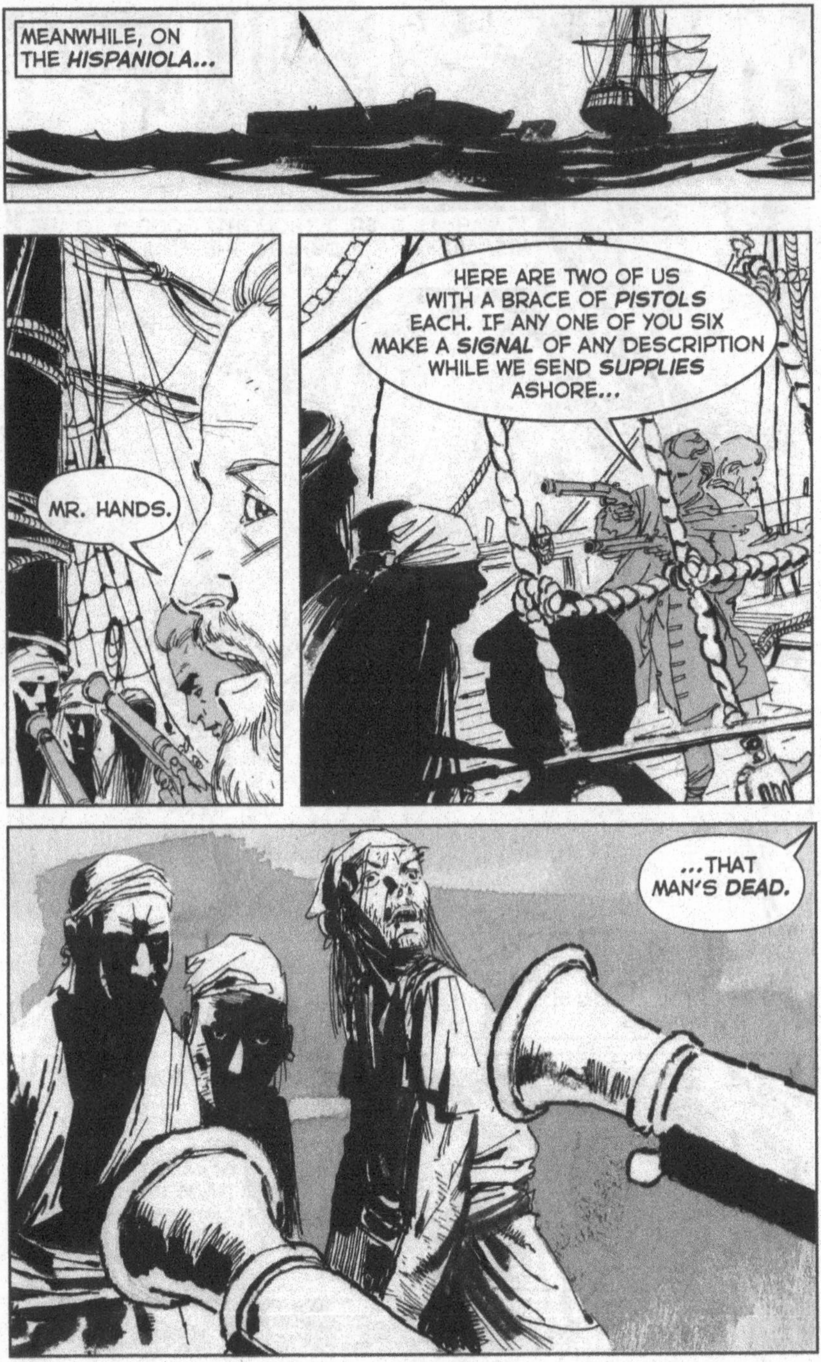
MEANWHILE, ON THE *HISPANIOLA*...
MR. HANDS.
HERE ARE TWO OF US WITH A BRACE OF *PISTOLS* EACH. IF ANY ONE OF YOU SIX MAKE A *SIGNAL* OF ANY DESCRIPTION WHILE WE SEND *SUPPLIES* ASHORE...
...THAT MAN'S *DEAD.*

DOCTOR LIVESEY HAD GONE ASHORE AND FOUND THE *STOCKADE* THAT WAS DRAWN ON THE MAP.

DOWN, DOGS!

NOW HE, CAPTAIN SMOLLETT, THE SQUIRE, AND THOSE LOYAL, WERE *ABANDONING* SHIP...

...AND TAKING AS MUCH AS THEY COULD WITH THEM. WHAT THEY COULD *NOT TAKE*, PARTICULARLY THE GUNS, AMMUNITION, AND GUNPOWDER, THEY THREW *OVERBOARD*.

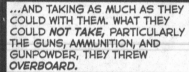

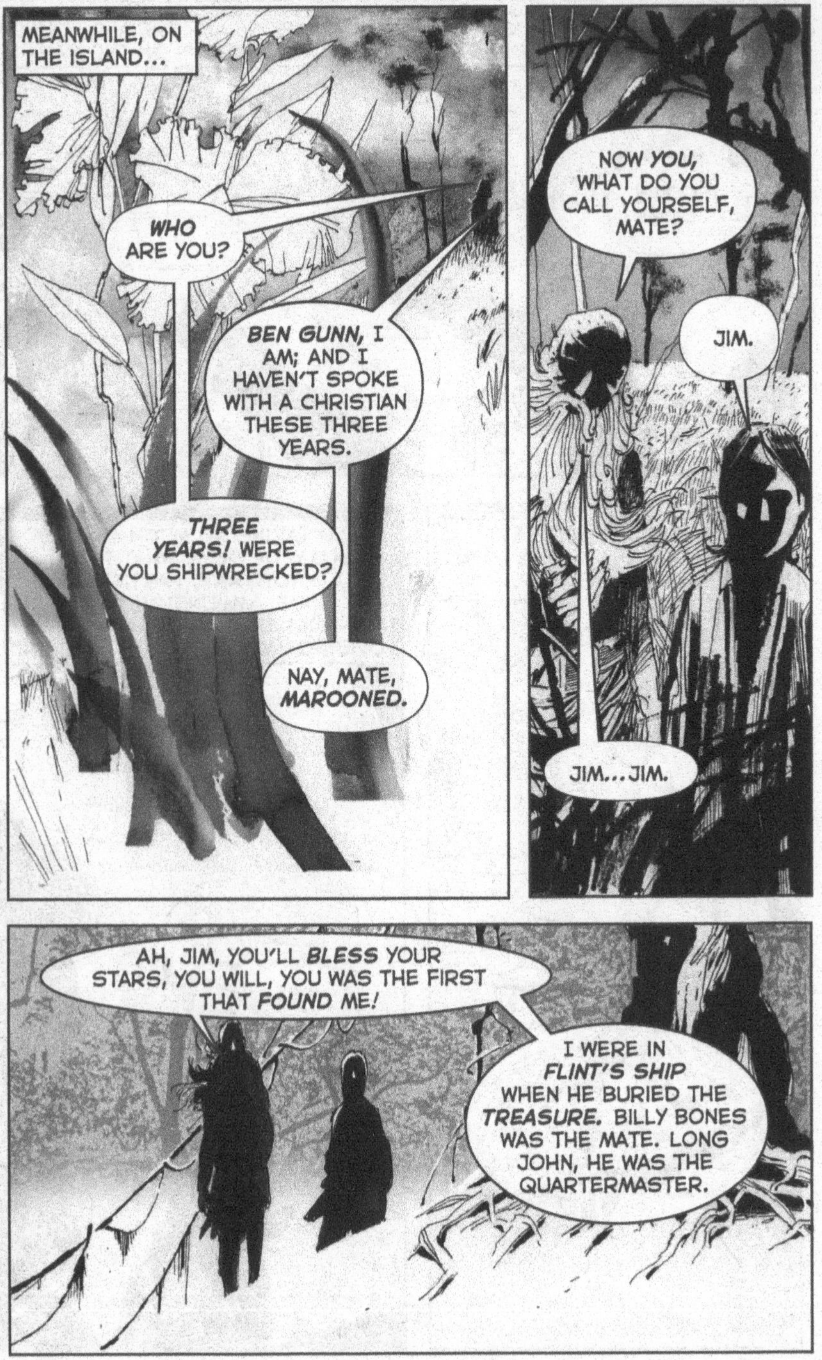
MEANWHILE, ON THE ISLAND...
WHO ARE YOU?
BEN GUNN, I AM; AND I HAVEN'T SPOKE WITH A CHRISTIAN THESE THREE YEARS.
THREE YEARS! WERE YOU SHIPWRECKED?
NAY, MATE, MAROONED.
NOW YOU, WHAT DO YOU CALL YOURSELF, MATE?
JIM.
JIM...JIM.
AH, JIM, YOU'LL BLESS YOUR STARS, YOU WILL, YOU WAS THE FIRST THAT FOUND ME!
I WERE IN FLINT'S SHIP WHEN HE BURIED THE TREASURE. BILLY BONES WAS THE MATE. LONG JOHN, HE WAS THE QUARTERMASTER.

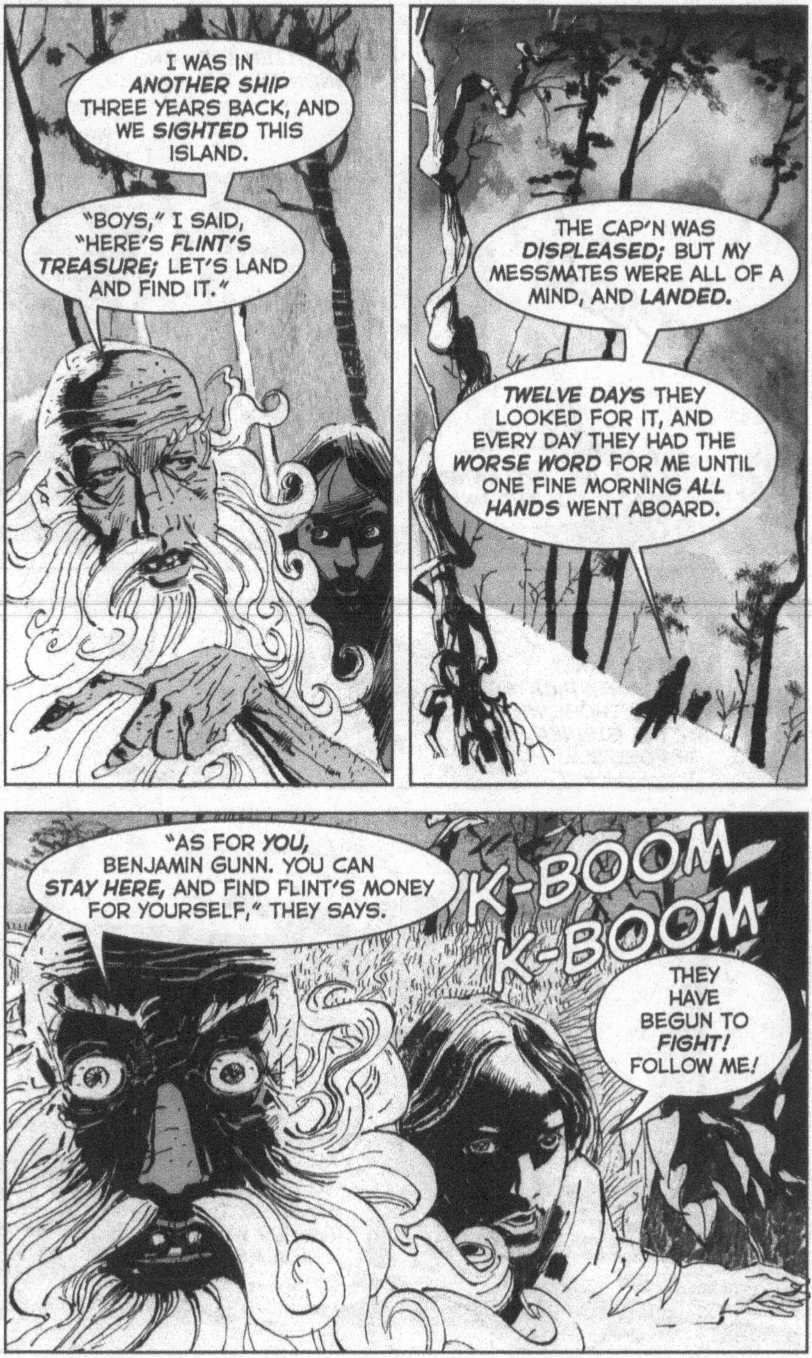
I WAS IN ANOTHER SHIP THREE YEARS BACK, AND WE SIGHTED THIS ISLAND.
"BOYS," I SAID, "HERE'S FLINT'S TREASURE; LET'S LAND AND FIND IT."
THE CAP'N WAS DISPLEASED; BUT MY MESSMATES WERE ALL OF A MIND, AND LANDED.
TWELVE DAYS THEY LOOKED FOR IT, AND EVERY DAY THEY HAD THE WORSE WORD FOR ME UNTIL ONE FINE MORNING ALL HANDS WENT ABOARD.
"AS FOR YOU, BENJAMIN GUNN. YOU CAN STAY HERE, AND FIND FLINT'S MONEY FOR YOURSELF," THEY SAYS.
K-BOOM
K-BOOM
THEY HAVE BEGUN TO FIGHT! FOLLOW ME!

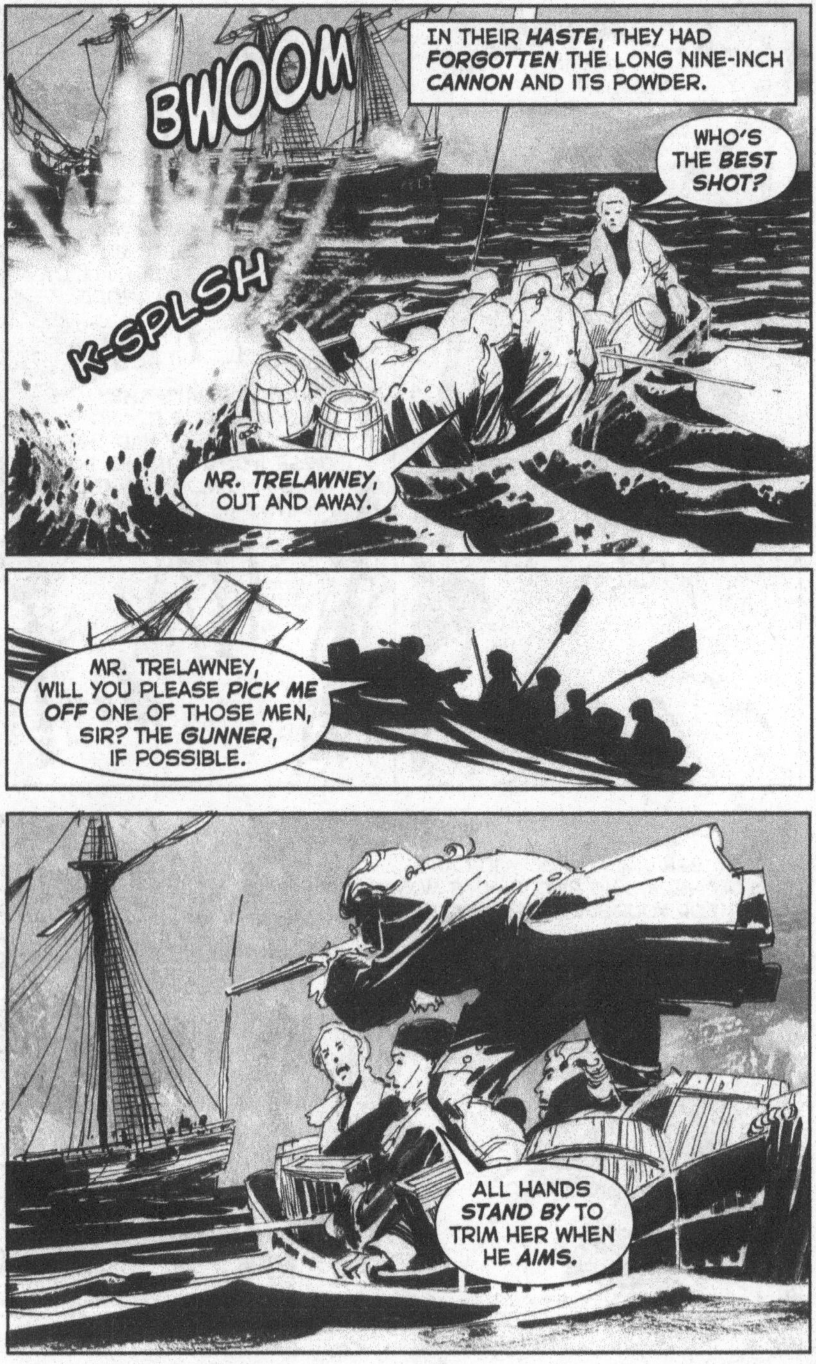
BWOOM
IN THEIR HASTE, THEY HAD FORGOTTEN THE LONG NINE-INCH CANNON AND ITS POWDER.
WHO'S THE BEST SHOT?
K-SPLSH
MR. TRELAWNEY, OUT AND AWAY.
MR. TRELAWNEY, WILL YOU PLEASE PICK ME OFF ONE OF THOSE MEN, SIR? THE GUNNER, IF POSSIBLE.
ALL HANDS STAND BY TO TRIM HER WHEN HE AIMS.

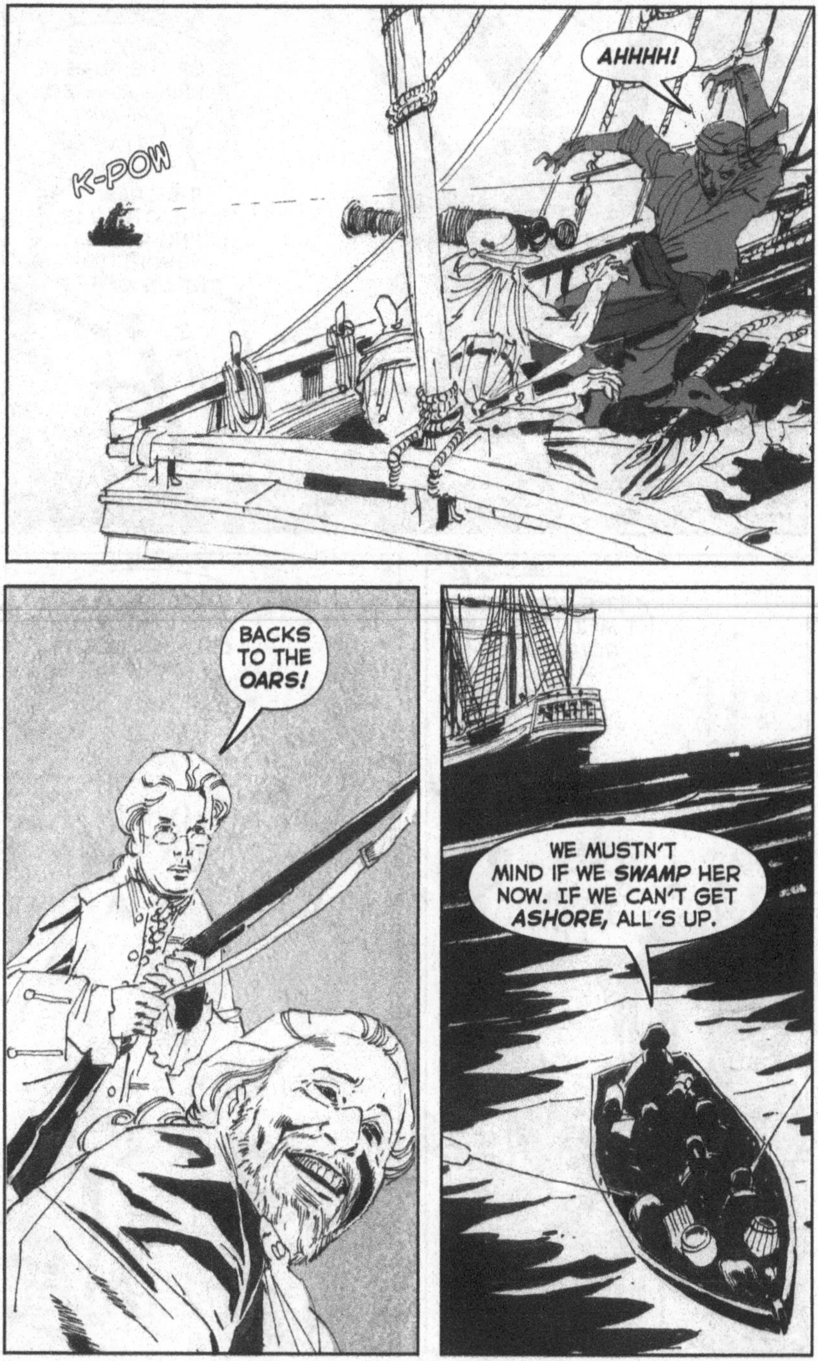
K-POW
AHHHH!
BACKS TO THE OARS!
WE MUSTN'T MIND IF WE SWAMP HER NOW. IF WE CAN'T GET ASHORE, ALL'S UP.

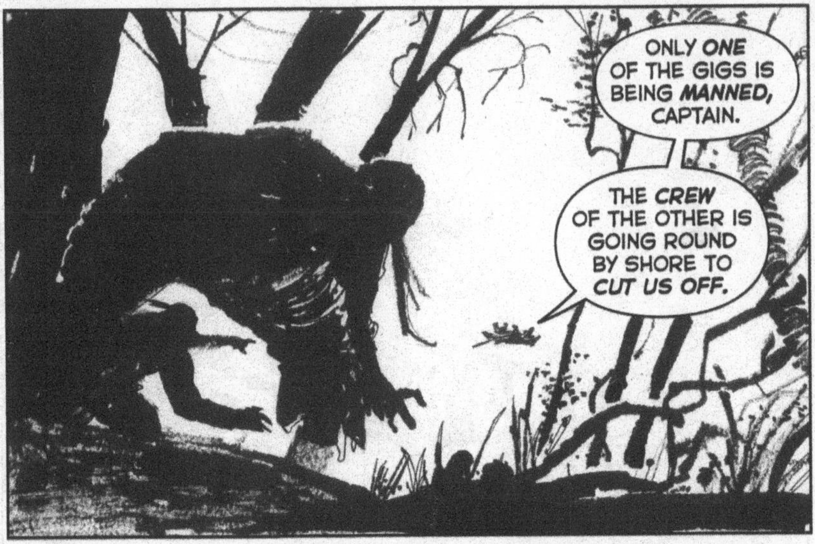
ONLY ONE OF THE GIGS IS BEING MANNED, CAPTAIN.
THE CREW OF THE OTHER IS GOING ROUND BY SHORE TO CUT US OFF.

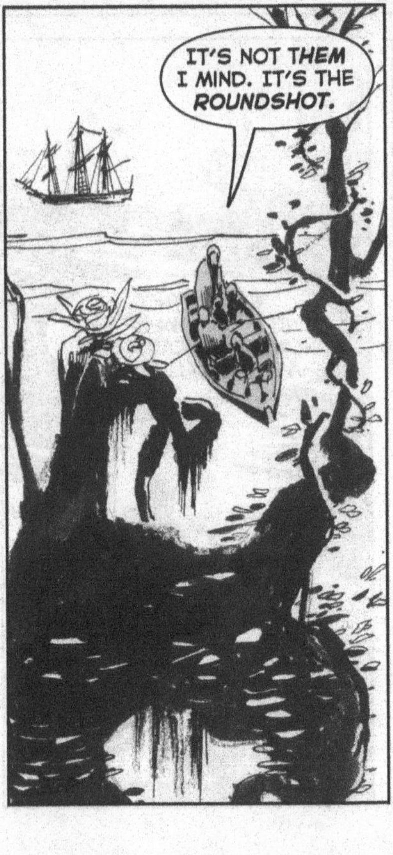
IT'S NOT THEM I MIND. IT'S THE ROUNDSHOT.

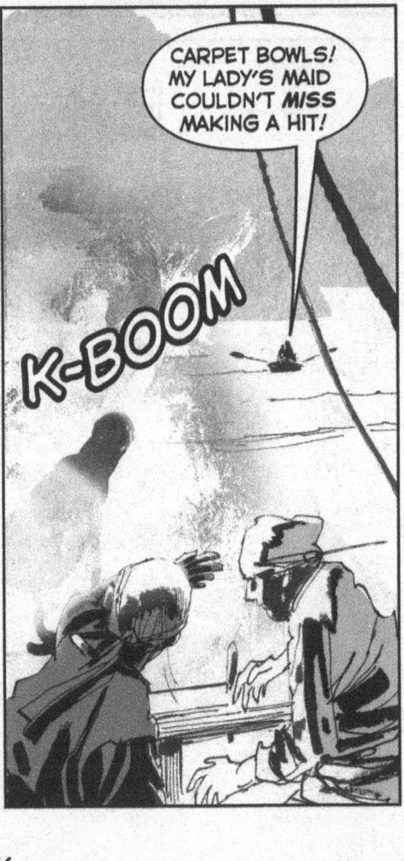
CARPET BOWLS! MY LADY'S MAID COULDN'T MISS MAKING A HIT!
K-BOOM

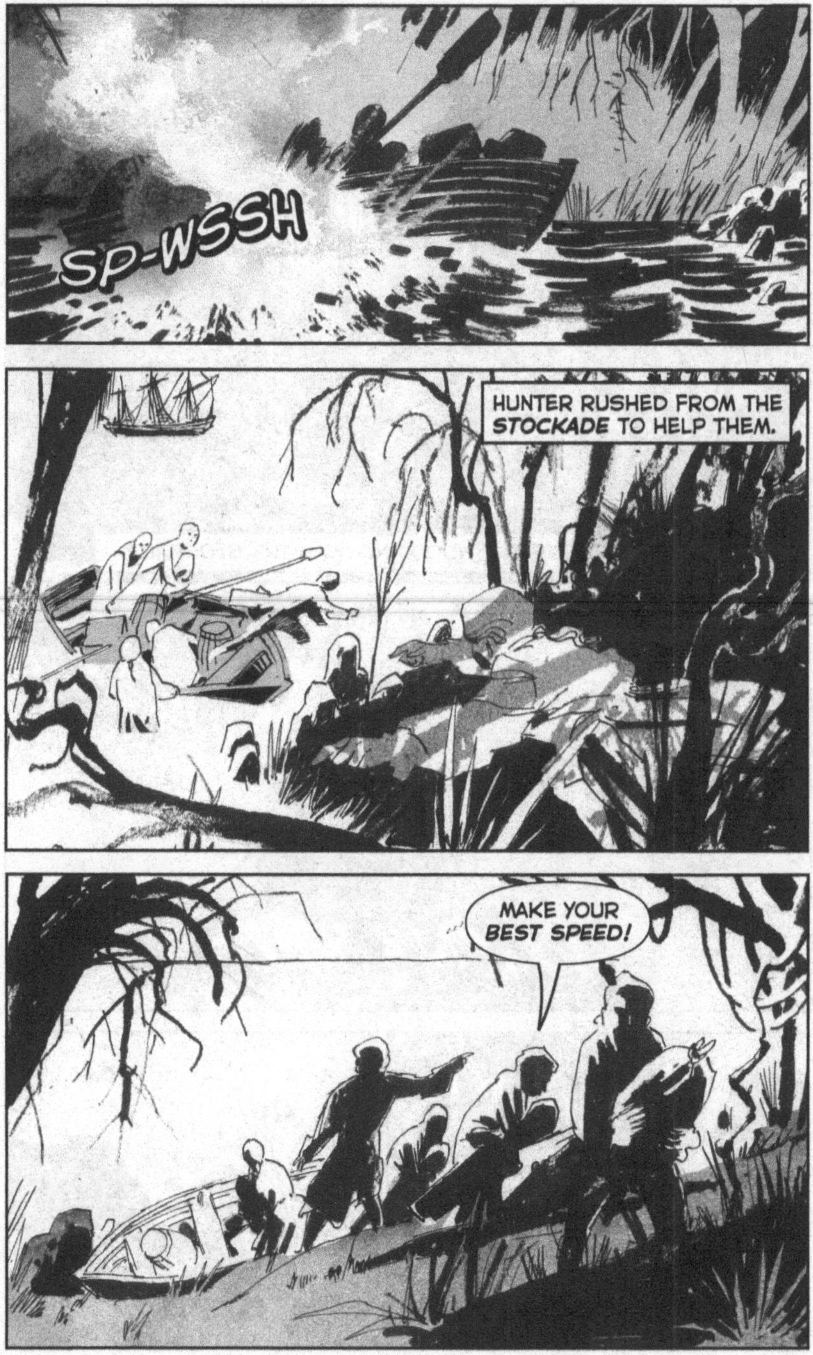
SP-WSSH
HUNTER RUSHED FROM THE STOCKADE TO HELP THEM.
MAKE YOUR BEST SPEED!

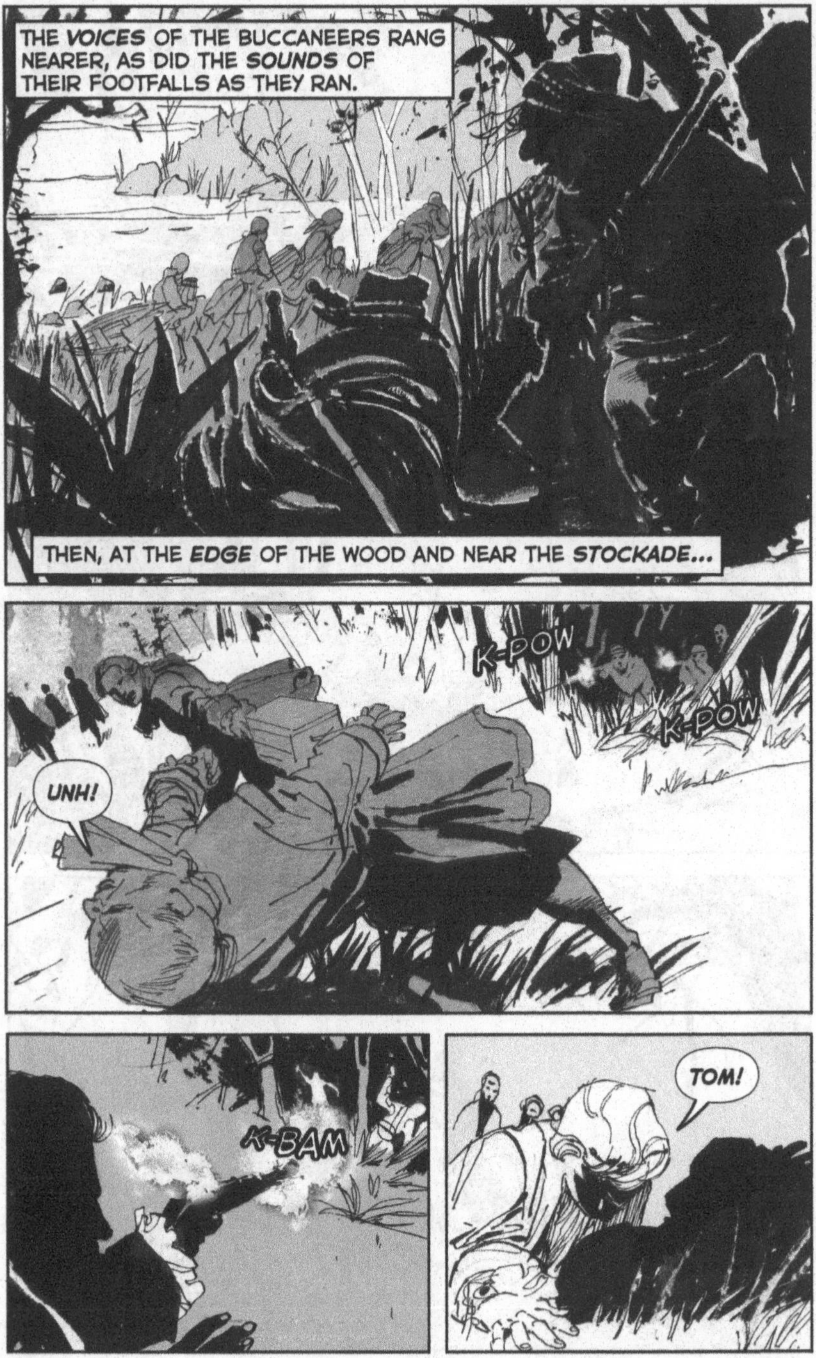
THE *VOICES* OF THE BUCCANEERS RANG NEARER, AS DID THE *SOUNDS* OF THEIR FOOTFALLS AS THEY RAN.
THEN, AT THE *EDGE* OF THE WOOD AND NEAR THE *STOCKADE...*
K-POW
K-POW
UNH!
K-BAM
TOM!

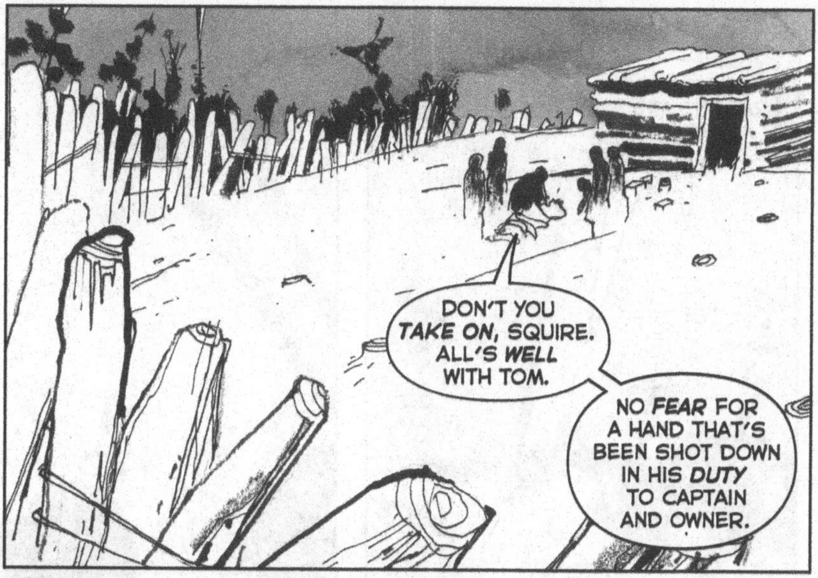
DON'T YOU *TAKE ON*, SQUIRE. ALL'S *WELL* WITH TOM.
NO *FEAR* FOR A HAND THAT'S BEEN SHOT DOWN IN HIS *DUTY* TO CAPTAIN AND OWNER.

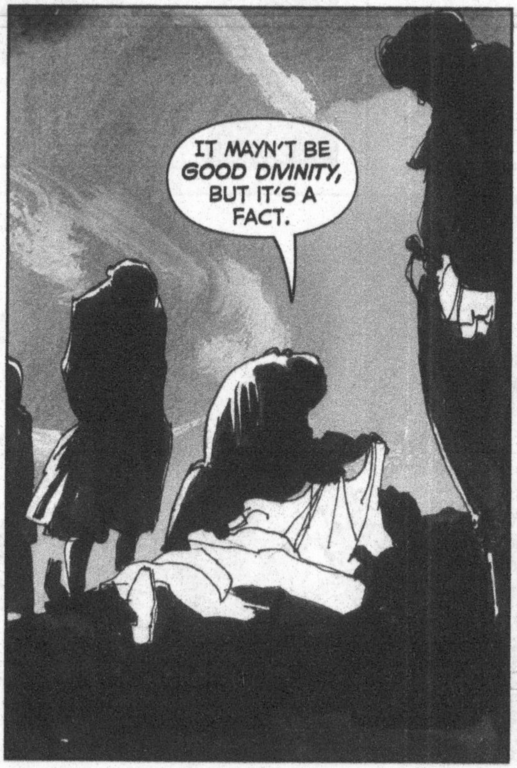
IT MAYN'T BE *GOOD DIVINITY,* BUT IT'S A FACT.

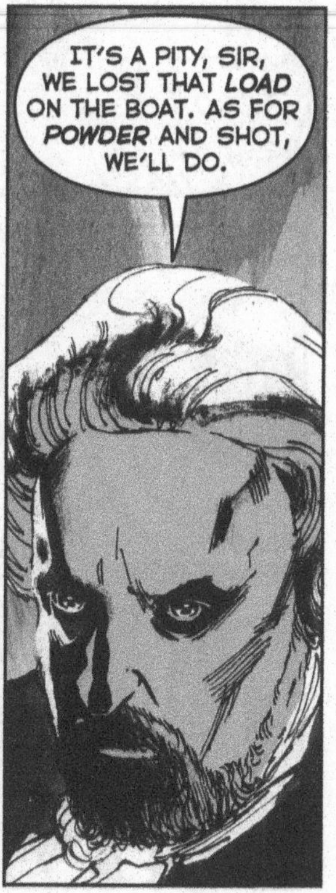
IT'S A PITY, SIR, WE LOST THAT *LOAD* ON THE BOAT. AS FOR *POWDER* AND SHOT, WE'LL DO.

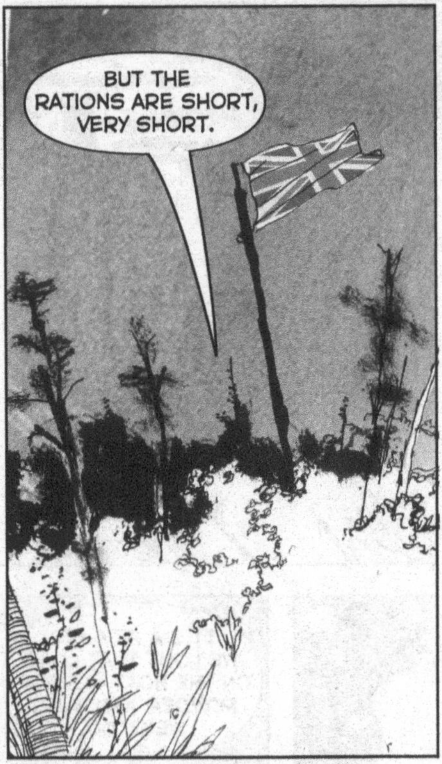
BUT THE RATIONS ARE SHORT, VERY SHORT.

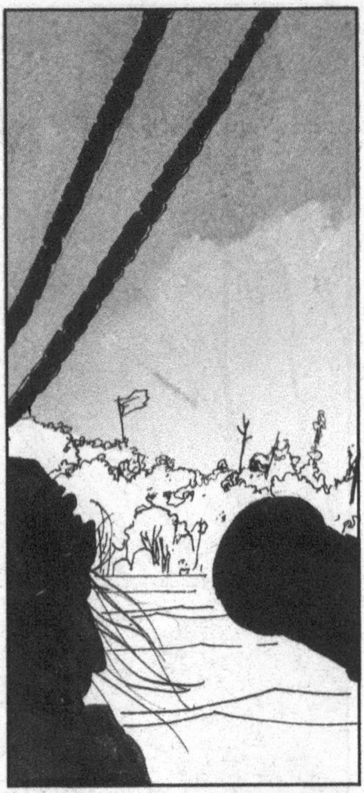

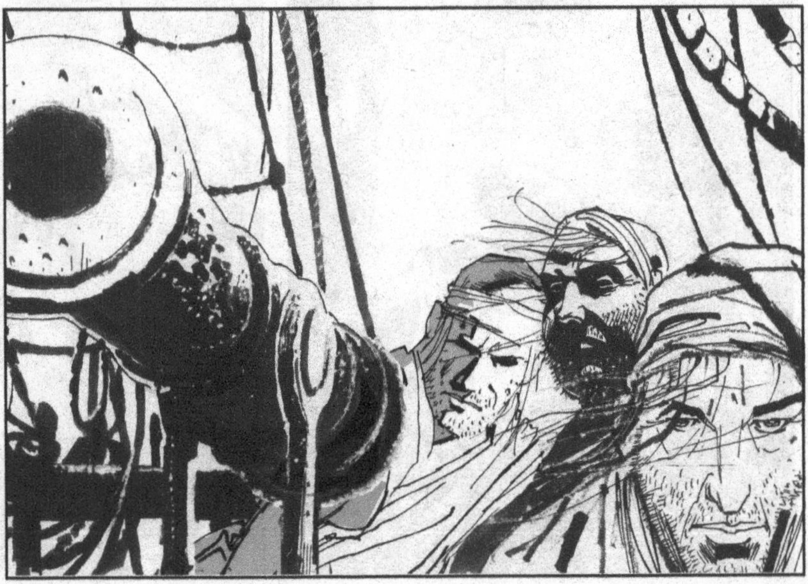

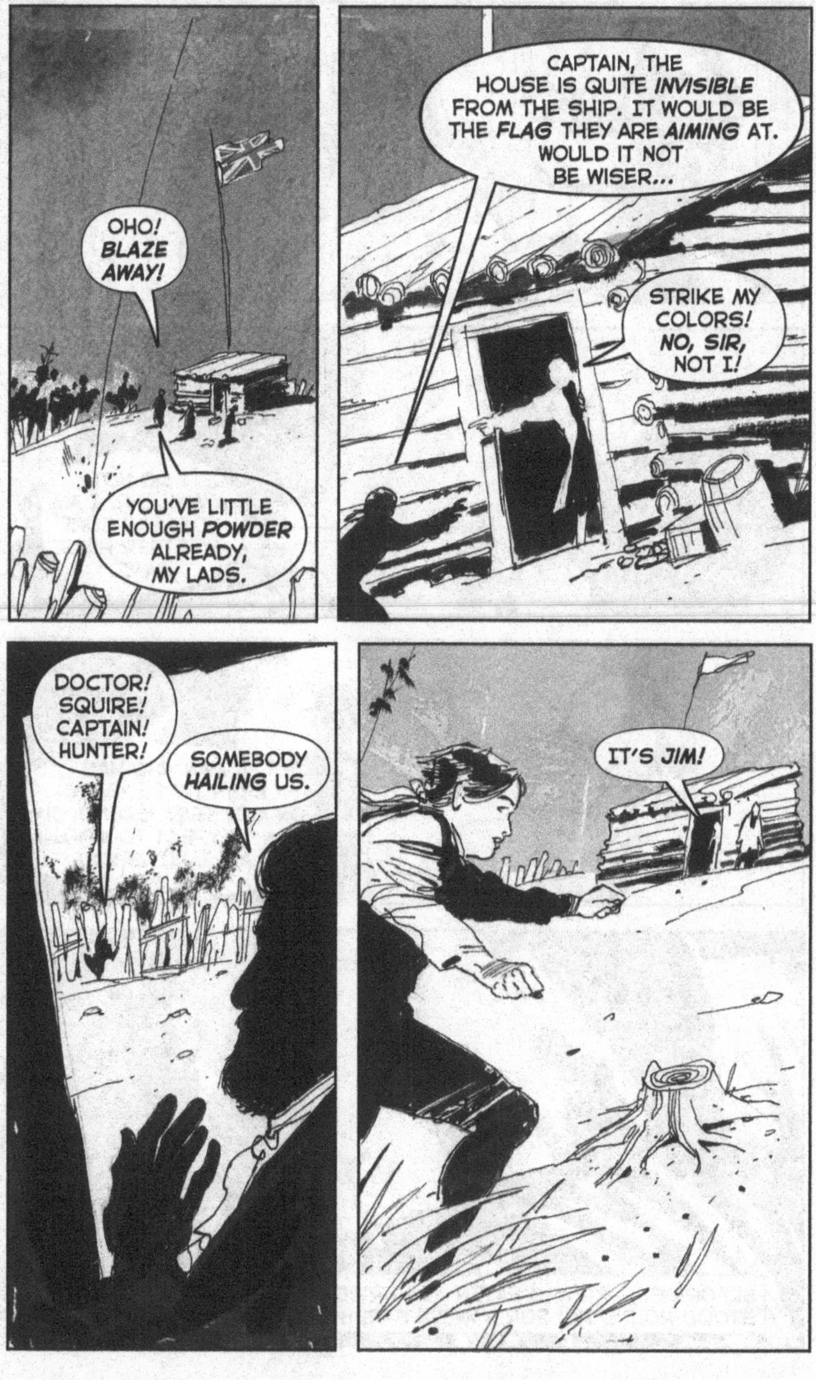
OHO! BLAZE AWAY!
YOU'VE LITTLE ENOUGH POWDER ALREADY, MY LADS.
CAPTAIN, THE HOUSE IS QUITE INVISIBLE FROM THE SHIP. IT WOULD BE THE FLAG THEY ARE AIMING AT. WOULD IT NOT BE WISER...
STRIKE MY COLORS! NO, SIR, NOT I!
DOCTOR! SQUIRE! CAPTAIN! HUNTER!
SOMEBODY HAILING US.
IT'S JIM!

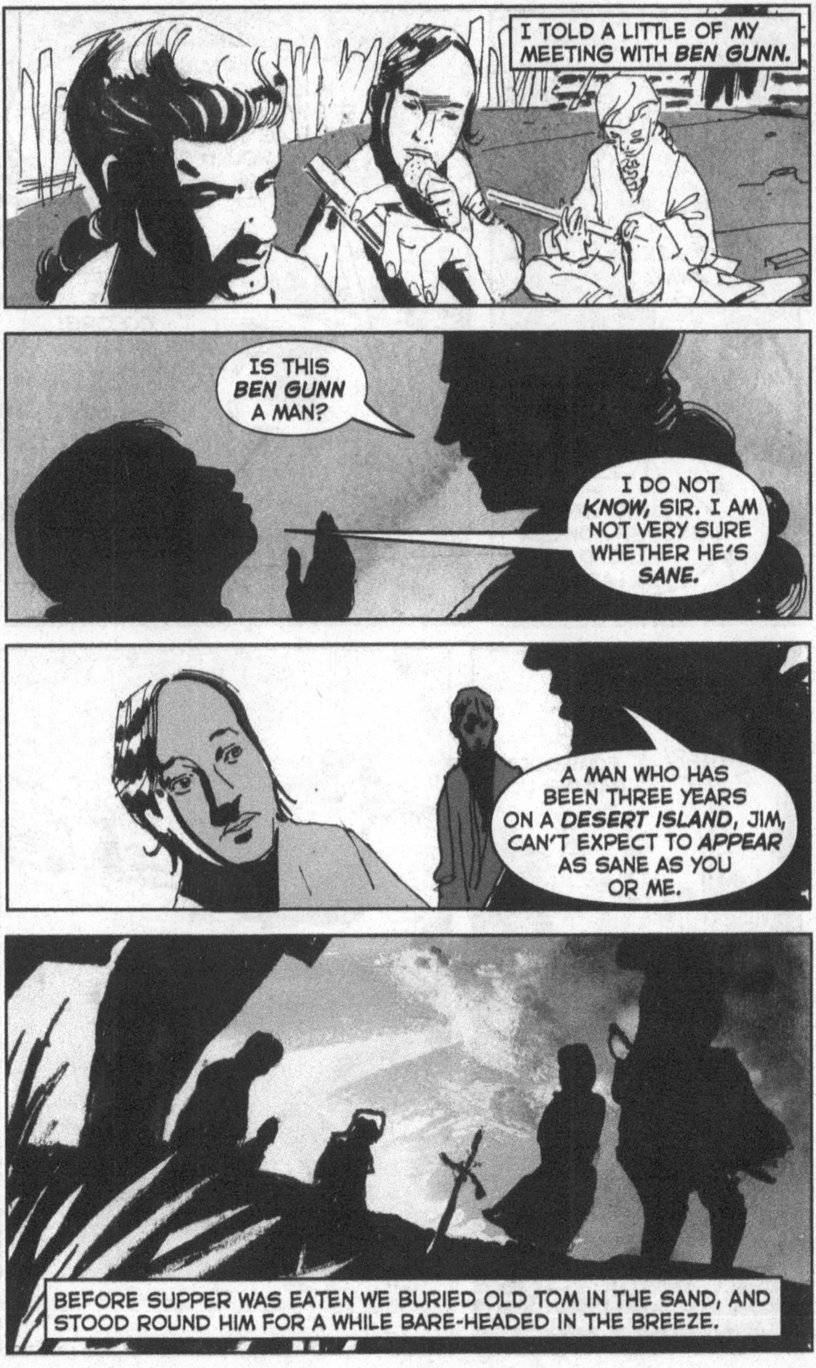
I TOLD A LITTLE OF MY MEETING WITH BEN GUNN.
IS THIS BEN GUNN A MAN?
I DO NOT KNOW, SIR. I AM NOT VERY SURE WHETHER HE'S SANE.
A MAN WHO HAS BEEN THREE YEARS ON A DESERT ISLAND, JIM, CAN'T EXPECT TO APPEAR AS SANE AS YOU OR ME.
BEFORE SUPPER WAS EATEN WE BURIED OLD TOM IN THE SAND, AND STOOD ROUND HIM FOR A WHILE BARE-HEADED IN THE BREEZE.

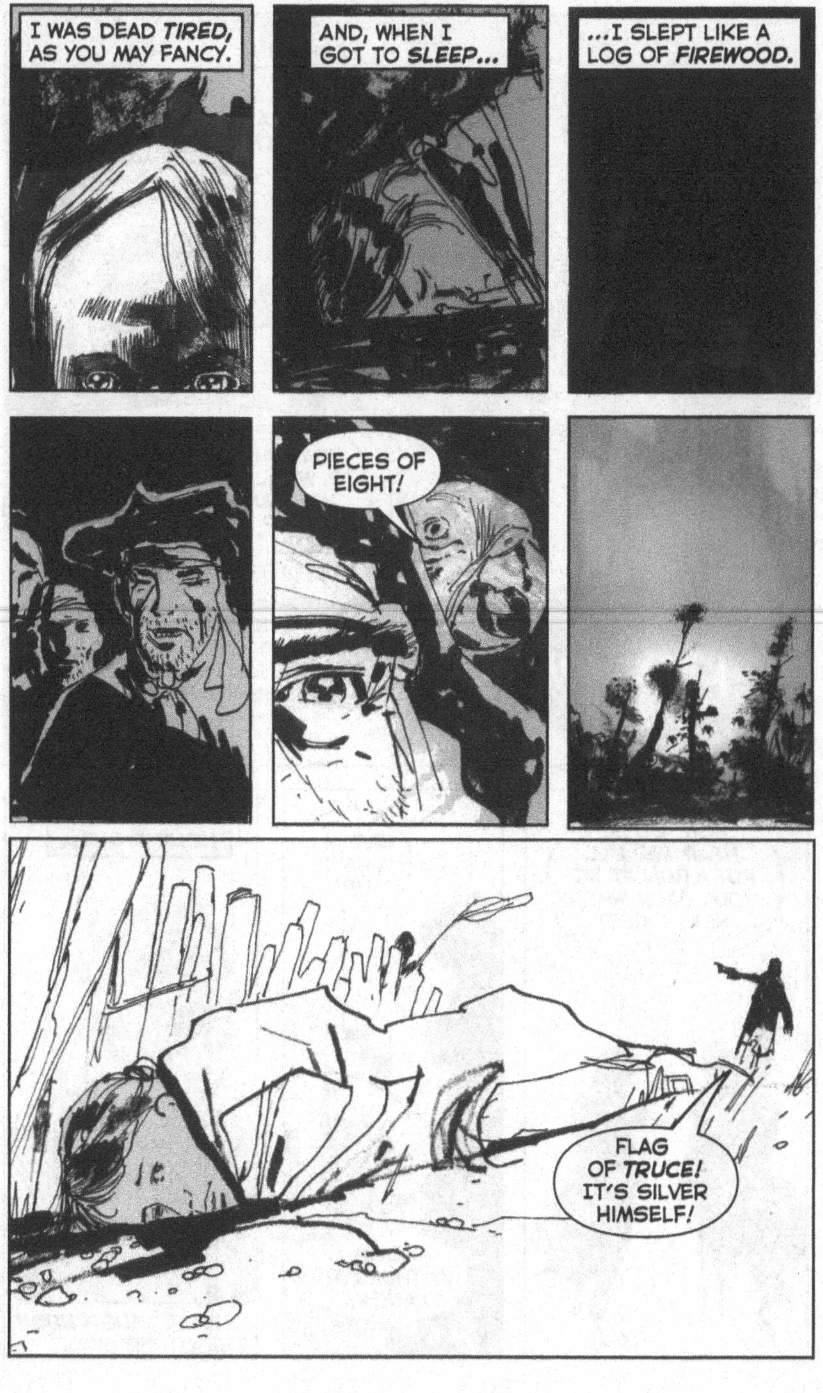
I WAS DEAD TIRED, AS YOU MAY FANCY.
AND, WHEN I GOT TO SLEEP...
...I SLEPT LIKE A LOG OF FIREWOOD.
PIECES OF EIGHT!
FLAG OF TRUCE! IT'S SILVER HIMSELF!

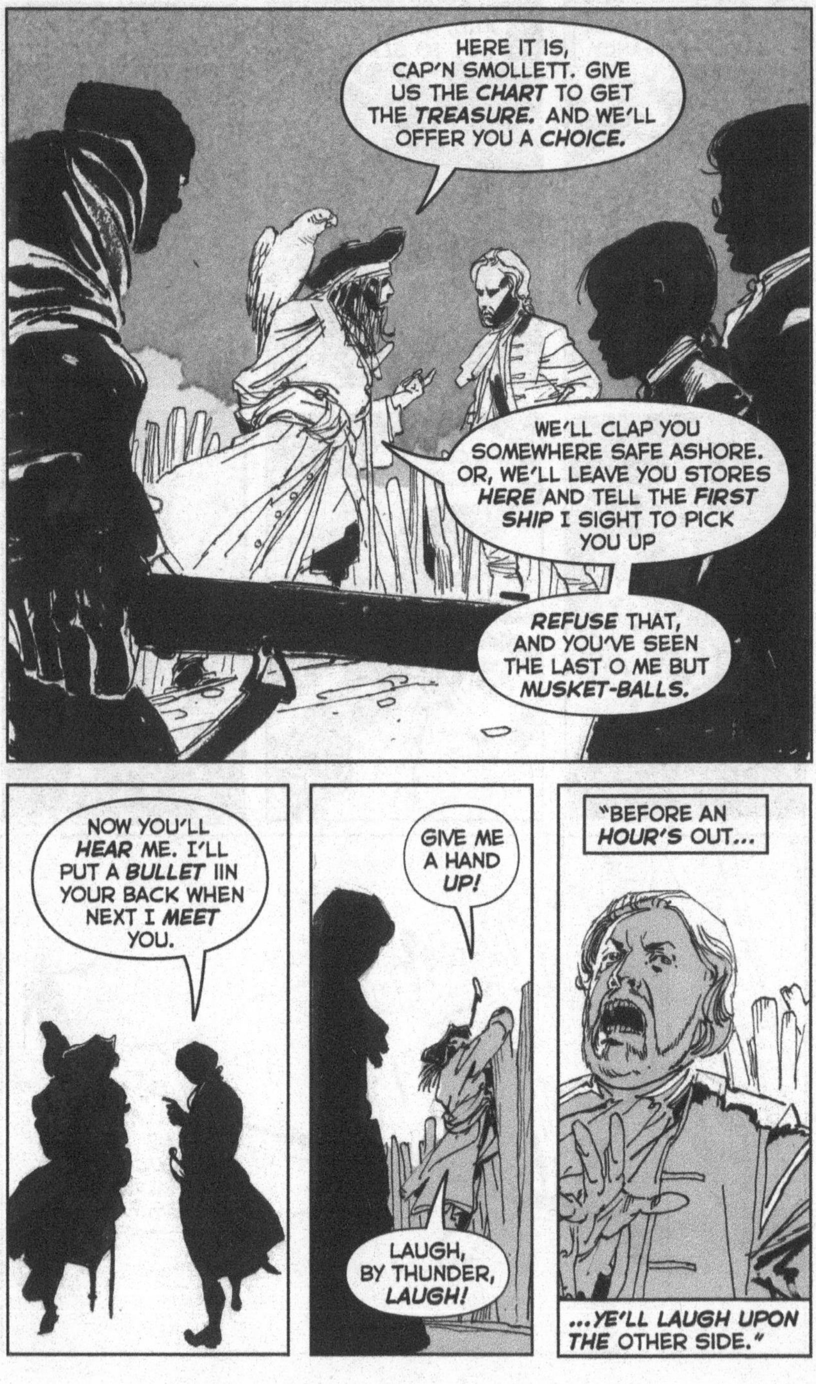
HERE IT IS, CAP'N SMOLLETT. GIVE US THE *CHART* TO GET THE *TREASURE.* AND WE'LL OFFER YOU A *CHOICE.*
WE'LL CLAP YOU SOMEWHERE SAFE ASHORE. OR, WE'LL LEAVE YOU STORES *HERE* AND TELL THE *FIRST SHIP* I SIGHT TO PICK YOU UP
REFUSE THAT, AND YOU'VE SEEN THE LAST O ME BUT *MUSKET-BALLS.*
NOW YOU'LL *HEAR* ME. I'LL PUT A *BULLET* IIN YOUR BACK WHEN NEXT I *MEET* YOU.
GIVE ME A HAND *UP!*
LAUGH, BY THUNDER, *LAUGH!*
"BEFORE AN *HOUR'S* OUT...
...YE'LL LAUGH UPON THE OTHER SIDE."

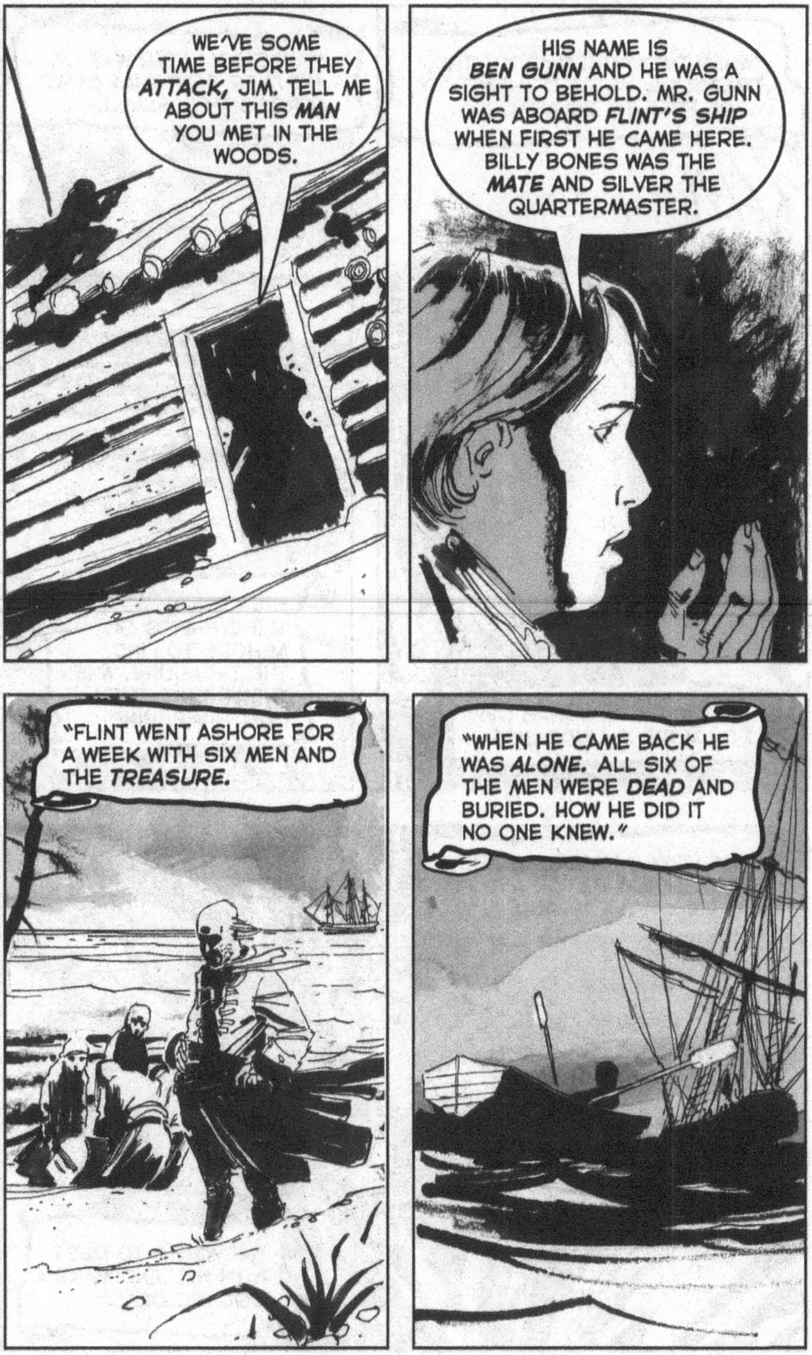
WE'VE SOME TIME BEFORE THEY ATTACK, JIM. TELL ME ABOUT THIS MAN YOU MET IN THE WOODS.
HIS NAME IS BEN GUNN AND HE WAS A SIGHT TO BEHOLD. MR. GUNN WAS ABOARD FLINT'S SHIP WHEN FIRST HE CAME HERE. BILLY BONES WAS THE MATE AND SILVER THE QUARTERMASTER.
"FLINT WENT ASHORE FOR A WEEK WITH SIX MEN AND THE TREASURE.
"WHEN HE CAME BACK HE WAS ALONE. ALL SIX OF THE MEN WERE DEAD AND BURIED. HOW HE DID IT NO ONE KNEW."

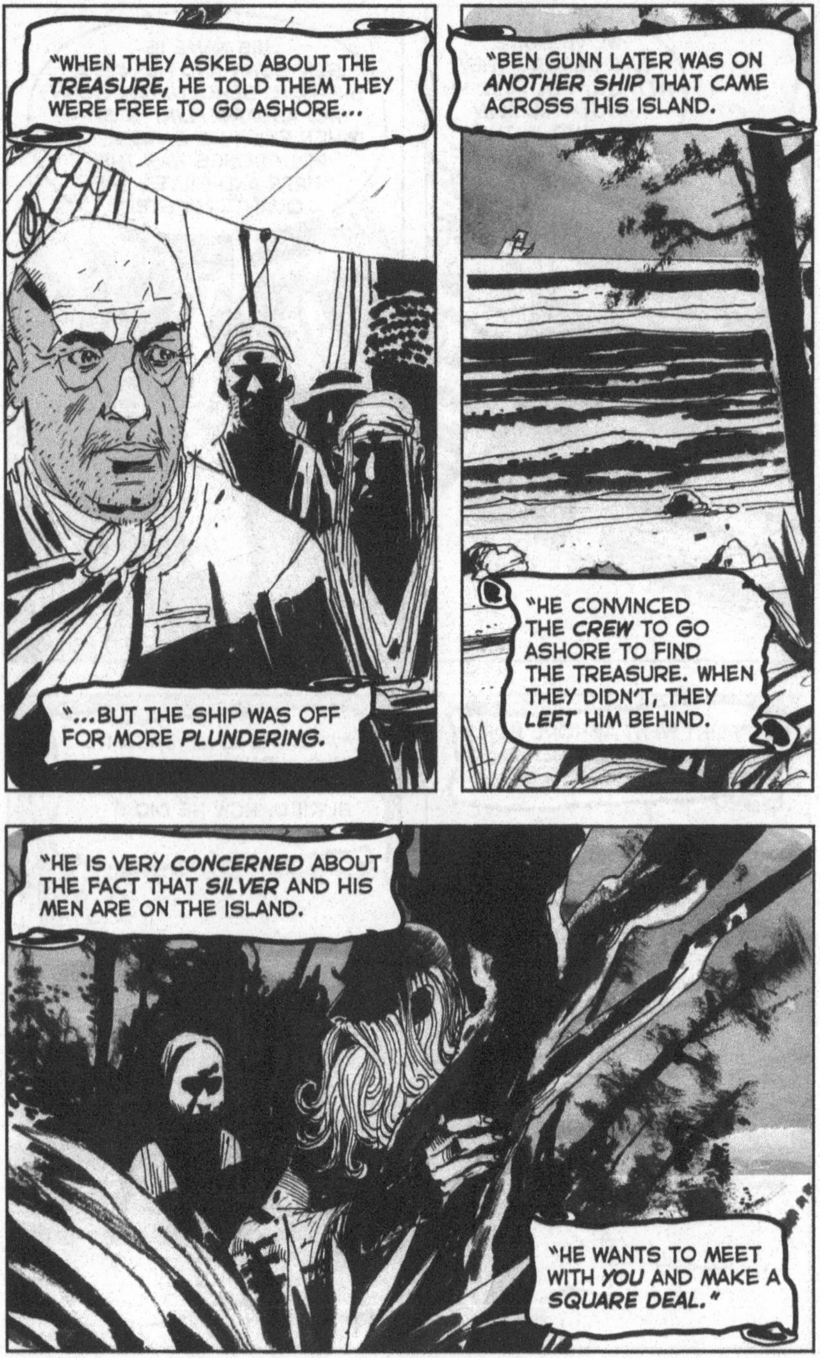
"WHEN THEY ASKED ABOUT THE TREASURE, HE TOLD THEM THEY WERE FREE TO GO ASHORE...
"...BUT THE SHIP WAS OFF FOR MORE PLUNDERING.
"BEN GUNN LATER WAS ON ANOTHER SHIP THAT CAME ACROSS THIS ISLAND.
"HE CONVINCED THE CREW TO GO ASHORE TO FIND THE TREASURE. WHEN THEY DIDN'T, THEY LEFT HIM BEHIND.
"HE IS VERY CONCERNED ABOUT THE FACT THAT SILVER AND HIS MEN ARE ON THE ISLAND.
"HE WANTS TO MEET WITH YOU AND MAKE A SQUARE DEAL."

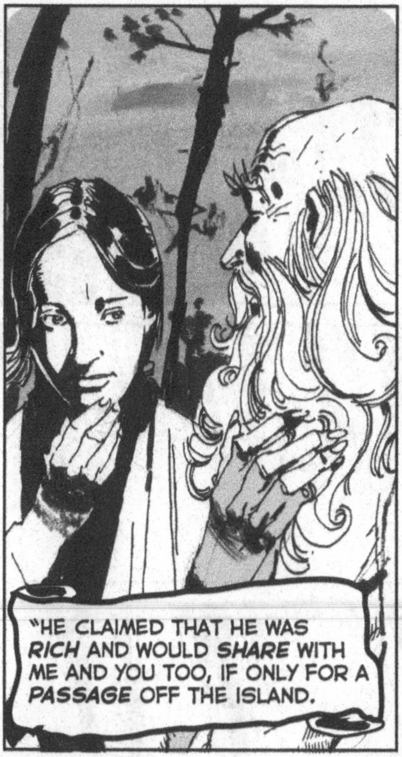
"HE CLAIMED THAT HE WAS RICH AND WOULD SHARE WITH ME AND YOU TOO, IF ONLY FOR A PASSAGE OFF THE ISLAND.

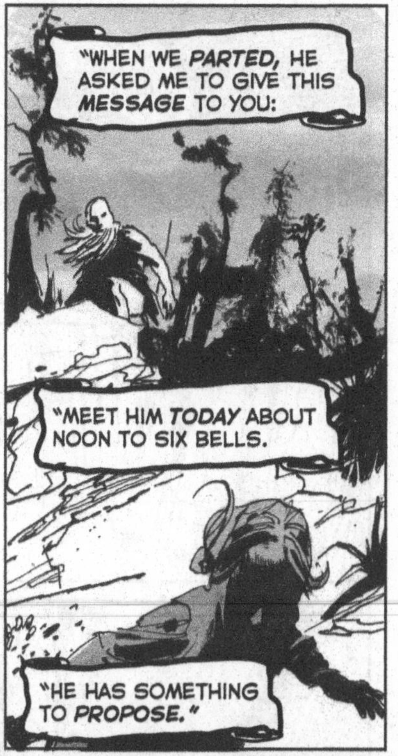
"WHEN WE PARTED, HE ASKED ME TO GIVE THIS MESSAGE TO YOU:
"MEET HIM TODAY ABOUT NOON TO SIX BELLS.
"HE HAS SOMETHING TO PROPOSE."

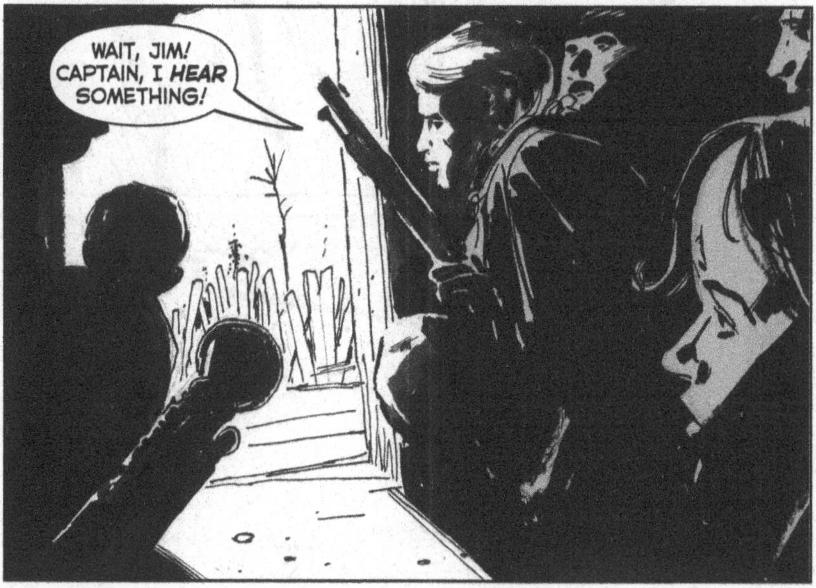
WAIT, JIM! CAPTAIN, I HEAR SOMETHING!

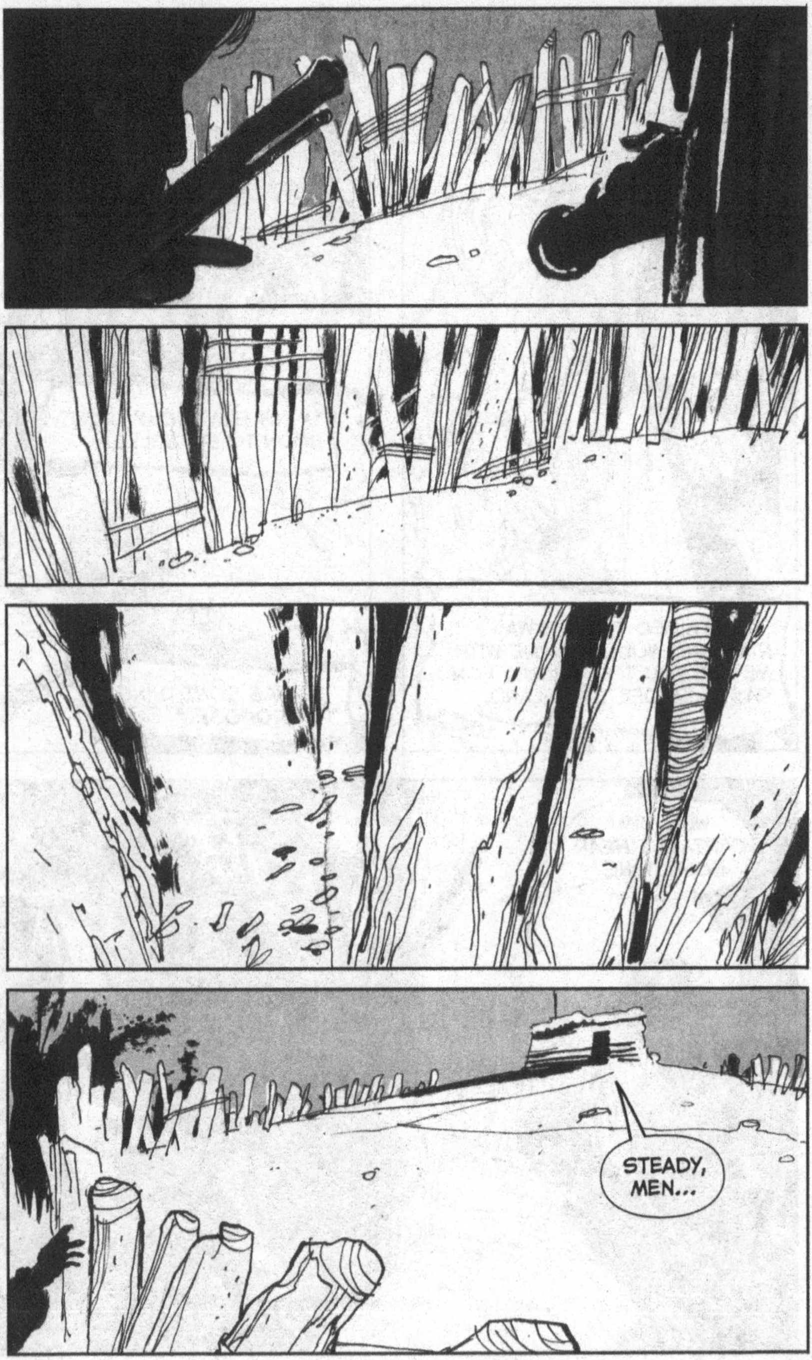
STEADY, MEN...

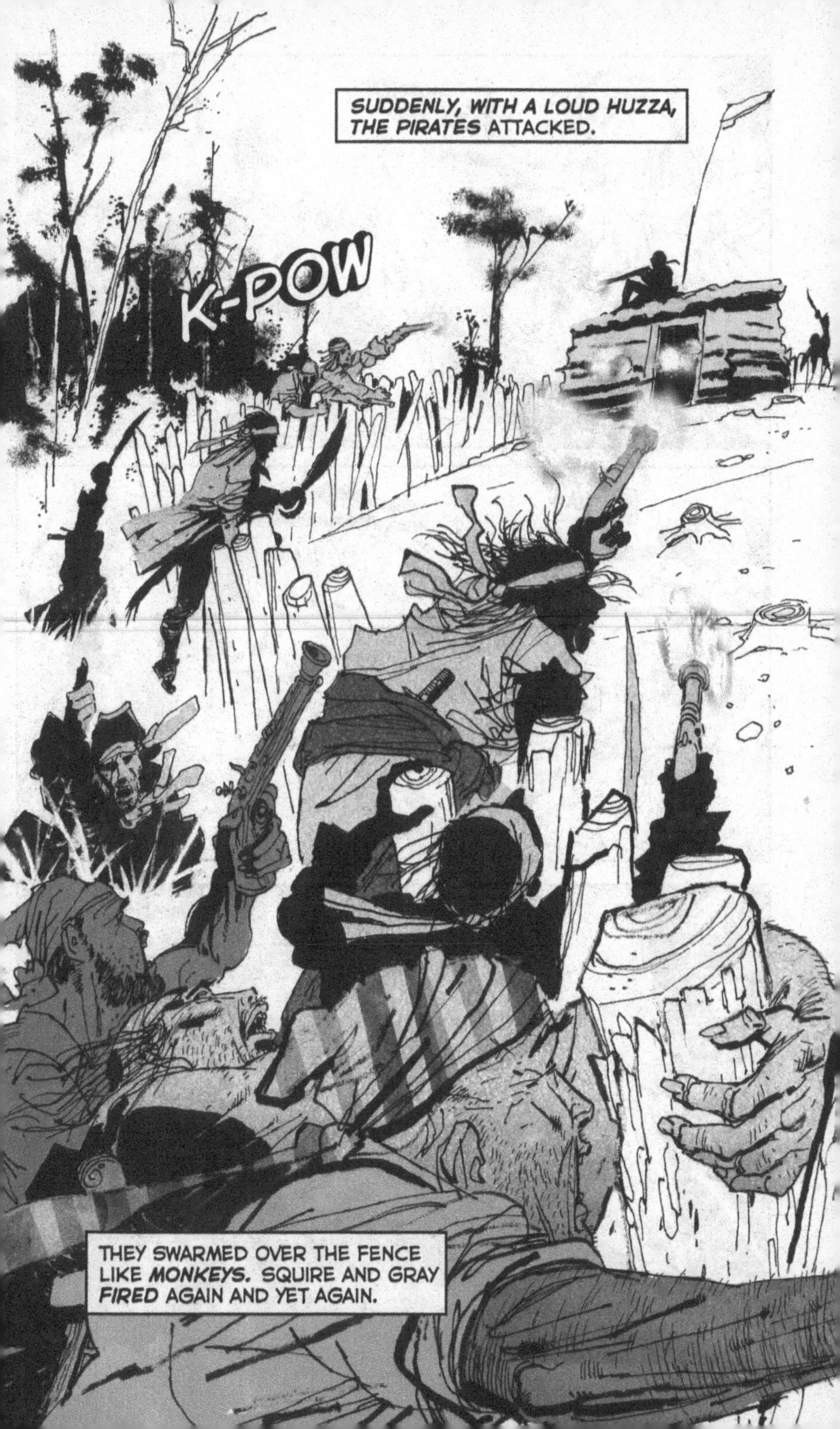
SUDDENLY, WITH A LOUD HUZZA, THE PIRATES ATTACKED.
K-POW
THEY SWARMED OVER THE FENCE LIKE MONKEYS. SQUIRE AND GRAY FIRED AGAIN AND YET AGAIN.

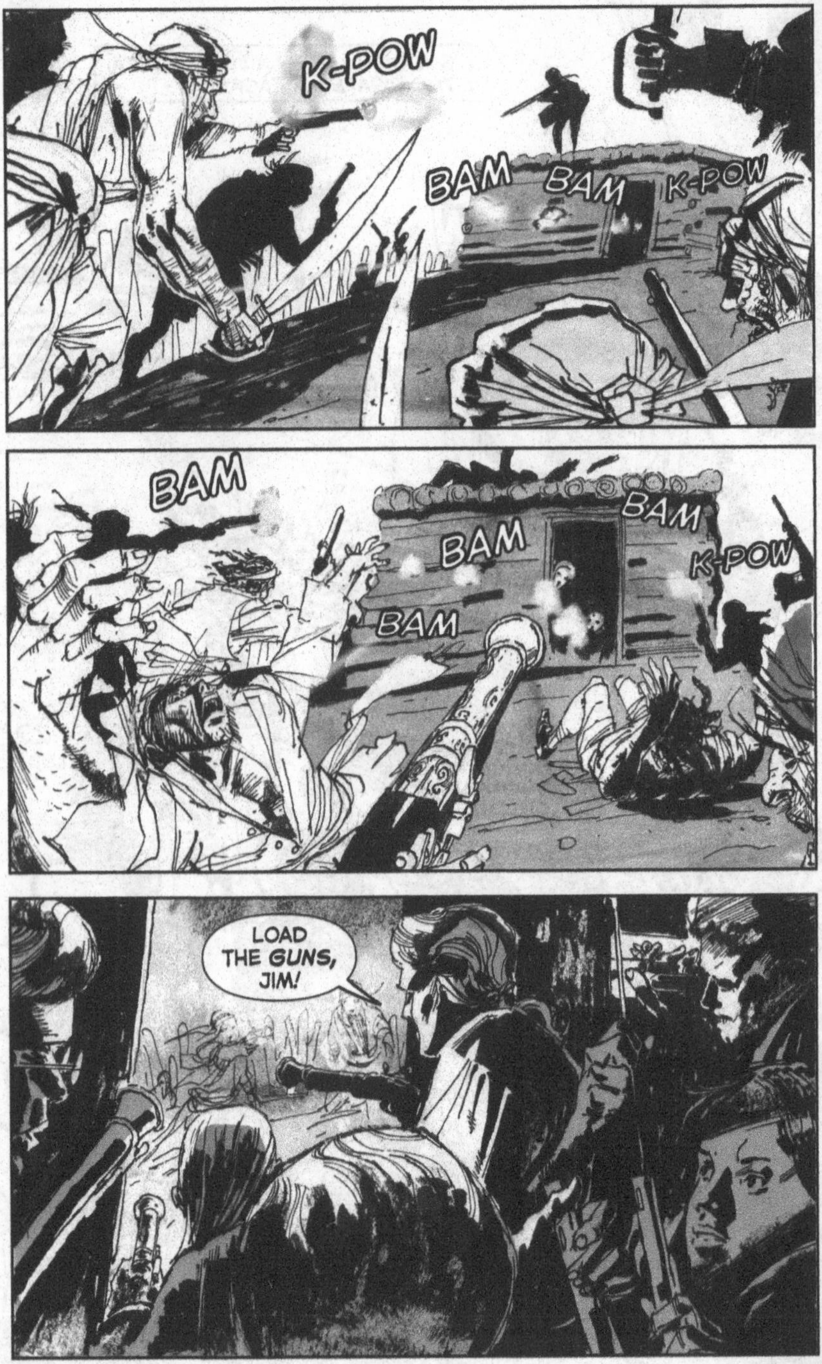
K-POW
BAM
BAM
K-POW
BAM
BAM
BAM
K-POW
BAM
LOAD THE GUNS, JIM!

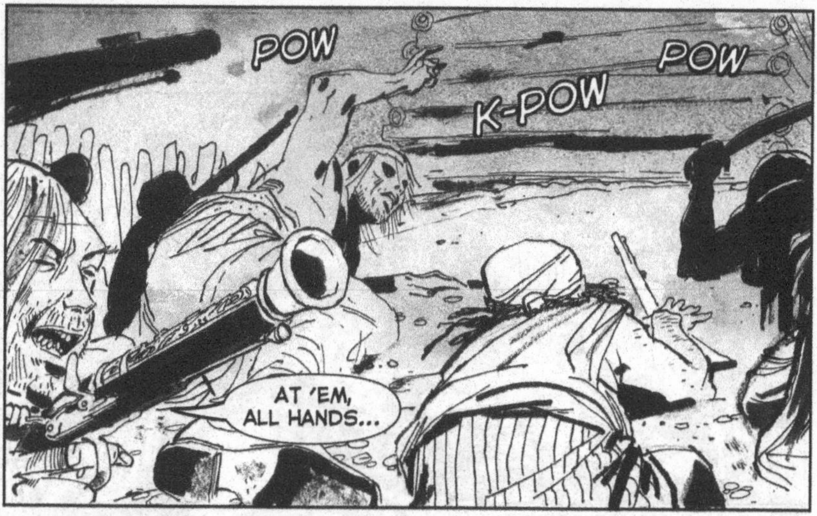
POW
K-POW
POW
AT 'EM, ALL HANDS...

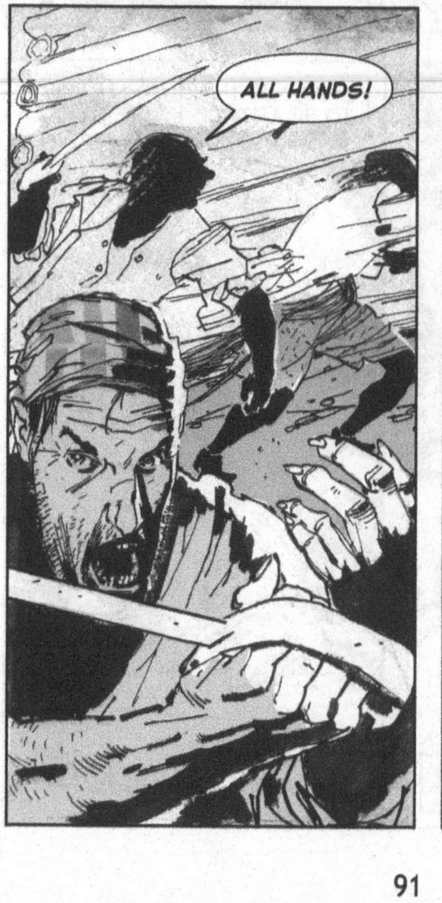
ALL HANDS!

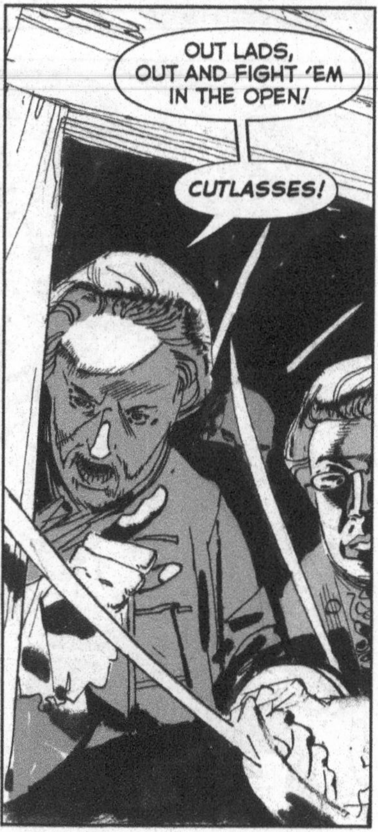
OUT LADS, OUT AND FIGHT 'EM IN THE OPEN!
CUTLASSES!

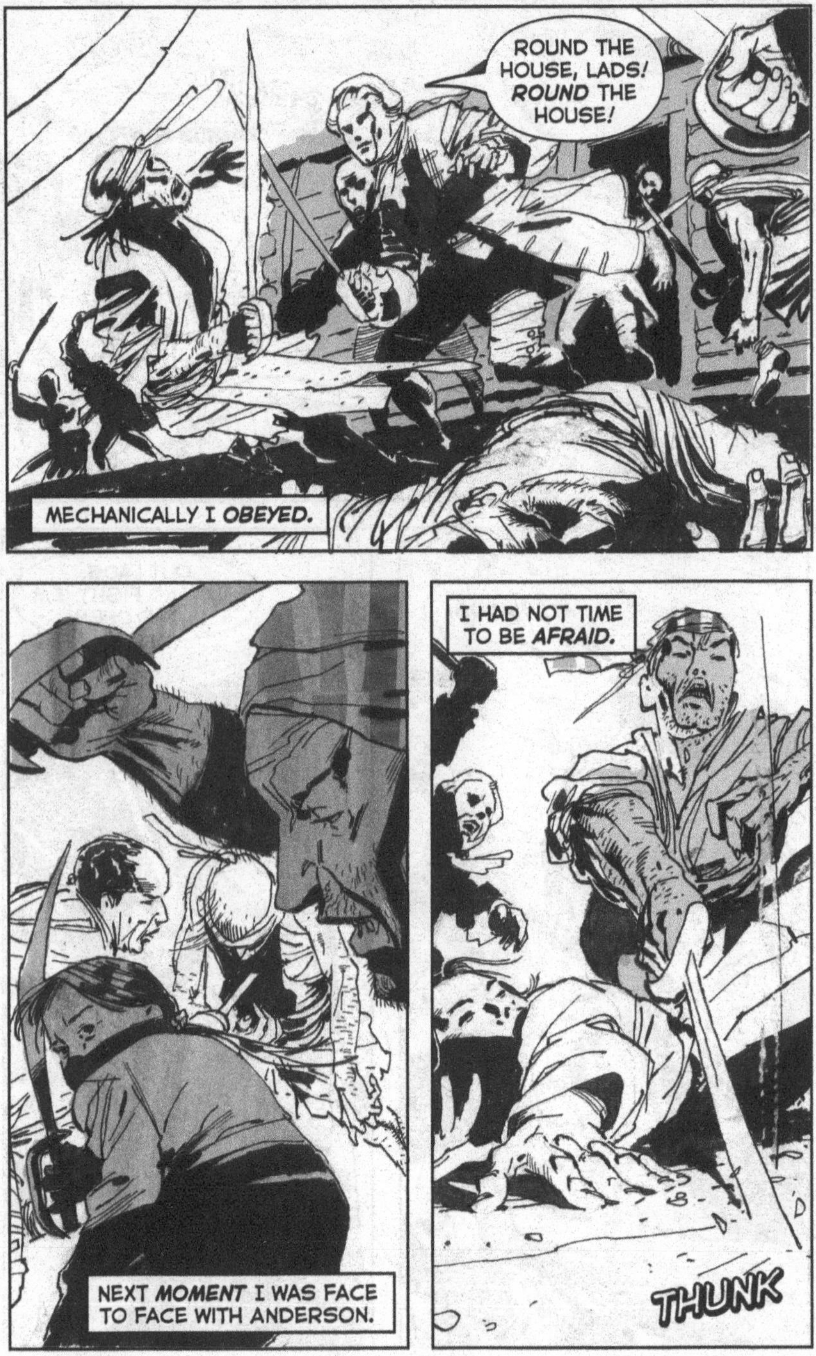
ROUND THE HOUSE, LADS! *ROUND* THE HOUSE!
MECHANICALLY I *OBEYED.*
NEXT *MOMENT* I WAS FACE TO FACE WITH ANDERSON.
I HAD NOT TIME TO BE *AFRAID.*
THUNK

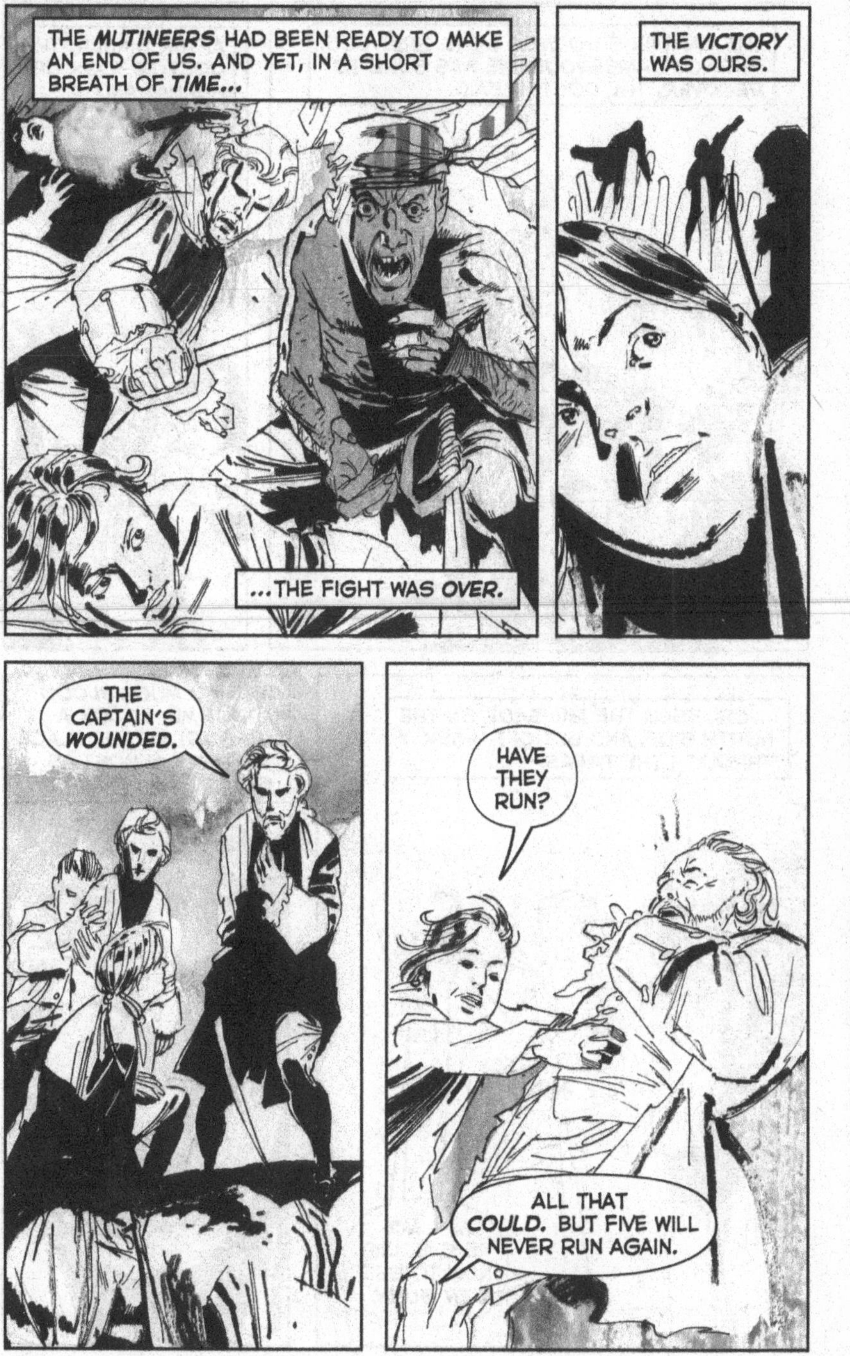
THE MUTINEERS HAD BEEN READY TO MAKE AN END OF US. AND YET, IN A SHORT BREATH OF TIME...
...THE FIGHT WAS OVER.
THE VICTORY WAS OURS.
THE CAPTAIN'S WOUNDED.
HAVE THEY RUN?
ALL THAT COULD. BUT FIVE WILL NEVER RUN AGAIN.

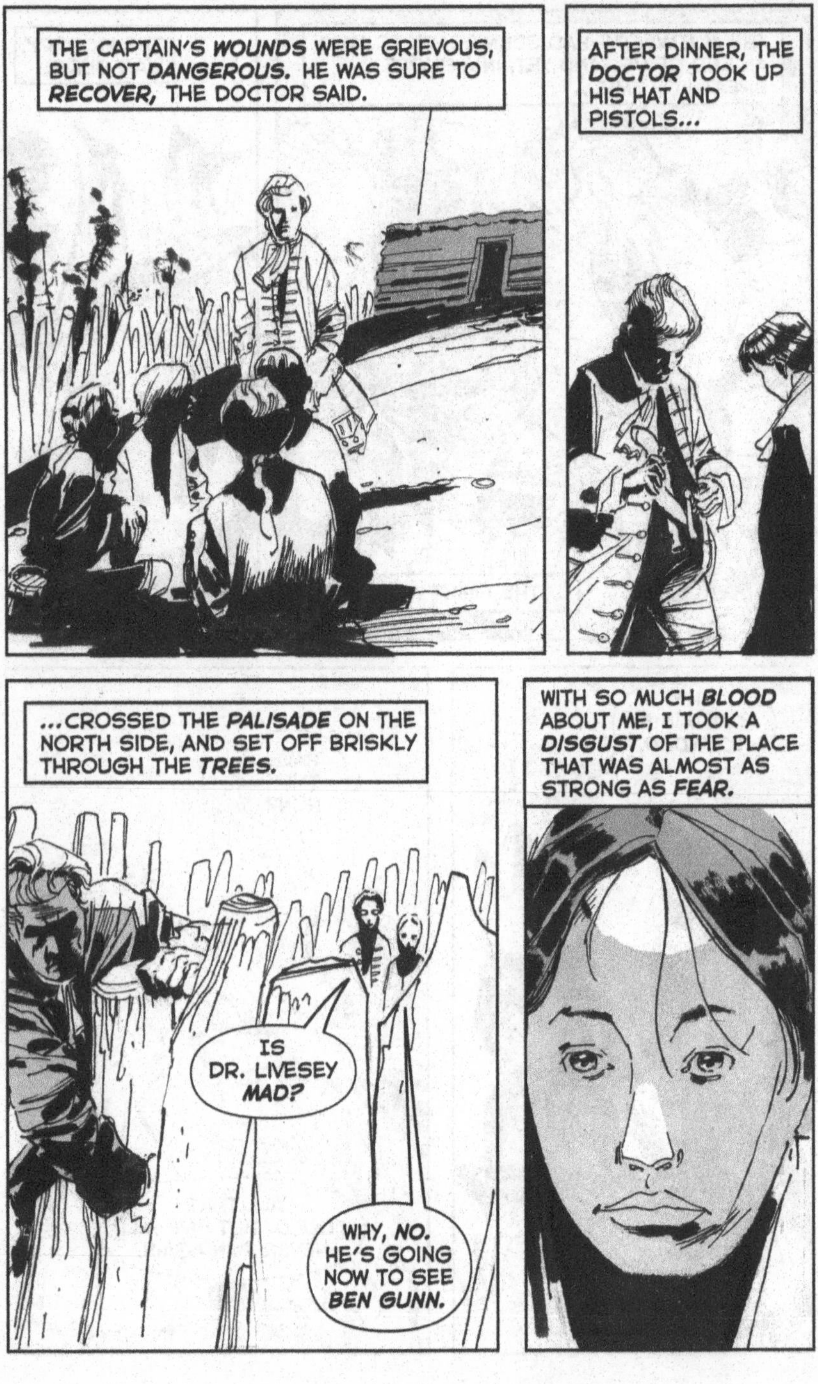
THE CAPTAIN'S WOUNDS WERE GRIEVOUS, BUT NOT DANGEROUS. HE WAS SURE TO RECOVER, THE DOCTOR SAID.
AFTER DINNER, THE DOCTOR TOOK UP HIS HAT AND PISTOLS...
...CROSSED THE PALISADE ON THE NORTH SIDE, AND SET OFF BRISKLY THROUGH THE TREES.
IS DR. LIVESEY MAD?
WHY, NO. HE'S GOING NOW TO SEE BEN GUNN.
WITH SO MUCH BLOOD ABOUT ME, I TOOK A DISGUST OF THE PLACE THAT WAS ALMOST AS STRONG AS FEAR.

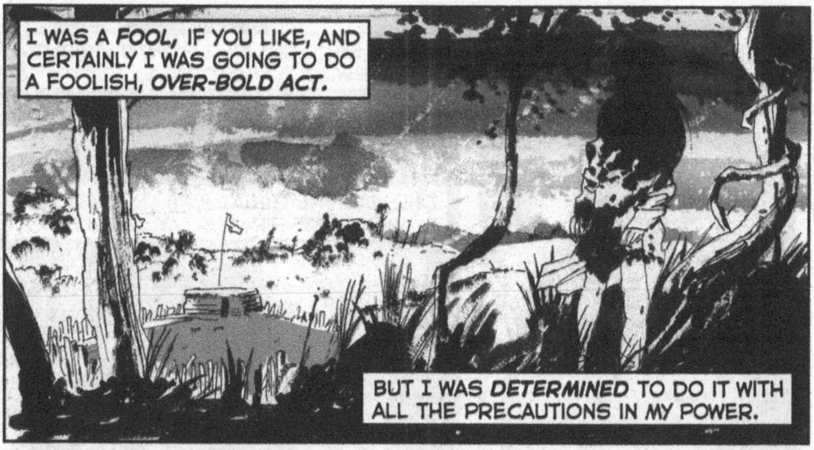
I WAS A *FOOL,* IF YOU LIKE, AND CERTAINLY I WAS GOING TO DO A FOOLISH, *OVER-BOLD ACT.*
BUT I WAS *DETERMINED* TO DO IT WITH ALL THE PRECAUTIONS IN MY POWER.

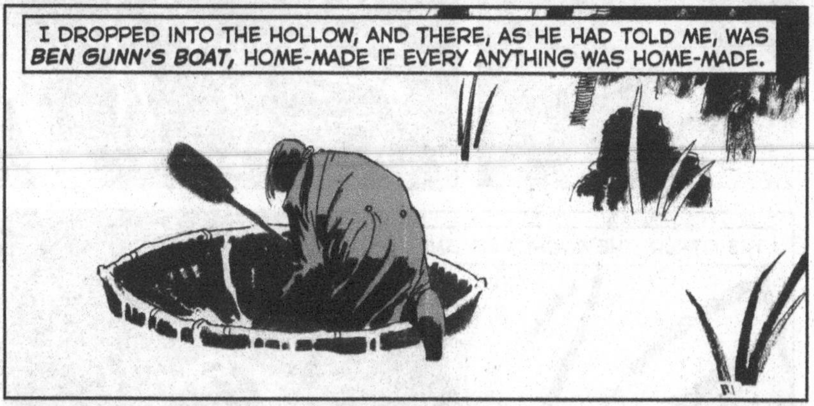
I DROPPED INTO THE HOLLOW, AND THERE, AS HE HAD TOLD ME, WAS *BEN GUNN'S BOAT,* HOME-MADE IF EVERY ANYTHING WAS HOME-MADE.

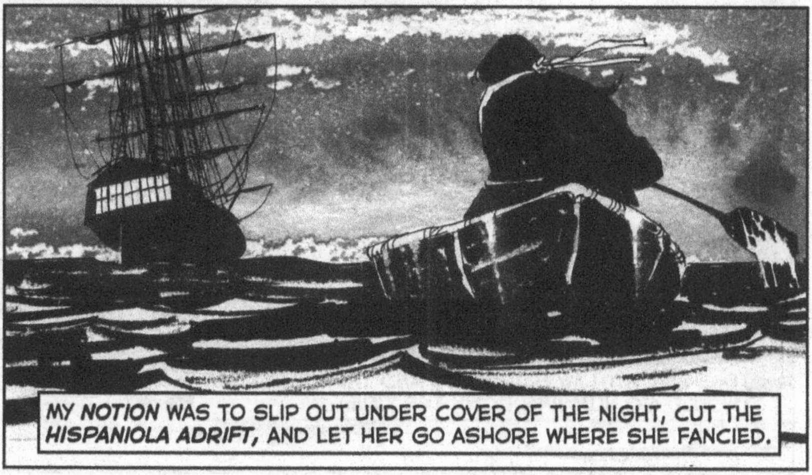
MY *NOTION* WAS TO SLIP OUT UNDER COVER OF THE NIGHT, CUT THE *HISPANIOLA ADRIFT,* AND LET HER GO ASHORE WHERE SHE FANCIED.

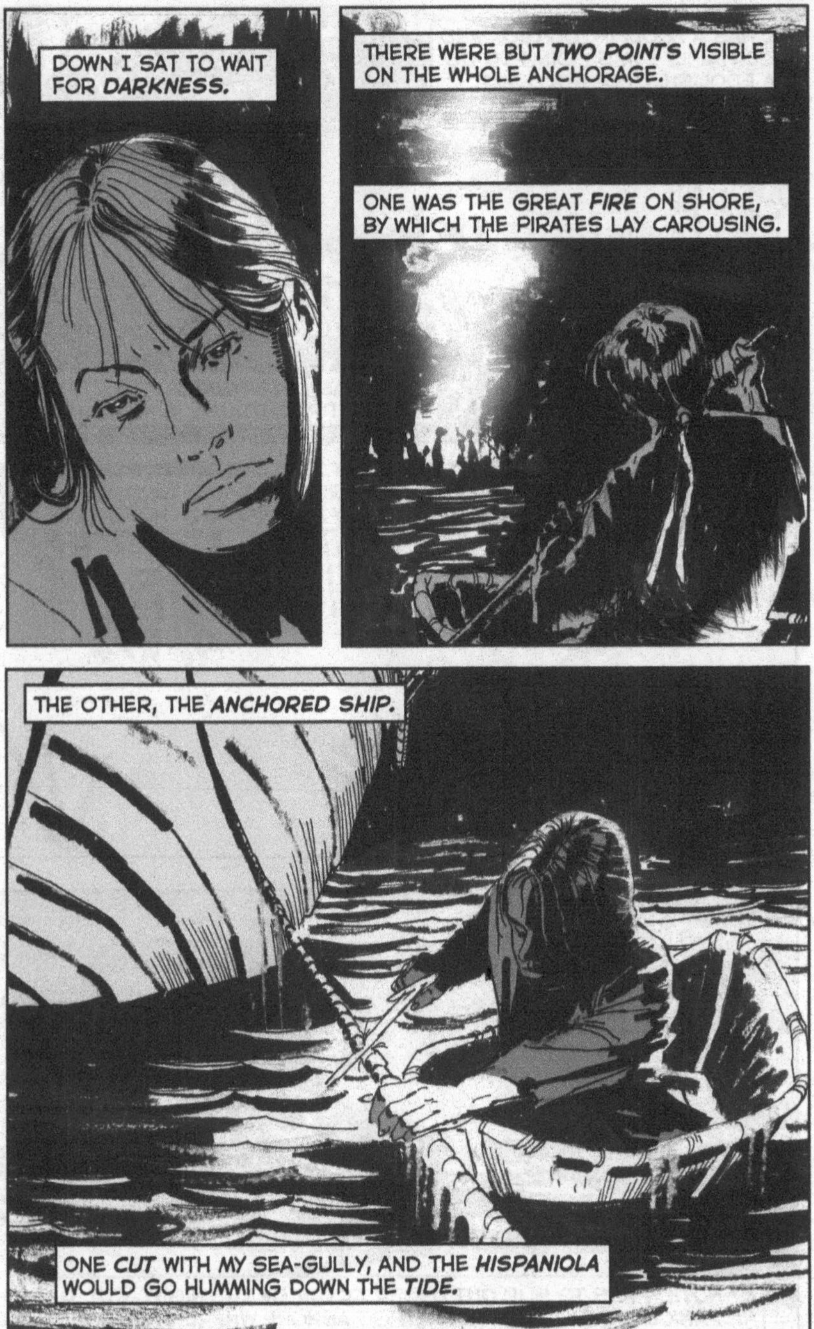
DOWN I SAT TO WAIT FOR DARKNESS.
THERE WERE BUT TWO POINTS VISIBLE ON THE WHOLE ANCHORAGE.
ONE WAS THE GREAT FIRE ON SHORE, BY WHICH THE PIRATES LAY CAROUSING.
THE OTHER, THE ANCHORED SHIP.
ONE CUT WITH MY SEA-GULLY, AND THE HISPANIOLA WOULD GO HUMMING DOWN THE TIDE.

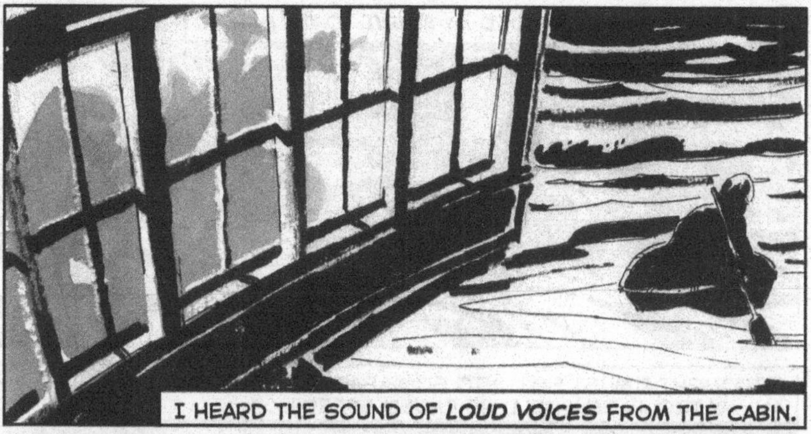
I HEARD THE SOUND OF *LOUD VOICES* FROM THE CABIN.

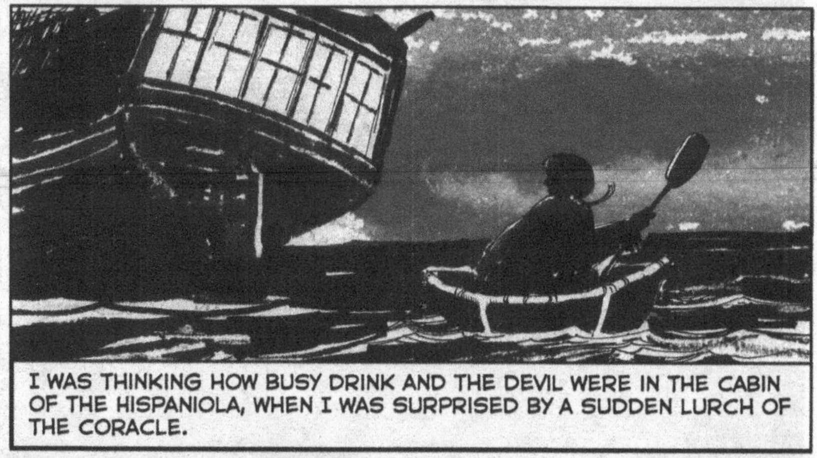
I WAS THINKING HOW BUSY DRINK AND THE DEVIL WERE IN THE CABIN OF THE HISPANIOLA, WHEN I WAS SURPRISED BY A SUDDEN LURCH OF THE CORACLE.

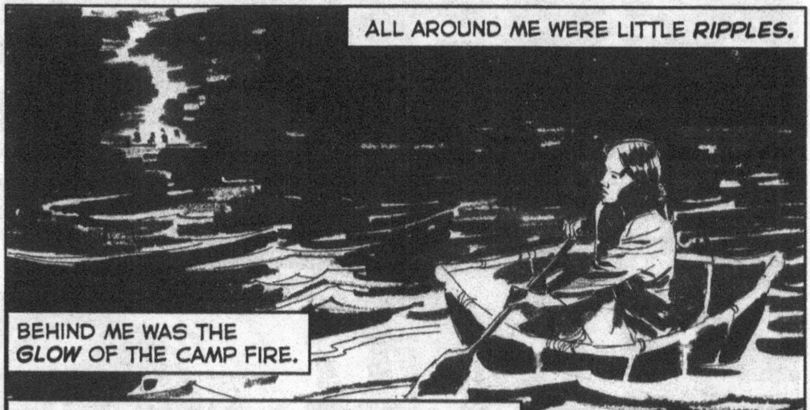
ALL AROUND ME WERE LITTLE *RIPPLES.*
BEHIND ME WAS THE *GLOW* OF THE CAMP FIRE.
THE CORACLE HEADED FOR THE *OPEN SEA.*

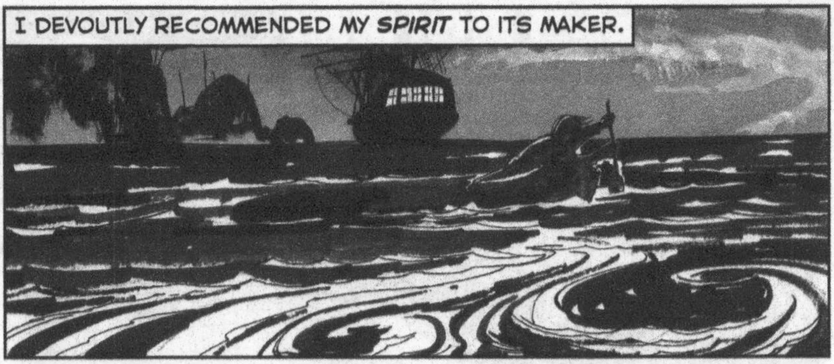
I DEVOUTLY RECOMMENDED MY SPIRIT TO ITS MAKER.

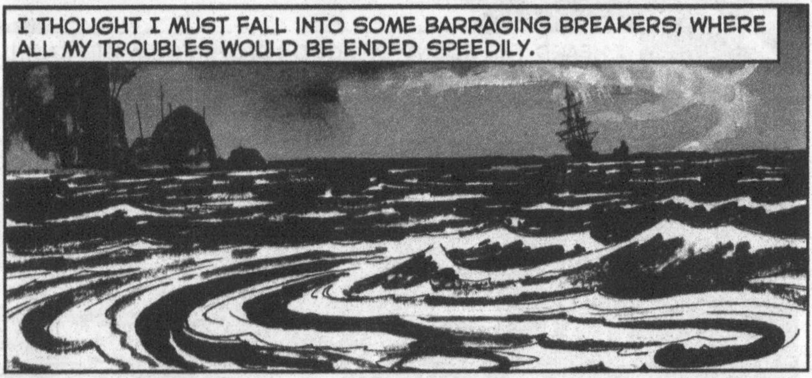
I THOUGHT I MUST FALL INTO SOME BARRAGING BREAKERS, WHERE ALL MY TROUBLES WOULD BE ENDED SPEEDILY.

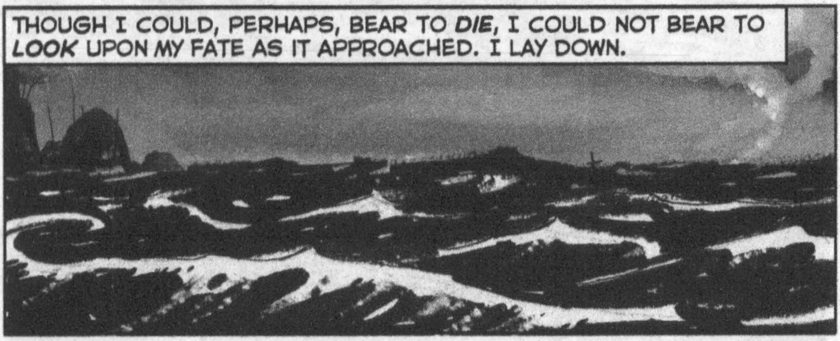
THOUGH I COULD, PERHAPS, BEAR TO DIE, I COULD NOT BEAR TO LOOK UPON MY FATE AS IT APPROACHED. I LAY DOWN.

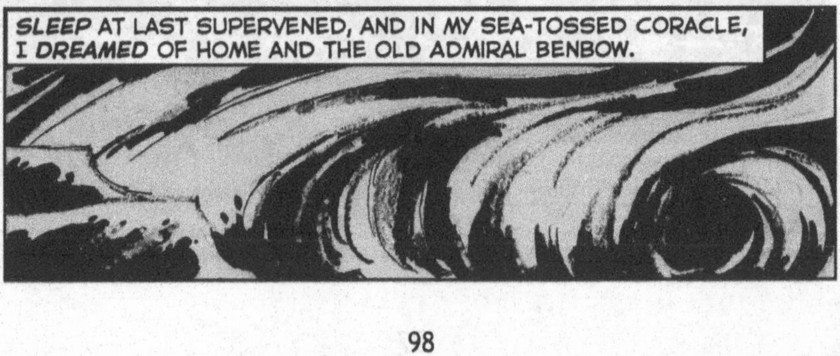
SLEEP AT LAST SUPERVENED, AND IN MY SEA-TOSSED CORACLE, I DREAMED OF HOME AND THE OLD ADMIRAL BENBOW.

IT WAS BROAD *DAY* WHEN I AWOKE, AND FOUND MYSELF TOSSING AT THE SOUTHWEST END OF *TREASURE ISLAND*.

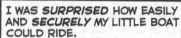

I WAS *SURPRISED* HOW EASILY AND *SECURELY* MY LITTLE BOAT COULD RIDE.

EVERY NOW AND AGAIN I GAVE A *WEAK STROKE* OR TWO TO TURN THE CORACLE TO SHORE.

THEN I BEHELD A *SIGHT* THAT CHANGED THE NATURE OF MY THOUGHTS.

THE *HISPANIOLA!*

99

TO AND FRO, THE *HISPANIOLA* *SAILED* BY SWOOPS AND DASHES. IT BECAME PLAIN TO ME THAT NOBODY WAS *STEERING*.

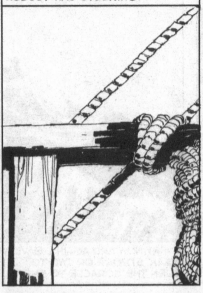

I SPRANG TO MY FEET AND *LEAPED*.

NOT A *SOUL* WAS TO BE SEEN.

THEN, THE *MAIN BOOM* SWUNG INBOARD, AND SHOWED ME THE LEE AFTER-DECK.

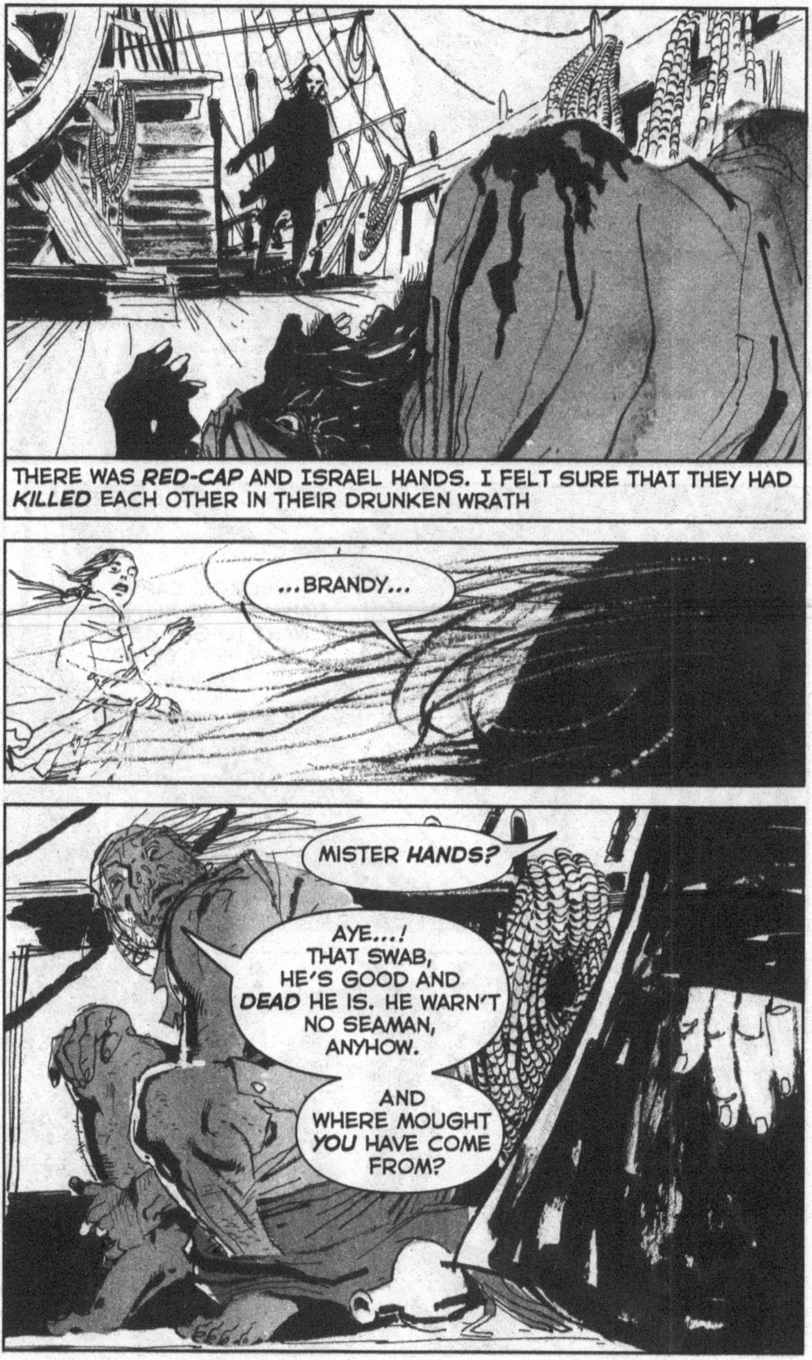
THERE WAS RED-CAP AND ISRAEL HANDS. I FELT SURE THAT THEY HAD KILLED EACH OTHER IN THEIR DRUNKEN WRATH
...BRANDY...
MISTER HANDS?
AYE...! THAT SWAB, HE'S GOOD AND DEAD HE IS. HE WARN'T NO SEAMAN, ANYHOW.
AND WHERE MOUGHT YOU HAVE COME FROM?

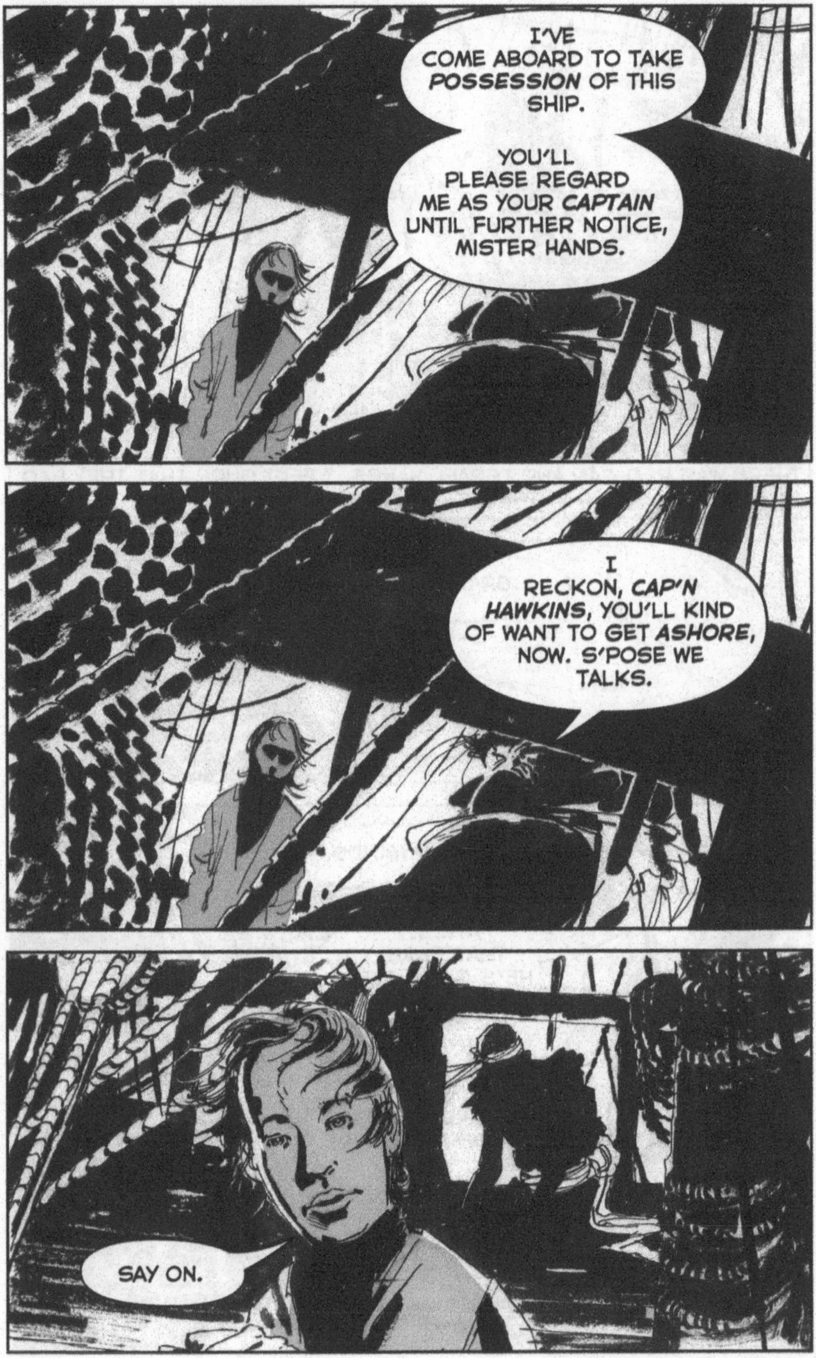
I'VE COME ABOARD TO TAKE *POSSESSION* OF THIS SHIP.
YOU'LL PLEASE REGARD ME AS YOUR *CAPTAIN* UNTIL FURTHER NOTICE, MISTER HANDS.
I RECKON, *CAP'N HAWKINS*, YOU'LL KIND OF WANT TO GET *ASHORE*, NOW. S'POSE WE TALKS.
SAY ON.

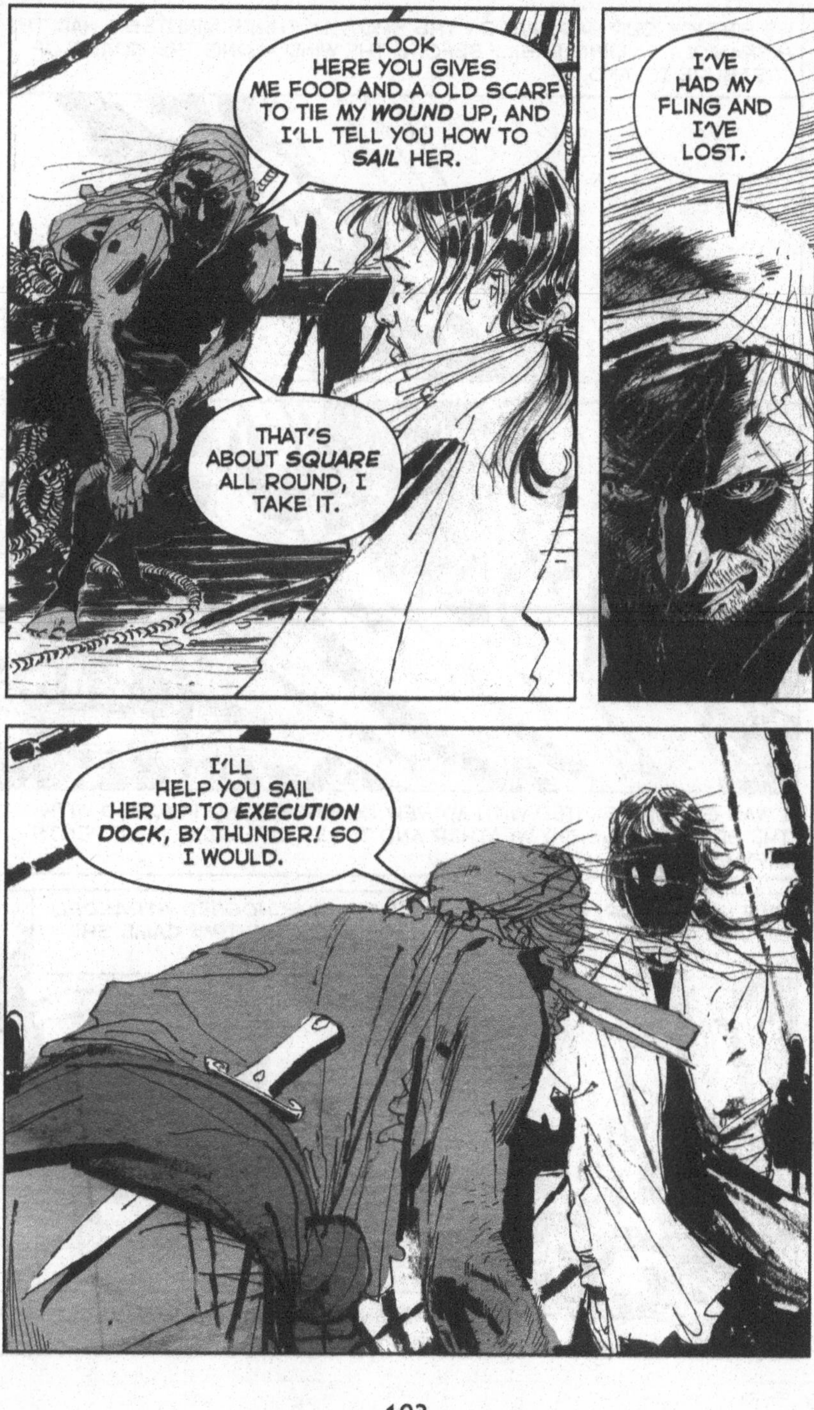
LOOK HERE YOU GIVES ME FOOD AND A OLD SCARF TO TIE MY *WOUND* UP, AND I'LL TELL YOU HOW TO *SAIL* HER.
THAT'S ABOUT *SQUARE* ALL ROUND, I TAKE IT.
I'VE HAD MY FLING AND I'VE LOST.
I'LL HELP YOU SAIL HER UP TO *EXECUTION DOCK*, BY THUNDER! SO I WOULD.

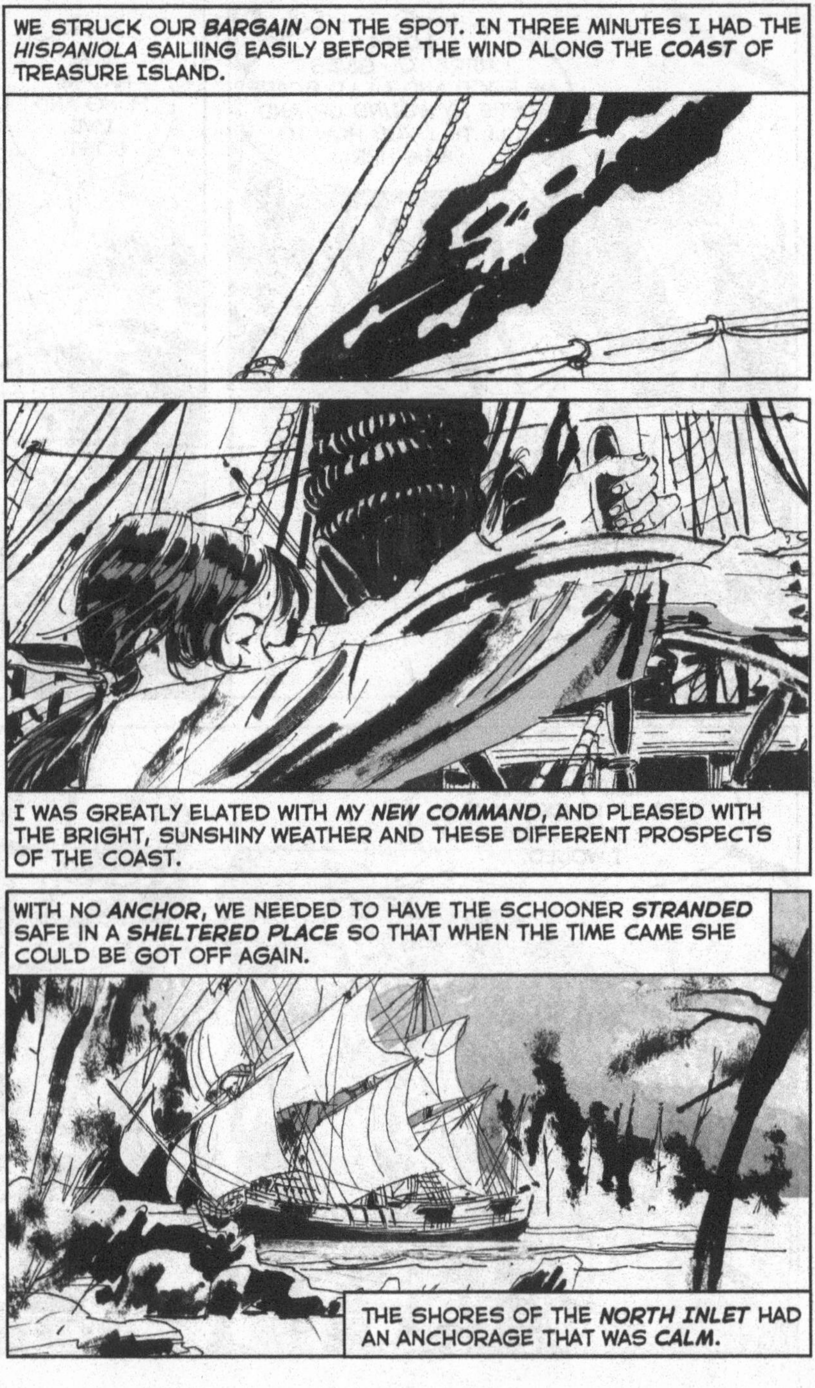
WE STRUCK OUR BARGAIN ON THE SPOT. IN THREE MINUTES I HAD THE HISPANIOLA SAILIING EASILY BEFORE THE WIND ALONG THE COAST OF TREASURE ISLAND.
I WAS GREATLY ELATED WITH MY NEW COMMAND, AND PLEASED WITH THE BRIGHT, SUNSHINY WEATHER AND THESE DIFFERENT PROSPECTS OF THE COAST.
WITH NO ANCHOR, WE NEEDED TO HAVE THE SCHOONER STRANDED SAFE IN A SHELTERED PLACE SO THAT WHEN THE TIME CAME SHE COULD BE GOT OFF AGAIN.
THE SHORES OF THE NORTH INLET HAD AN ANCHORAGE THAT WAS CALM.

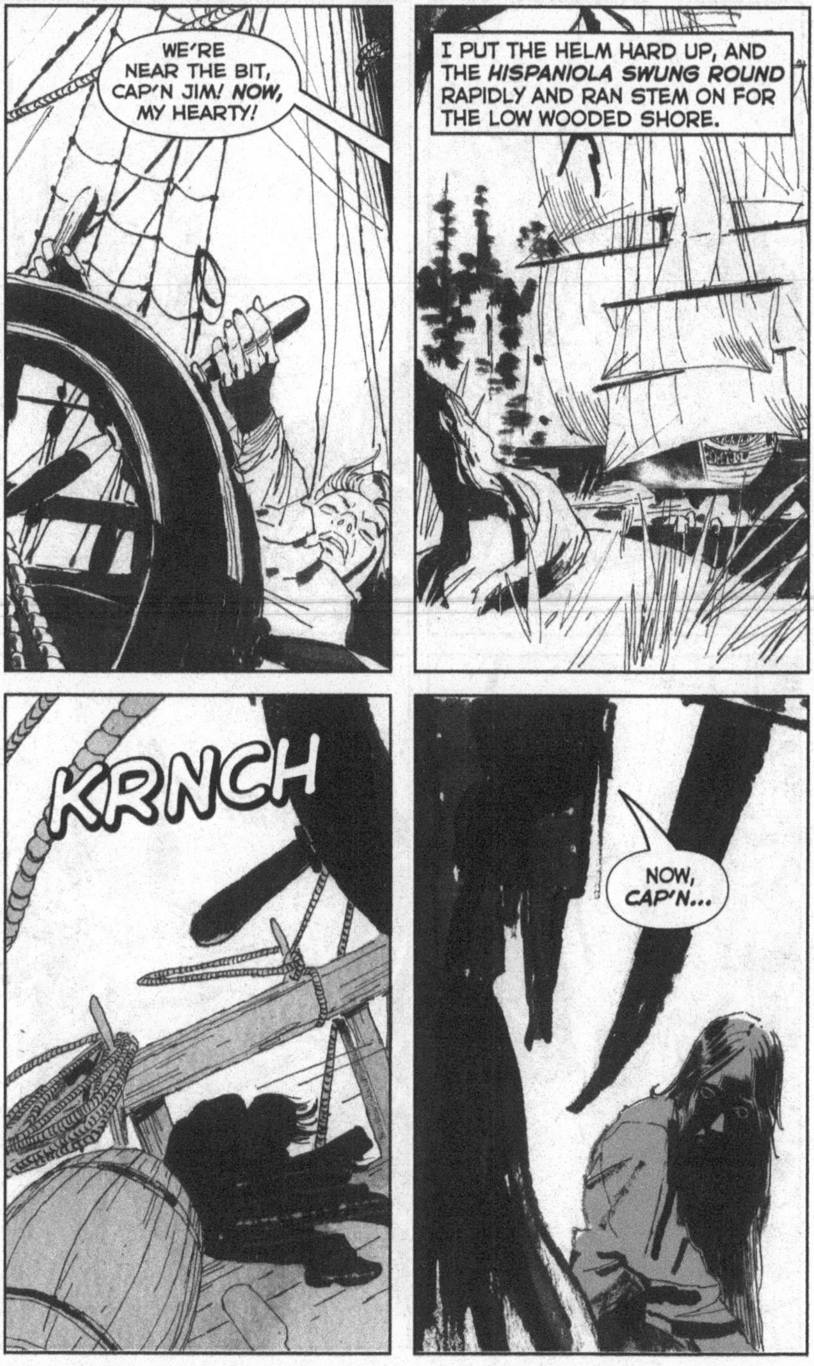
WE'RE NEAR THE BIT, CAP'N JIM! NOW, MY HEARTY!
I PUT THE HELM HARD UP, AND THE HISPANIOLA SWUNG ROUND RAPIDLY AND RAN STEM ON FOR THE LOW WOODED SHORE.
KRNCH
NOW, CAP'N...

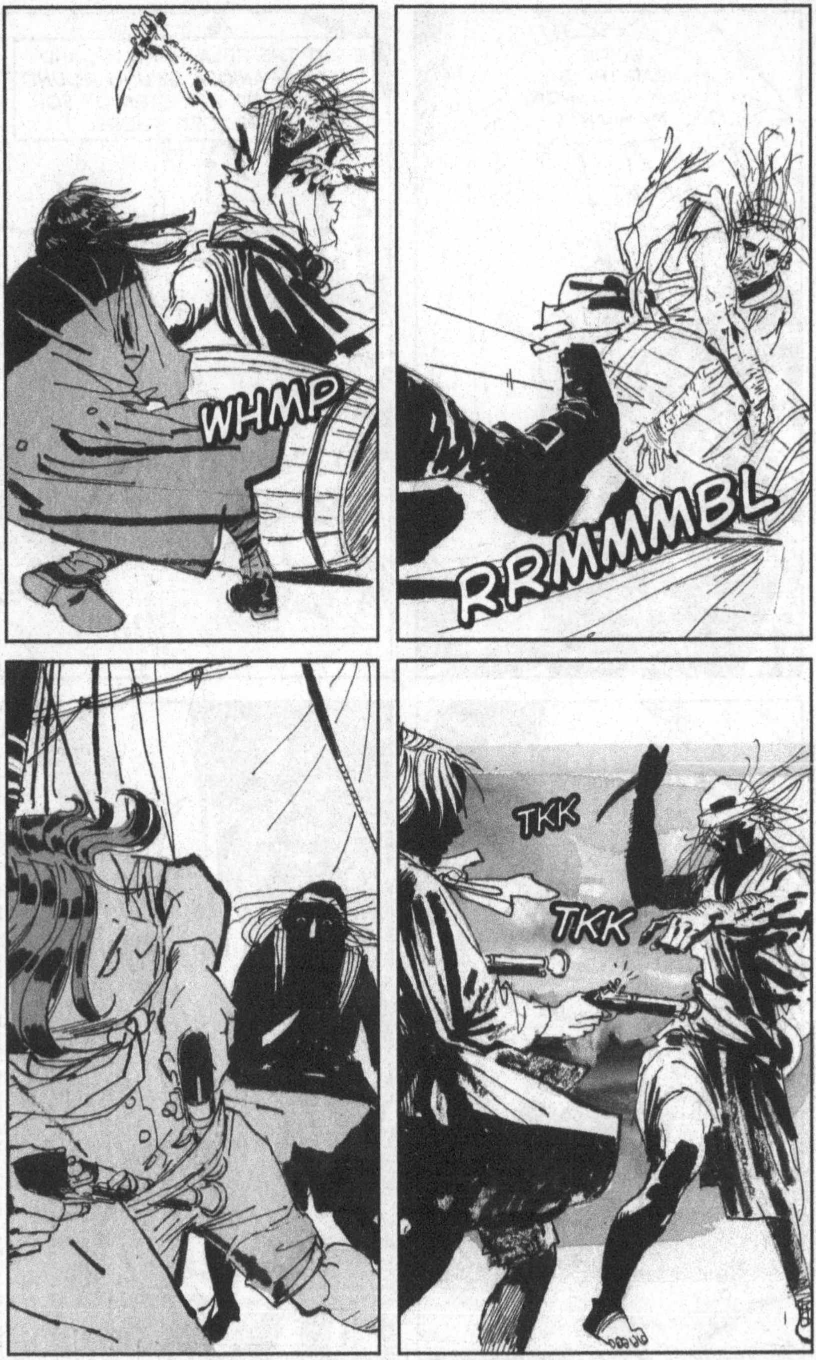
WHMP
RRMMMMBL
TKK
TKK

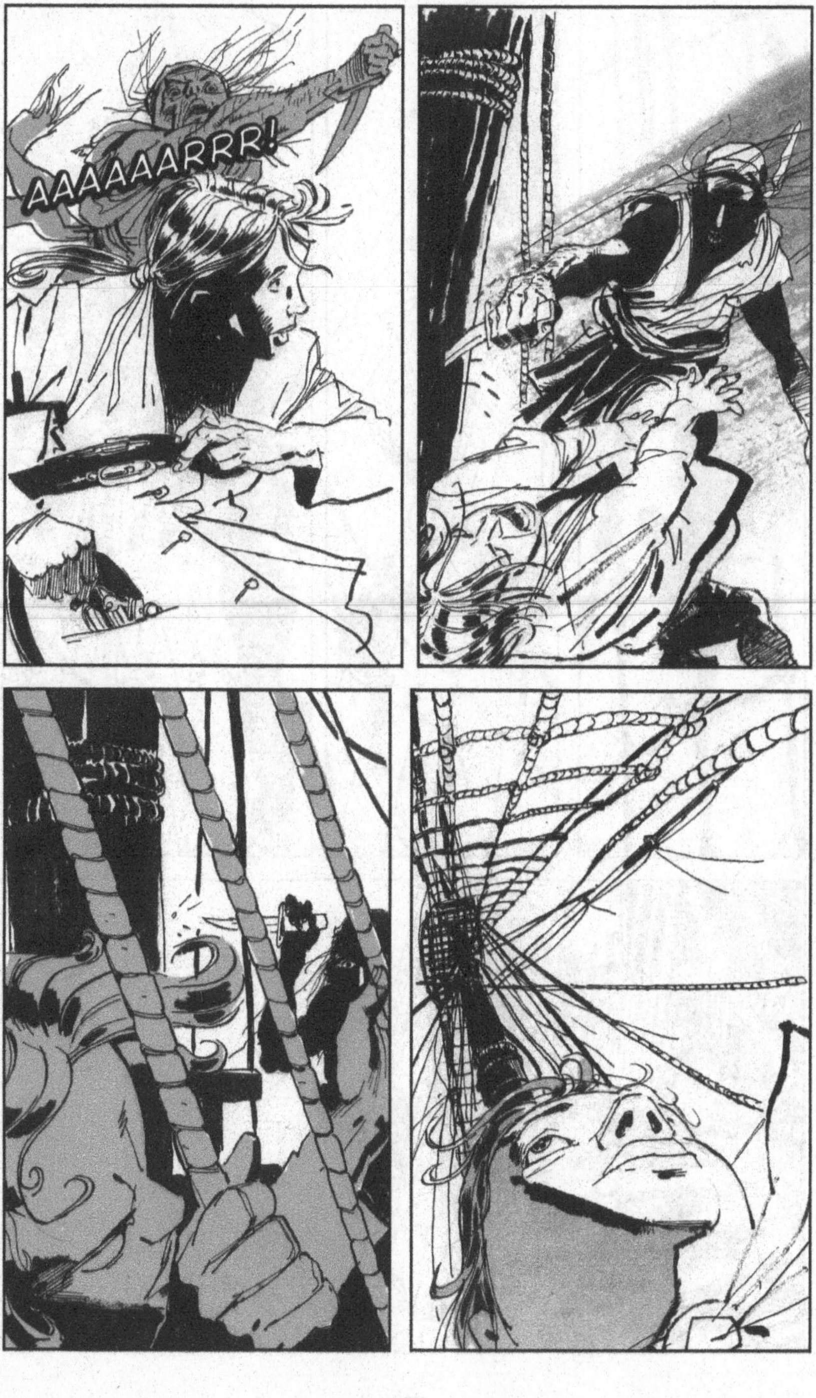
AAAAAAARRRR!

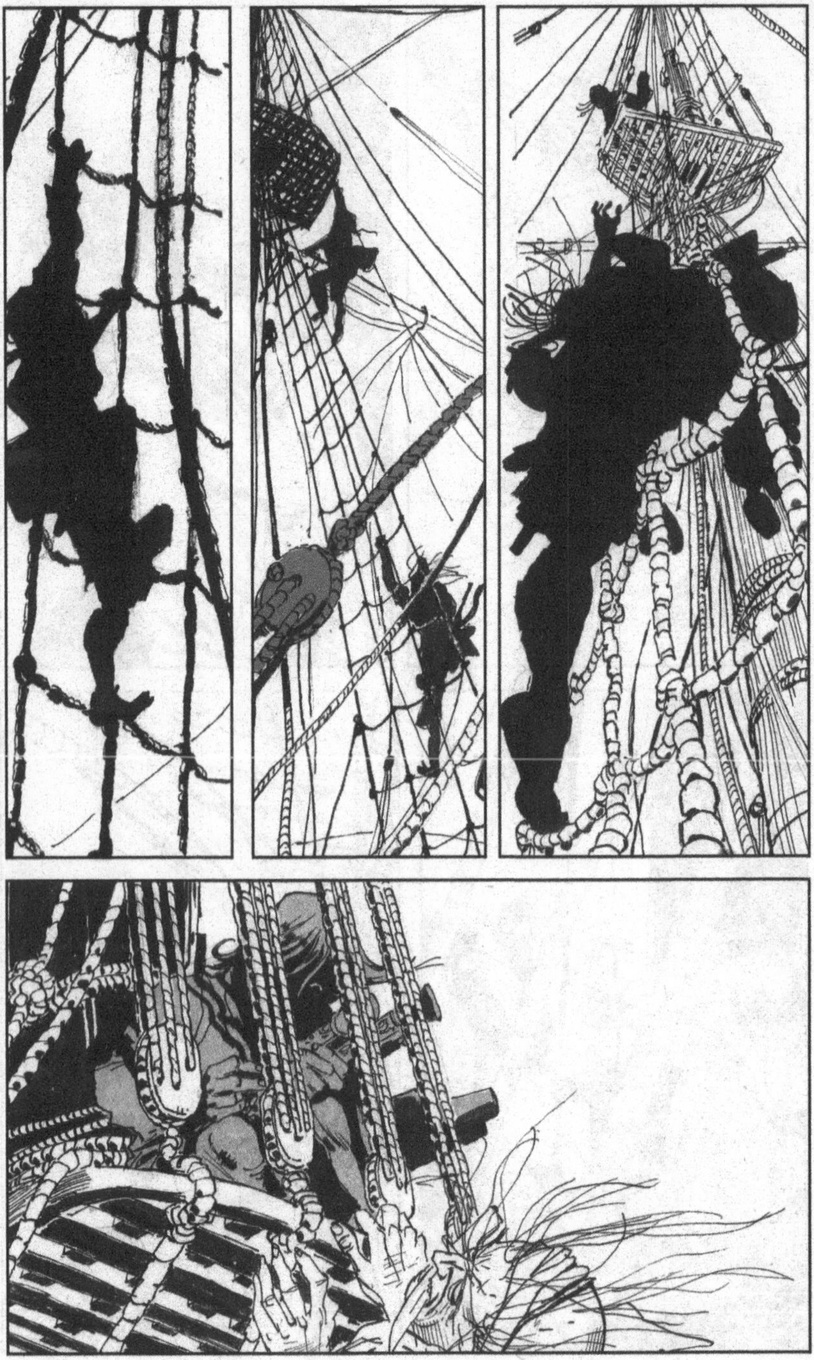

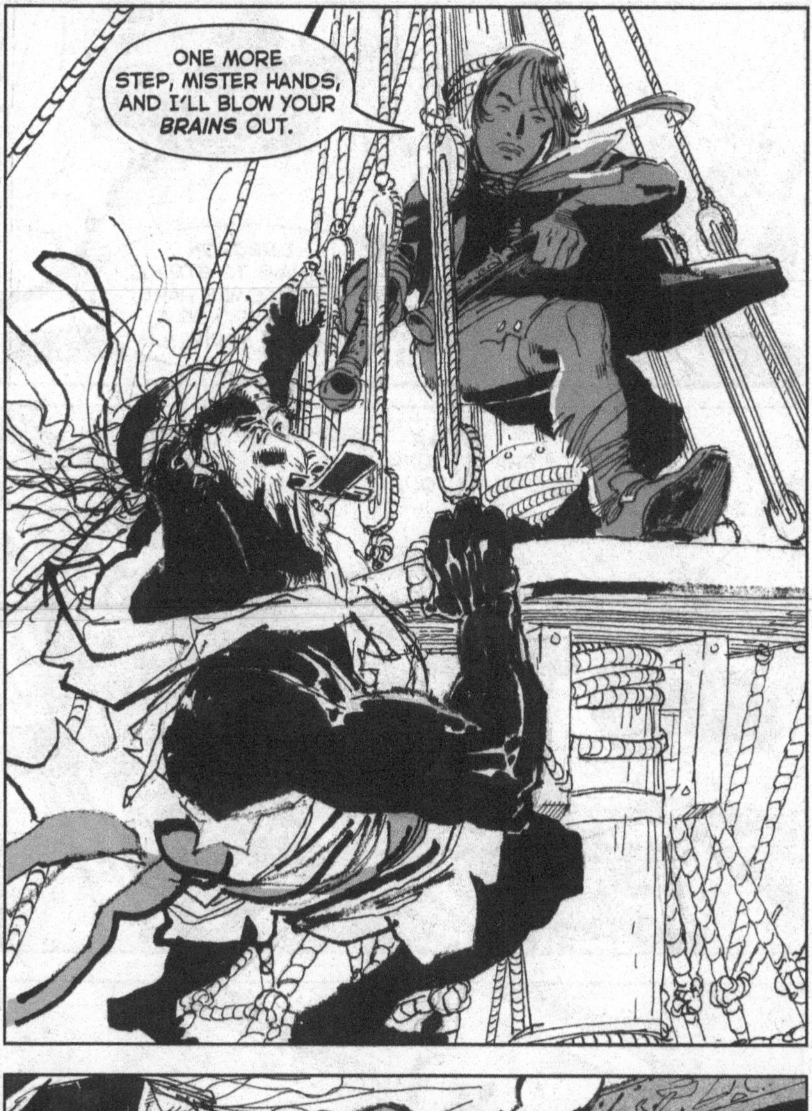
ONE MORE STEP, MISTER HANDS, AND I'LL BLOW YOUR BRAINS OUT.

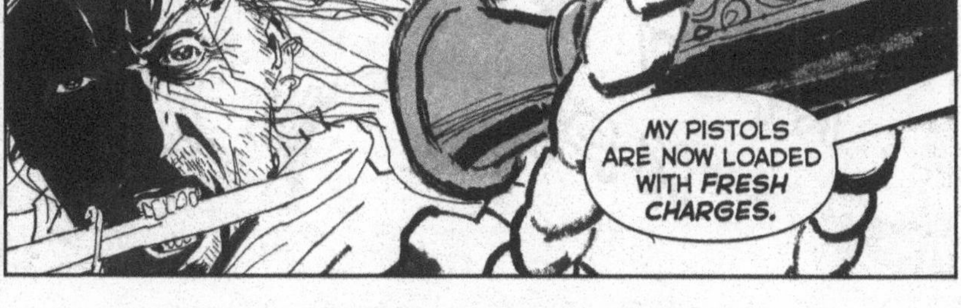
MY PISTOLS ARE NOW LOADED WITH FRESH CHARGES.

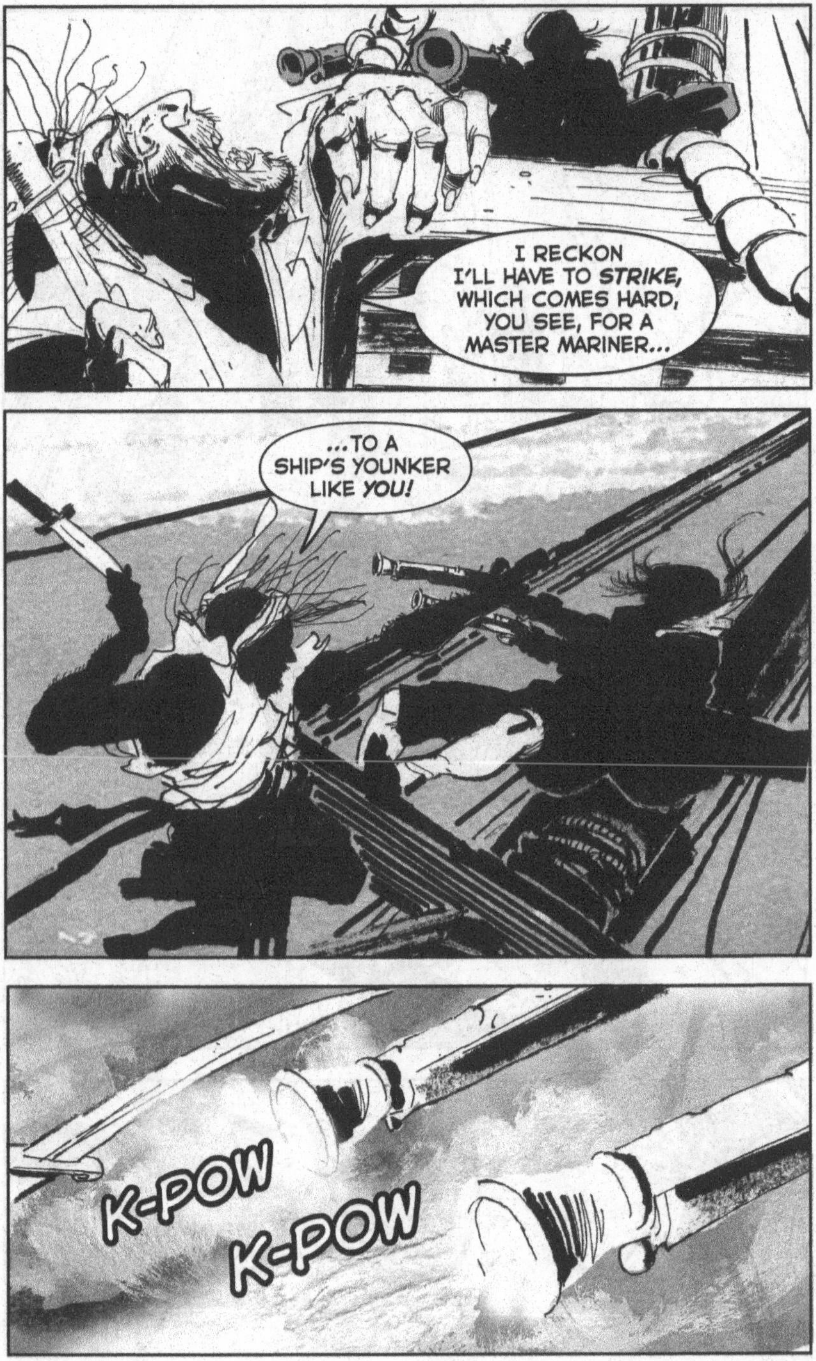
I RECKON I'LL HAVE TO *STRIKE,* WHICH COMES HARD, YOU SEE, FOR A MASTER MARINER...
...TO A SHIP'S YOUNKER LIKE *YOU!*
K-POW
K-POW

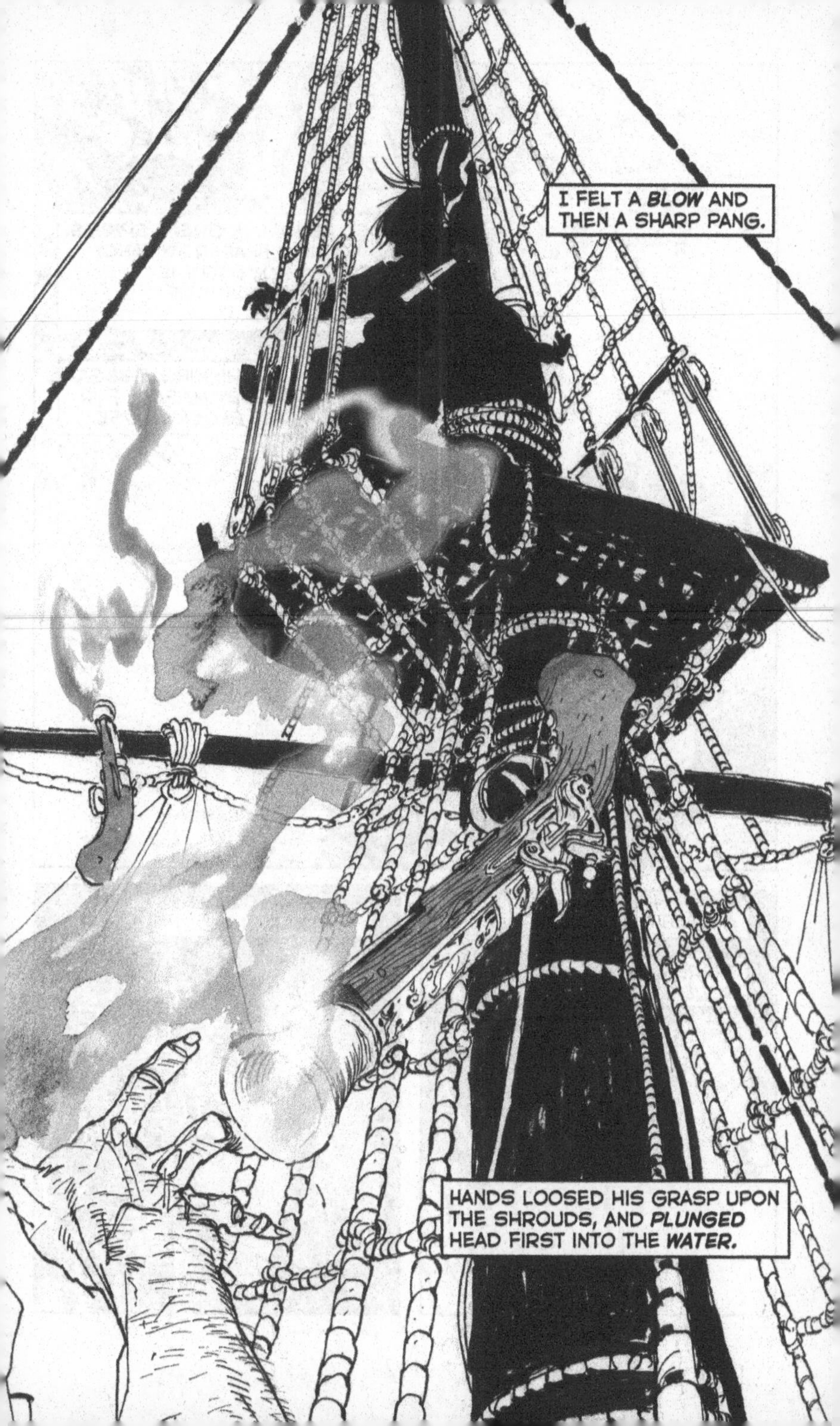
I FELT A *BLOW* AND THEN A SHARP PANG.
HANDS LOOSED HIS GRASP UPON THE SHROUDS, AND *PLUNGED* HEAD FIRST INTO THE *WATER.*

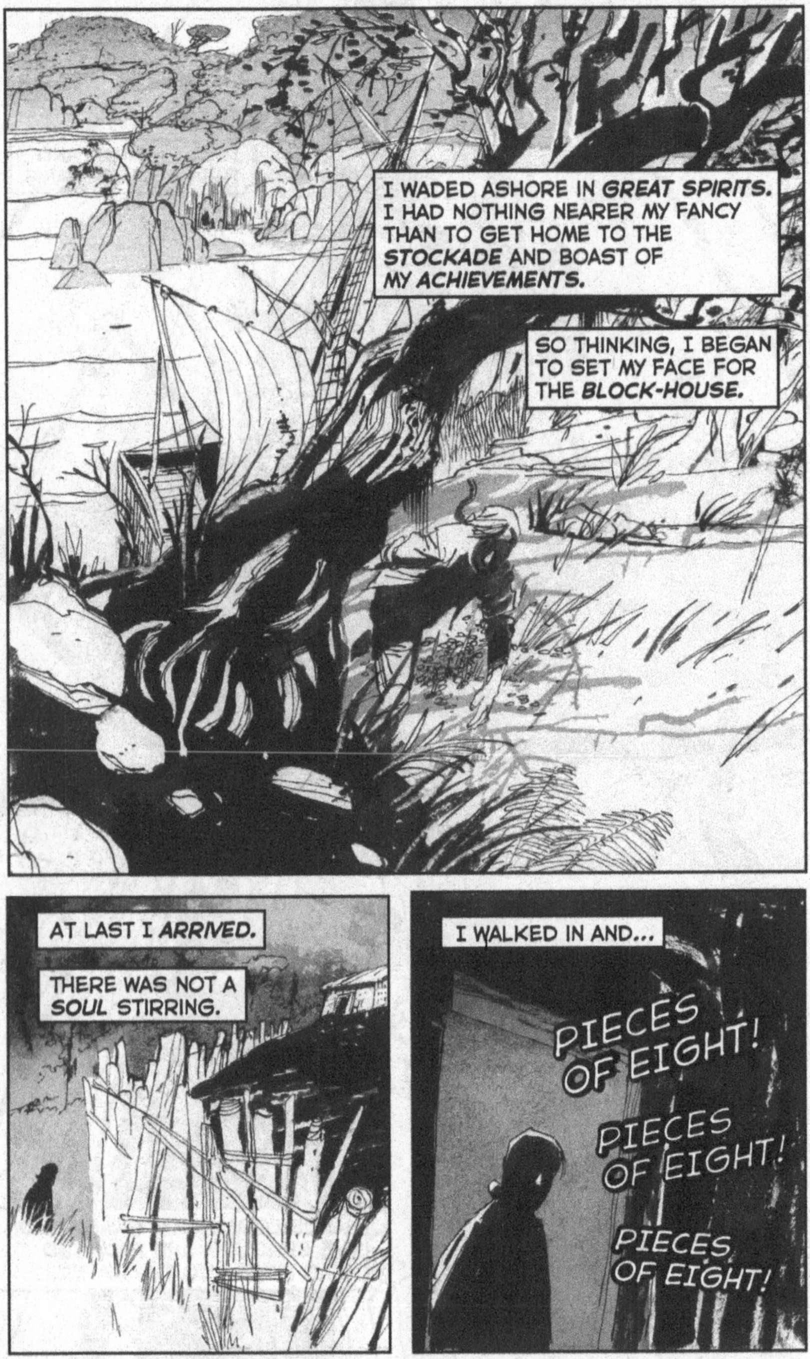
I WADED ASHORE IN GREAT SPIRITS. I HAD NOTHING NEARER MY FANCY THAN TO GET HOME TO THE STOCKADE AND BOAST OF MY ACHIEVEMENTS.
SO THINKING, I BEGAN TO SET MY FACE FOR THE BLOCK-HOUSE.
AT LAST I ARRIVED.
THERE WAS NOT A SOUL STIRRING.
I WALKED IN AND...
PIECES OF EIGHT!
PIECES OF EIGHT!
PIECES OF EIGHT!

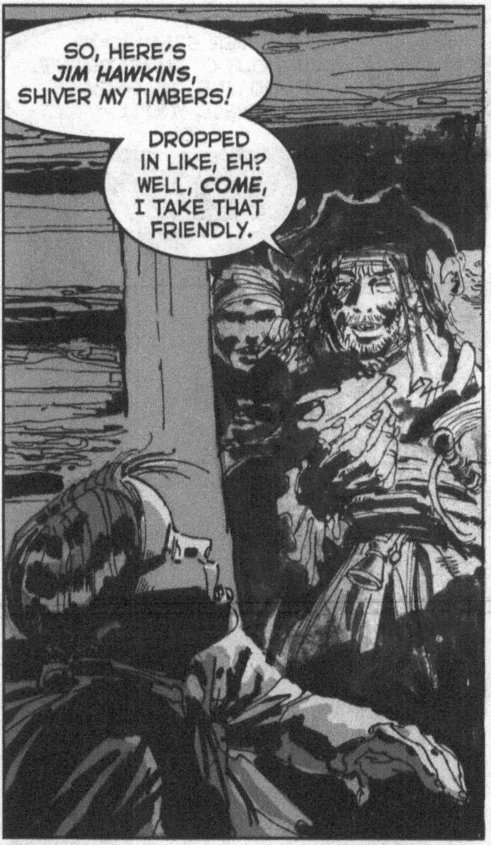
SO, HERE'S *JIM HAWKINS*, SHIVER MY TIMBERS!
DROPPED IN LIKE, EH? WELL, *COME*, I TAKE THAT FRIENDLY.

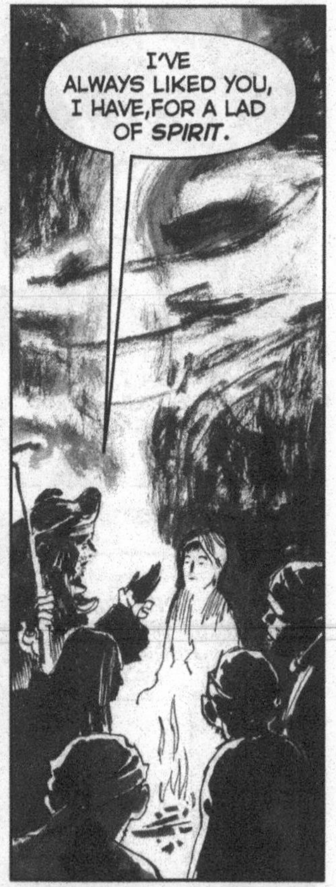
I'VE ALWAYS LIKED YOU, I HAVE, FOR A LAD OF *SPIRIT*.

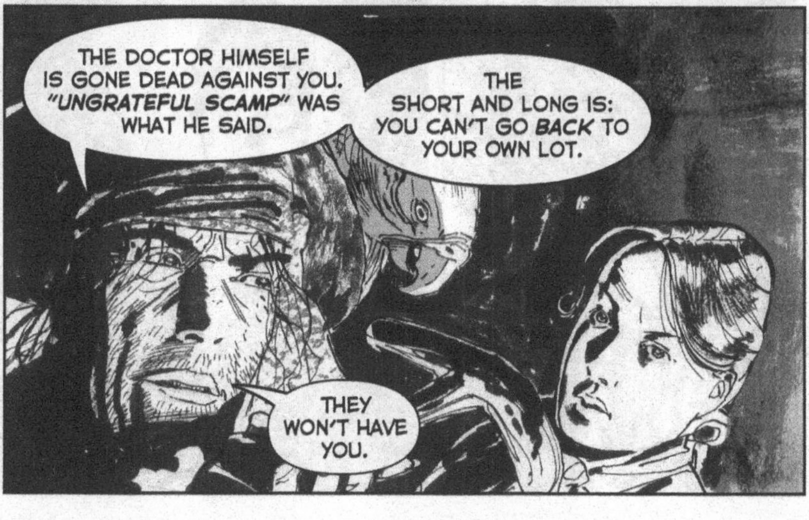
THE DOCTOR HIMSELF IS GONE DEAD AGAINST YOU. *"UNGRATEFUL SCAMP"* WAS WHAT HE SAID.
THE SHORT AND LONG IS: YOU CAN'T GO *BACK* TO YOUR OWN LOT.
THEY WON'T HAVE YOU.

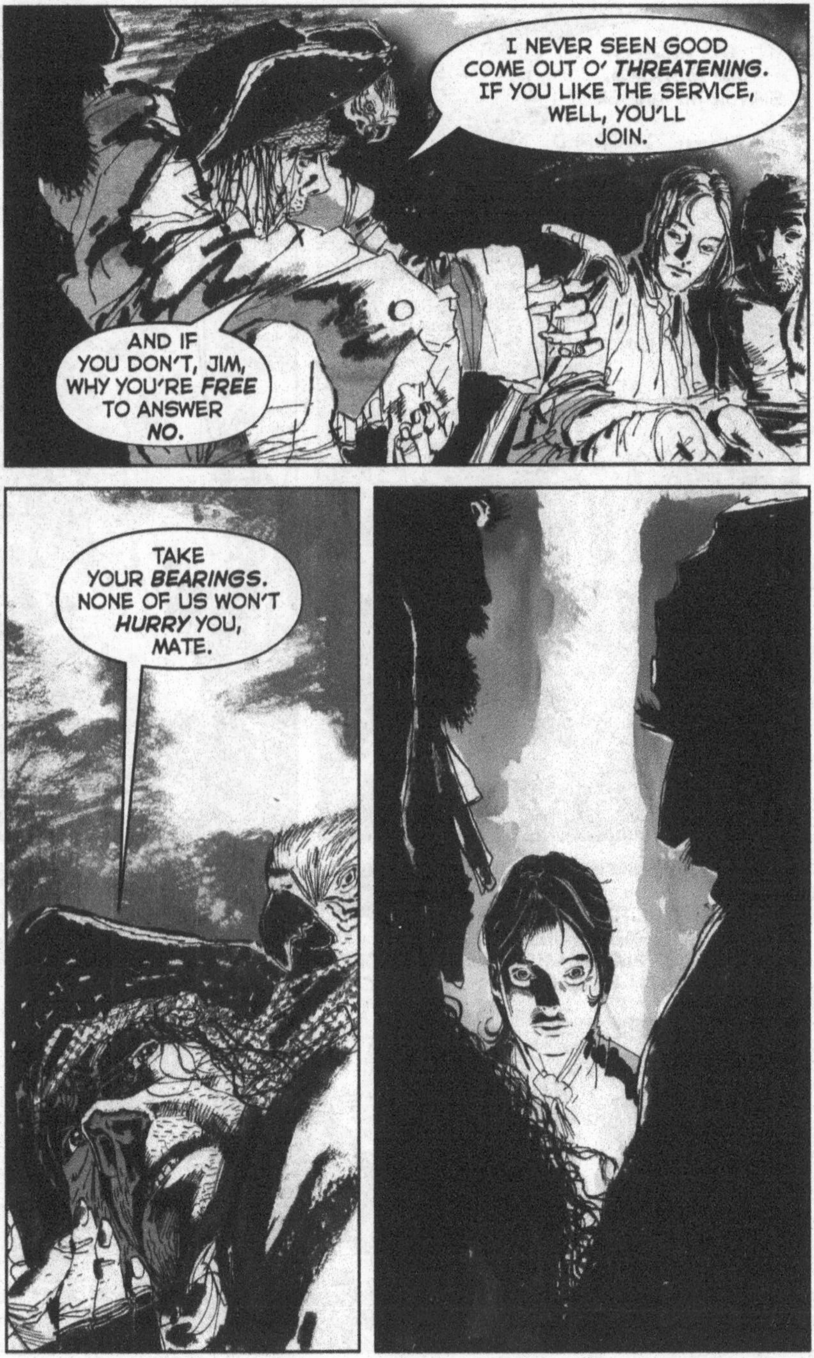
I NEVER SEEN GOOD COME OUT O' THREATENING. IF YOU LIKE THE SERVICE, WELL, YOU'LL JOIN.
AND IF YOU DON'T, JIM, WHY YOU'RE FREE TO ANSWER NO.
TAKE YOUR BEARINGS. NONE OF US WON'T HURRY YOU, MATE.

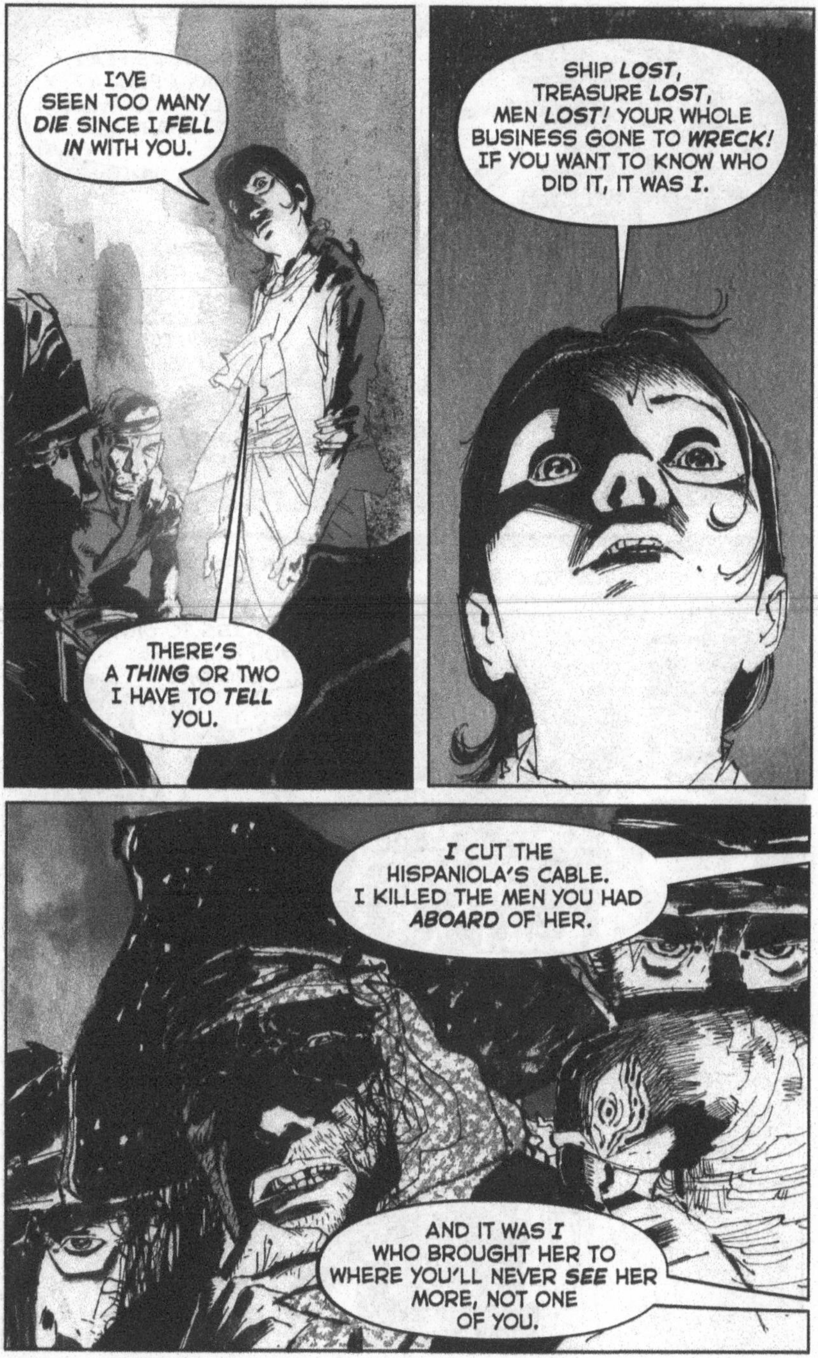
I'VE SEEN TOO MANY DIE SINCE I FELL IN WITH YOU.
THERE'S A THING OR TWO I HAVE TO TELL YOU.
SHIP LOST, TREASURE LOST, MEN LOST! YOUR WHOLE BUSINESS GONE TO WRECK! IF YOU WANT TO KNOW WHO DID IT, IT WAS I.
I CUT THE HISPANIOLA'S CABLE. I KILLED THE MEN YOU HAD ABOARD OF HER.
AND IT WAS I WHO BROUGHT HER TO WHERE YOU'LL NEVER SEE HER MORE, NOT ONE OF YOU.

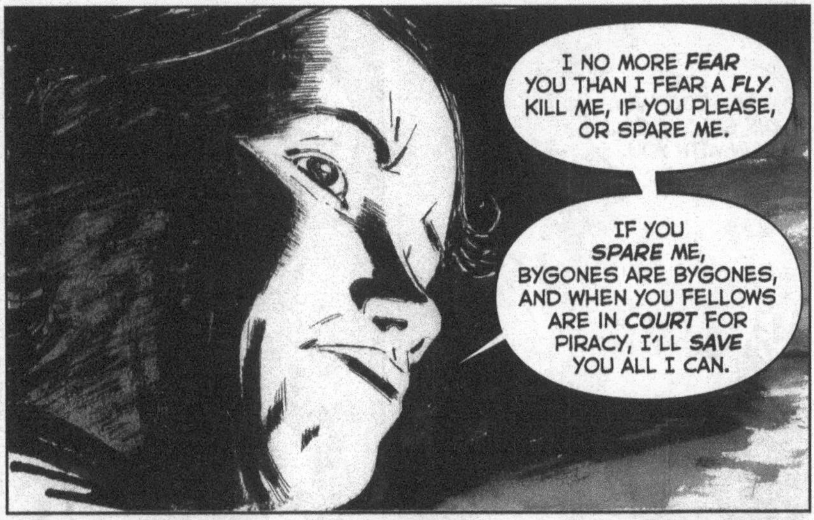
I NO MORE *FEAR* YOU THAN I FEAR A *FLY*. KILL ME, IF YOU PLEASE, OR SPARE ME.
IF YOU *SPARE* ME, BYGONES ARE BYGONES, AND WHEN YOU FELLOWS ARE IN *COURT* FOR PIRACY, I'LL *SAVE* YOU ALL I CAN.

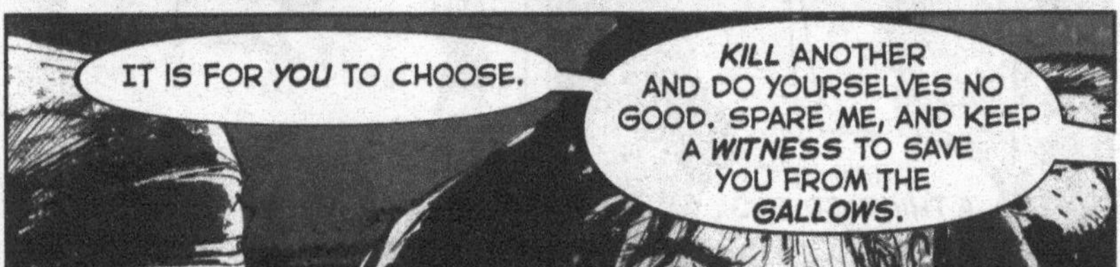
IT IS FOR *YOU* TO CHOOSE.
KILL ANOTHER AND DO YOURSELVES NO GOOD. SPARE ME, AND KEEP A *WITNESS* TO SAVE YOU FROM THE *GALLOWS*.

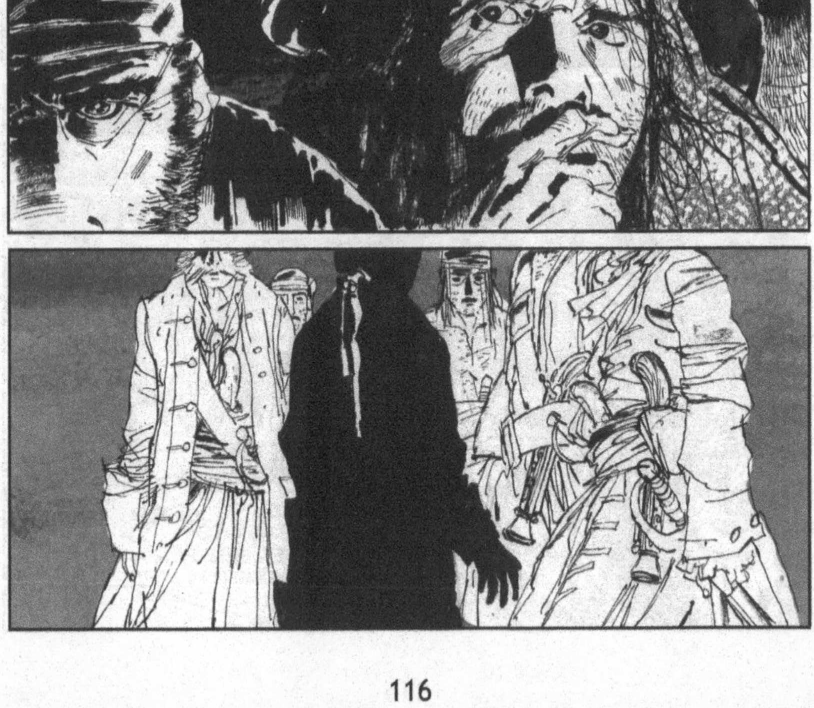

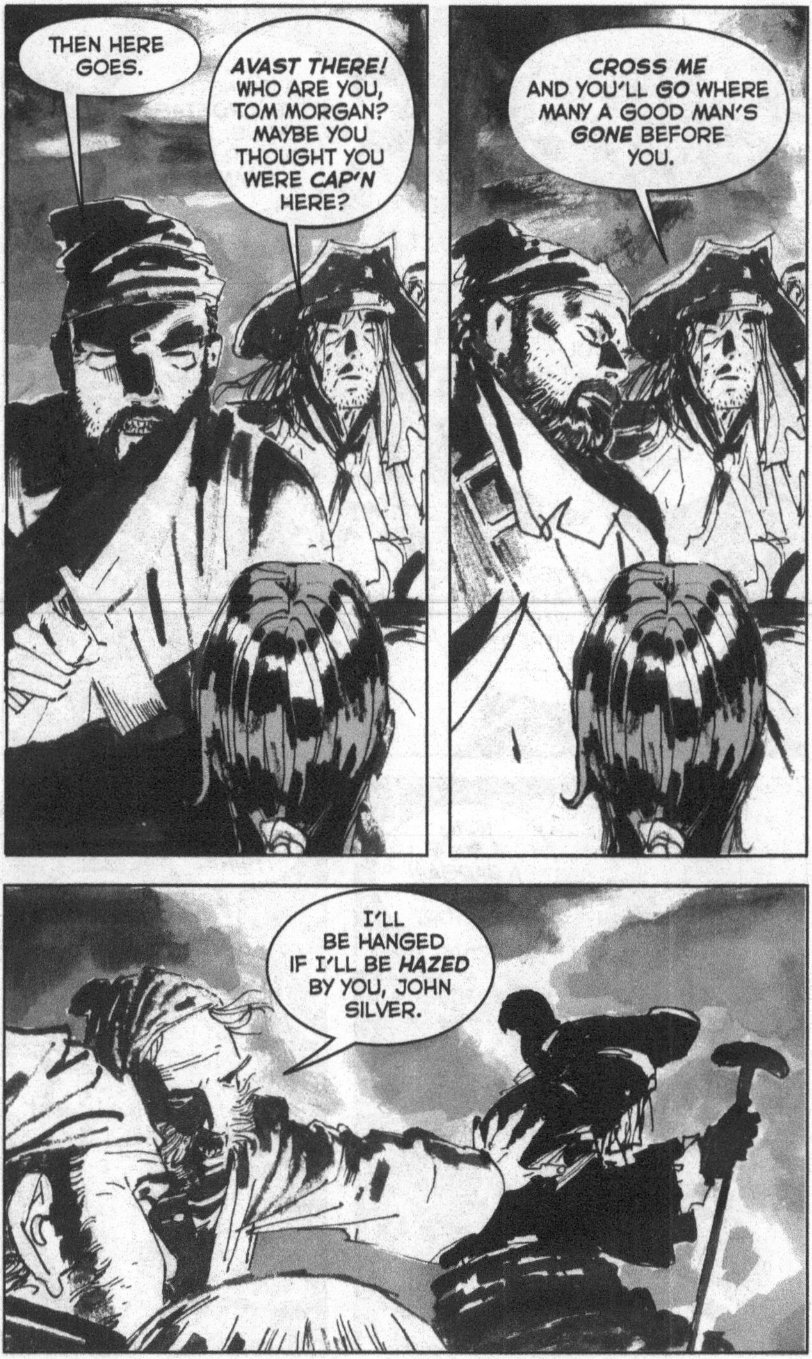
THEN HERE GOES.
AVAST THERE! WHO ARE YOU, TOM MORGAN? MAYBE YOU THOUGHT YOU WERE CAP'N HERE?
CROSS ME AND YOU'LL GO WHERE MANY A GOOD MAN'S GONE BEFORE YOU.
I'LL BE HANGED IF I'LL BE HAZED BY YOU, JOHN SILVER.

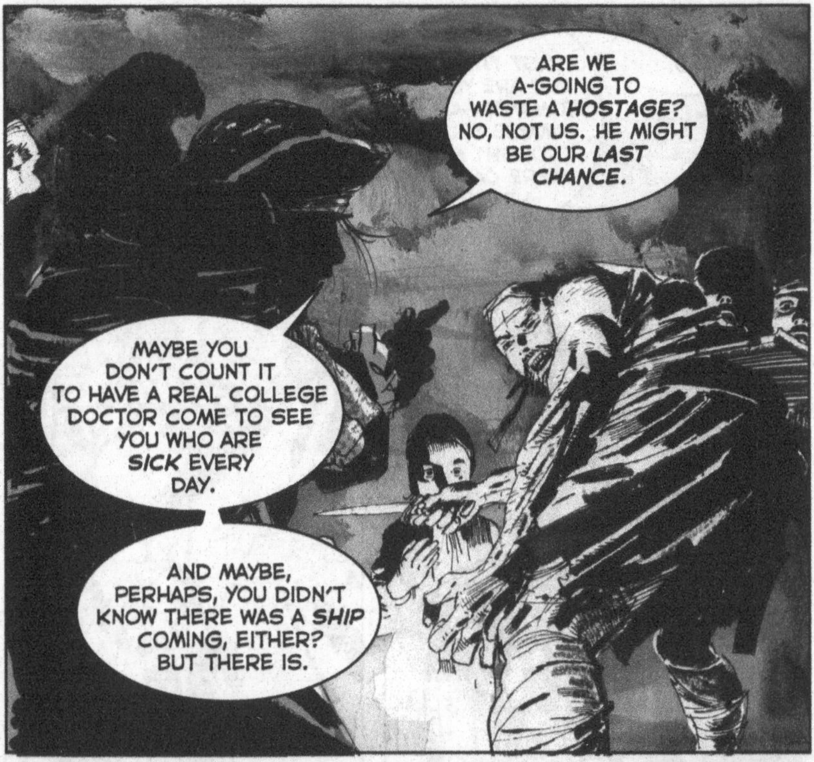
ARE WE A-GOING TO WASTE A HOSTAGE? NO, NOT US. HE MIGHT BE OUR LAST CHANCE.
MAYBE YOU DON'T COUNT IT TO HAVE A REAL COLLEGE DOCTOR COME TO SEE YOU WHO ARE SICK EVERY DAY.
AND MAYBE, PERHAPS, YOU DIDN'T KNOW THERE WAS A SHIP COMING, EITHER? BUT THERE IS.

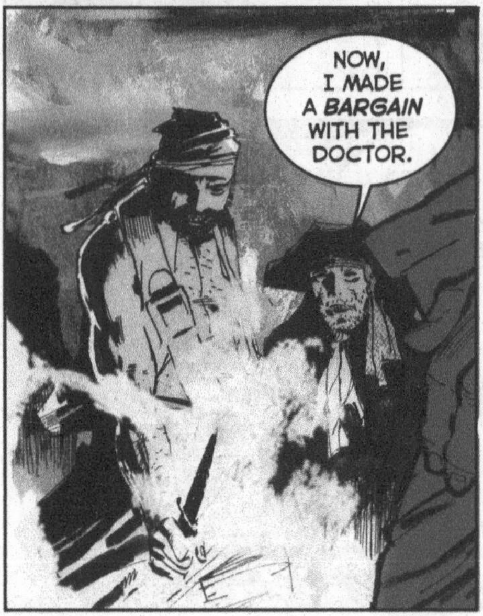
NOW, I MADE A BARGAIN WITH THE DOCTOR.

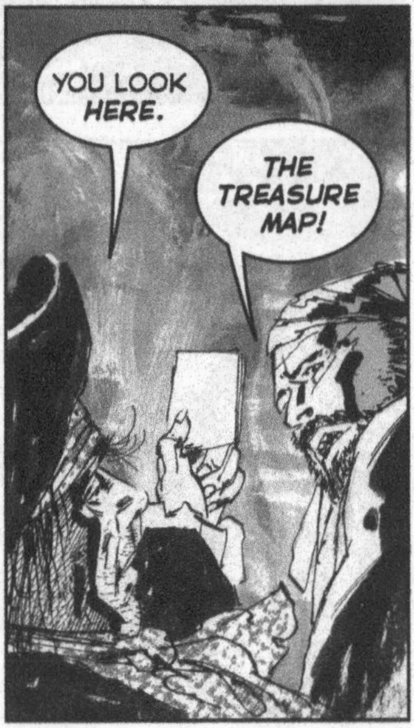
YOU LOOK HERE.
THE TREASURE MAP!

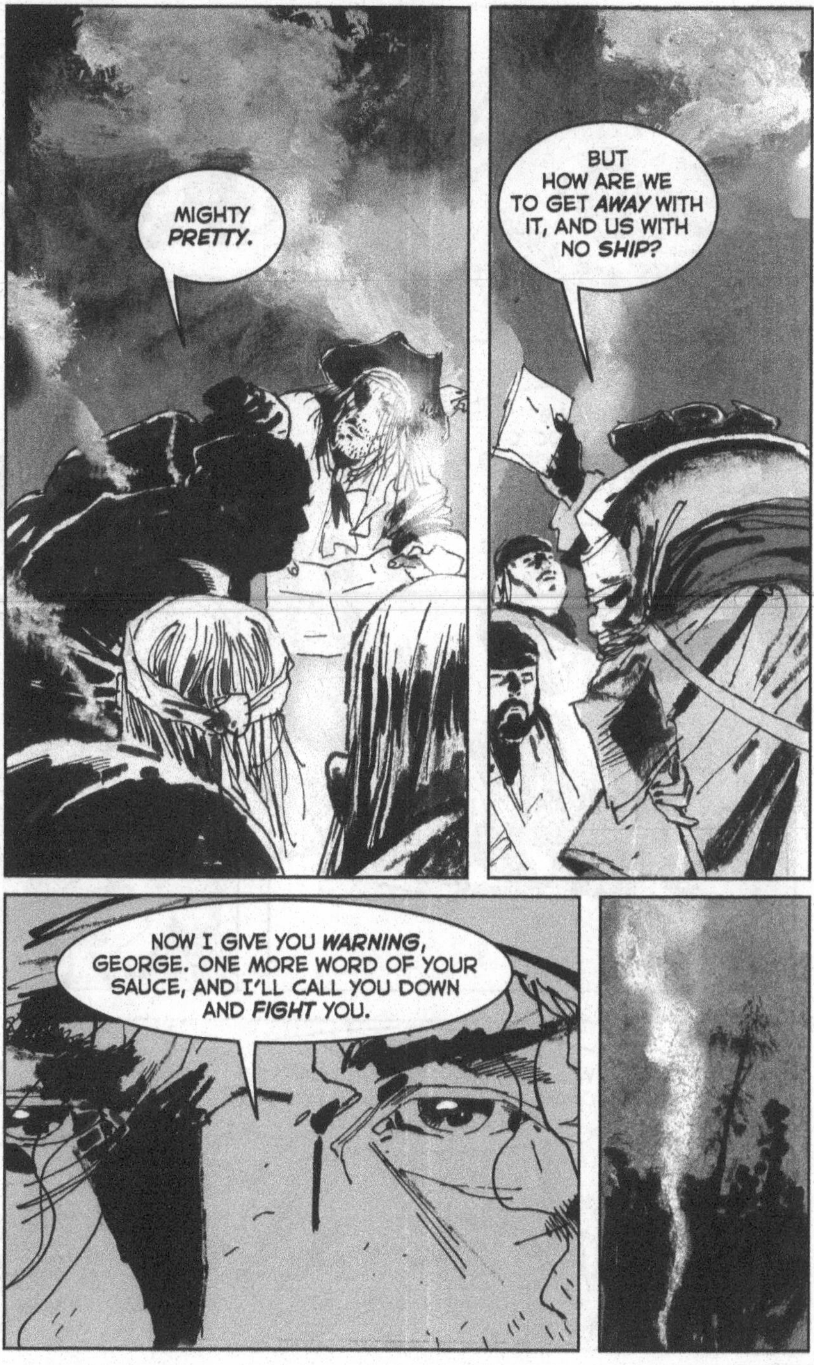
MIGHTY PRETTY.
BUT HOW ARE WE TO GET AWAY WITH IT, AND US WITH NO SHIP?
NOW I GIVE YOU WARNING, GEORGE. ONE MORE WORD OF YOUR SAUCE, AND I'LL CALL YOU DOWN AND FIGHT YOU.

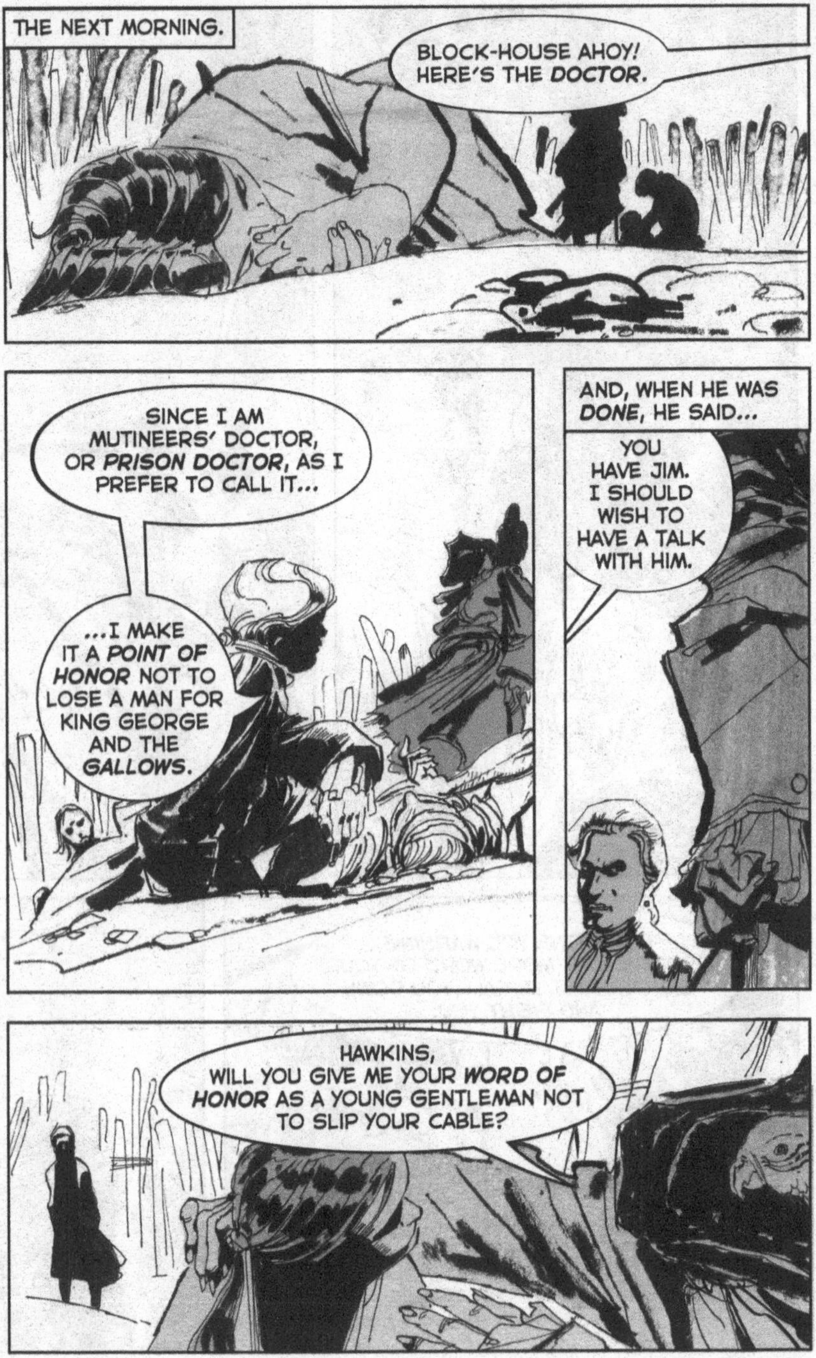

THE NEXT MORNING.
BLOCK-HOUSE AHOY! HERE'S THE *DOCTOR*.
SINCE I AM MUTINEERS' DOCTOR, OR *PRISON DOCTOR*, AS I PREFER TO CALL IT...
...I MAKE IT A *POINT OF HONOR* NOT TO LOSE A MAN FOR KING GEORGE AND THE *GALLOWS*.
AND, WHEN HE WAS *DONE*, HE SAID...
YOU HAVE JIM. I SHOULD WISH TO HAVE A TALK WITH HIM.
HAWKINS, WILL YOU GIVE ME YOUR *WORD OF HONOR* AS A YOUNG GENTLEMAN NOT TO SLIP YOUR CABLE?

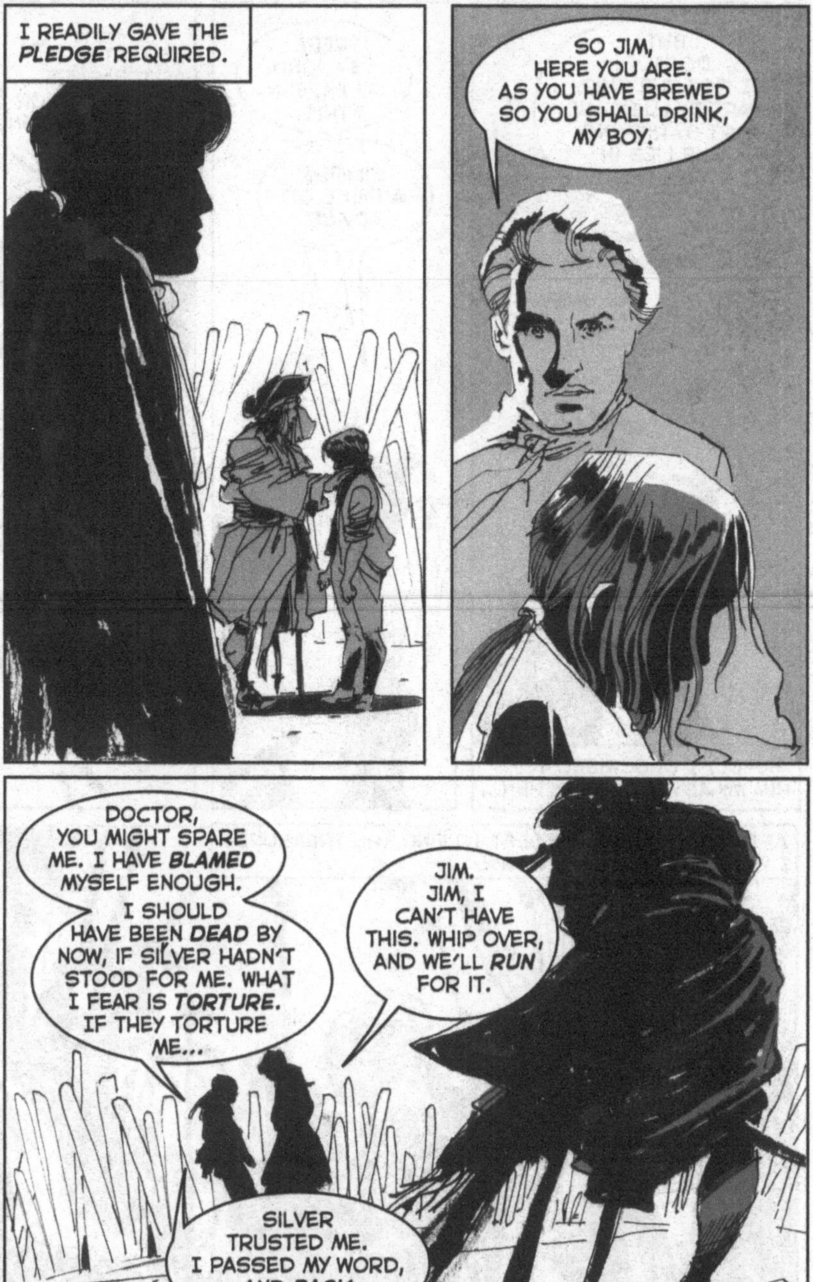
I READILY GAVE THE PLEDGE REQUIRED.
SO JIM, HERE YOU ARE. AS YOU HAVE BREWED SO YOU SHALL DRINK, MY BOY.
DOCTOR, YOU MIGHT SPARE ME. I HAVE BLAMED MYSELF ENOUGH.
I SHOULD HAVE BEEN DEAD BY NOW, IF SILVER HADN'T STOOD FOR ME. WHAT I FEAR IS TORTURE. IF THEY TORTURE ME...
JIM. JIM, I CAN'T HAVE THIS. WHIP OVER, AND WE'LL RUN FOR IT.
SILVER TRUSTED ME. I PASSED MY WORD, AND BACK I GO.

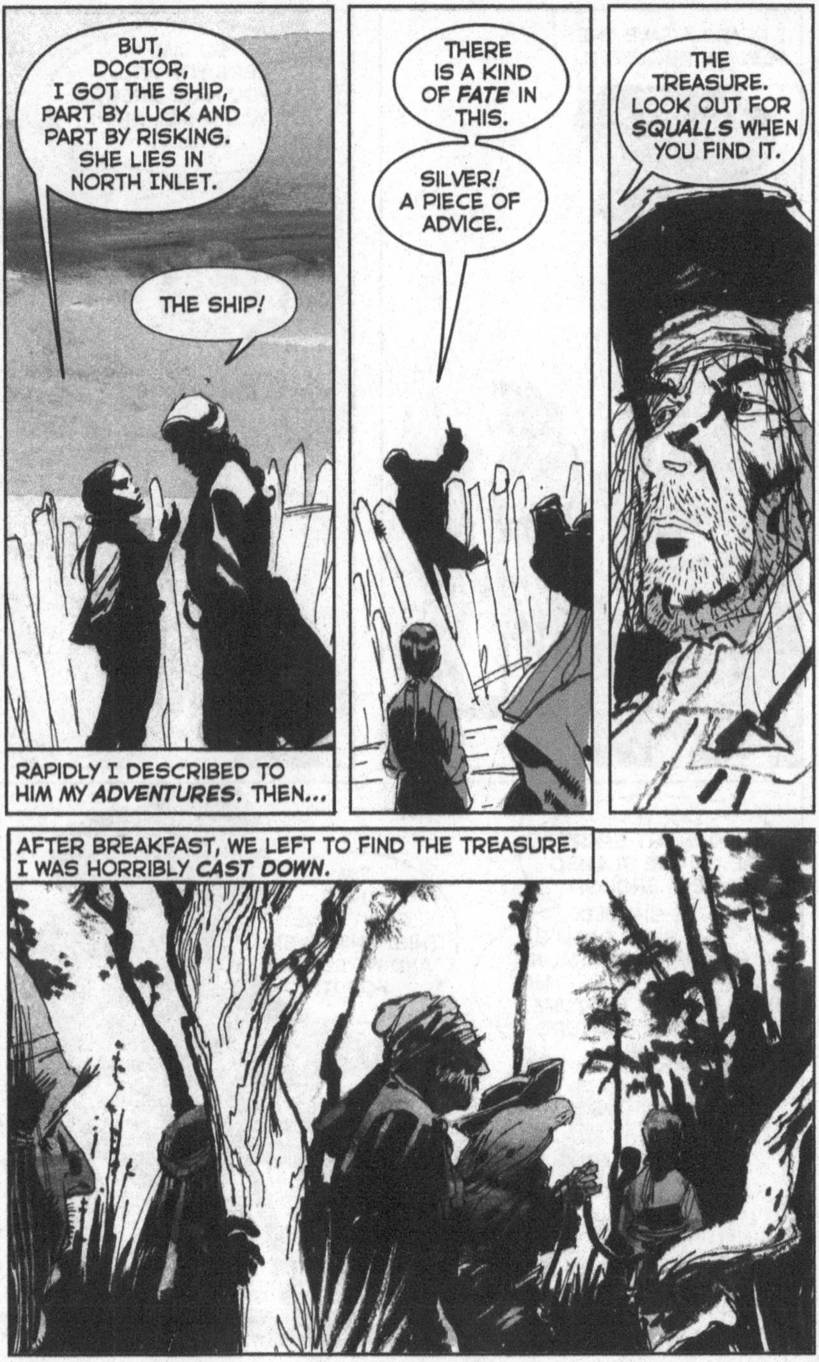

RAPIDLY I DESCRIBED TO HIM MY *ADVENTURES*. THEN...
BUT, DOCTOR, I GOT THE SHIP, PART BY LUCK AND PART BY RISKING. SHE LIES IN NORTH INLET.
THE SHIP!
THERE IS A KIND OF *FATE* IN THIS.
SILVER! A PIECE OF ADVICE.
THE TREASURE. LOOK OUT FOR *SQUALLS* WHEN YOU FIND IT.
AFTER BREAKFAST, WE LEFT TO FIND THE TREASURE. I WAS HORRIBLY *CAST DOWN*.

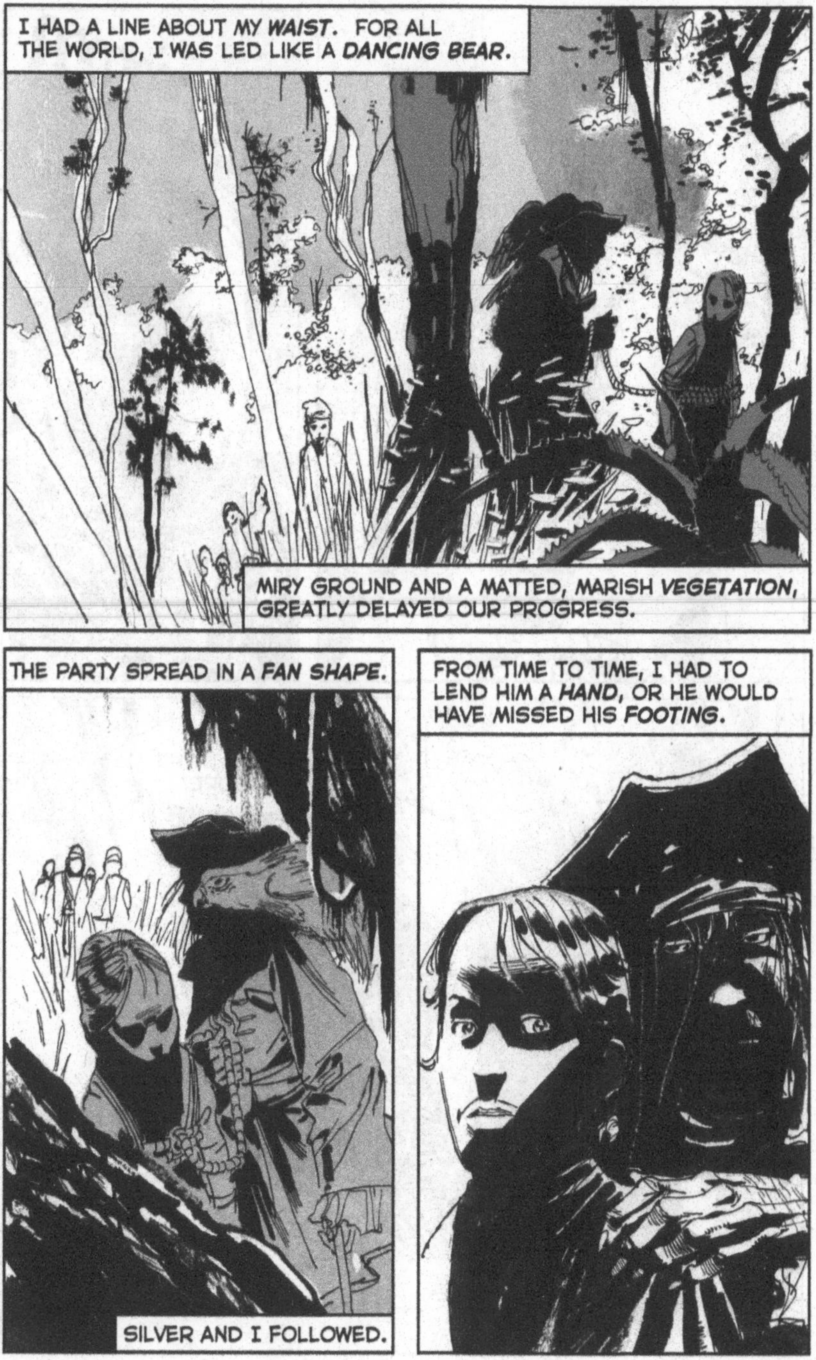
I HAD A LINE ABOUT MY *WAIST*. FOR ALL THE WORLD, I WAS LED LIKE A *DANCING BEAR*.
MIRY GROUND AND A MATTED, MARISH *VEGETATION*, GREATLY DELAYED OUR PROGRESS.
THE PARTY SPREAD IN A *FAN SHAPE*.
SILVER AND I FOLLOWED.
FROM TIME TO TIME, I HAD TO LEND HIM A *HAND*, OR HE WOULD HAVE MISSED HIS *FOOTING*.

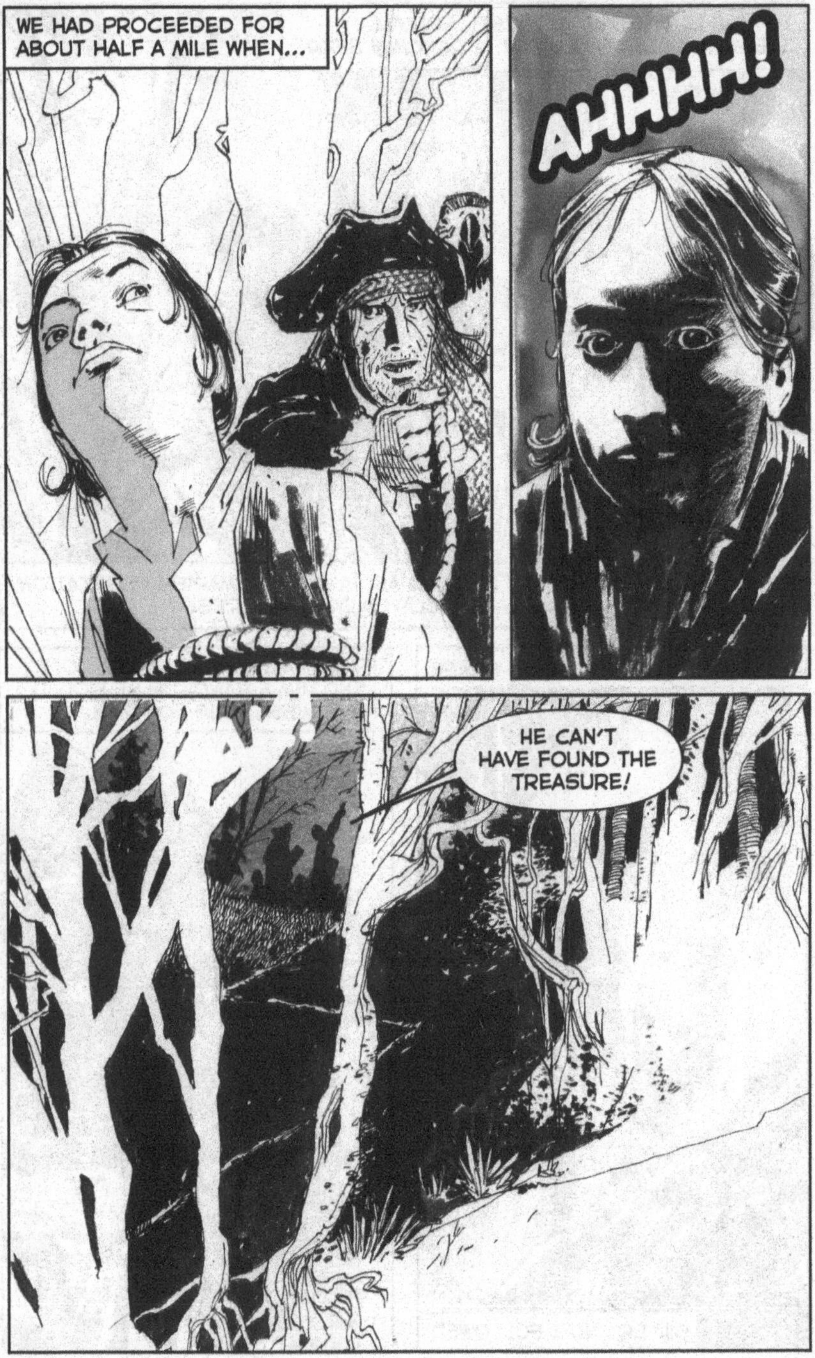
WE HAD PROCEEDED FOR ABOUT HALF A MILE WHEN...
AHHHH!
HE CAN'T HAVE FOUND THE TREASURE!

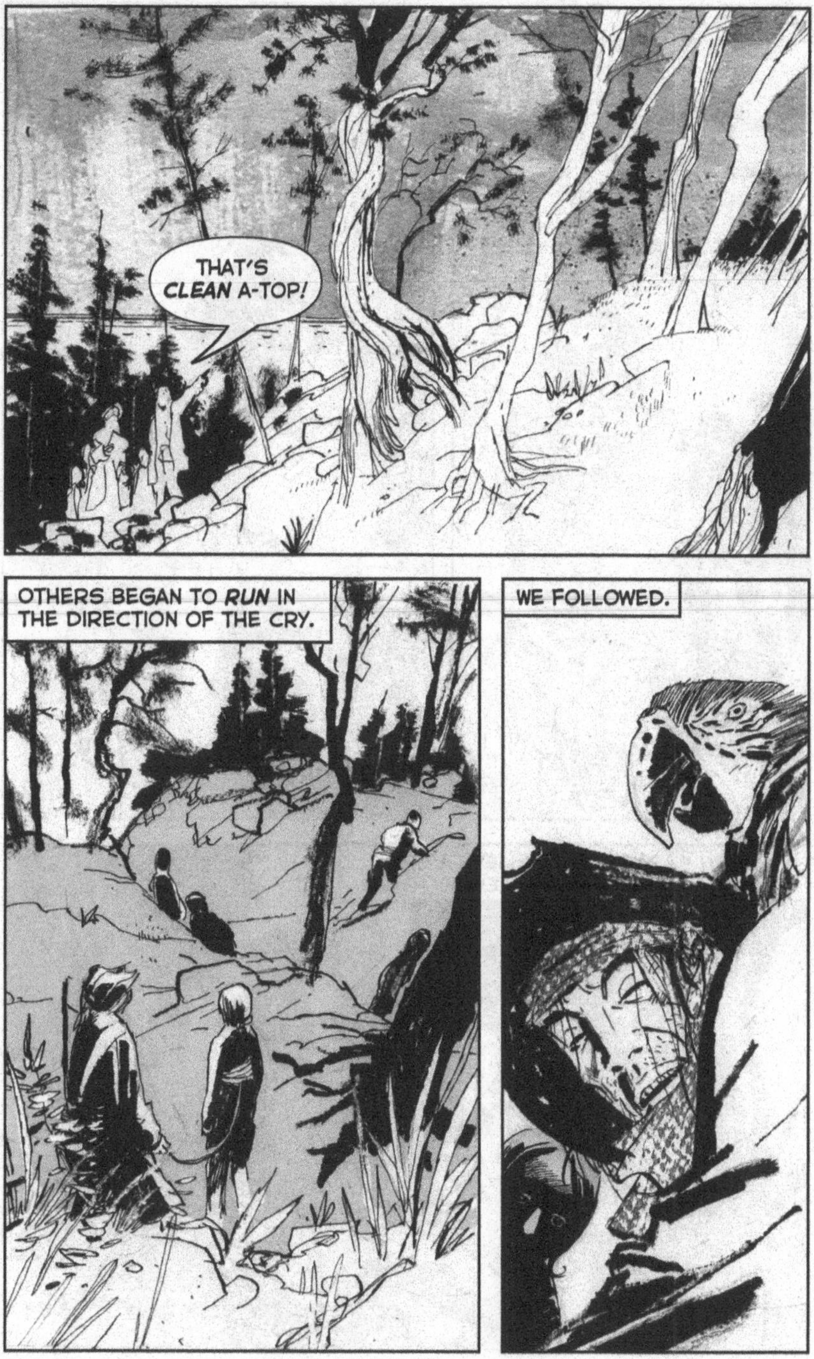
THAT'S CLEAN A-TOP!
OTHERS BEGAN TO RUN IN THE DIRECTION OF THE CRY.
WE FOLLOWED.

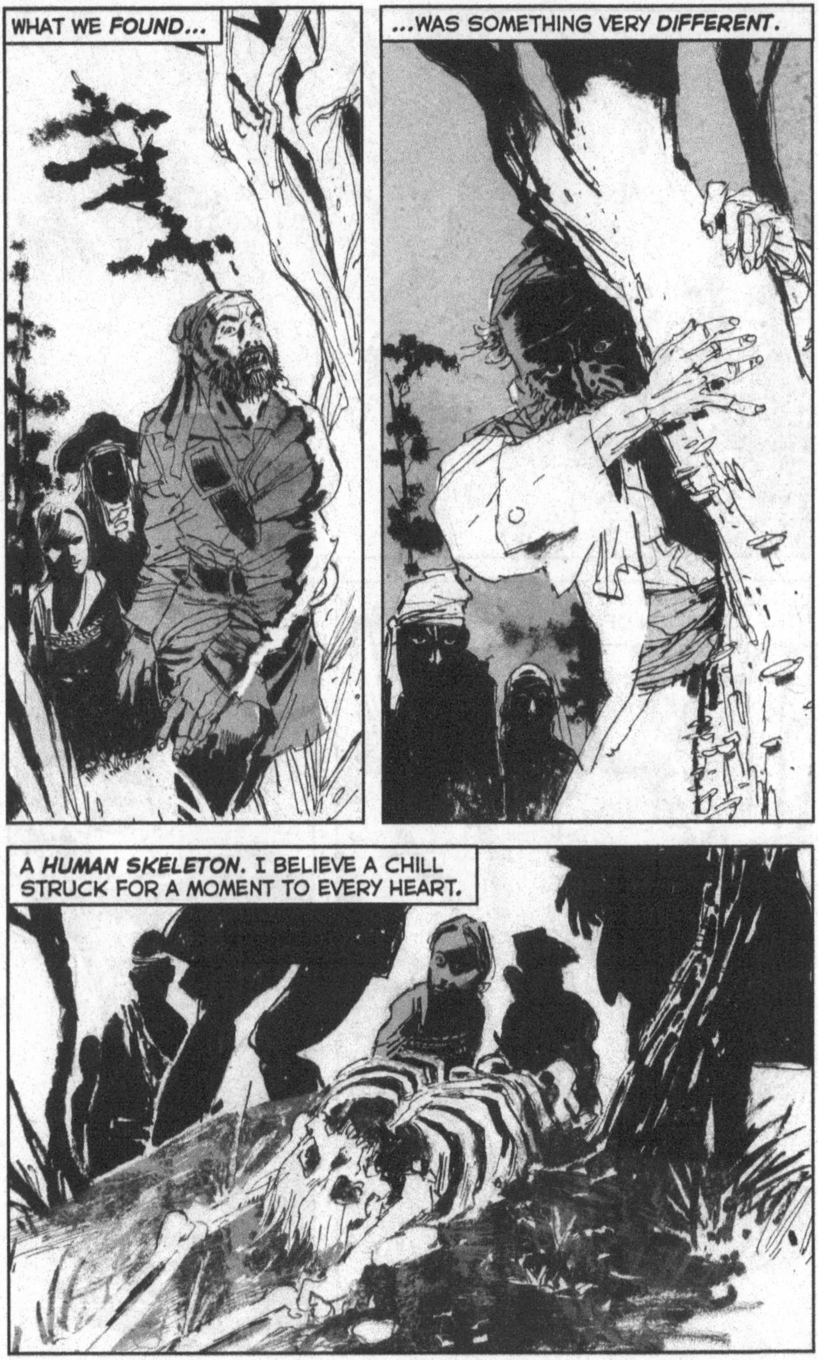
WHAT WE *FOUND*...
...WAS SOMETHING VERY *DIFFERENT*.
A *HUMAN SKELETON*. I BELIEVE A CHILL STRUCK FOR A MOMENT TO EVERY HEART.

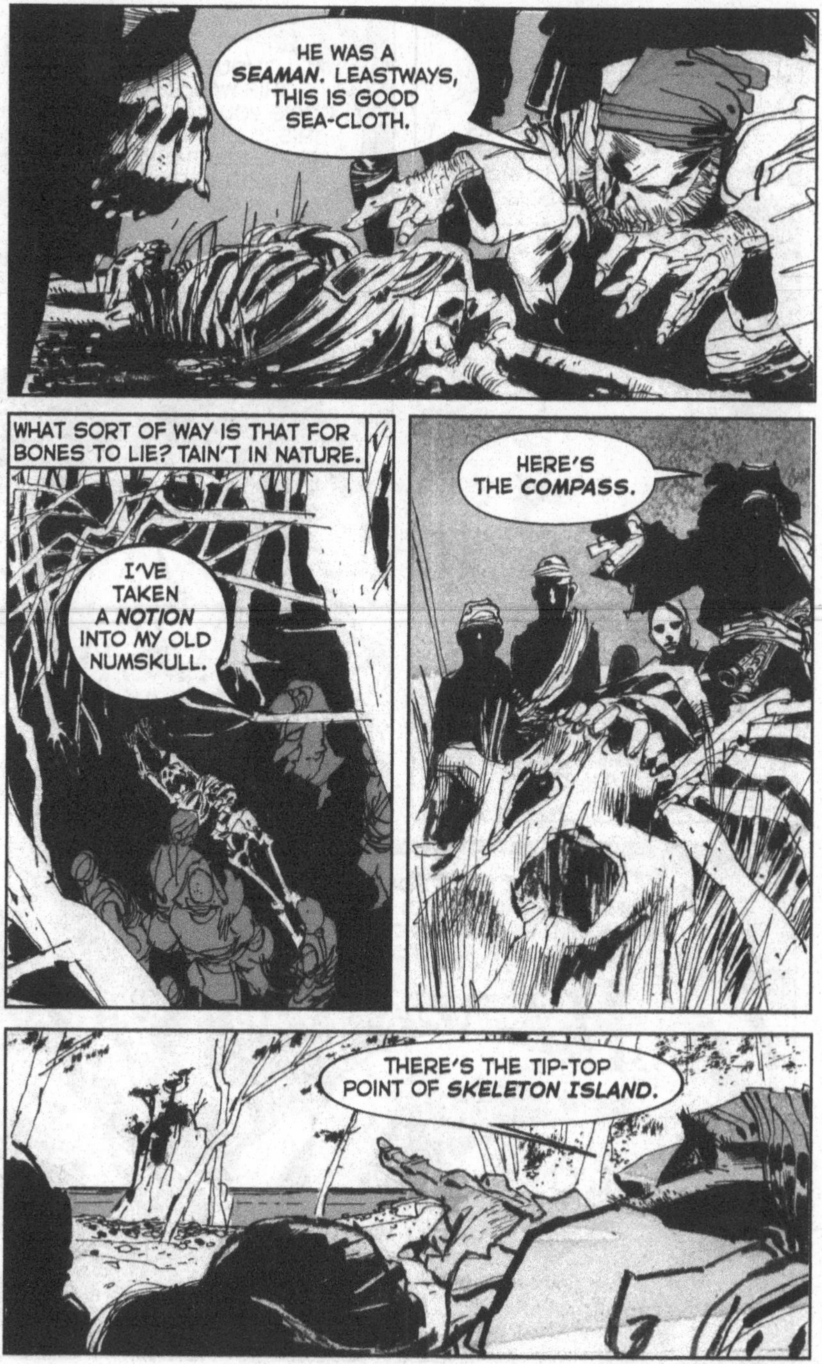
HE WAS A SEAMAN. LEASTWAYS, THIS IS GOOD SEA-CLOTH.
WHAT SORT OF WAY IS THAT FOR BONES TO LIE? TAIN'T IN NATURE.
I'VE TAKEN A NOTION INTO MY OLD NUMSKULL.
HERE'S THE COMPASS.
THERE'S THE TIP-TOP POINT OF SKELETON ISLAND.

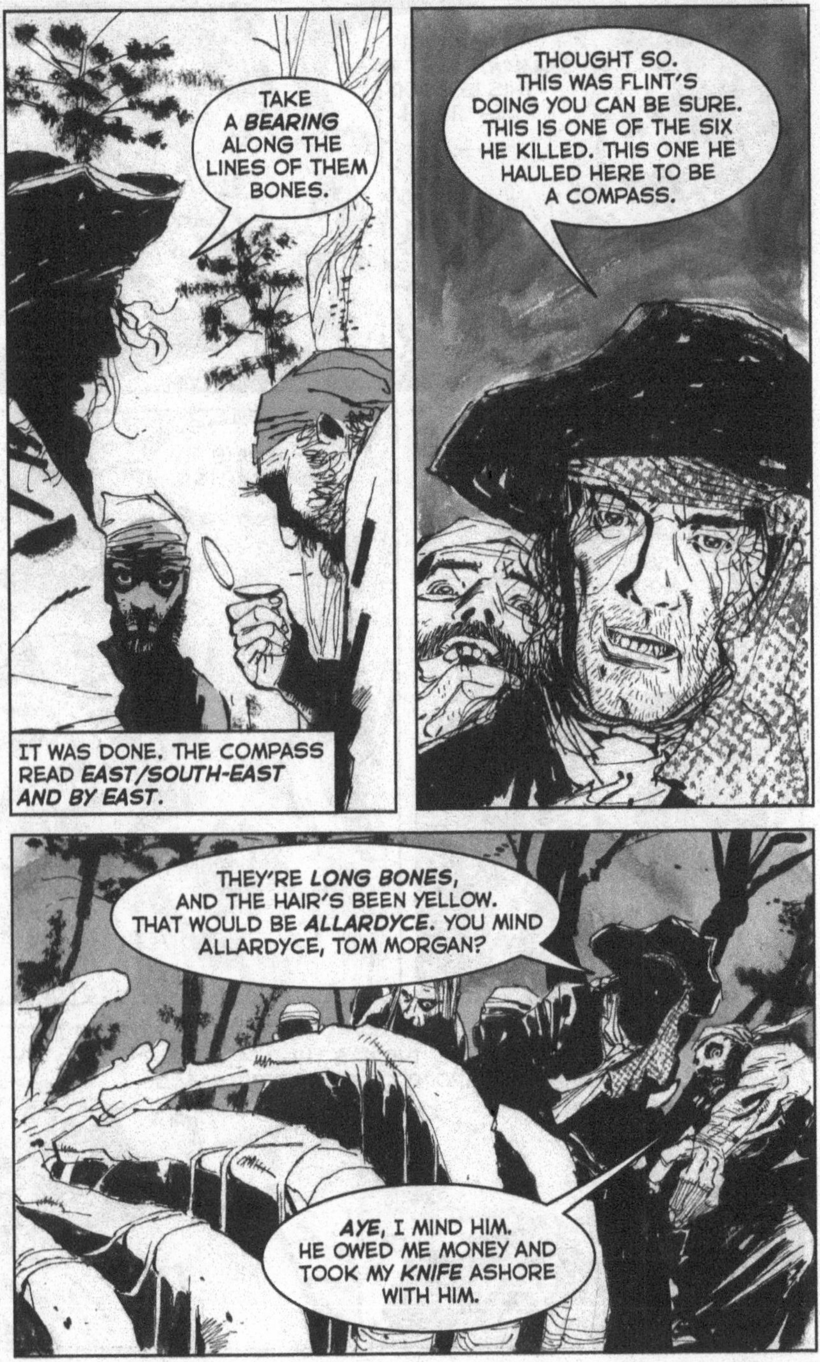
TAKE A *BEARING* ALONG THE LINES OF THEM BONES.
IT WAS DONE. THE COMPASS READ *EAST/SOUTH-EAST AND BY EAST*.
THOUGHT SO. THIS WAS FLINT'S DOING YOU CAN BE SURE. THIS IS ONE OF THE SIX HE KILLED. THIS ONE HE HAULED HERE TO BE A COMPASS.
THEY'RE *LONG BONES*, AND THE HAIR'S BEEN YELLOW. THAT WOULD BE *ALLARDYCE*. YOU MIND ALLARDYCE, TOM MORGAN?
AYE, I MIND HIM. HE OWED ME MONEY AND TOOK MY *KNIFE* ASHORE WITH HIM.

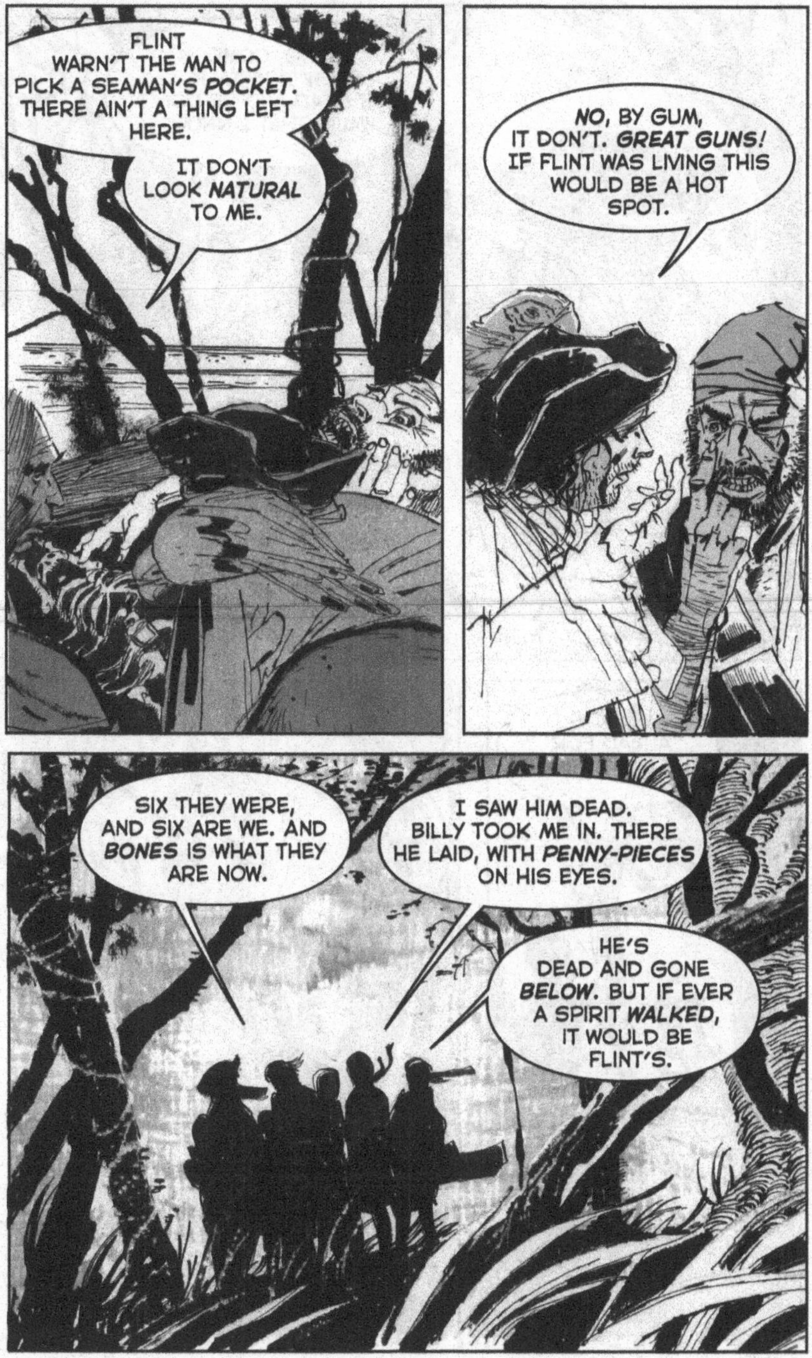
FLINT WARN'T THE MAN TO PICK A SEAMAN'S *POCKET*. THERE AIN'T A THING LEFT HERE.
IT DON'T LOOK *NATURAL* TO ME.
NO, BY GUM, IT DON'T. *GREAT GUNS!* IF FLINT WAS LIVING THIS WOULD BE A HOT SPOT.
SIX THEY WERE, AND SIX ARE WE. AND *BONES* IS WHAT THEY ARE NOW.
I SAW HIM DEAD. BILLY TOOK ME IN. THERE HE LAID, WITH *PENNY-PIECES* ON HIS EYES.
HE'S DEAD AND GONE *BELOW*. BUT IF EVER A SPIRIT *WALKED*, IT WOULD BE FLINT'S.

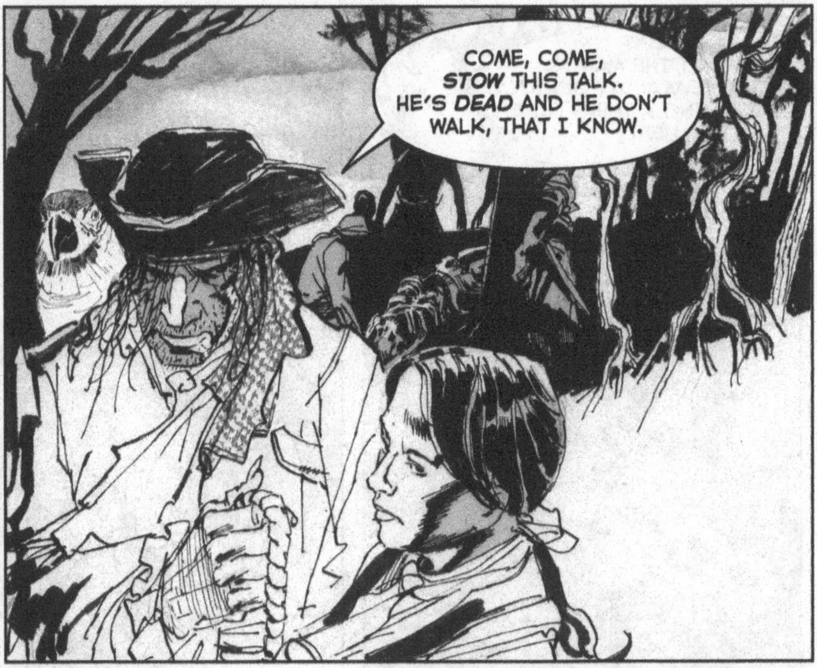
COME, COME, STOW THIS TALK. HE'S DEAD AND HE DON'T WALK, THAT I KNOW.

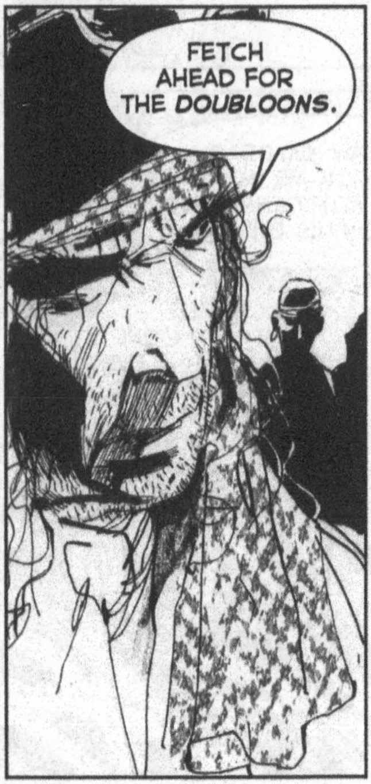
FETCH AHEAD FOR THE DOUBLOONS.

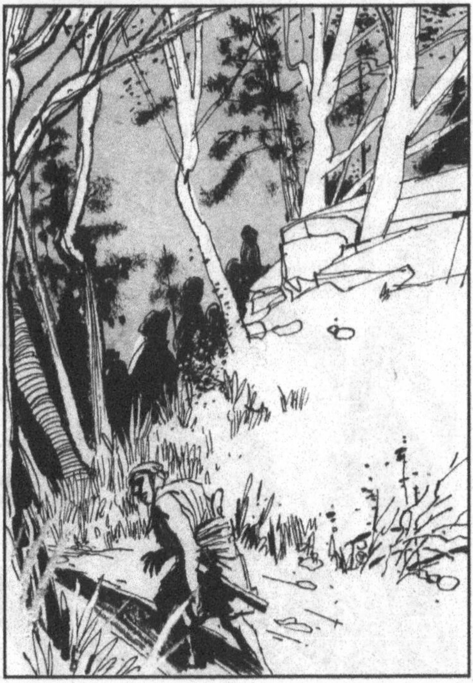

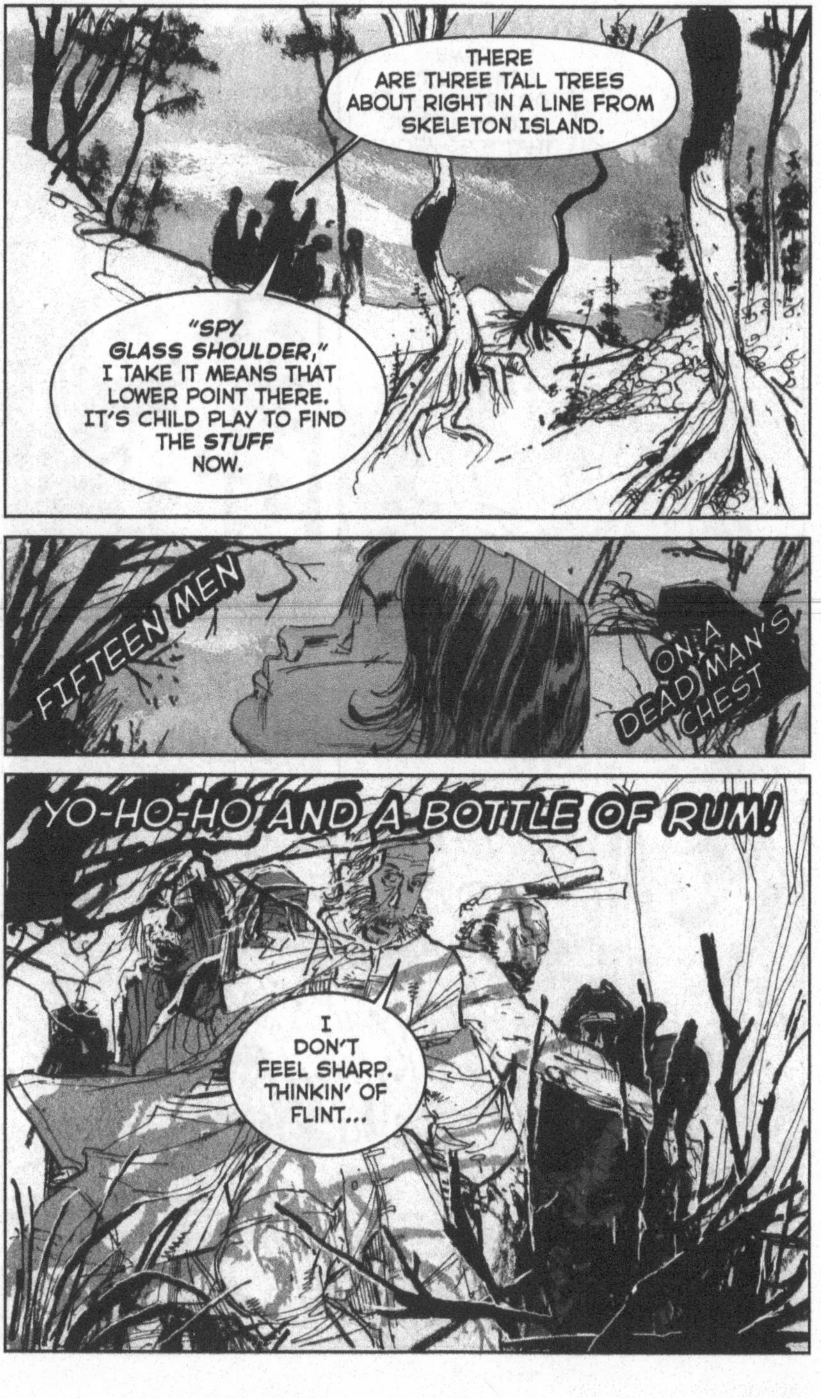
THERE ARE THREE TALL TREES ABOUT RIGHT IN A LINE FROM SKELETON ISLAND.
"SPY GLASS SHOULDER," I TAKE IT MEANS THAT LOWER POINT THERE. IT'S CHILD PLAY TO FIND THE *STUFF* NOW.
FIFTEEN MEN
ON A DEAD MAN'S CHEST
YO-HO-HO AND A BOTTLE OF RUM!
I DON'T FEEL SHARP. THINKIN' OF FLINT...

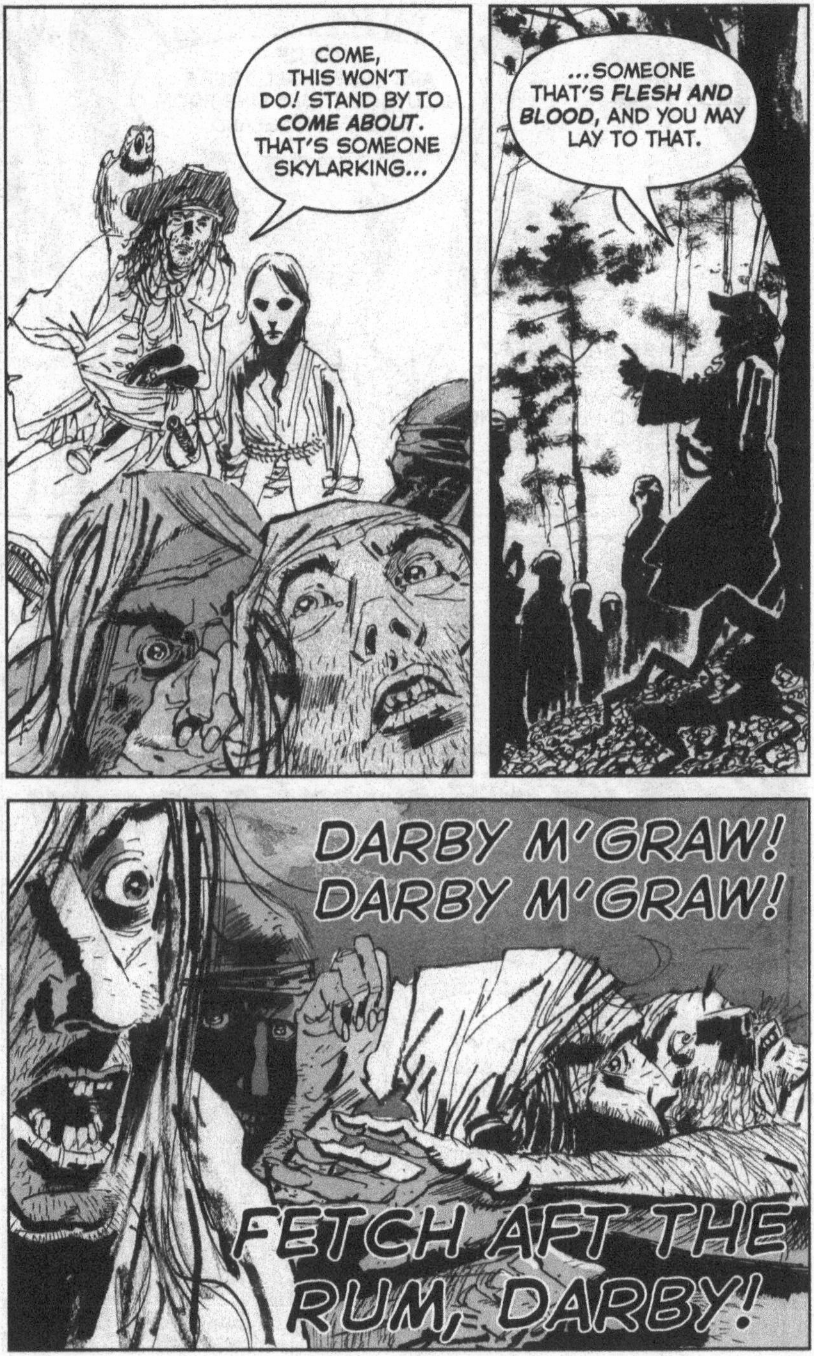
COME, THIS WON'T DO! STAND BY TO COME ABOUT. THAT'S SOMEONE SKYLARKING...
...SOMEONE THAT'S FLESH AND BLOOD, AND YOU MAY LAY TO THAT.
DARBY M'GRAW! DARBY M'GRAW!
FETCH AFT THE RUM, DARBY!

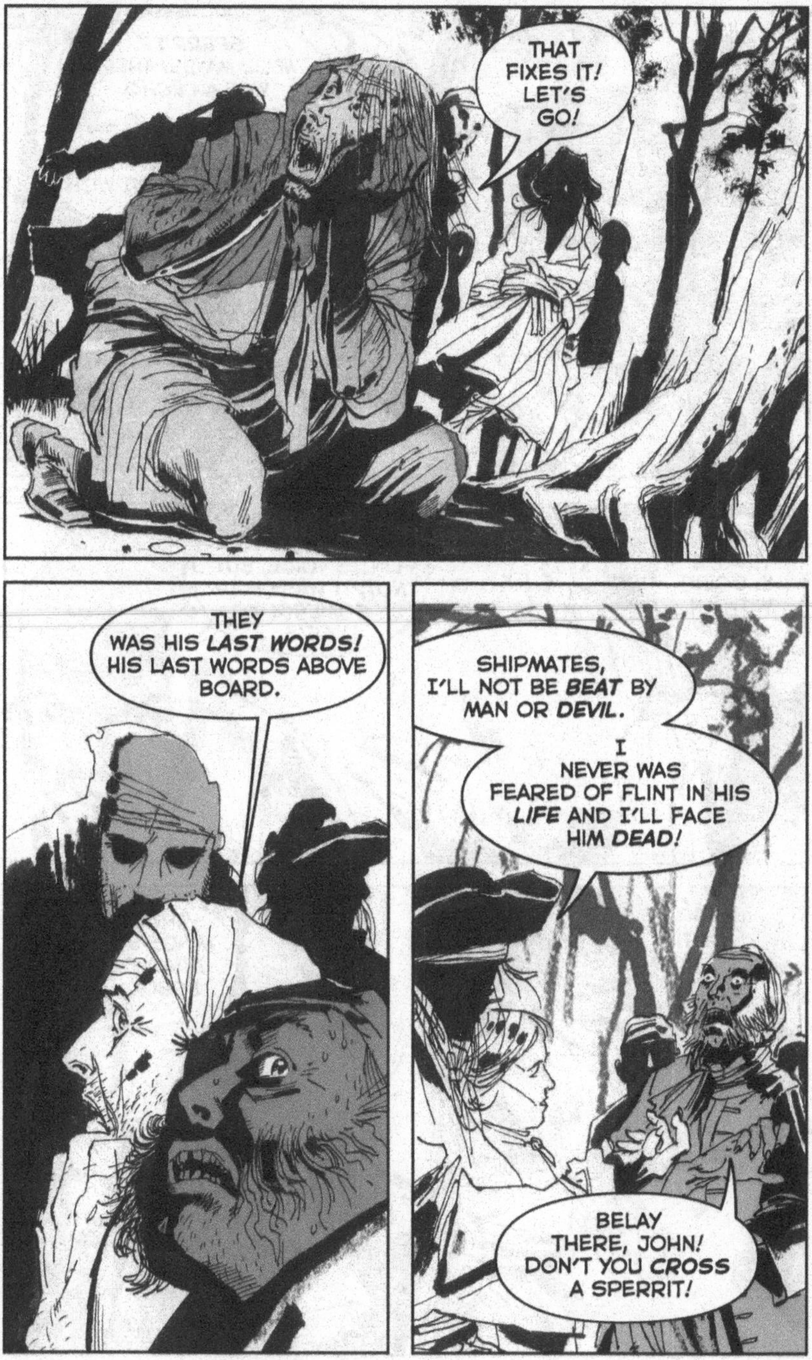
THAT FIXES IT! LET'S GO!
THEY WAS HIS LAST WORDS! HIS LAST WORDS ABOVE BOARD.
SHIPMATES, I'LL NOT BE BEAT BY MAN OR DEVIL.
I NEVER WAS FEARED OF FLINT IN HIS LIFE AND I'LL FACE HIM DEAD!
BELAY THERE, JOHN! DON'T YOU CROSS A SPERRIT!

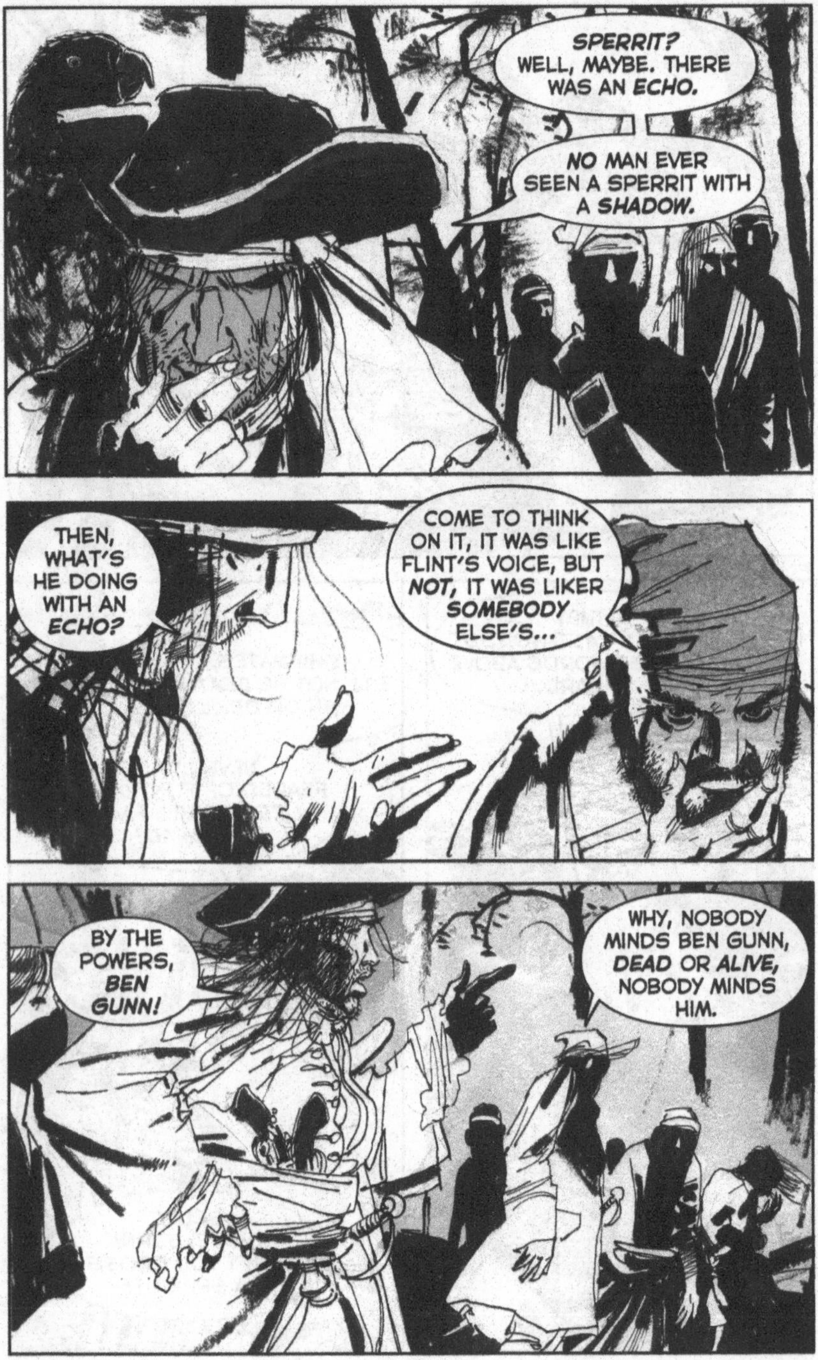
SPERRIT? WELL, MAYBE. THERE WAS AN ECHO.
NO MAN EVER SEEN A SPERRIT WITH A SHADOW.
THEN, WHAT'S HE DOING WITH AN ECHO?
COME TO THINK ON IT, IT WAS LIKE FLINT'S VOICE, BUT NOT, IT WAS LIKER SOMEBODY ELSE'S...
BY THE POWERS, BEN GUNN!
WHY, NOBODY MINDS BEN GUNN, DEAD OR ALIVE, NOBODY MINDS HIM.

IT WAS EXTRAORDINARY HOW THEIR *SPIRITS* HAD RETURNED.

NOT LONG AFTER, HEARING NO FURTHER *SOUND,* THEY SHOULDERED THE TOOLS AND SET FORTH AGAIN.

WE SOON FOUND THE NEXT MARKER, A *TALL TREE.*

IT WAS HARD FOR ME TO KEEP UP WITH THE *RAPID PACE* OF THE TREASURE-HUNTERS.

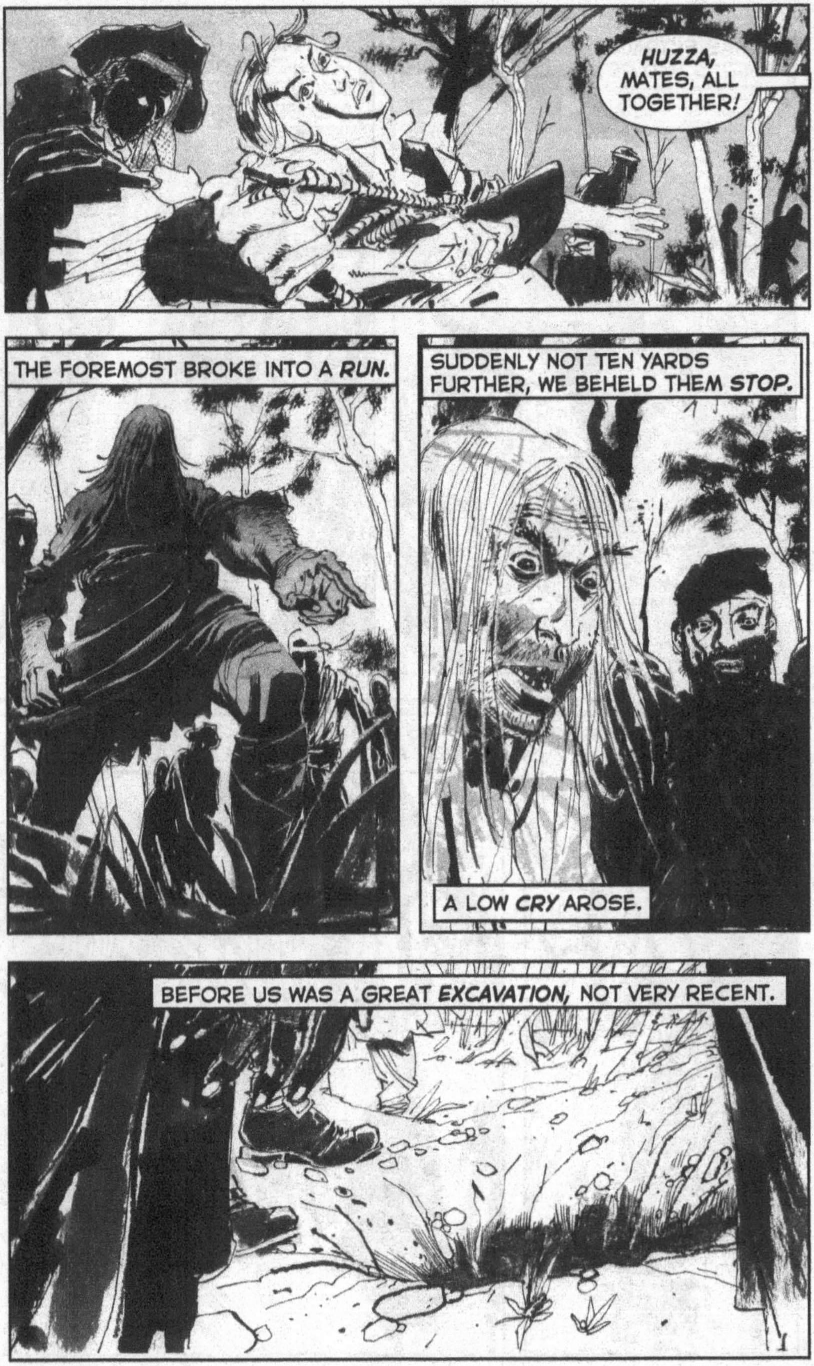
HUZZA, MATES, ALL TOGETHER!
THE FOREMOST BROKE INTO A RUN.
SUDDENLY NOT TEN YARDS FURTHER, WE BEHELD THEM STOP.
A LOW CRY AROSE.
BEFORE US WAS A GREAT EXCAVATION, NOT VERY RECENT.

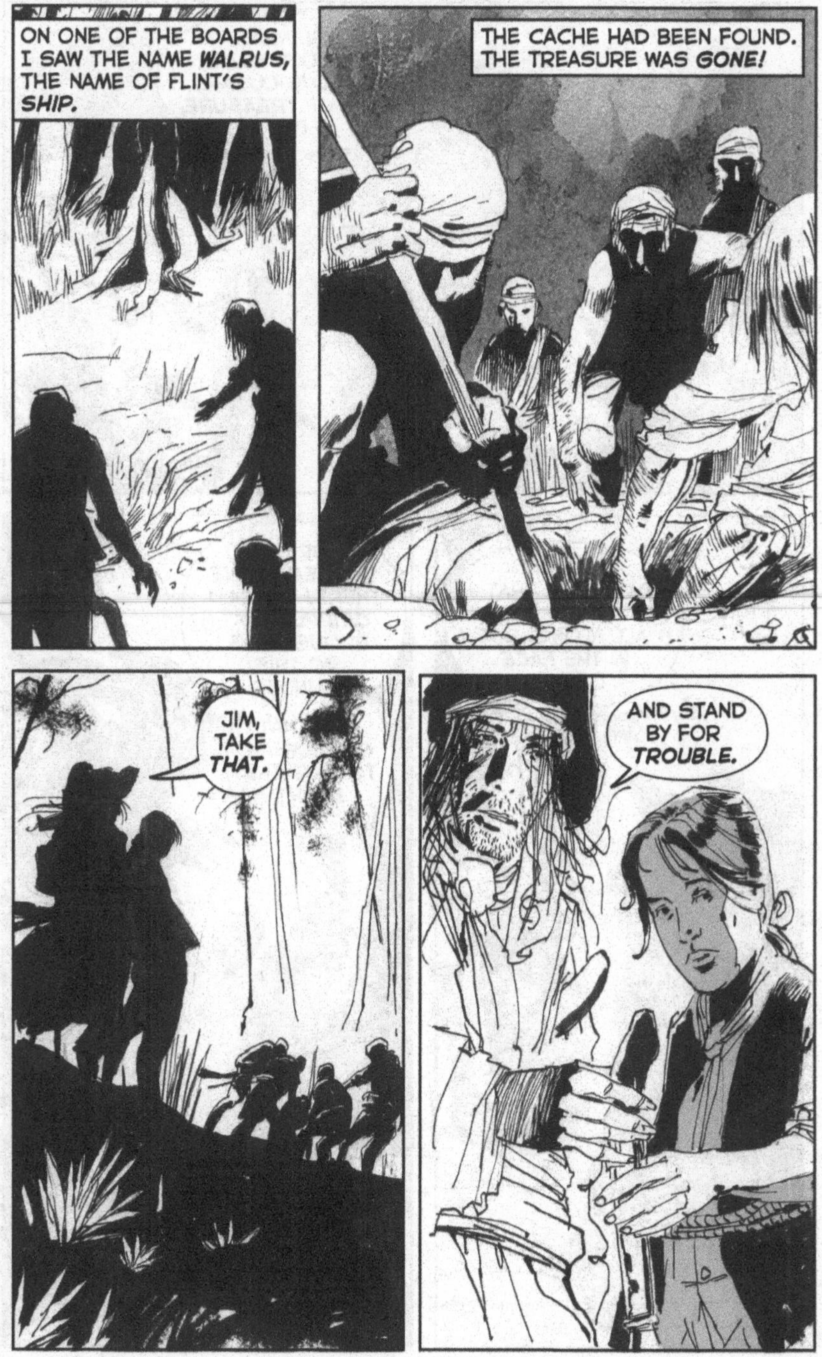
ON ONE OF THE BOARDS I SAW THE NAME *WALRUS*, THE NAME OF FLINT'S *SHIP.*
THE CACHE HAD BEEN FOUND. THE TREASURE WAS *GONE!*
JIM, TAKE *THAT.*
AND STAND BY FOR *TROUBLE.*

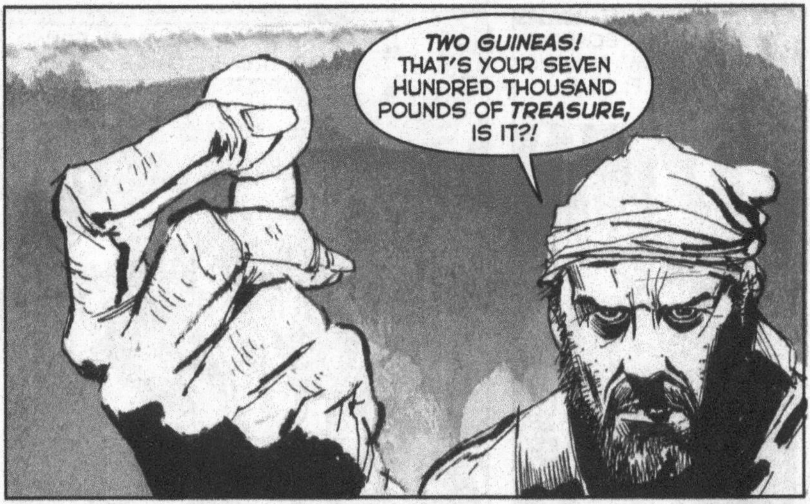
TWO GUINEAS! THAT'S YOUR SEVEN HUNDRED THOUSAND POUNDS OF TREASURE, IS IT?!

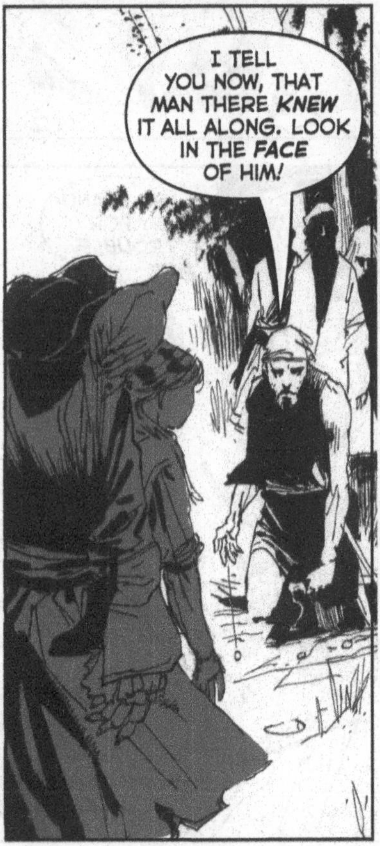
I TELL YOU NOW, THAT MAN THERE KNEW IT ALL ALONG. LOOK IN THE FACE OF HIM!

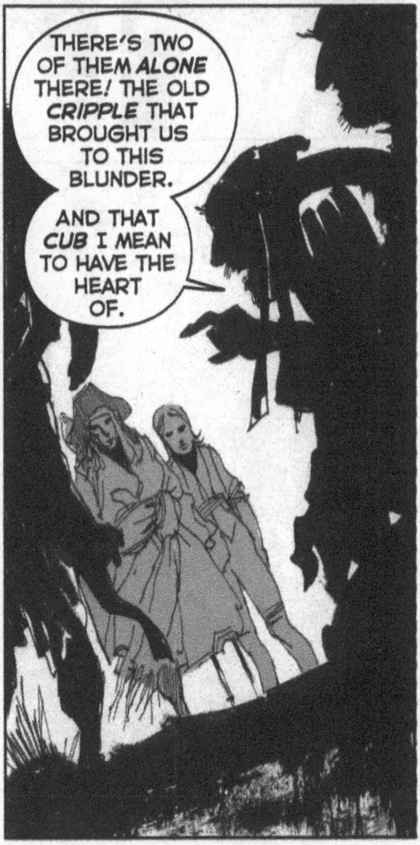
THERE'S TWO OF THEM ALONE THERE! THE OLD CRIPPLE THAT BROUGHT US TO THIS BLUNDER.
AND THAT CUB I MEAN TO HAVE THE HEART OF.

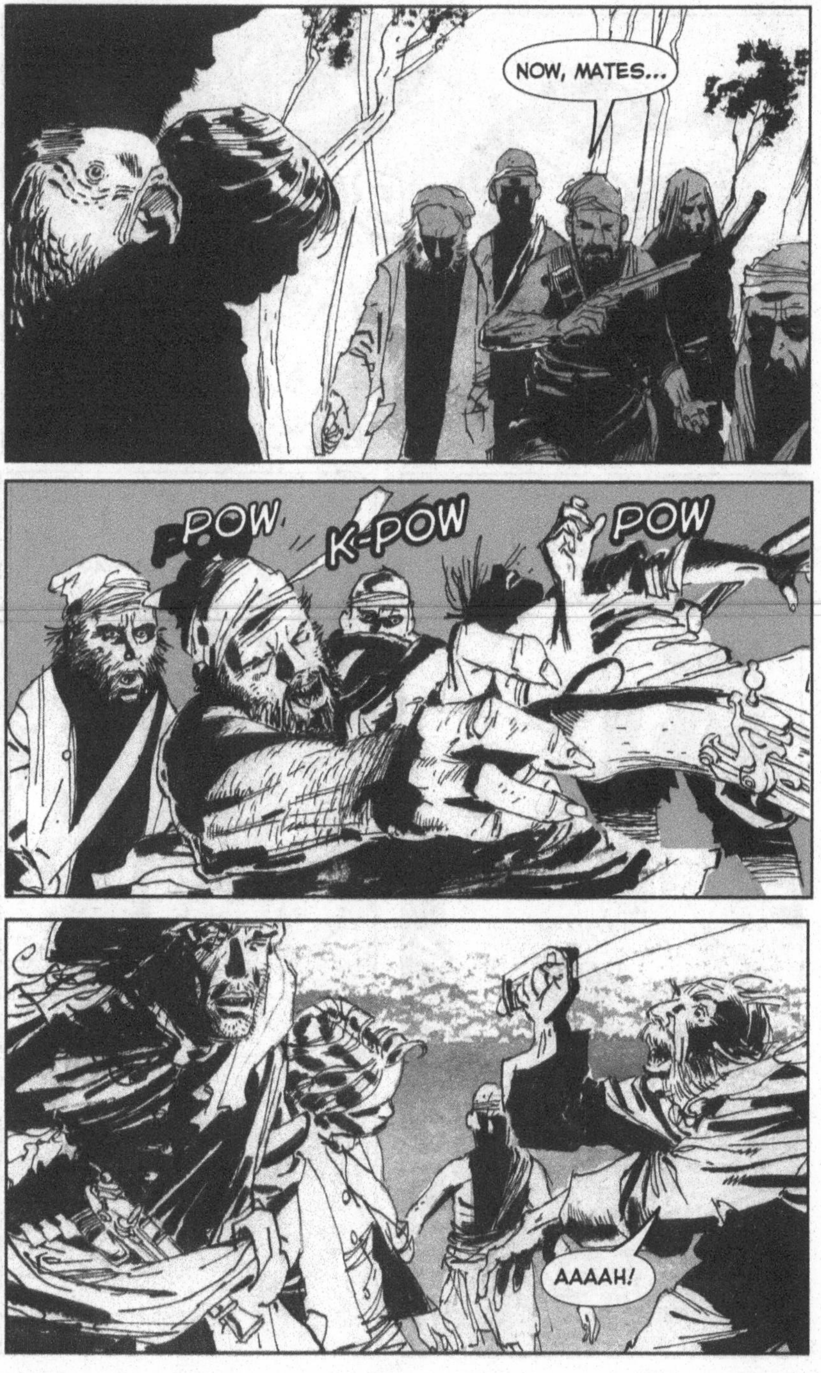
NOW, MATES...
POW
K-POW
POW
AAAAH!

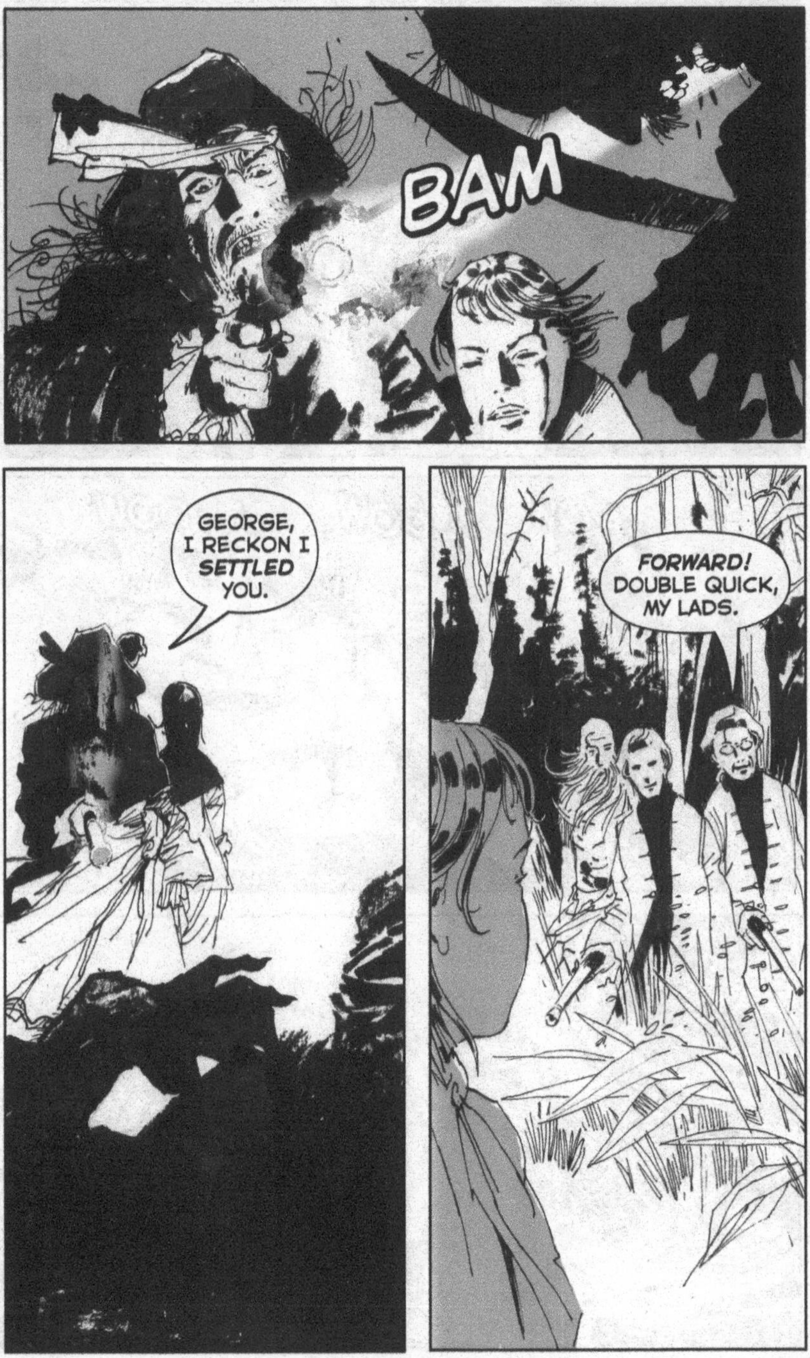
BAM
GEORGE, I RECKON I SETTLED YOU.
FORWARD! DOUBLE QUICK, MY LADS.

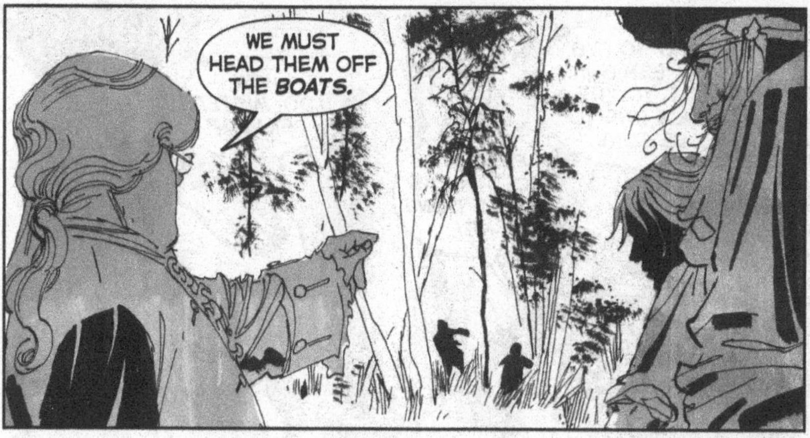
WE MUST HEAD THEM OFF THE *BOATS.*

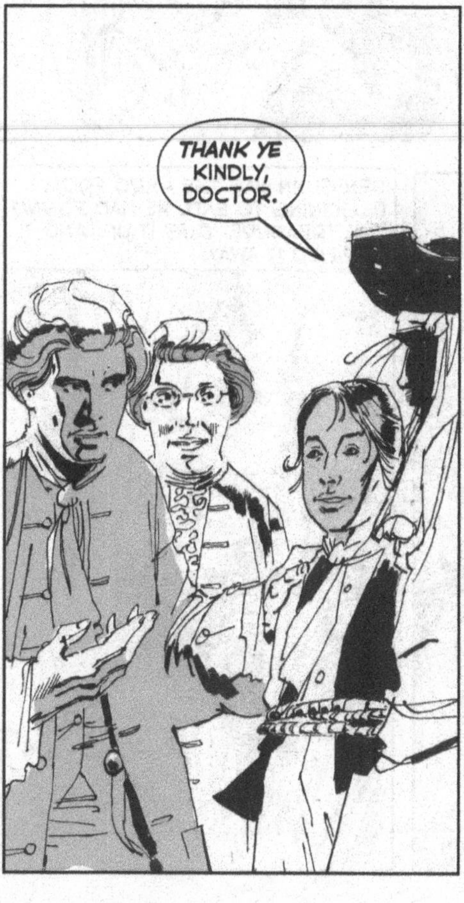
THANK YE KINDLY, DOCTOR.

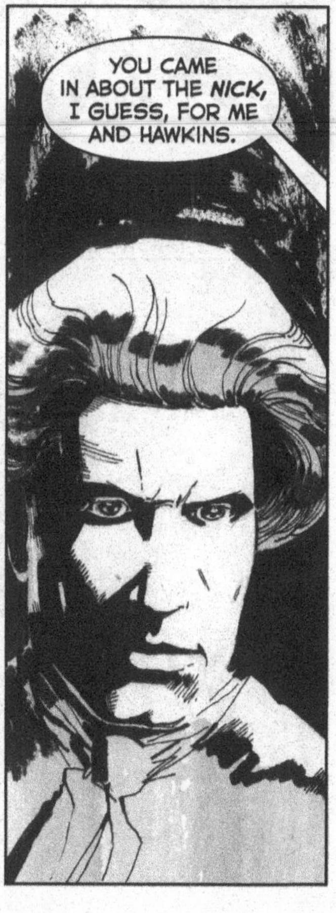
YOU CAME IN ABOUT THE *NICK,* I GUESS, FOR ME AND HAWKINS.

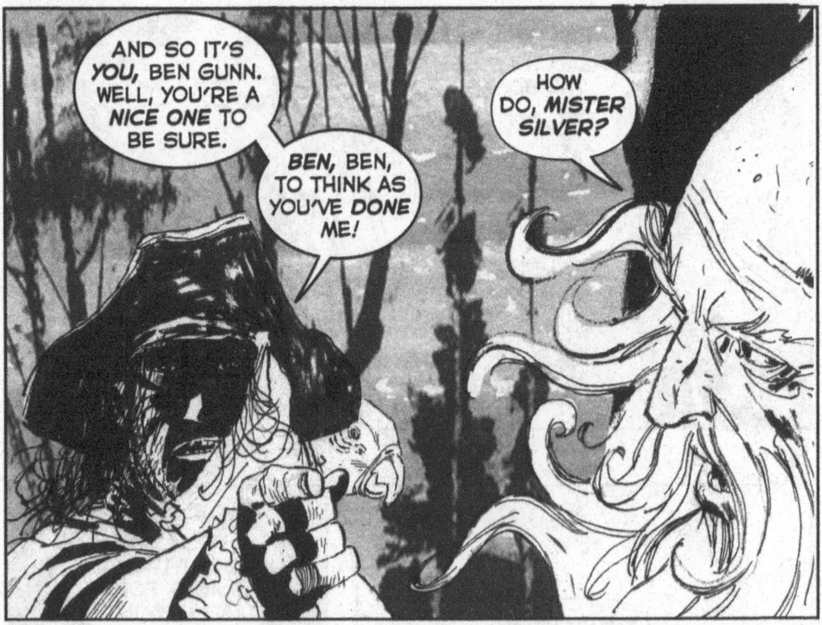
AND SO IT'S YOU, BEN GUNN. WELL, YOU'RE A NICE ONE TO BE SURE.
BEN, BEN, TO THINK AS YOU'VE DONE ME!
HOW DO, MISTER SILVER?

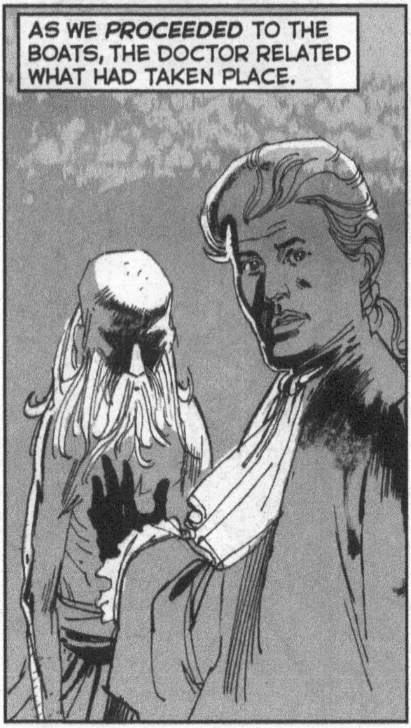
AS WE PROCEEDED TO THE BOATS, THE DOCTOR RELATED WHAT HAD TAKEN PLACE.

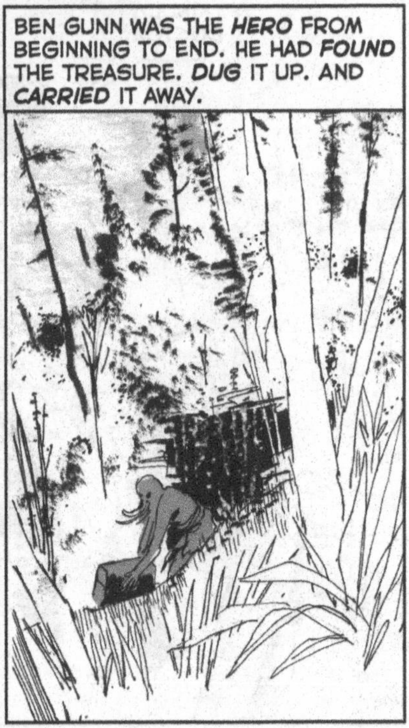
BEN GUNN WAS THE HERO FROM BEGINNING TO END. HE HAD FOUND THE TREASURE. DUG IT UP. AND CARRIED IT AWAY.

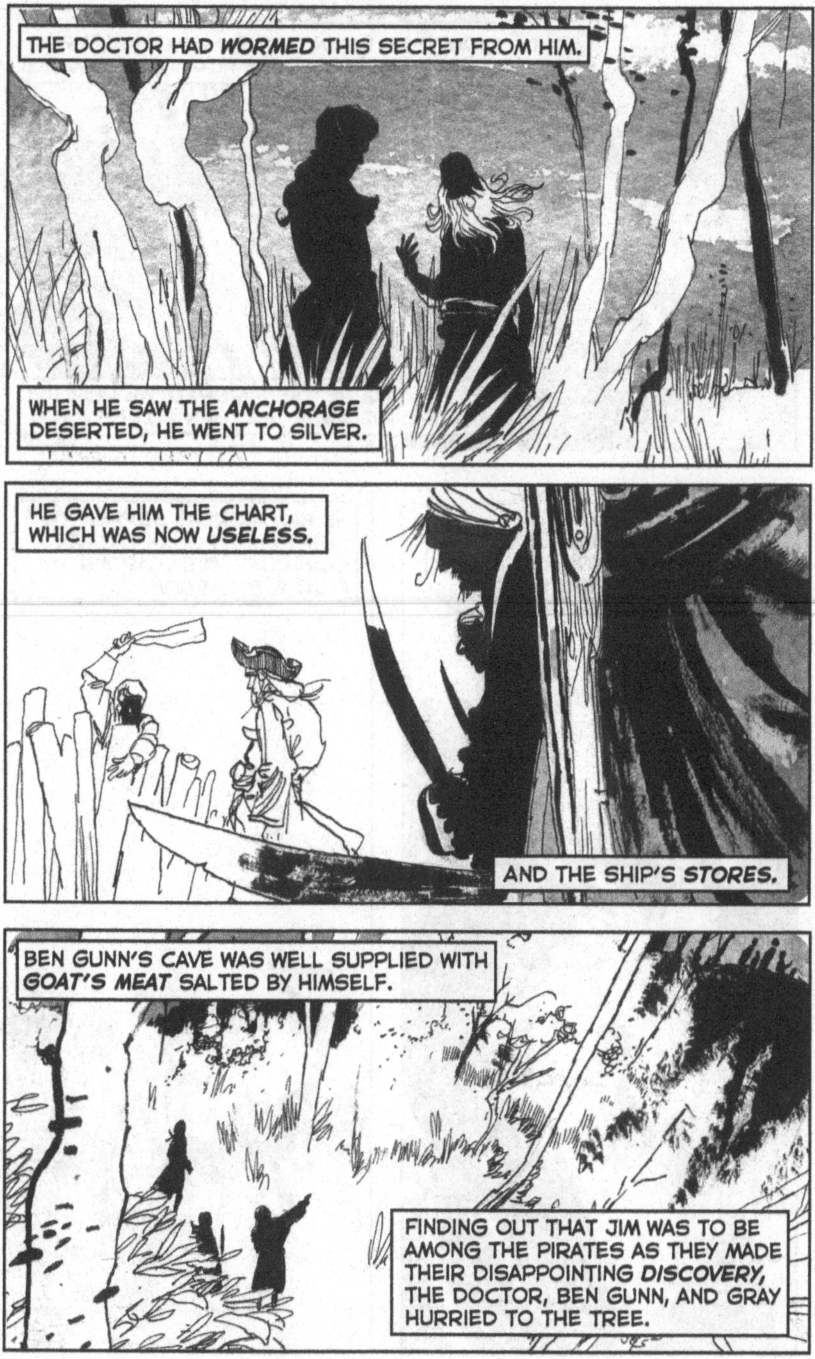
THE DOCTOR HAD WORMED THIS SECRET FROM HIM.
WHEN HE SAW THE ANCHORAGE DESERTED, HE WENT TO SILVER.
HE GAVE HIM THE CHART, WHICH WAS NOW USELESS.
AND THE SHIP'S STORES.
BEN GUNN'S CAVE WAS WELL SUPPLIED WITH GOAT'S MEAT SALTED BY HIMSELF.
FINDING OUT THAT JIM WAS TO BE AMONG THE PIRATES AS THEY MADE THEIR DISAPPOINTING DISCOVERY, THE DOCTOR, BEN GUNN, AND GRAY HURRIED TO THE TREE.

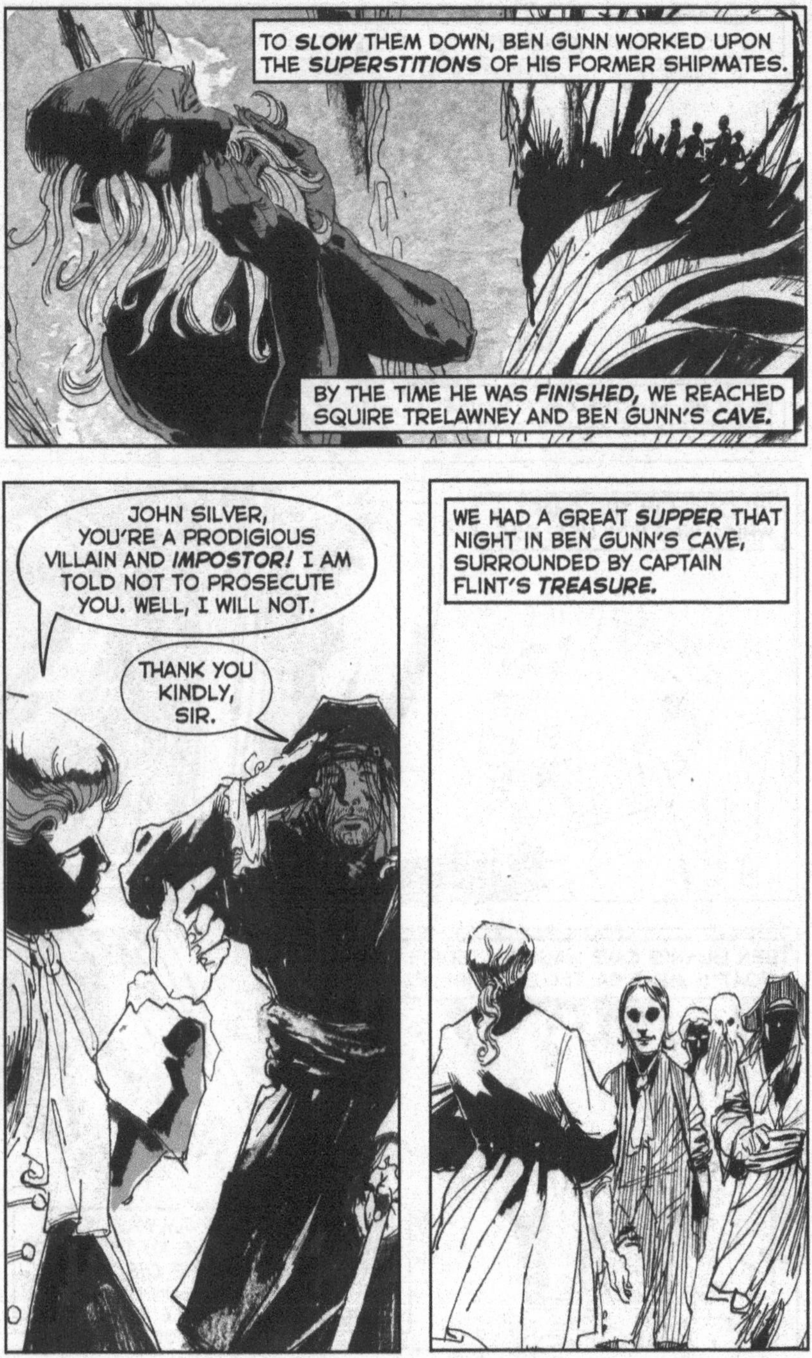
TO SLOW THEM DOWN, BEN GUNN WORKED UPON THE SUPERSTITIONS OF HIS FORMER SHIPMATES.
BY THE TIME HE WAS FINISHED, WE REACHED SQUIRE TRELAWNEY AND BEN GUNN'S CAVE.
JOHN SILVER, YOU'RE A PRODIGIOUS VILLAIN AND IMPOSTOR! I AM TOLD NOT TO PROSECUTE YOU. WELL, I WILL NOT.
THANK YOU KINDLY, SIR.
WE HAD A GREAT SUPPER THAT NIGHT IN BEN GUNN'S CAVE, SURROUNDED BY CAPTAIN FLINT'S TREASURE.

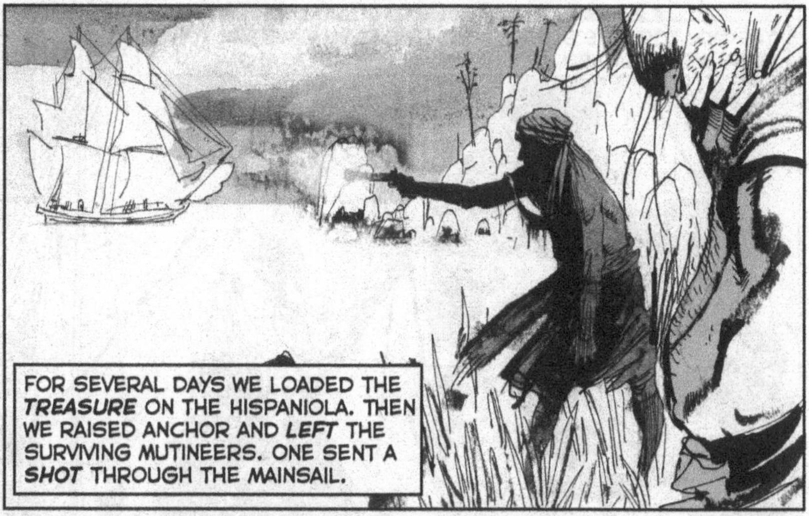
FOR SEVERAL DAYS WE LOADED THE TREASURE ON THE HISPANIOLA. THEN WE RAISED ANCHOR AND LEFT THE SURVIVING MUTINEERS. ONE SENT A SHOT THROUGH THE MAINSAIL.

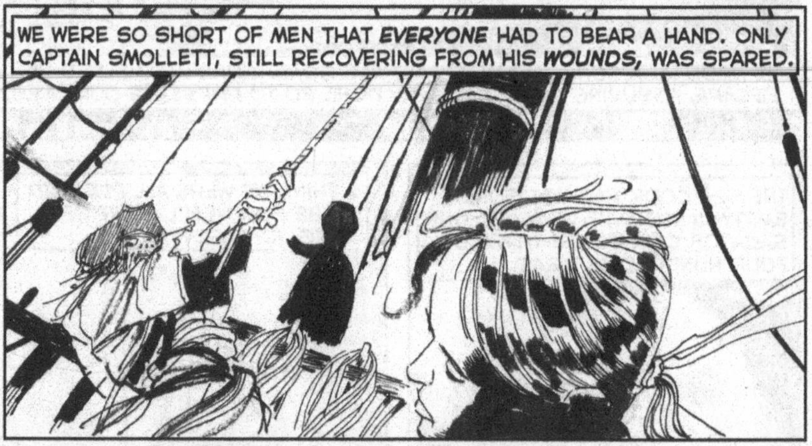
WE WERE SO SHORT OF MEN THAT EVERYONE HAD TO BEAR A HAND. ONLY CAPTAIN SMOLLETT, STILL RECOVERING FROM HIS WOUNDS, WAS SPARED.

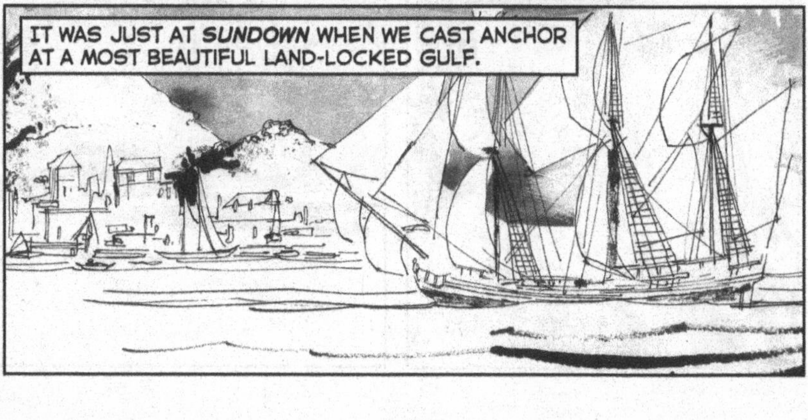
IT WAS JUST AT SUNDOWN WHEN WE CAST ANCHOR AT A MOST BEAUTIFUL LAND-LOCKED GULF.

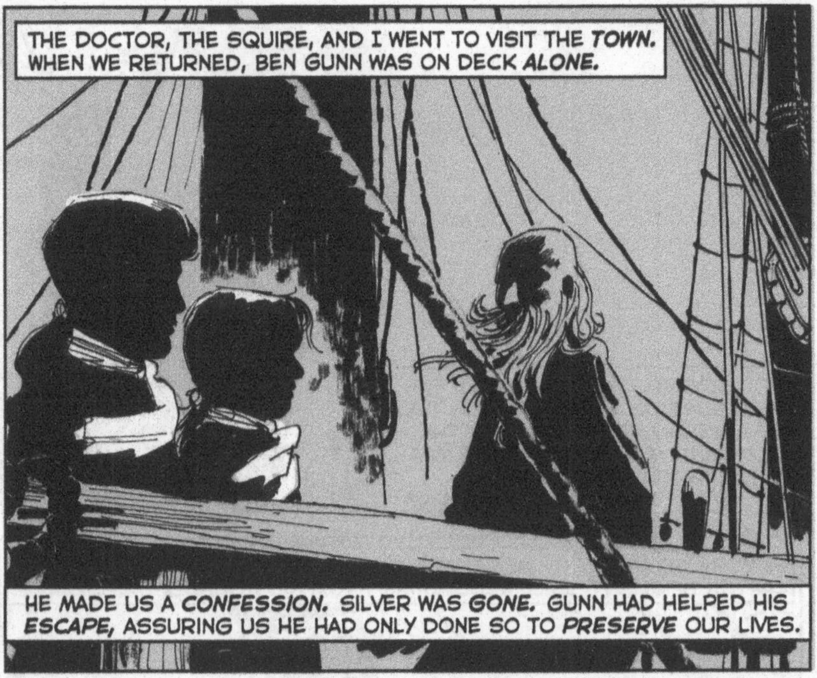
THE DOCTOR, THE SQUIRE, AND I WENT TO VISIT THE TOWN. WHEN WE RETURNED, BEN GUNN WAS ON DECK ALONE.
HE MADE US A CONFESSION. SILVER WAS GONE. GUNN HAD HELPED HIS ESCAPE, ASSURING US HE HAD ONLY DONE SO TO PRESERVE OUR LIVES.

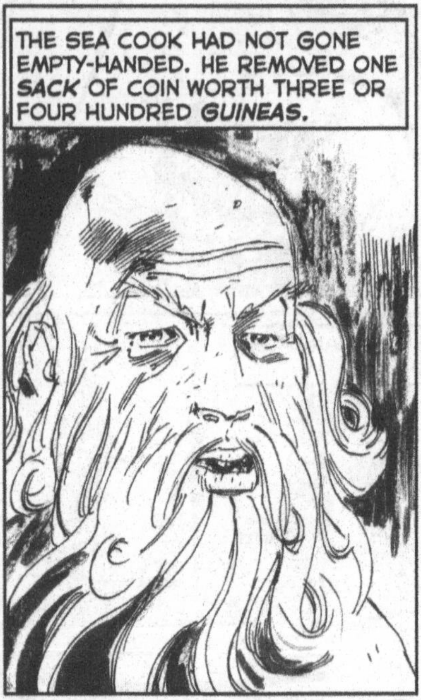
THE SEA COOK HAD NOT GONE EMPTY-HANDED. HE REMOVED ONE SACK OF COIN WORTH THREE OR FOUR HUNDRED GUINEAS.

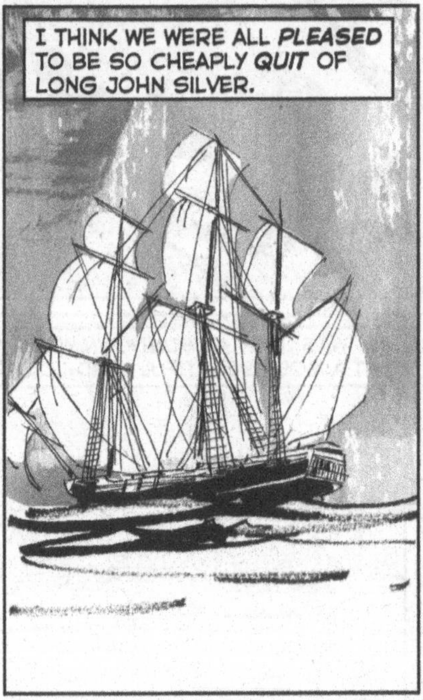
I THINK WE WERE ALL PLEASED TO BE SO CHEAPLY QUIT OF LONG JOHN SILVER.

TO MAKE A LONG STORY SHORT, WE MADE A *GOOD CRUISE* HOME. ALL OF US HAD AN AMPLE *SHARE* OF THE TREASURE, AND USED IT WISELY OR *FOOLISHLY*, ACCORDING TO OUR NATURE.

OF SILVER WE HAVE HEARD *NO MORE.*

THAT FORMIDABLE *SEAFARING MAN* WITH ONE LEG HAS AT LAST *GONE* CLEAN OUT OF MY LIFE.

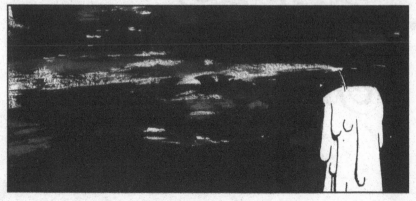

THE WORST DREAMS THAT EVER I HAVE ARE WHEN I HEAR THE SURF BOOMING ABOUT ITS COASTS.
OR WHEN I START UPRIGHT IN BED, WITH THE SHARP VOICE OF CAPTAIN FLINT STILL RINGING IN MY EARS.
PIECES OF EIGHT!
PIECES OF EIGHT!
THE END

THE MAKING OF

ROBERT LOUIS STEVENSON'S

Treasure Island

"I did look forward, with some intimidation, to creating my own take on the look and feel of this novel."

—Tim Hamilton

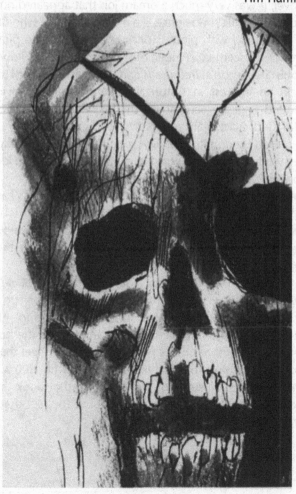

TIM HAMILTON TALKS ABOUT
Treasure Island

When Byron Preiss approached me with the offer of adapting and illustrating *Treasure Island* as a graphic novel, it was very much a dream job that appeared right out of the blue. I was once like many other kids who had a fascination with pirate stories and treasure. No pirate story ever seemed as ingeniously put together as Robert Louis Stevenson's *Treasure Island*. Even as an adult I still held an interest in historical subject matter revolving around English sailing ships, the real life stories of Captain Kidd, Blackbeard and New World explorers.

Even though I'm not always comfortable with adapting work that seems perfect in its original form, I did look forward, with some intimidation, to creating my own take on the look and feel of this novel. Other artists have done their verson, and I avoided looking at them while working on mine. In fact, I never saw any of the movie versions of *Treasure Island,* even as a kid. I was busy watching the monster movies!

Though intimidated by adapting *Treasure Island,* I was nevertheless drawn into the process by the strong characters and colorful atmosphere. Each setting—the attack on the Admiral Benbow Inn, the trip on the boat and the adventure on the island—had its own feel that I enjoyed bringing to visual life. I stayed up till 1:00 A.M. many nights illustrating scenes from the book just because it was fun to do. I forgot about the fact that it was a job.

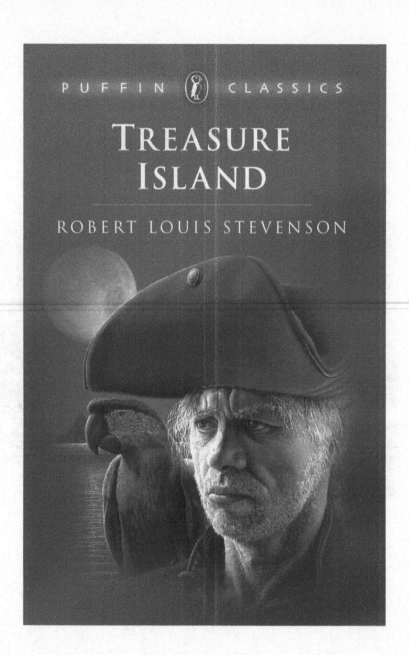

PUFFIN CLASSICS

TREASURE ISLAND

ROBERT LOUIS STEVENSON

Tim adapted his story from this Puffin Classics edition of *Treasure Island*.

Treasure Island
CONCEPT SKETCHES

A sailing ship.

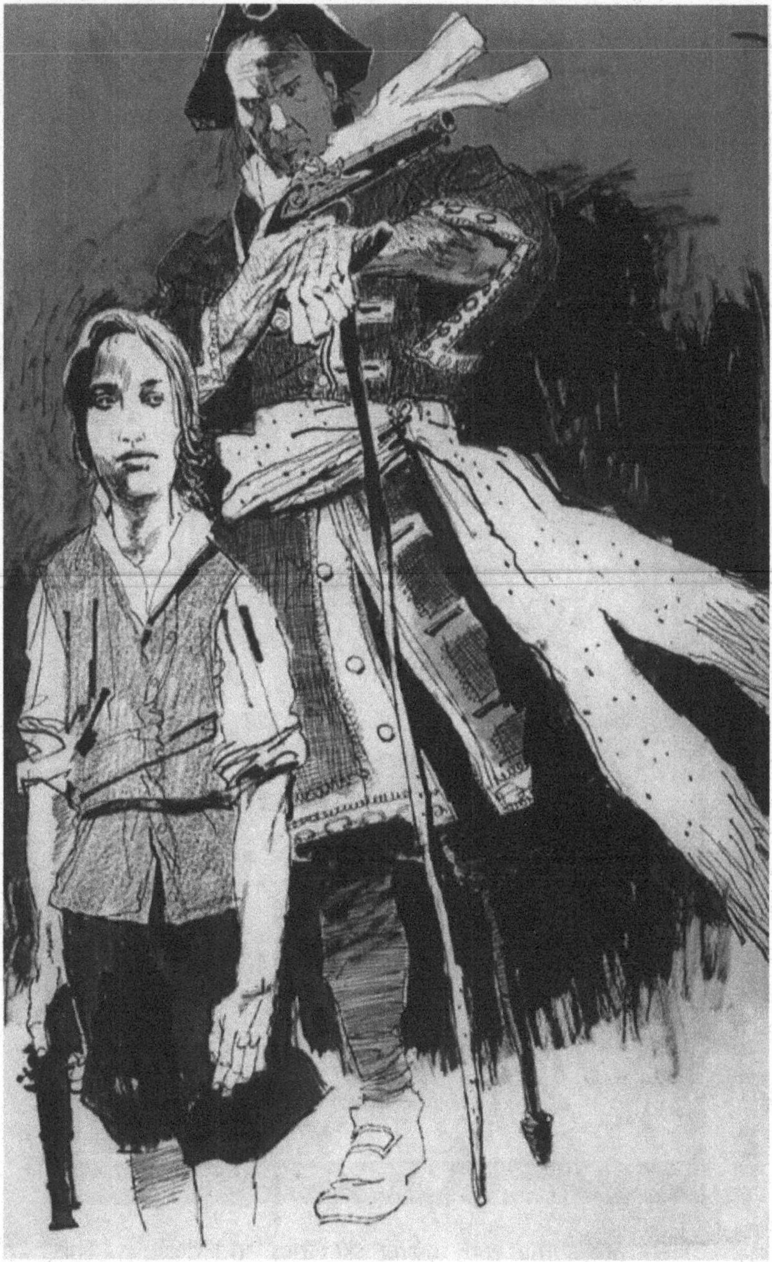

Jim Hawkins and Long John Silver

COVER GALLERY

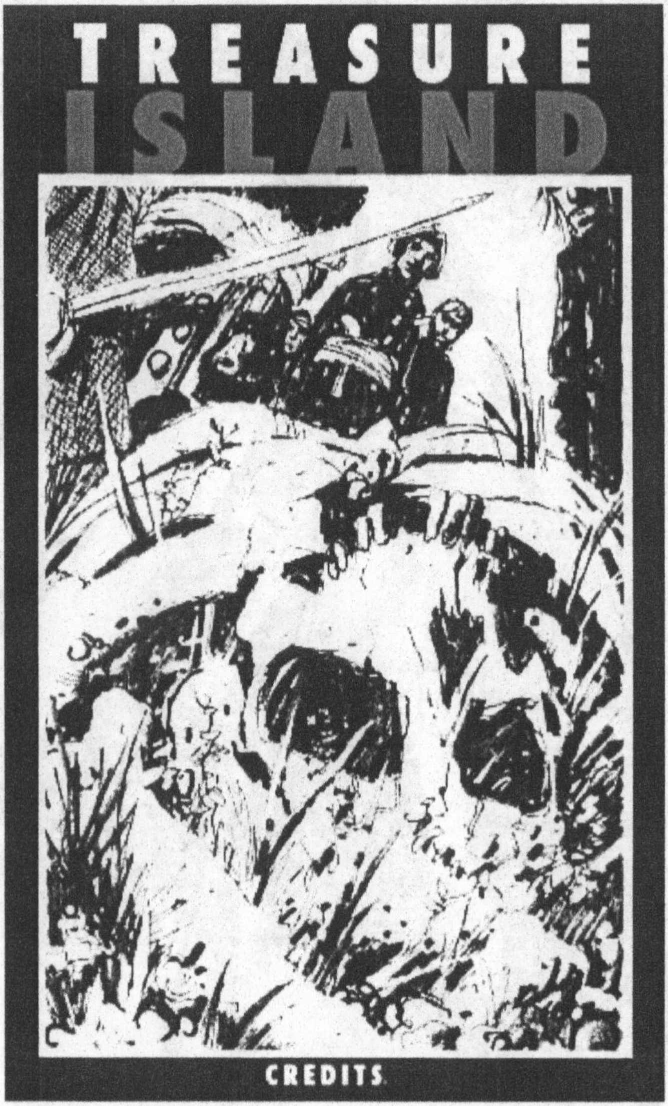
TREASURE
ISLAND
CREDITS

Here are some early cover sketches and designs. This page features a sketch complete with a suggested design with indication for title and credits.

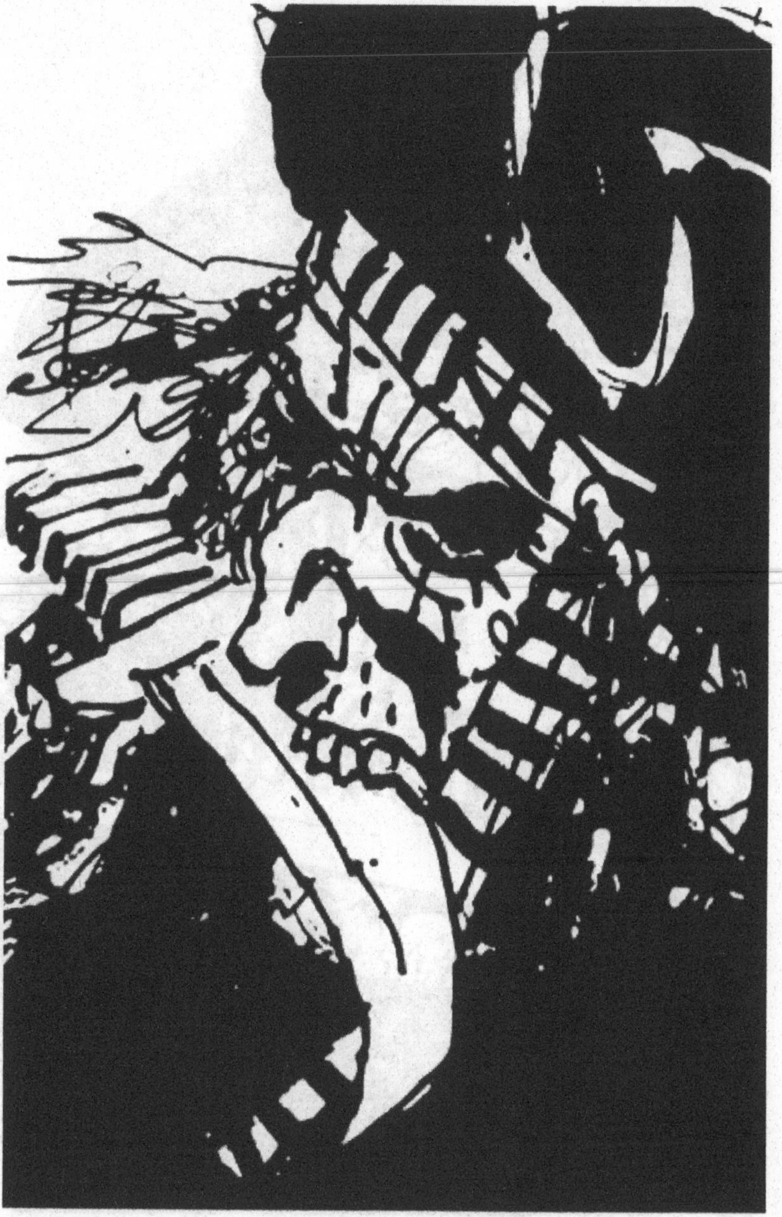

A closeup of a pirate.

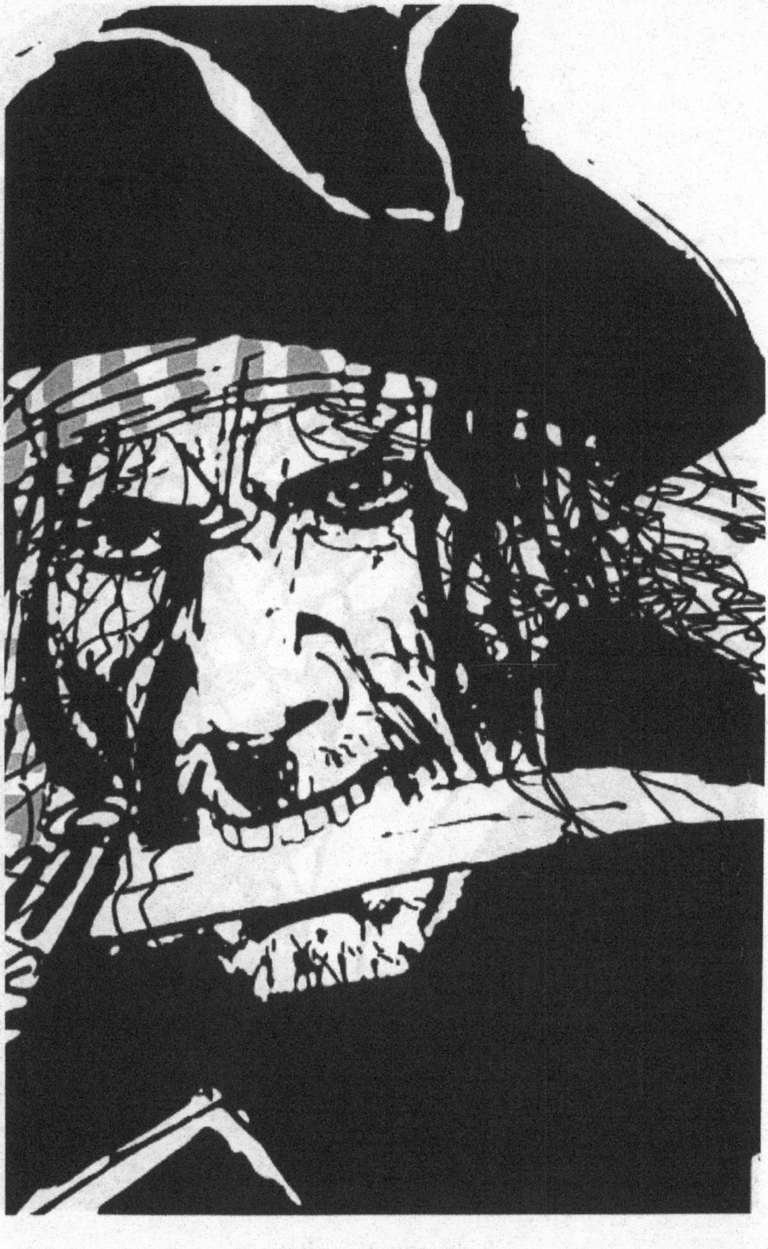

This sketch was ultimately picked for the final cover, with some suggested revisions.

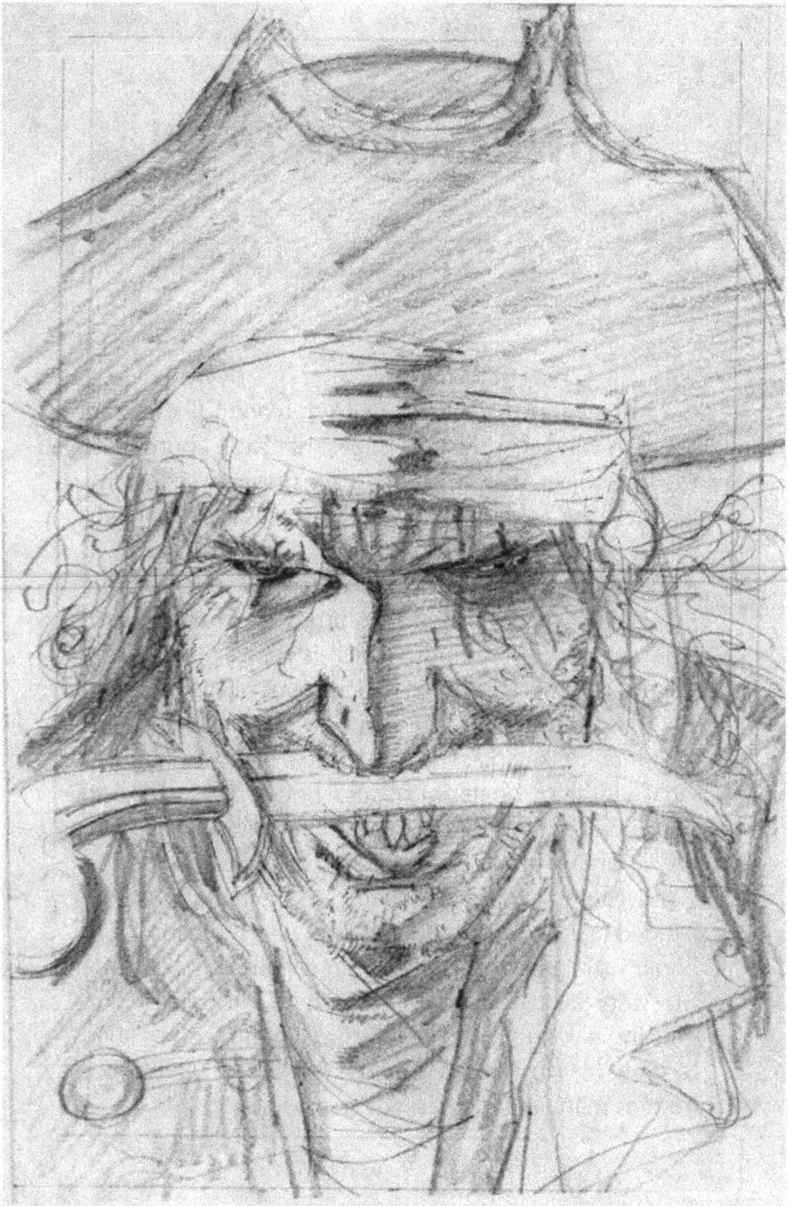

Here is the finished pencil art for the final cover, incorporating revisions. Note the differences between the final sketch, and the starting point on the previous page.

HOW TIM WORKED ON
Treasure Island

In creating the art for *Treasure Island* I first looked through various art history books that were appropriate to the subject matter. I ended up gravitating towards Japanese art, as much of that art involves the ocean and nature, and *Treasure Island* takes place mostly on an island and at sea. I also looked at the work of Kathe Kollwitz. Her art depicted the common people often in dark and moody settings, which is how I pictured the Benbow Inn and the poor difficult lives of the pirates.

I also did historical research, as the action of *Treasure Island* takes place in the 1700s. I had to find out what clothing, boats, guns and houses looked like in that time period. I found this info in various places, but the library was the main source of my research.

Because of the many characters in *Treasure Island*, I needed real life models and faces to play the parts in the book. Taking pictures of friends in various lighting made the story all the more interesting to illustrate. When drawing a young man like Jim Hawkins as much as I had to draw him in *Treasure Island*, I needed to see his face from as many different angles as possible.

In laying out the book itself I first drew thumbnails—small sketches of the art with a marker so I could see where all the lights and shadows would be placed. This also helped me figure out how to clearly tell the story. I approach storytelling in a cinematic way, and I take inspiration from film history. I study what movie directors like Alfred Hitchcock and Akira Kurosawa have done and learn what I can from them.

After I finished the thumbnails, I transferred the art to Bristol board and made sure the faces of the various characters looked like who they should be before I inked the art with India ink.

When I inked the pencil art for *Treasure Island*, I used whatever tool I needed to get the look I wanted. I used metal pen nibs, good brushes, old damaged brushes, grease crayon and even a wooden stick I carved myself. After that I scanned the pages into the computer and, using the software Photoshop, added gray tones to the art. I then checked for any mistakes. Then I sent the digital files of the art to the publisher to be lettered and printed.

A *Treasure Island* PAGE FROM SKETCH TO INKS

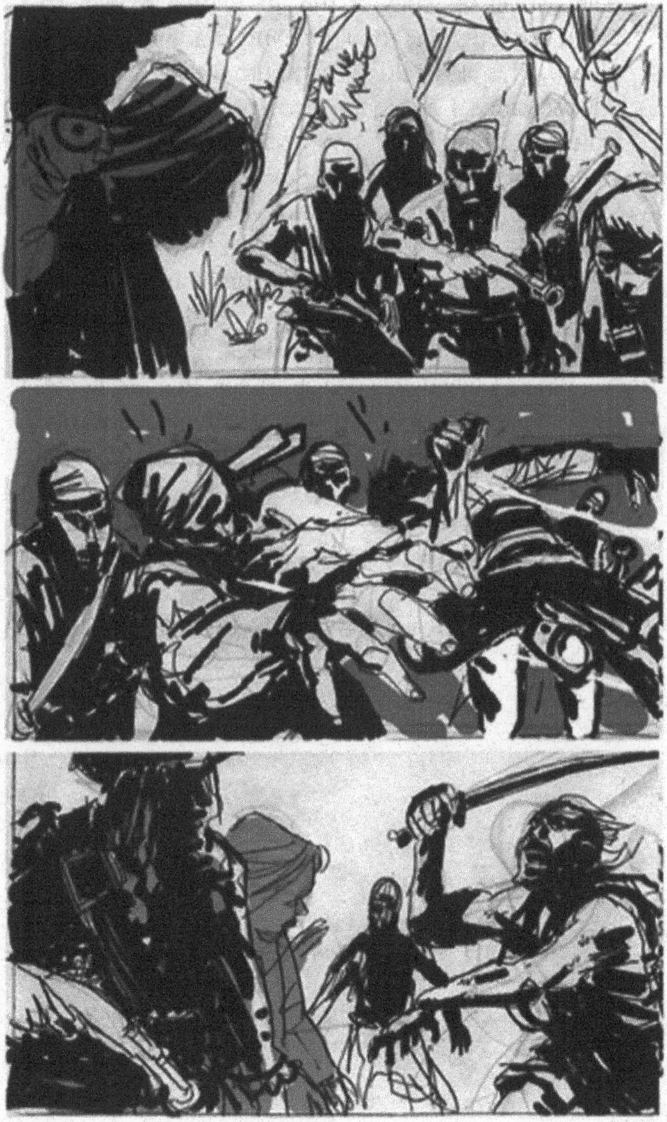

A rough sketch of a page.

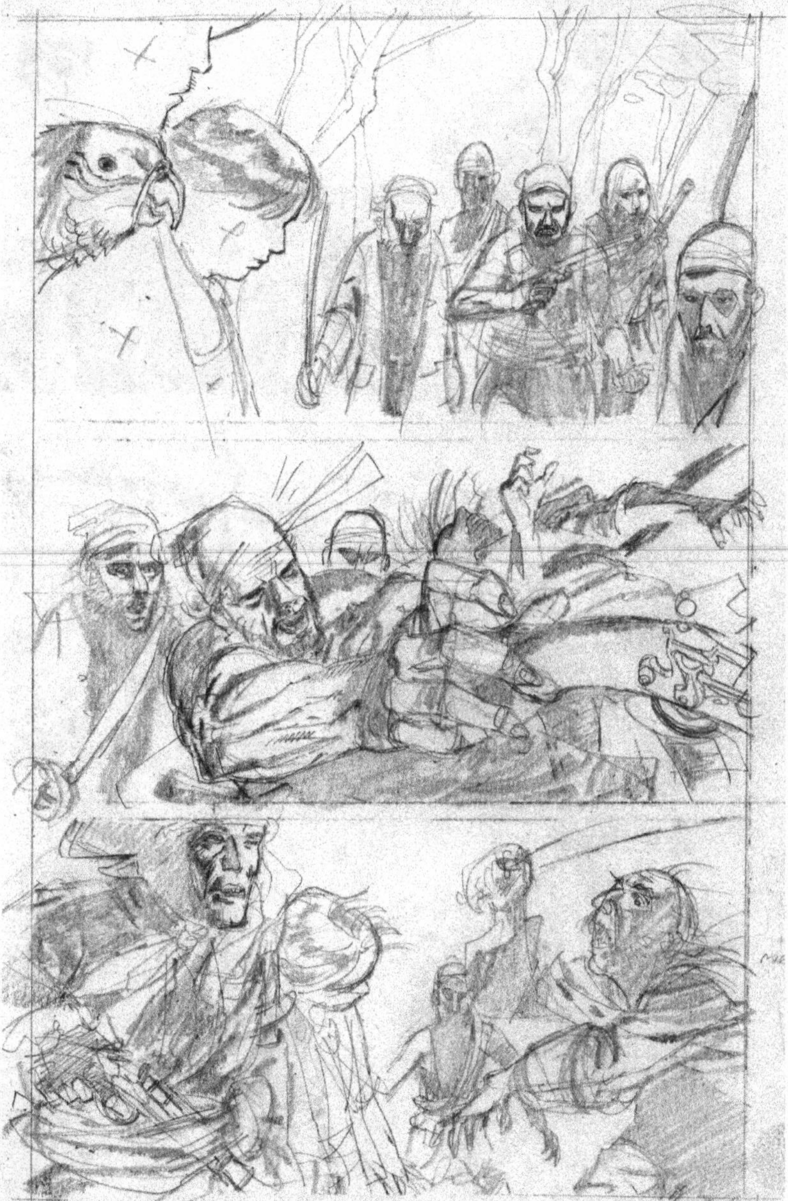

The same page in finished pencil form. Note the detail added to the faces.

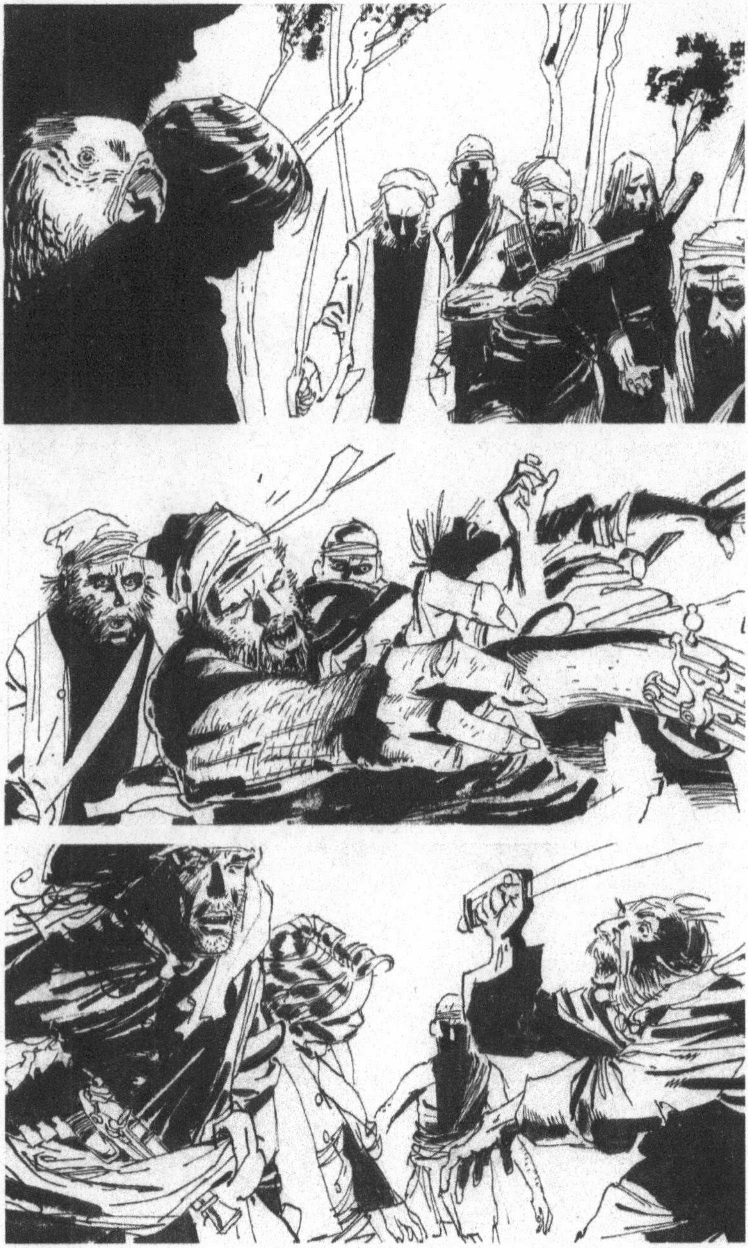

The fully inked page. All that remains now is for the lettering to be added.

A ROGUE'S GALLERY OF MODELS

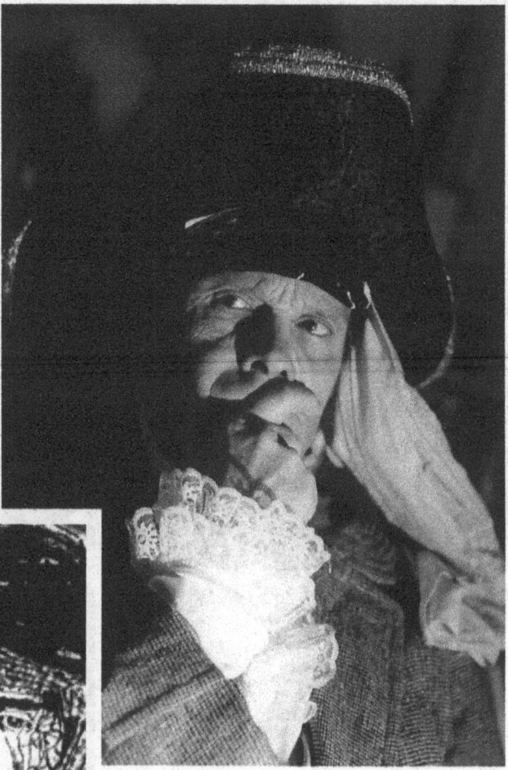

TED LEWIN

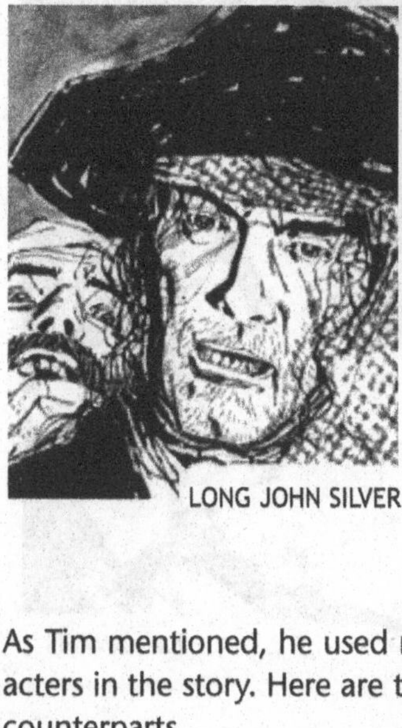

LONG JOHN SILVER

As Tim mentioned, he used models for a number of the characters in the story. Here are the real life models and their story counterparts.

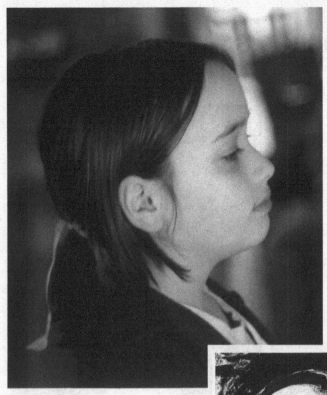

AARON BRAUN

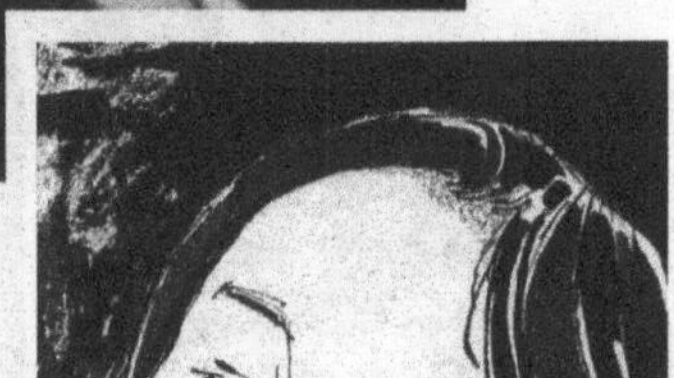

JIM HAWKINS

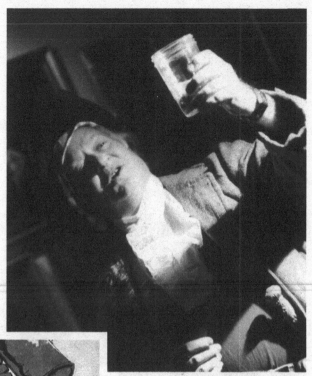

HARVEY WILSON

BILLY BONES

ANDREW DAVENPORT

SQUIRE TRELAWNEY

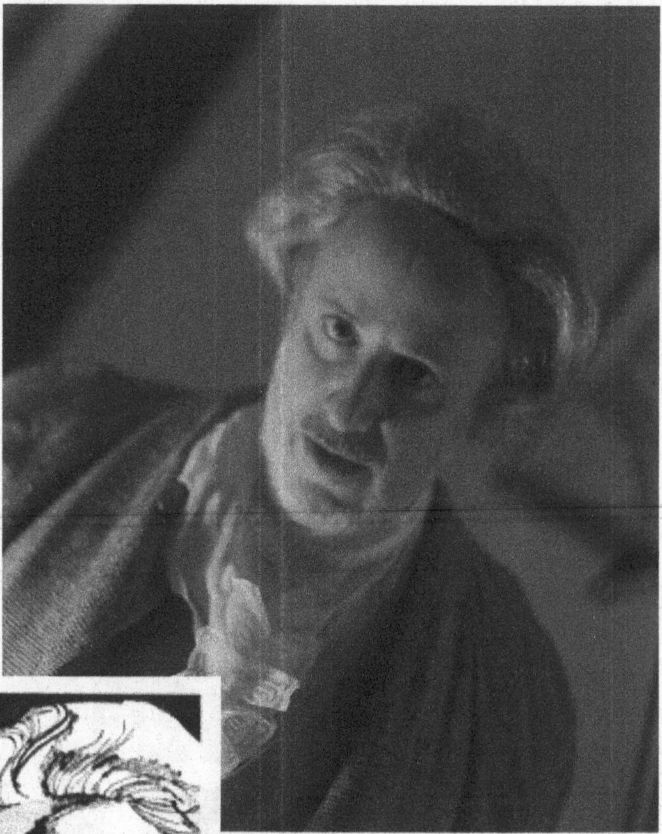
JACOB BRAUN

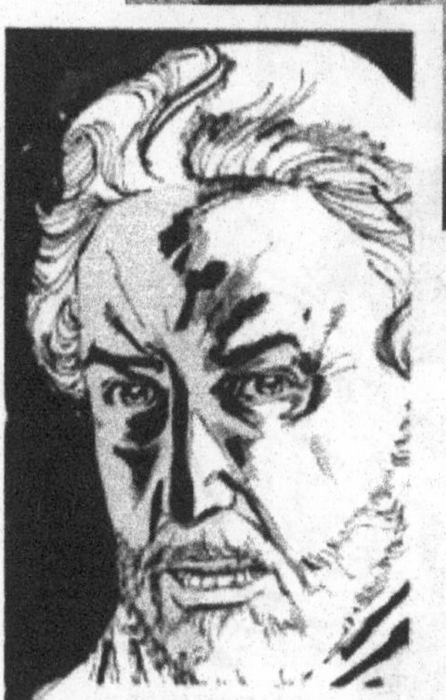
CAPTAIN SMOLLETT

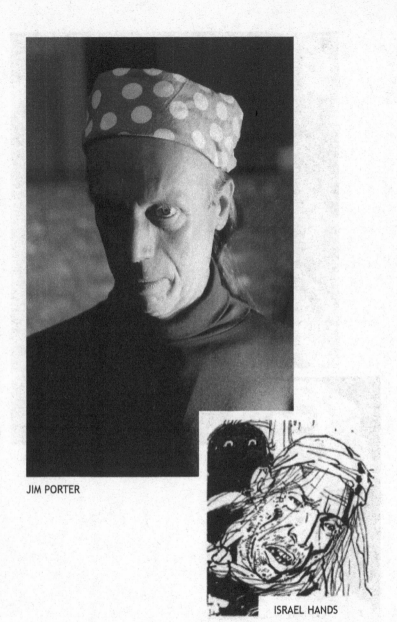

JIM PORTER

ISRAEL HANDS

TIM HAMILTON'S BREAKDOWNS

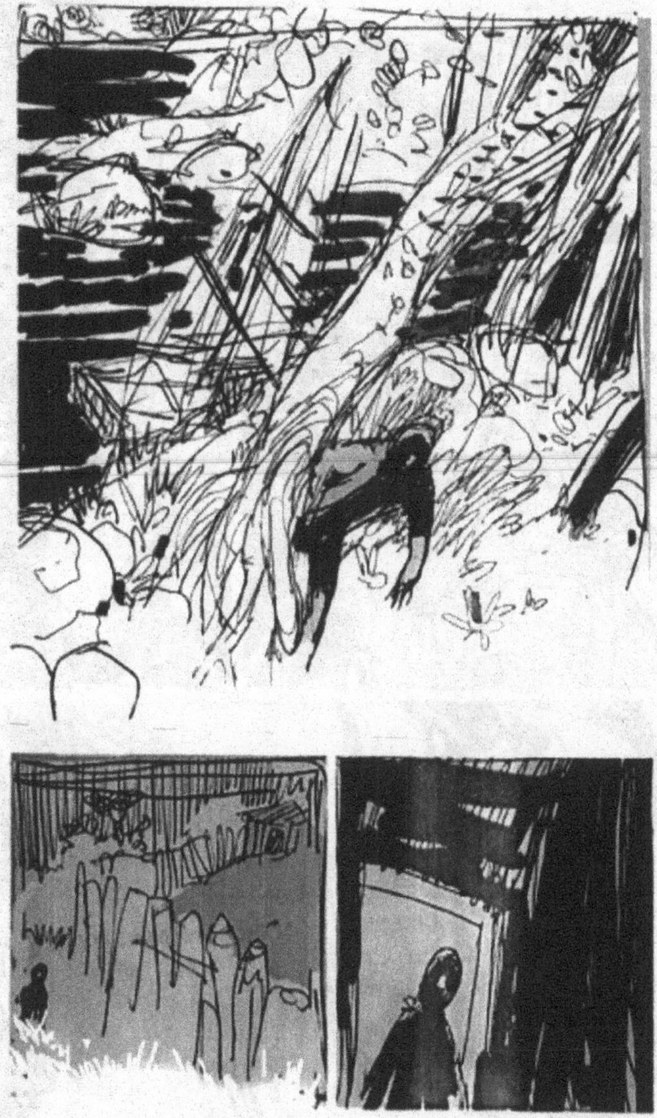

Here is a unique opportunity to see the art breakdowns for a scene in a graphic novel. Compare this six-page sequence with the finished art.

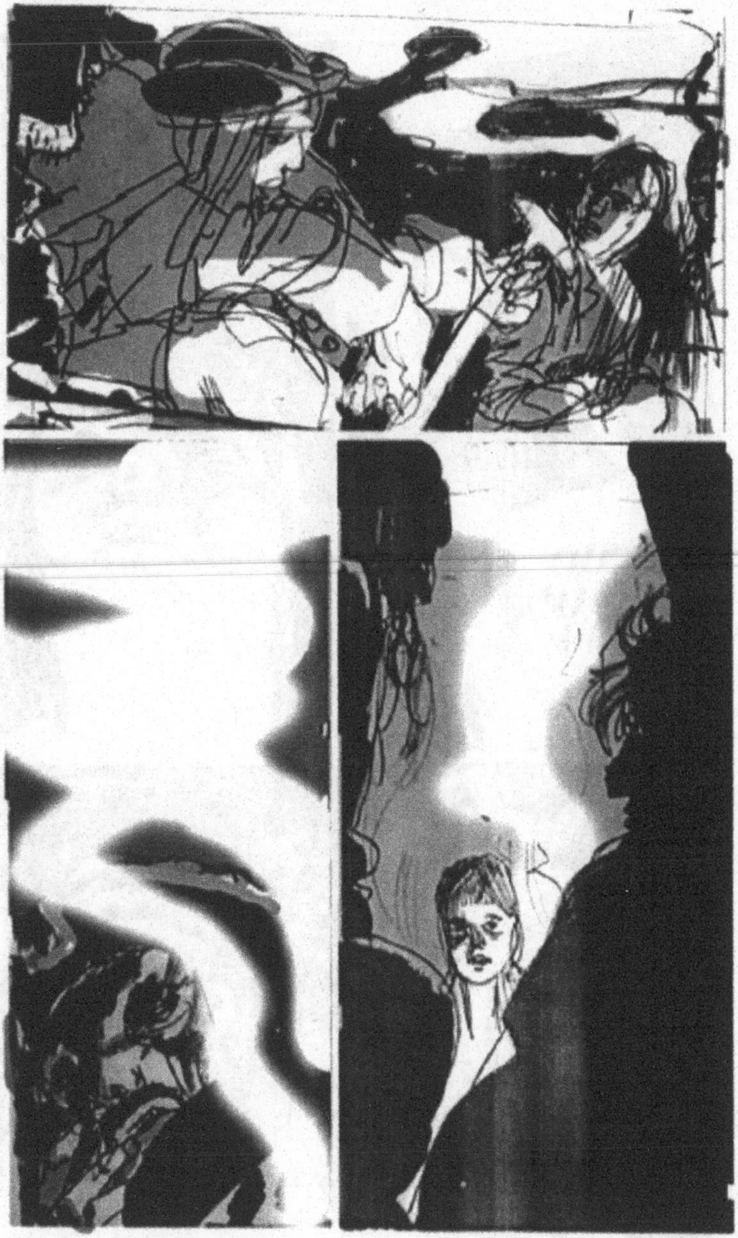

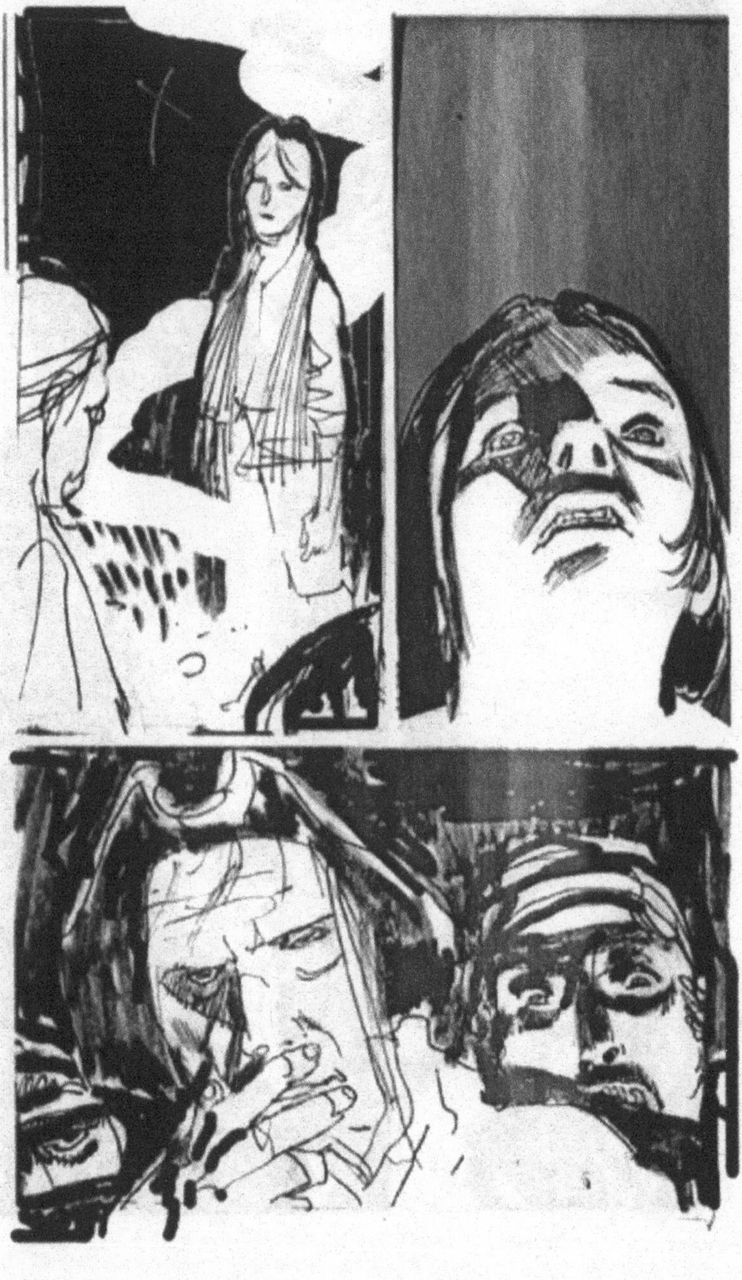

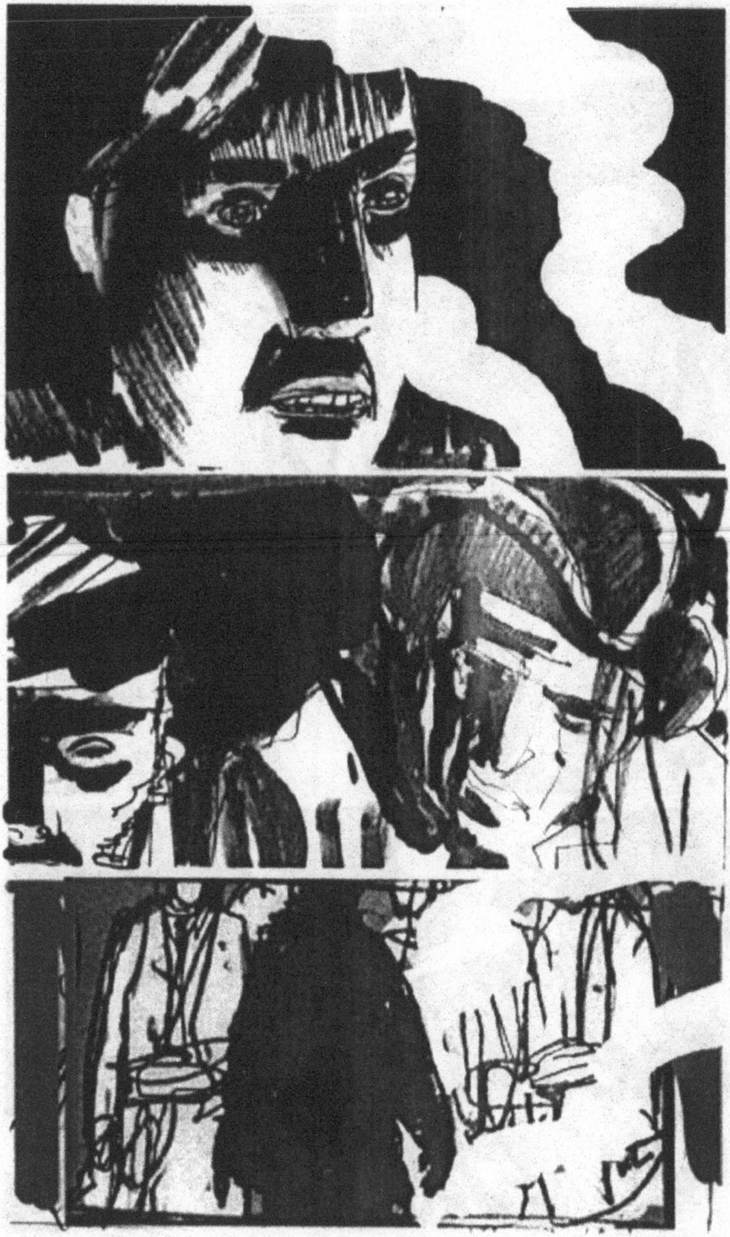

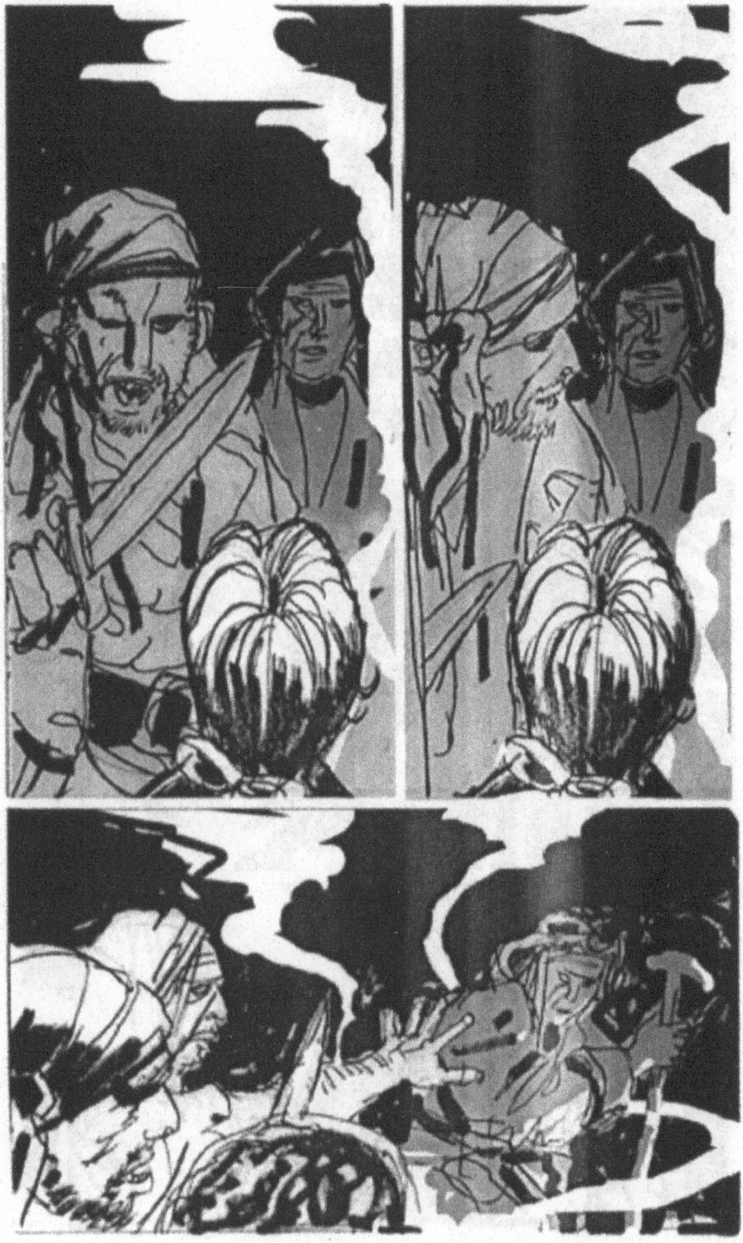

ROBERT LOUIS STEVENSON (1850-94) was born into a famous Edinburgh engineering family. His middle name was originally Lewis, but he changed the spelling, while keeping the pronunciation. His father wanted him to study law, and although Robert was called to the Scottish Bar, he made little effort to become successful as a lawyer since he was already trying to make his mark in the world of literature.

While travelling in Europe among somewhat Bohemian circles he met his future wife, an American called Fanny van de Grift Osbourne. She already had a son, Lloyd, by a previous marriage. One day in 1881, Lloyd and his step-father sketched a map of a treasure island, and Lloyd casually said how nice it would be to have a book about it. Fired by the idea, Robert Louis Stevenson created *Treasure Island* and, with his emphasis not just on plot, but also on character, revolutionized the writing of adventure stories. Other famous adventure novels, such as *Kidnapped*, followed, as well as the beautiful *A Child's Garden of Verses*.

TIM HAMILTON began working as an illustrator after graduating from the Art Institute of Pittsburgh in 1987. His first regular assignment illustrating comics was the 1980s comic book series *The Trouble with Girls* written by Gerard Jones. In the 90s Tim worked on a variety of comics including *Aliens* and *Comic's Greatest World for Dark Horse Comics*. At DC Comics he worked on *Justice League Europe, Green Lantern, Green Lantern Quarterly,* and *Justice League International*. He also illustrated books for Marvel, Malibu, Defiant and Broadway comics. While working for Marvel, Tim created conceptual art involving proposed toys and animated projects for Toybiz. Tim continued his art education at Pratt Institute in the late 90s and now works in New York City as a graphic designer/illustrator. He regularly writes and illustrates humorous comics for *Nickelodeon* Magazine and has produced art for the *New York Times Book Review, Cicada, King Features* and *Serializer.net*.